W9-BNW-109

DEC == 2014

A FANTASTIC FAMILY WHIPPLE NOVEL

WAR *OF THE* WORLD RECORDS

MATTHEW WARD

razOr
bill

AN IMPRINT OF PENGUIN GROUP (USA)

razOr bill

A division of Penguin Young Readers Group
Published by the Penguin Group
Penguin Group (USA) Inc., 345 Hudson Street
New York, New York 10014, U.S.A.

USA / Canada / UK / Ireland / Australia / New Zealand / India / South Africa / China
Penguin.com
A Penguin Random House Company

ISBN: 978-1-59514-691-5

Library of Congress Cataloging-in-Publication Data

Ward, Matthew (Children's writer)
War of the world records : a Fantastic family Whipple novel / Matthew Ward.
pages cm
Summary: When the rivalry between the Whipples and the Goldwins escalates to an all-out war as the World Record World Championships draw near, recordless Arthur Whipple and his unlikely ally Ruby Goldwin unravel the mystery of the Lyon's Curse and the secrets of their fathers' shared past.
ISBN 978-1-59514-691-5 (hardback)
[1. Families--Fiction. 2. World records--Fiction. 3. Competition (Psychology)--Fiction. 4. Mystery and detective stories.] I. Title.
PZ7.W2153War 2014
[Fic]—dc23
2014028360

Printed in the United States of America

1 3 5 7 9 10 8 6 4 2

*For Wendie and
Henry & Miles,
whom I'd be proud to have on my
side in a blood feud anytime.*

WHAT REMAINS TO BE SEEN

It was unclear how the human thigh bone came to be sticking out of the seventeenth turret on the World's Largest Sandcastle. It was, however, looking more and more likely that its builder would be disqualified.

The world-record certifier for the twelfth annual Castle Classic snapped his rulebook shut, then trudged off across the beach to determine just how the bone had entered the sand supply. After examining all the sand-removal sites in view, he followed the builder's wheelbarrow tracks to an opening in the cliffside and disappeared within.

The crowd of sandcastle spectators murmured. There was no doubt the builder, now distraught at the prospect of forfeiting his hard-won record, had scooped up the bone by accident in his frenzy to finish construction in the allotted time. But the bone's origin remained a mystery. The common consensus was that the femur had simply washed ashore after a routine raid on a bone smuggler's boat, as random bones had been known to do in the area.

This theory, however, was quickly proved wrong when the certifier burst from the cave screaming.

The police were promptly called to the scene.

"Coming through!" barked the beak-nosed man in the thick, black overcoat as he pushed past the crowd at the cave opening, hardly glancing at the multispired fortress of sand that towered twenty-five feet over his head between the surf and the cliffside. "Let me see him! Where is he?"

The man charged into the shallow cavern now bustling with police and made his way to the place where three officers crouched over the floor with brushes and small metal implements in their hands.

Embedded in the ground between them lay a human skeleton, completely intact, apart from its right femur bone. On its left index finger, it wore a heavy gold ring.

"Ah yes, Inspector Smudge," started a policeman with what looked to be a high-ranking hat. "I'm—"

As Inspector Smudge took in the scene, the hopeful smirk fell from his face like a man from a cliff. "What is the meaning of this?!" he cried. "These aren't the remains of our fugitive. These bones have clearly been here for years, and Mr. Smith only disappeared off the Whipples' boat last night!"

"Yes, Inspector," said the high-ranking-hatted officer.

2

"I'm afraid the call to you may have been a bit premature. The first officer to arrive thought this may have been your man—this Sammy 'the Spatula' character—seeing as how the Whipple shipwreck occurred less than a mile offshore from here. Apparently thought his body might've washed up overnight and provided a bit of a buffet for the local sea life."

"Ha!" sneered the inspector. "I've seen shore crabs do quite a number on seawater stiffs before, but never anything like this. Looks decades old, this one. Surely just some other would-be gangster who got what was coming to him. Cases usually go unsolved of course. But who am I to stand in the way if these hoodlums want to kill each other off? As much as I'd love to further my record for Most Solved Cases, I shall happily sacrifice if it means a few less criminals in this world."

A medium-built, spry-looking man in a gray trench coat stepped out from behind Inspector Smudge and pointed at the skeleton's left hand.

"What do you think about the ring, Inspector?" he said brightly. "Interesting markings there, aren't they?"

"Ahh, Greenley," said the inspector, closing his eyes and rubbing his temples. "Interesting though it may be, the ring is a distraction. It'll no doubt aid in the identification of this unlucky individual, but as we have established this is not our man, that information is utterly irrelevant to us. Any other dazzling insights, Detective Sergeant?"

"No, sir," replied D.S. Greenley, less brightly.

"Well," the inspector sighed, "this has been a disappointment. I had hoped the tip we got this morning from the man in that coastal cookery shop claiming to see Mr. Smith alive was a mistake, but now it seems we must regard it as a legitimate sighting." He returned his dark, broad-brimmed hat to his head. "All right, Greenley. Let's leave it to the local police to sort out this mess, shall we? What we need to do is get ourselves back to Saltcliffe Station and wait for Mr. Smith to make his move. If he is indeed alive, that train will be his only way out of the area. We'll catch him there as he attempts to flee, and he'll be back in shackles before teatime."

• • •

Arthur Whipple had the misfortune of being nearest the doorway when the knock came.

He had hardly been able to sleep that night and had crept from his bedroom just prior to sunrise, before anyone else in the house had risen. As he wandered past the entry hall on his way to the kitchen, he was nearly startled out of his slippers by a violent thumping at the front door.

Upon collecting his wits, he decided the knocking sounded far too urgent to wait for Wilhelm—the Whipples' butler and World's Strongest German—to answer it. So he walked to the door and opened it himself.

He immediately wished he hadn't.

It did not seem possible that the man outside the door could look any angrier. But then the man recognized the mousy-haired twelve-year-old boy who had opened the door for him.

4

"Ah!" cried Inspector Smudge, throwing up his arms in exasperation. "I can't stand to look at him, Greenley! Get him out of my sight!"

"Really sir?" said Greenley with a yawn. The typically wide-eyed detective looked as though he had not slept in some time.

"Out of my sight—now!" ordered Smudge.

"Yes, sir," said Detective Sergeant Greenley.

Inspector Smudge whirled about and stormed off down the steps.

The sergeant turned to Arthur with an apologetic smile. "Pardon us, Arthur—nice to see you again, by the way— but would you mind fetching your parents? The inspector would like a word."

"Of course, D.S. Greenley," said Arthur. "I believe they're still in bed, but . . ."

The sergeant sighed. "I'm afraid nothing short of the grave will stop the inspector this morning."

"Right," said Arthur.

He returned two minutes later with his mother and father, strategically positioning himself behind his parents as Smudge stamped back up to the doorway.

"Good morning, Inspector," said Arthur's father, Charles, with half-open eyelids. "A bit early for a friendly visit I'd say. What seems to be the trouble?"

"Oh nothing, Mr. Whipple," Smudge grumbled. "Just thought I'd stop in to deliver the morning paper in case you'd missed it." With that, he removed a bulging newspaper from his coat and hurled it at Arthur's father.

Mr. Whipple caught the paper with a grimace, then held it up to the light.

Spanning *The World Record*'s front page was a photograph of Inspector Smudge and a dozen policemen holding spatulas next to a stack of barrels at a train station.

It looked to Arthur like any of the other record-breaking property-seizure photos that typically graced the pages of *The Record*—except for one small detail. Over Smudge's shoulder in the top left corner, a circular section of the background had been enlarged to show a dark figure suspended in midair, dangling from the handles of what appeared to be a rolling pin. The figure wore an all-black chef's uniform—complete with puffy, black chef's hat—like some sort of culinary cat burglar. The rolling pin in the figure's grasp straddled a taut stretch of rope, which the figure was using as a zip line to glide toward an open door on the side of a steaming freight train.

The headline above screamed: TREACHEROUS WHIPPLE CHEF ALIVE AND ON THE RUN!

"Sammy?" gasped Arthur's father.

"Oh, Charles," cried his mother.

A sudden, relieved smile formed on Arthur's face—but he quickly hid it behind his hand.

Luckily, Smudge failed to notice. "Indeed," the inspector snarled, "it would seem your chef has cheated both death and justice yet again. First, he manages not to have his body wash up in a cave yesterday morning, and then last night he stages a spatula-smuggling operation to divert law enforcement from a brazen train getaway!" Noticing the confused expressions on the Whipples' faces, the inspector threw up his hand in a dismissive gesture. "I hope it makes you happy knowing you and your son have unleashed a dangerous criminal into the world. After his numerous attempts on your lives and now his blatant fleeing of the law, I trust you harbor no further delusions as to Mr. Smith's innocence. But fear not, dear Whipples—however you may hinder her course, Justice shall prevail in the end!"

Arthur's parents stood clutching the newspaper, unable to look away from the photograph.

"Come on, Greenley," snapped the inspector. "We haven't an hour of daylight to spare."

"Yes, sir," yawned the sergeant. He tipped his hat to Arthur and his parents and said, "Morning, Whipples," then turned to follow the inspector, who had already stormed back down the front steps.

Mr. Whipple closed the door behind the detectives and put his hand on his son's shoulder. "You see, Arthur?" he said, pressing the newspaper into the boy's chest. "Chin up. Sammy may have betrayed us, but at least he's not dead. We must count our blessings. Now go rouse your brothers and sisters. We've got to get on with our lives and get back to work."

When his parents had left the room, Arthur unfolded the newspaper and stared once more at the grainy blown-up image of Sammy the Spatula. He smiled to himself and started flipping to the section where the story continued.

His progress, however, was soon halted by a certain striking photograph on page 2.

There at the top of the page was a picture of a grinning skeleton, half-buried in sand. Below it was a small close-up of the skeleton's bony fingers, one of which wore a distinctive metal ring. The accompanying headline read:

BURIED TREASURER!

Grim curiosity getting the better of him, Arthur couldn't help but take a peek at the article below:

> A human skeleton discovered in a coastal cave by a record certifier at the Castle Classic sandcastle-building competition on Saturday has been identified as the remains of Bartholomew Niven, former treasurer for the Ardmore Association Board of Directors.

Arthur squinted at the last words of the opening sentence. He had heard the Ardmore Association mentioned before, but he had never learned much about the organization beyond its name. He knew it was somehow involved with the publication of the *Amazing Ardmore Almanac of the Ridiculously Remarkable* and the certification of certain world records not listed in *Grazelby's Guide to World Records and Fantastic Feats*, the publication that sponsored his own family's record breaking. But since Mr. Whipple had prohibited any of his children from ever reading it, this knowledge was of little use. Arthur gnawed his lip and continued the article.

> There was some preliminary speculation that the skeleton could be the crab-eaten remains of the Whipple family's former chef, escaped convict Sammy "the Spatula" Smith, after he jumped off the family's frigate just before it sank to the sea floor on Friday (in yet another apparent example of the so-called Lyon's Curse that has plagued that family in recent weeks).

Arthur shuddered. It was hard to believe it had been less than two days since the Current Champion had sunk. *They couldn't sink Sammy, though, could they?* he thought. *Guess that's what Inspector Smudge meant about Sammy's body not washing up in a cave. Seems the Lyon's Curse hasn't completely caught up to us after all then, doesn't it?* He tried to sound confident when he said this in his mind, but he only shuddered again when he thought about just how close the curse had come. He went back to reading.

> Smith, however, was quickly ruled out when the coroner determined the man in question had been deceased for over twenty years. (Furthermore, Smith would be seen alive on more than one occasion that day. SEE FRONT PAGE.)
>
> The ring on the skeleton's hand, which features the Ardmore treasurer's seal, ultimately led to the discovery of the man's identity.

Arthur re-examined the photograph of the skeleton's ring. At the center of its broad, rounded face the ring bore the emblem of a jeweled, five-pointed crown. Each of the crown's points, however, ended in a sharp, curving flame, so that the crown appeared to be made of fire.

Pretty, Arthur thought, *but certainly not the Most* Practical *Piece of Headgear Ever Invented*. He traced the symbol with his finger, then returned to the article.

> The evidence of the ring was quickly corroborated by aging dental records, confirming the skeleton to be none other than Bartholomew Niven, the lost Ardmore treasurer. Cause of death has yet to be determined.
>
> Niven was last seen alive some twenty-five years ago, just before he and the rest of the Ardmore Board of Directors seemingly vanished without a trace. The disappearance of the entire board, which had been public at the time, proved something of a mystery. But it seemed to solve itself a month later, when the *Ardmore Almanac* appeared on newsstands across the globe just as it always had done before. The public assumed the board had simply gone underground to avoid the pressures of such a highly competitive field. The discovery of Niven, however, suggests there has been a new treasurer on the Ardmore board for some time.
>
> Indeed, with the deep and active treasury the Ardmore Association clearly possesses (evidenced not least by its new, record-breaking contract with the Goldwins, who broke more records at last week's Unsafe Sports Showdown than any other family), a successor to Niven would

surely be required for the management of its finances. The identities of any such board members, however, remain a secret. Ardmore's chief legal representative, Malcolm Boyle, gave a brief statement regarding the organization's current governance by this unnamed shadow board: "The Association feels that separating its board of directors from its record-publishing pursuits pulls the spotlight from its leadership and places it on the amazing world-record breakers it sponsors, where the spotlight belongs."

And so, despite the discovery of Niven's remains, it seems the identity of the current treasurer may never be revealed.

Arthur gulped and looked at the photo of the skeleton again. He did not know what to make of what he'd just read, which involved events occurring long before he was born and an organization he knew next to nothing about. What Arthur did know was how very glad he was that the skeleton in the photo was not Sammy the Spatula's. His father had been right about counting his blessings.

Arthur closed the newspaper and glanced about him to make sure no one was watching. Then he reached into his pocket and slid out the secret message he'd received inside a birthday cake one day earlier. He unfolded the letter and began reading its closing lines for the tenth time that morning:

Stay strong, mate. Your all the hope I've got in this world.

11

Until we meet again . . .

Your Greatful Freind,
Sammy

Arthur stood staring at the words another moment, then—with a sharp breath—returned the letter to his pocket and went to fetch the others.

DINNER IS SEVERED

There are few scenarios quite so disheartening as being beaten by your rivals, deprived of your boat, and betrayed by your chef—all in the same week.

As the seven-day span that included the Unsafe Sports Showdown, the sinking of the *Current Champion*, and the disappearance of Sammy the Spatula drew to a close, a heavy fog settled over the Whipple estate and in the minds of those who lived there.

The Whipples' usual stream of record breaking slowed to a mere trickle. Cordelia could only muster the energy to complete the bottom half of her Eiffel Tower, which barely scraped out a world record for Largest Structure Constructed Entirely from Sugar Cubes, and though Simon finished the Longest Single Piece of Music Ever Composed for the Accordion, it was depressingly dirge-like and nearly unlistenable. The octuplets—Penelope, Edward, Charlotte, Lenora, Franklin, Abigail, Beatrice, and George—busied themselves with the record for Most Bubble Wrap Popped in Forty-Eight Hours. Meanwhile, two-year-old Ivy and her teddy bear, Mr. Growls, went the Longest Time for a Stuffed Toy and Its Owner to Wear a Single Set of Matching Outfits, which consisted solely of two plain gray ponchos. Henry, who had been the only member of his family to pull out a world record against the Goldwins at the Unsafe Sports Showdown, was in no better spirits than the rest of his siblings. After having the Ten-Eighty so tragically snatched out from under his nose, he endeavored to develop a new penny-farthing stunt he could be the first to execute—but all he could come up with was the Lemon Twist (a single airborne spin while balancing a lemon on his chin).

In short, Arthur's siblings scarcely knew what to do with themselves. Sammy's apparent betrayal had hit them all hard, and their recent Unsafe Sports trouncing by the Goldwin family had not helped matters. Having never suffered such a defeat before, they were staggered by the strange, aching feeling that accompanied it.

This was nothing new for Arthur, of course. He had failed at every world record he'd ever attempted. But as much as he hated to see his siblings in such a state, he had never felt closer to them. For the first time in his life, he finally had something in common with his brothers and sisters—if only for a short while.

14

As Friday morning dawned, the fog began to lift.

The Whipples had been dreading their prearranged dinner with the Goldwins all week, but when the day actually arrived, it proved just the thing to pull them out of their gloom. Realizing the evening would yield fresh opportunities for competition, the Whipple children found themselves suddenly invigorated. Surely, the best way to regain their pride was to win it back from those who had stolen it from them in the first place.

Arthur also found himself strangely looking forward to the Goldwins' dinner party, but for decidedly different reasons. Despite several attempts to contact her, he had not seen Ruby Goldwin, his newly enlisted detective partner, since the night the *Current Champion* sank—and he could hardly wait to show her the message he'd received from Sammy. The sooner they resumed their investigation, he figured, the sooner they might clear Sammy's name.

And so, before the clock had struck seven, Arthur and his family took their places on the World's Largest Pedal-Powered Tricycle—which served as their leisurely mode of transportation—and promptly engaged the pedals located below each of their seats. A system of cranks, gears, and chains whirred into motion, and the whole contraption lurched forward down the drive.

• • •

As the Whipples pulled up to the front of the Goldwin residence, Arthur was reminded of his last visit to the grounds

15

of what had been known to him then as the Crosley estate. Though the house's exterior had been elegantly refinished and all the trees perfectly pruned, the renovations were not enough to hide its similarities to the nightmare realm he had entered not so long ago in search of a missing model rocket.

The oversized tricycle had hardly reached a complete stop, when the house's front doors swung open and out stepped Rex Goldwin, followed by the entire Goldwin family. The look of the Goldwins all standing there at the front of their house gave Arthur the sense that he had stepped into some sort of living, breathing advertisement. But exactly which product that advertisement was trying to sell, he couldn't quite pinpoint. Clothing? Real estate? Skin cream? Toothpaste? All of these seemed likely contenders. *Wow*, Arthur thought. *They're like an advertisement for a company that makes advertisements.*

He then noticed Ruby at the back of the group, and the idyllic image was shattered. There was something in the girl's green eyes and dark, tousled hair that now reminded him of recklessness and danger and uncertainty—in a surprisingly appealing way.

"Welcome, welcome, dear Whipples!" Rex exclaimed through a sparkling grin as Arthur's family alighted from their vehicle.

"Good evening, Mr. and Mrs. Goldwin," Mr. Whipple said with a sociable smile. Whatever his past grievances with Rex Goldwin, he seemed to be trying to make the best of the situation now.

16

"Ah, took the trike, did we?" said the chisel-cheeked host. "How delightful!"

"Gosh, Dad," said Roland, the eldest Goldwin child present. "It's been ages since we've taken out our fourteen-seat bicycle, hasn't it? I'd say it's time we dusted the old thing off."

"I'd say you're right, Son," said Rex. "Certainly beats walking when one is feeling sluggardly, does it not?"

Mr. Whipple's expression dropped ever so slightly, but he remained otherwise unfazed. "It does indeed, Mr. Goldwin."

"We're so glad you all could make it, Lizzie," said Rita Goldwin, beaming as she stepped forward to hug Mrs. Whipple.

"Of course, Mrs. Goldwin," Mrs. Whipple replied, doing her best to hide her discomfort with Rita's spontaneous hugs. "The invitation was most generous." She took a breath, then exhaled. "Especially after what happened the last time we invited you . . ."

Rex smiled. "Don't say another word about it, Mrs. Whipple. We're just happy you're safe now. You will not be bothered by any murderous chefs or their freakishly sized clown associates tonight." With that, he bowed down and gingerly kissed her hand.

Just then, a giant Great Dane bounded forward from the back of the group and licked Rex on the mouth with a tongue nearly the size of his head. Rita shrieked and pulled her children close to her.

"Hamlet, no!" cried Arthur's sister Abigail as she chased after her dog.

17

The Great Dane sat back on his haunches and panted cheerfully.

"I'm so sorry, Mr. Goldwin," said Abigail when she had caught up to him. "We've been training round the clock for the upcoming dog-kissing semifinals, but I'm afraid he hasn't mastered his kissing signals quite yet."

Rex wiped his mouth on his sleeve and gave a jovial smile. "Perfectly understandable," he said. "You can hardly expect a dog to behave like a gentleman, can you?"

When Rita saw the dog was under control, she slowly loosened her grip on her children. "I suppose not," she said with a nervous chuckle. "How foolish of me to assume other people's animals conduct themselves as ours do."

"Now dear," Rex assured his wife, "it's only a dog. Don't let its grubbiness disturb you too deeply."

"Of course, dear," Rita replied, exhaling. She straightened her skirt and turned to Arthur's parents with an uneasy smile. "You'll have to forgive us if we're a bit put off by your canine. It's just that, with the sort of breeds we keep, we're used to seeing dogs employed more often as pet *feed* than as pets—but please, don't imagine for a moment we think any less of you for the slightly filthy nature of your preferred animal companion."

"We really are sorry about that," said Mrs. Whipple. "I assure you, Mrs. Goldwin, it won't happen again. Is there some place outside where our dog can wait for us during dinner?"

Abigail frowned. "But I've barely played with him all day," she protested. "He'll be lonely."

18

"Abigail," Mrs. Whipple said firmly, "I warned you if you couldn't keep Hamlet under control, he would not be able to dine with us. Now do as you're told."

The little girl hung her head. "Yes, ma'am," she sighed. "Let's go, Hammie."

Hamlet panted excitedly and crouched forward, allowing Abigail to climb onto her usual spot on his back.

"I know just the spot for him," said Rita. "If you'll simply follow me through the house, we can put him in the garden, close to where we keep the other animals."

Her daughter Roxy—the recent rocket-stick champion—gave a sneaky smile. "But not *too* close, of course."

• • •

Arthur was eager for formal greetings to come to an end so he might have a private word with Ruby about the urgent investigation that awaited them. But as soon as he stepped through the Goldwins' doorway, he found himself rather distracted. It was as if, by crossing the threshold, he had stepped out of the past and into the future.

The walls, ceilings, and floors of the Goldwin house were all gleaming white, its furniture and artwork providing the only accents of color. The decor would not have looked out of place on a space station built by a race of Martians with an exceptionally clean design sense—or perhaps by Swedish people.

"Impressive, isn't it?" Rex grinned. "You just can't beat the timeless elegance and graceful beauty of molded plastics."

"Is that what this is?" asked Arthur's father.

"Of course," said Rex. "With wood and plaster feeling so hopelessly old-fashioned these days, we opted for a more modern approach. After gutting the interior of the old Crosley house, we reconstructed it from scratch with 100 percent man-made materials. You'll notice the floors are made of distinctive Umbrian vinyl Corlite; the carpets and upholstery of fine Luxurethane; the window fabrics of alluring Styron and Crylitate. In fact, apart from its antique facade, there isn't a single natural material employed anywhere in the house's construction—earning it the world record for Lowest Ratio of Natural to Man-Made Materials Used in the Construction of a Single Family Dwelling."

"Makes it a breeze to clean as well," Rita said with a pointed glance to the Whipples' Great Dane, "in case of *foreign contaminants*. The self-cleaning mechanism is always just a button-press away. And this is only the front room, of course," she added excitedly. "Wait till you see the rest of it."

"That's right," said Rex. "Luckily, we've got a bit of time to kill before dinner is ready. Chef Bijou is quite the perfectionist, you see. He's been working on this meal for three days now. It'll do us well to work up our appetite. Let's just pop out to take care of the animals, and then we'll have the full tour."

He escorted the group back outside through a pair of towering doors at the rear of the room. The party emerged onto a terrace, which separated the Goldwin house from the large, well-groomed woodland behind it.

"Just down these steps is an area where we sometimes train our own animals. Rodney—you've got feeding privileges this week—why don't you show Miss Whipple the stake she can chain her canine to for the time being? And double-check to make sure it's clean. Might make the dog uncomfortable if it knew the chain's usual purpose."

"My pleasure," said the blond-haired boy as he stepped forward.

"Oh," said Mrs. Whipple, catching a glimpse of the heavy, but clean-looking chain at the bottom of the stairs. "Very well, Abigail. Go on and, er, chain Hamlet to the stake."

"All right," said Arthur's sister from her seat on the dog's back. "Come on, Hammie."

The dog wagged his tail happily at the sound of his own name as his unhappy rider guided him down the steps with Rodney Goldwin.

When Hamlet's collar had been attached to the chain and stake, he woofed a goodbye to Abigail, who began trudging back toward the others.

"Hey," said Ruby's four-year-old sister Rowena from the edge of the terrace, "I know what will cheer her up. Let's show the Whipples *our* pets. Can we? Can we?"

"Well," said Mrs. Goldwin, holding back a smile, "I suppose so. But no excessive frolicking with the animals. We haven't got time for a deep-pore cleansing before dinner. For them or for you."

Rita led the rest of the group down the terrace steps,

through the trees, and into a large clearing, which was almost entirely occupied by a miniature, cartoonish version of the Goldwin house.

"Welcome," Rita announced, "to the pride of the Goldwin estate!" Her face lit up as she spoke. "Some of the world's most prized animals make their residence here, and we are honored to call ourselves their caretakers. Now please, allow me to introduce them."

Rita grasped the handle on the trapezoidal front door and hinged it inward.

Arthur felt his pulse quicken slightly as he strained to see any trace of the creatures that reportedly ate dogs for dinner. He ventured a small step closer and—*whoosh!*—a scaly, sharp-toothed snout lunged at him from out of the shadows.

Arthur lurched back in terror and stumbled to the ground. He braced himself for the inevitable mauling—but just before the creature's needle-filled mouth could reach him, it jerked to a halt with a loud *clink*. The Goldwins promptly burst into laughter.

It was then that Arthur noticed the tautly pulled chain at the back of the creature's neck, keeping it from crossing the threshold.

"Now, now, Ransley," Rita Goldwin chuckled as she addressed the lizard, "it seems some of our guests are a little on the jittery side. Remember what I've told you about first impressions."

The lizard stared blankly forward, as if it didn't actually

understand English. Rita Goldwin didn't seem to notice.

"Being the Fastest Lizard on Earth," she explained to her bewildered guests, "Ransley is our little greeter—aren't you, Ransley? Yes you are!" She bent down and pinched the lizard's cheeks—or whatever it is that lizards have on the sides of their faces—and gave them an affectionate jiggle.

Arthur then noticed another detail about the scaly-skinned creature: it was wearing a satin waistcoat. And a bow tie.

Rupert Goldwin, the black-haired boy who had alerted Smudge and the Execution Squad to Sammy's escape aboard the *Current Champion*, offered his hand to Arthur and pulled him to his feet. "Dry your eyes, Arthur," he said with a chuckle as Arthur dusted himself off. "Black spiny-tailed iguanas are almost exclusively plant-eaters, as everybody knows—so unless you've got a head of cabbage in your back pocket, you're completely safe from this one. Can't say the same for all of them, though."

"No you can't, Son," his father agreed. "Let's meet them, shall we?"

Rex turned to flip a switch on the side of the house, and a lurid neon sign fizzled into view over the front door. Beneath the image of a blinking blue martini glass tilting to the lips of a smiling lizard face, the words LIZARD LOUNGE buzzed in glowing green letters.

"Welcome," said Rex, gesturing to the miniaturized doorway, "to the Lizard Lounge."

23

Mr. Whipple cleared his throat. "Um, yes. Thank you, Mr. Goldwin. But well, is it really necessary to show us the inside? A bit small for all of us, isn't it?"

Arthur noticed his father's face was slightly flushed.

"Not at all, Charlie," Rex said with a grin. "There's plenty of room. Unless, of course, you've got a fear of our four-legged friends here . . ."

"No, it's not that," said Mr. Whipple. "It's. . . . Never mind, Mr. Goldwin. After you."

Rex shrugged and ducked through the short, narrow door. Mr. Whipple drew a deep breath, then ducked in after him, the rest of the group following just behind. Once inside, Rex flipped a second light switch, treating Arthur and his family to another remarkable sight. Just like the outside of the Lizard Lounge, its interior was a small-scale caricature of the Goldwins' main house, with ultra-modern furniture and decor—but with one major difference: all of its inhabitants were lizards. The room in which the party now stood was divided by clear plexiglass walls into separate enclosed units, each containing a different lizard species, all of which were dressed in assorted party attire.

Arthur marveled at the wide array of classy-looking creatures. Reclining on a chaise longue behind the plexiglass wall to his left lay a massive monitor lizard wearing a red cocktail dress. Overhead, gliding from wall to wall above a plexiglass ceiling were hundreds of small, winged lizards, each wearing a tiny silk scarf. A nearby wall plate read: *Draco dussumieri* (SOUTHERN FLYING LIZARD), FAST-EST GLIDING LIZARD ON EARTH.

There was also a Mexican beaded lizard in a mariachi jacket, a chameleon in a feather boa, and in the largest chamber, an enormous Komodo dragon in a burgundy velvet smoking jacket with a gold-rimmed monocle strapped over its right eye.

"So, what do you think?" beamed Rita Goldwin.

"I must admit, Mrs. Goldwin," said Arthur's mother, "I don't know if I've ever seen so many record-breaking lizards in one place . . . certainly not all in costume."

"Oh, but these aren't just *any* record-breaking lizards," Rita insisted. "They're *show* lizards. Each of them has taken top honors at the world's most prestigious lizard shows: Craggs, Westmonster, Terrarium International—we've won them all."

"Impressive," Mrs. Whipple said politely, "isn't it, Charles?"

Mr. Whipple gave a start and wiped a bead of sweat from his brow. "Hmm? Oh—yes, of course, dear. But shouldn't we be—"

"May I pet them, Mrs. Goldwin?" Abigail interrupted, her little hands and face plastered against the clear partition that held the Komodo dragon.

"Why, of course, dear!" Rita replied, before Arthur's father could object. She turned and slid open a door behind her to reveal a rack of strange-looking garments. "Just put on one of our patent-pending Saurian Suits and you can move freely from room to room."

When Abigail had put on the tough, padded suit over

25

her clothes and placed the steel-visored helmet on her head, she looked like a cross between a deep-sea diver and a knight in armor.

"You're all set!" said Rita. "Now, even with the suit on, you might want to steer clear of Ramón, our Mexican beaded lizard. He's been a bit cranky lately and we're all out of anti-venom—and he just happens to be the Most Venomous Lizard on Earth. Oh, and do mind the Komodo dragon; Ridgely's weekly feeding isn't until tomorrow and he's chewed through another one of his muzzles, so you might not want to get too close to his mouth. . . . But other than that—enjoy!"

Arthur watched nervously as Abigail stepped through the sliding door that led to the first compartment. He had yet to be convinced his first reaction to the Lizard Lounge had not been the appropriate one. Despite their darling outfits—or perhaps because of them—the building's inhabitants still made him exceedingly uneasy. As his sister frolicked from one chamber to another, Arthur couldn't shake the fear that the next lizard would be the one to attack.

He looked over to his father and found him breathing heavily and wiping the back of his neck in between frequent glances to the floor and ceiling. It seemed he was nervous about the lizards too.

Meanwhile, Rita Goldwin continued to enlighten her guests about the fascinating world of show lizards. ". . . Which is why the current judging system in the Jaws and Claws category needs a serious overhaul," she concluded, pausing for the first time in several minutes.

Arthur's father clapped his hands together. "Well then," he blurted in a breathy voice. "This has all been very informative, Mr. and Mrs. Goldwin, but I'm sure we could all use some fresh air now." He mopped his brow again, then cupped his hands to his mouth and called out toward the Komodo dragon enclosure, "Abigail—time to go!"

Rex turned to him with a sly smile. "A bit cramped for you in here is it, Charlie? I see some things never change...."

Mr. Whipple's face froze.

"I must say," Rex continued, "it's refreshing for us mere mortals to see that even an icon like the great Charles Whipple has *some* sort of weakness—though I'd hardly call it that. No—I'd say you're just more sensitive to your surroundings than most men, wouldn't you, Charlie?"

Arthur's father looked as if he might collapse or explode—or both—at any moment. But before Mr. Whipple could do either of these things, Rex simply said, "Very well. We've seen enough of the Lizard Lounge, haven't we? I'm sure Rita could go on forever about her precious pets, but we've still got one more stop on the tour before dinner. So let's get back to the house, shall we?"

Mr. Whipple exhaled. Abigail exited the inner chambers and grudgingly removed her Saurian Suit, and soon the party had made its way back out into the night air. Mr. Whipple's color and demeanor returned to normal.

As the Lizard Lounge faded from view, Arthur was finally able to relax. He'd convinced himself a house full

27

of lethal lizards could lead to nothing but calamity, and he was glad to have been mistaken.

• • •

"And here we have the crown jewel of our humble home," Rex announced as he ushered the group through a vault-like door. "The Goldwin family trophy room!"

Arthur and his family were met by a spectacular sight. Golden cups and statuettes spun on motorized pedestals, shimmering under the chamber's accented lighting. Plexiglass display cases housed hundreds of record-breaking artifacts and vast collections, while video screens looped footage of the Goldwins' record-setting endeavors.

As much as Arthur hated to admit it, the Whipple family's trophy room looked almost ancient in comparison.

"Please, feel free to browse," Rex grinned as he joined his guests. "But be warned: all the cases are thoroughly theft-proof, so don't get any ideas!"

The party dispersed throughout the room, and Arthur marveled at the Goldwins' unique array of awards. In a display case entitled "The Perfect Teeth of the Goldwin Men," six sets of chomping dentures, cast from the mouths of Rowan, Radley, Randolf, Rodney, Rupert, Roland, and Rex clacked in time to "Twinkle, Twinkle, Little Star." The adjacent exhibit, entitled "The Goldwins: More International Beauty Pageant Wins than Any Other Family," displayed spinning beauty queen crowns from each of the Goldwin women—with the exception of Ruby.

"Very proud of all our ladies," said Rex Goldwin, stepping up alongside Arthur. "Though I'm afraid Ruby's record breaking history is rather limited. With so many children, of course, one of them is bound to fall through the cracks. But one out of twelve ain't bad, eh?"

Arthur chuckled uneasily and stepped away from the host. He glanced behind him to the doorway, where Ruby stood brooding against the wall. The instant their eyes met, Ruby's darted away, finding a nearby section of floor to rest on.

Arthur couldn't help but be reminded of a certain unanswered question—and recognized a rare opportunity to solve it. If he ever hoped to uncover the mysterious world record Ruby had claimed to hold at their first meeting, surely this was the place to look.

He turned with new purpose to the next display. There, a battered pair of boxing gloves dangled over a photo of Roland Goldwin with his fist in the face of some poor, unrecognizable boy. The accompanying plaque read: MOST PUNCHES LANDED IN A SINGLE MATCH. Beside it, Arthur was surprised to find that Roland's brother Rupert also held the record for Most Punches Landed in a Single Match, but in ice hockey rather than boxing. More surprising still was that—according to the following exhibit—little Rowena held the same distinction in junior badminton.

Arthur made a mental note not to cross any of the three preceding Goldwins, then continued his search.

In the next display case, a riding crop and tennis racquet had been positioned to form an X between a pair

29

of framed photographs. Each of the photos contained a handsome young man posing in a different sport-themed scenario—the boy on the left standing in a stable, holding a riding crop, while the boy on the right held a tennis racquet against his shoulder and sat on a locker room bench. Sharing the same perfect skin and teeth and the same expertly styled sandy-blond hair, the two boys were identical in appearance, apart from the contrasting colors of their sleeveless pullovers. So similar was their appearance, in fact, that Arthur might have assumed both photos were of the same person, had the accompanying plaques not specified otherwise.

Just then, Arthur was joined by his mother and several of his younger siblings as Rita Goldwin herded them forward.

"Oh yes," the hostess beamed, gesturing to the display, "these are the twins! Have I mentioned they're traveling the world right now on the Clapford Fellowship?"

"Very impressive," nodded Mrs. Whipple.

"Yes, well, Rayford and Royston have always excelled in the realm of academia. Truly, the only thing that can match their aptitude for academic study is their knack for sport—which led to their recruitment by the Ardmore Academy before they were even five years old. Here's Rayford's world record for Fastest Furlong on Horseback—and Royston's record for Fastest Tennis Serve Ever Recorded. Goodness, I do miss them sometimes. . . ." She stroked the photographs with a far-off look in her eye, before blinking it away. "Oh my," she said, "I've done it again." Always

30

going on about my own children and never inquiring after the children of others—how rude of me. . . . So, tell me Lizzie—how many of *your* children have been selected by elite schools to spend their lives traveling the world on academic and athletic scholarships?"

"Oh," said Mrs. Whipple, slightly taken aback, "well, Abigail spent a semester in Saskatchewan last year living with a family of wolves through the Canadian Lupine Exchange Program. . . ."

"Oh yes," Rita cut in, shifting her gaze to Abigail and overenunciating her words, "*that* must have been *so* much *fun* for you, Abbie! You got to live with the puppy dogs, didn't you?"

Abigail looked up with a confused yet polite expression.

Rita turned back to Mrs. Whipple and whispered, "It really is adorable she doesn't realize how disgusting that is. Honestly, what a good mother you are for letting her think that wandering the wilderness with those beasts is anything like world travel!"

Though Mrs. Whipple could have gone on to mention Franklin's stint with the Royal Naval Academy, or Cordelia's apprenticeship at the Institute for Medical and Architectural Research, or Henry's YesterGear sponsorship, she instead said nothing and simply smiled.

"Ah, well," said Rita, "so much more to see, Lizzie. Have you had a chance to view Randolf's trophies for Fastest Trophy Polishing?"

As his mother was whisked away again by the host-

31

ess, Arthur turned to look for Ruby, but found she was no longer in the room. He then discovered a half-open door where he'd last seen her standing and peeked inside.

An angular indoor fountain spouted from the center of the dim, candle-lit chamber. There, on the fountain's outer ledge, reading an old cloth-bound book, sat Ruby. Arthur stepped inside.

"Done gawking?" said Ruby without looking up from her book.

"What? No," said Arthur. "I was just, um . . ." His voice trailed off. "So," he said a moment later, taking a seat a few feet from her on the fountain's edge, "what's that you're reading?"

"*Poise and Poisonousness*," she replied. "One of the last novels Joss Langston wrote before her untimely death. I'm just at the part where Elsie discovers Mr. Billowy has self-ishly sullied her sister's honor, and decides to even the score by stirring arsenic into his cognac while he's out dancing a quadrille."

Arthur grimaced.

Apparently sensing his unease, Ruby added, "You've heard of Joss Langston—*Crime and Credulousness? Corpse and Culpability? Southanger Cemetery?*"

"Not really."

"Classic Victorian noir. Some of the finest femmes fatales ever to wield a cleaver while wearing a corset. I just finished *Lass and Laceration*, and I'm moving on to *Man-slaughter Park* as soon as I get through this one."

"Hmm," said Arthur. "Sounds, um, engrossing. So what is this place anyway?"

"The reflection room," she said. "Rita saw it in a magazine I think. 'No modern home is complete without a room in which to relax and reflect on one's unity with the universe' or some such. Doesn't get much use." Ruby paused, looking up from her book for the first time. She dipped her hand in the fountain and let the water drain through her fingers. "But perhaps we should do a bit of *reflecting* of our own," she said cryptically. She closed her book and set it beside her on the ledge, then walked to the doorway. Peering cautiously out into the trophy room, she quietly shut the door.

"So," she said, turning back to Arthur, "what are we to do with our investigation now? You know, now that Sammy's been seen alive?"

"Hmm?" said Arthur. "Oh, right—the investigation. I've been meaning to—"

"I mean," Ruby cut in as she sat herself back down, "I was thrilled to see him on the front page of *The Record*, clearly not dead, and I wanted to believe he was innocent— but this skipping-town business, without a word to anyone. . . . It's a bit hard to swallow, don't you think?"

"I know," replied Arthur, unable to conceal a sudden smirk. "If only there were some way to know for sure he was telling the truth. . . ."

He then slipped Sammy's note out of his pocket and handed it to Ruby.

33

"What's this?" she said.

"Read it."

Ruby unfolded the paper. She hadn't held it open for two seconds before she exclaimed, "What? Where did you get this?"

Arthur glanced to the door to make sure it was still closed, then whispered, "It was delivered to me inside a belated birthday cake the day after the *Current Champion* sank."

"And you're just showing it to me now?" Ruby shot back.

"I tried to call you all this week," Arthur explained, "but the boy answering the phone said you'd just be a minute, only to leave me waiting for hours every time."

"Sounds like Rupert's idea of a joke," Ruby said with a scowl.

"I nearly achieved the Longest Time to Hold a Telephone Line at one point," Arthur added, "but it went dead at thirteen and a half hours, just ten minutes short of the record."

"Yep," said Ruby. "That's Rupert all right."

She returned to Sammy's letter. When she had finished reading, she looked up at Arthur and smiled. "I told you he was grateful."

Ruby handed Sammy's note back to Arthur, then scrunched up her face. "So, if Sammy didn't put the poison in the galley, then who did? Either Smudge is completely crooked and planting evidence, or someone else managed to get it aboard the ship that night."

34

"But who? Besides Inspector Smudge and the Execution Squad, it was only our two families and the ship's crew who ever set foot aboard the *Current Champion*, as far as I know."

"Well," scowled Ruby. "I wouldn't put it past Smudge or the Execution Squad, for starters." Then, with a nod to the trophy room door she muttered, "Or anyone in my family, really. . . . And how well do you know the crew?"

"Not very well, I guess," Arthur admitted. "Besides the regular staff, we hire an assortment of sailors and deckhands off the docks to handle the rigging and whatnot."

"And is it possible one of them might have accepted a bribe from the giant and the dwarf—Messrs. Overkill and Undercut—to plant the poison?"

"I guess so. They *are* a bit of a salty bunch, come to think of it."

"They usually are," Ruby nodded. "And as the ship is now a permanent addition to the sea floor—and the physical evidence is in the possession of Inspector Smudge, I'm afraid we've come to a bit of a stall here. It seems we'll have to find some other way to track down our culprits. Any ideas?"

"Well, I've already tried contacting the Unsafe Sports Committee to see if the giant and the dwarf turned up in any of their photographs or film footage, but they were too busy fighting the lawsuits from this year's Showdown to be of any help. So, I don't think we'll get anywhere that way either. But we've got to come up with something, wouldn't you say? So we're not just sitting on our hands, waiting for

35

our villains to make their next move?"

"Indeed, Detective Whipple," Ruby replied. "Anything less would simply be bad police work. How's tomorrow for a comprehensive case meeting?"

"Well, I'm attempting the record for Balancing Most Wine Glasses on Chin tomorrow morning, but as soon as that's over, I've got the rest of the day free."

Ruby couldn't help but roll her eyes ever so slightly at Arthur's mention of the record attempt. "Fine," she said. "We'll rendezvous at the Undertakers' Graveyard at noon."

"Hang on," Arthur protested, "can't we pick somewhere—"

"I am having a meeting in a graveyard one way or another," Ruby said firmly. "I still haven't forgiven you for the last time you had one without me. Be thankful I'm not demanding we meet at midnight."

"Very well then," Arthur sighed. "I'll—"

Just then, the door burst open and Ruby's mother poked her head through the doorway.

"Come on, you two," she said. "We know you have no interest in trophies and awards, but that's no reason to be antisocial. I'm sure the Whipples don't want their underachieving son dragged down any further by your influence, dear."

"Of course they don't," said Ruby.

After Rita had escorted the two of them back into the trophy room, Rex gathered the rest of the group. "All right, then," he declared, "I think we've sufficiently exhausted the anteroom now. . . ."

"Anteroom?" puzzled Mr. Whipple. "But I thought—"

"Oh, no," Rex replied. "This is merely the entryway. The main trophy chamber is just through there. . . ."

The Whipples followed their host through yet another plastic portal to find themselves in a huge circular room. Every inch of its high, curving wall was covered with sparkling plaques.

Arthur gaped at the sight. Reminded of his earlier mission, he took a deep breath and set about scanning each new award, hoping to finally locate the one with Ruby's name on it.

"My, my," said Mr. Whipple after a stretch of dumbfounded silence. "This is *almost* as big as our own wall of plaques back home—isn't it, children?"

Rex turned to him and smiled. "Right you are, Charlie. Your record for Largest Wall of Plaques in a Family Residence is indeed safe for the time being."

Arthur's father put on an unmistakably proud face—but their host hadn't finished.

"Yes, we realized early on that *one* wall simply would not be enough for us. . . ."

Rex pressed a button in a concealed panel to his right, and the curving wall of plaques split down the center and slid open to reveal: a second wall of plaques. This in itself was easily enough to wipe the smirk off Mr. Whipple's face, but as soon as the first wall had come to a halt, the second wall split apart as well, unveiling yet another plaque-covered wall behind it.

37

The Whipples' jaws dropped.

Hopelessly overwhelmed, Arthur officially called off his search. It would take hours to read so many plaques. If he was going to discover Ruby's secret world record, it would not be like this.

"Yes, yes," Mr. Whipple said a moment later. "Three walls of plaques—a clever gimmick to be sure. But what of it? Clearly, most of these awards have not even been officially certified, seeing as you only broke your thousandth record a few weeks ago at the Birthday Extravaganza."

"It's true, Charlie," said Rex. "That was our thousandth record . . . for *this* season. I mean, surely you've heard the news by now."

Mr. Whipple cocked his head to one side. "And what news would that be?"

"Well," Rex replied, "as a result of our performance at the Unsafe Sports Showdown, the International World Record Federation has ruled to acknowledge all the unregistered records we'd quietly broken in the years before our new contract with the *Ardmore Almanac*. So as it turns out, we now officially hold more records than the legendary Nakamoto family—your old sparring partners! Of course, we do still trail your family by a fair margin, but I'd say going from amateur to world's second best in a matter of weeks isn't half bad. Really, I'm shocked you hadn't heard before. It's all in the new edition of the *Ardmore Almanac*, out today. You do read the *Almanac*, don't you, Charlie?"

Arthur's father arched his eyebrows and opened his

mouth in such a way that no kind words could have come from it, but he was promptly cut off by a burst of static, as the image of a thin-mustached man in a towering chef's hat appeared on a nearby viewscreen.

"Monsieur Goldween," the chef declared, "deenair eez sairved."

• • •

Arthur was famished. Since the time of Sammy the Spatula's arrest, the Whipples had been auditioning various chefs to fill the position but had yet to find anyone with even half of Sammy's talent. This week's candidate, Chef Stefan Mulch-mann, was famous for his extensive menu of gourmet casseroles. Arthur had initially been taken in by the dishes' enticing-sounding names, but he grew increasingly amazed at the number of otherwise-delicious foods that suddenly became unpalatable once the word "casserole" was added to their titles. After a week of trying to make the best of pizza casserole, roast beef casserole, sweet-and-sour casserole, macaroni casserole, taco casserole, and all-you-can-eat buffet casserole, Arthur had been inspired to attempt the record for Longest Time to Survive without Food. (Unfortunately, when Beatrice had smuggled an uncasseroled sausage link from the kitchen that morning and offered to divide it amongst her siblings, Arthur had forgotten all about his ongoing fast until he had already broken it.)

Needless to say, he was very much looking forward to having a meal away from home.

And so, as he peered down at the pea-sized splotch in the middle of his plate, he couldn't help but feel a bit disappointed.

"But where's all the food?" said Beatrice.

"Hush, Beatrice," said Arthur's mother. "Don't be rude."

"Not at all, Mrs. Whipple," said Rex, grinning from across the Goldwins' white, kidney-shaped dining table. "This is hardly your everyday spread. As you can see, Chef Bijou painstakingly pares down each cut of meat and every handpicked vegetable until all that remains is an absolutely ideal specimen. Tonight's meal, I'm happy to report, will break his own record for Smallest Portioned Five-Star/Four-Course Dinner Ever Prepared, further cementing his title for Most Records in Petite Cuisine. Why, come to think of it, Charlie, this must remind you a bit of your own former chef. Sammy the Spatula's work never had the same focus on premium quality that Bijou's does, but it was fairly groundbreaking in its own right, wasn't it? What a shame he got you to believe in him, only to try and murder you all again like that. I hear they nearly caught him boarding the first train he could sneak himself onto—"

"If you don't mind, Mr. Goldwin," said Arthur's father, "I'd rather not discuss our former chef at this time. Still a bit of a tender subject, I'm afraid."

"Oh, I completely understand, Charlie. I can't imagine the heartbreak of having a member of one's own trusted staff commit such a betrayal. Fortunately, we've never had to experience anything like that, since each of our staff has come fully recommended by the Ardmore Association. Just one of the many perks of membership, of course. You should really think of coming over—I know the Association would love to have you. . . ."

Arthur thought back to the last place he'd heard the Ardmore Association mentioned, in an article about the discovery of a deceased board member at a sandcastle competition. He wondered if Rex had read that article, too.

"I'm afraid I'd rather not discuss the Ardmore Association either, Mr. Goldwin," said Arthur's father.

"Well then," Rex replied. "Since it seems I'm failing so miserably as your host, perhaps you might tell us what you *would* like to discuss."

"Forgive me," Mr. Whipple grumbled, "if, after such a *hearty* meal, I don't have the stomach for recounting one of the worst disasters in our family's history, or for hearing a recruitment talk from an organization whose past members turn up as skeletons. And while we're on the subject, perhaps you can shed some light on this shadowy board of directors running the show these days. We know they've added one new member at the very least. So tell me, Mr. Goldwin: who is the new treasurer? Friend of yours, is he?"

Mrs. Whipple dropped her fork, which clattered loudly against her empty plate.

Rex Goldwin did not miss a beat. "Wish I knew, Charlie. You'd think with the record-breaking deal we've made we'd be privy to that information, wouldn't you? But alas, we're just as much in the dark about the board of directors as anybody else. Of course, you're more than welcome to your opinions, Charlie. Chef Bijou's cuisine, as well as the Ardmore Association, are certainly not for everyone. I had hoped you were forward-thinking enough to embrace them—but I wonder if your resistance stems from another source altogether. It would seem by your behavior in the Lizard Lounge that you have not entirely overcome the past." Rex's eyes narrowed as he flashed a roguish grin. "Surely you're not still sore about that business at *Norbury*, are you? I mean honestly, Charlie, that was ages ago—and you've more than proved yourself since then."

Mr. Whipple said nothing. At the mention of the word "Norbury," Arthur noticed his father's face become sullen and pale, its features frozen into an unnatural expression.

"Look, Charlie," Rex declared, "why don't we let bygones be bygones and set the record straight once and for all? For my part, I hold no grudge—but if you're still intent on carrying out this imagined little feud of yours, why don't we at least have some fun with it? The World Record World Championships are coming up in a couple of months, you know. . . ."

Arthur's heart fluttered with equal parts excitement and anxiety, just as it always did at the mention of the WRWC.

The World Record World Championships, of course, is a week-long tournament—organized every two years by the International World Record Federation—in which the world's greatest world-record breakers travel across the globe to compete for universal fame and fortune. After seven days and more than a thousand record-setting events, awards are given in various categories to the entrants who have collected the most world records. The highest of these awards is the World Record World Championship Cup, presented at the end of the tournament to the Family to Hold the Most World Records on Earth. The Whipples had managed to bring home the cup at the past three championships, despite Arthur's failure to even qualify for a single event. Still, Arthur had always dreamt that one day he might have some small part in his family's success.

His father remained speechless as Rex continued his proposal. "What would you say to signing an official rivalry contract for this year's tournament, eh, Charlie? Now, I know you're not used to such heated competition, and what with the poorly timed return of this Lyon's Curse and these unfortunate catastrophes it keeps causing, I can see why you might not want to take on anything else at the moment. But then again, what better way to show the world you're still the undisputed Record-Breakingest Family on Earth?"

"Forgive me, Mr. Goldwin," Arthur's mother cut in. "But what exactly is a rivalry contract?"

"Why, it's hardly anything at all, Mrs. Whipple," Rex replied. "Just a way to keep things interesting. Simply offers a few advantages to the winning party—and a few penalties to the loser."

"And what sort of penalties would those be exactly?"

"Oh, just that if one of our families wins the Championship Cup, the other would excuse themselves from any future

43

events in which the winner is participating—for a specified period of two years. So as to ease the competition and give the winner a better chance of keeping the cup longer."

Mrs. Whipple shook her head and turned to her husband, who was rubbing his jaw in deep thought. "I don't know, Charles," she said. "The possible advantages scarcely seem worth the risk."

Before her husband could answer, Rex interjected, "I completely understand, Mrs. Whipple. The penalties—however minor—would, of course, make it harder for the losing family to close the gap between the winning family after the championships. So, if you're not one hundred percent confident yours will come out on top, it really doesn't make sense for you to jeopardize your standing any further. I must say I'm flattered, though. Who ever would imagine the Whipples could have even the slightest doubt going up against a family of newcomers like ours? Unless, of course, Charlie is thinking about Norbury again. . . ."

Arthur's father choked on a fleck of truffled veal from their microscopic dinner but promptly cleared his throat. "There is no doubt, Mr. Goldwin," he said, ignoring the stern look on his wife's face. "We accept."

"Very well then," Rex said as he stood from his chair. "I'll have our lawyer draft the official papers, and we can get this under way." He pushed a button in a wall panel behind him and spoke into the speaker grille beside it. "Mr. Boyle, would you bring us the Ardmore paperwork?"

A moment later, a high-foreheaded man with dark,

44

puffily coiffed hair and huge black-rimmed glasses stepped into the room. His tiny, insect-like eyes peered lazily from behind the massive lenses as if gazing up from twin petri dishes. They blinked every few seconds, confirming they were still live specimens.

"Ah yes," said Rex. "Malcolm Boyle, meet the Whipples, our new rivals. Mr. Boyle here is chief legal representative for the Ardmore Association."

The corners of Mr. Boyle's mouth twitched upward to form the subtlest, wryest of smiles on an otherwise expressionless face. He stepped forward without a word and hefted a massive briefcase onto the table, then popped the clasps open with his thumbs to reveal a second, smaller briefcase, which he promptly popped open to reveal a third. From out of this briefcase he removed a stack of papers and set them before Arthur's father, while the Whipples looked on in disbelief. "Pleasure to meet you, Mr. Whipple," the lawyer said finally in a low, languid voice that was both unhurried and oddly precise. "If you would just sign and date this official Intention of Rivalry form—in triplicate—your rivalry may commence." He removed a gold pen from his jacket and circled a few key points on the contract as he skimmed over them out loud. "Penalties in effect for two years following the championships' end. . . . All disputes to be resolved by dueling . . . yada yada yada. . . . Standard boilerplate."

"Goodness," said Mr. Whipple as he reached the end of the form, "all our names have already been typed in here. If I didn't know any better, I'd say you drafted this long

45

before we arrived here tonight. Why, you must be the Fastest Typist on the Planet, Mr. Boyle."

"My personal record-breaking skills—though impressive—are immaterial in these proceedings, Mr. Whipple," said Mr. Boyle. The corners of his mouth twitched upward once more. Then he held out the pen. "Simply sign and date in triplicate."

Mr. Whipple took the pen from the lawyer. He gave a momentary glance to his wife, who widened her eyes and shook her head in silent protest. Then, catching a glimpse of the crooked smirk on Rex's face, Arthur's father lowered the pen and signed the form.

"There we are, Mr. Whipple," said Rex, smiling as he extended his arm across the table. "It's settled."

Mr. Whipple stood to grasp his rival's hand. "May the best family win," he said.

"And we will," Rupert snickered just loud enough for Arthur to hear.

The air hung heavy with tension.

"Now," Rex declared, "let us kick off our official rivalry the old-fashioned way—with a cutthroat game of hide-and-seek!"

UNJUST DESSERTS

Uncle Mervyn, the Whipples' longtime personal record certifier (and godfather to the Whipple children), stood calibrating his stopwatch on the terrace behind the Goldwin house, where he had been summoned to officiate. Mrs. Waite, the Whipples' plump, silver-haired housekeeper, stood beside him holding two-year-old Ivy, the youngest Whipple child, to whom she served as unofficial nanny. Ivy held her matching teddy bear, Mr. Growls, who was currently dressed like a ninja.

The members of the two teams spread themselves out across the area, warming up for the critical match to come, as Mr. Boyle approached Uncle Mervyn from across the terrace.

"Always fascinated me," the lawyer said casually, "this Oath of Impartiality you certifiers swear to uphold."

"Required by the IWRF, of course," said Uncle Mervyn, still fussing with his watch, "but it's an oath I'd gladly take nonetheless."

"Seems a bit absurd, though, doesn't it," Mr. Boyle said dryly, "not to show preference for the people closest to you? The ones who pay your salary? The ones who trust you with their deepest secrets? I know I couldn't do it." The corners of his mouth twitched upward. "Lucky for me, we lawyers are required to take no such oath."

Mrs. Waite stepped forward. "I'm not sure I like your tone, Mr. Boyle," she said, linking her free arm in Uncle Mervyn's. "I've not been around record breaking long, but in my short time with the Whipples, Mervyn has already proved himself the World's Most Honest, Most Reliable, Most Trustworthy Soul on the Planet." She placed her cheek against his grizzled beard and added quietly, "Not to mention the Sweetest."

Uncle Mervyn's cheeks turned rosy as he straightened a clump of thinning gray hair on top of his head. "Why, thank you, Mrs. Waite," he stammered. "You—you are quite remarkable yourself."

"So, Mr. Boyle," the woman concluded with a mischievous grin, "please refrain from your pointed comments—unless you'd like to find yourself facing the business end of an angry housekeeper's feather duster."

"Forgive me, Mrs. Waite," said Mr. Boyle, his tiny eyes blinking behind his massive glasses. "I meant no disrespect."

"Dis-re-speck!" chirped Ivy.

48

Arthur smiled at Mrs. Waite's noble defiance and at the sound of his little sister's voice. Then, following his family's lead, he moved away from the terrace and began stretching his muscles against a nearby tree—which he promptly discovered was like no other tree he had ever encountered.

The first thing he noticed was how strangely clean and squishy its bark felt. He then stepped back to find its branches were identical on either side of its trunk, so that from where he stood, the tree appeared to be perfectly symmetrical. He studied the other trees around him and realized they all shared the same odd quality. Clearly, something had changed since his prior visit to the Crosley estate.

It then struck him his fingers were coated in a clear gel that looked and smelled like tree sap, but with none of its stickiness.

Two trees over, Arthur's little brother George held up a goo-covered hand and asked, "What's wrong with this tree, Dad?"

Mr. Whipple, busy studying his own upturned palm, appeared just as baffled.

Rex Goldwin, however, was quick to answer. "Don't tell me your old dad's never let you climb a Sim-o-Tree before! Really, Charlie, you've got to get with the times. *Actual* trees are a thing of the past—the future's all about Sim-o-Trees. This place was absolutely teeming with actual trees when we bought it, but with a little bit of vision on our part, we transformed this overgrown, grimy little grove into the Largest Synthetic Woodland on the Planet."

"And with Sim-o-Trees," his wife added, "you never have to worry about leaves falling off and dirtying up the ground—or getting that disgusting tree sap all over your hands and clothes."

Her six-year-old son, Randolf, began rubbing the seat of his trousers onto the tree behind him, then turned it to face the Whipples. "See?" he said.

"Hmm," said Mr. Whipple, rubbing his fingers together in the unidentified ooze. "But what's this then?" he asked.

"Pine-scented disinfectant hand soap," Rita replied. "Only comes in the top-of-the-line models. The more you climb, the cleaner you get. I'd like to see you try that in a normal tree!"

"And to cap it off," said Roland, "our fabricated forest here has just been recognized by the Intercontinental Hide-and-Seek Commission as an Optimum Field of Play, the highest distinction in the sport. . . ."

"But don't be too intimidated," added Roxy. "We'll try and go easy on you."

"Oh, don't worry about us," Cordelia replied.

"Yeah," said George. "Do your worst."

After winning the coin toss, the Goldwins chose to hide first—as is the usual preference in premier division hide-and-seek. They took their places at the hiding line as the Whipples circled around the giant Sim-o-Tree that served as home base.

Uncle Mervyn raised his megaphone. "On my mark," he announced, "seekers may commence countdown. And . . ."

Arthur felt his throat go dry as a woozy feeling rushed over him. He doubled over and gave a violent gagging cough. He would have felt rather embarrassed, had half his family members not done the very same a moment later.

"Goodness, Whipples!" said Rex, turning back to face his opponents. "What on earth is the matter? Word of advice: you might not want to burst out in spontaneous coughing once the hide-and-seek match actually begins. Sort of makes it difficult to conceal your position, don't you think?"

Arthur's father, hands on his knees and wheezing like the rest of his family, cocked his head toward Rex Goldwin and rasped, "What did you put out here?"

Rex looked puzzled. "What do you . . . ? Ohhh—you're not having a bad reaction to the Sim-o-Trees, are you? I'm told it takes a few months for the advanced polymers to stabilize, and that in the meantime, they might give off a slightly noxious gas, which may cause temporary dizziness and respiratory trauma to the unconditioned. But we're so used to being surrounded by plastics, we haven't noticed it! Ohhh—I really feel terrible about this. I should have warned you—I sometimes forget that not everyone has upgraded to the luxury of plastics like we have."

Another bout of coughing broke out amongst the Whipples.

Mr. Boyle stepped forward. "I think you'll find this covered in Article Seventeen of the Intention of Rivalry form: 'Rival A shall not be held liable for any health

51

complications of Rival B resulting from side effects of artificial vegetation.'"

"Ooh," said Rex. "It does say that, doesn't it? Not to worry, though—you'll all be right as rain in just a few minutes. Deep breaths now." Rex checked his watch a moment later and added, "Hmm. I really wish we could delay the start time, but it is already on the books."

His eldest daughter Rosalind spoke up. "We could always fit them with gas masks from the new Reek Chic collection, couldn't we, Dad? Sure to improve their wardrobe at the very least. . . ."

"That won't be necessary," Arthur's father wheezed. He gritted his teeth and stifled a cough. "Let's get on with it."

"Very well, Charlie," said Rex as both families returned to their starting points. "Good luck to you."

Uncle Mervyn, still wheezing himself, lifted the megaphone to his lips and cried feebly, "Go!"

The Goldwins scattered into the surrounding fake forest while Arthur and his family did their best to stand up straight and count down from one hundred.

". . . five, four, three, two, one," the Whipples coughed at last. "Ready or not, here we come!"

● ● ●

An hour and a half after leaving home base, the Whipples had largely adapted to the effects of the Sim-o-Trees, but had yet to find a single member of the Goldwin family.

Arthur had been assigned the specialized position of

"flusher," whose job it was to wander alone and flush out any hiders he might stumble upon. So far, he had stumbled upon a plastic owl, three plastic squirrels, and a section of synthetic shrubbery that looked exactly like Rita Goldwin from ten paces away, but nothing yet that would qualify as an actual human being.

As he crept into an exceptionally dark section of Sim-o-Trees, Arthur glimpsed a hint of movement to his right and lunged toward it, only to discover a live barn owl swooping off with a plastic field mouse in its talons. Arthur had no trouble identifying with the disappointment the owl would shortly be experiencing.

Arthur turned around with a sigh but was halted in his tracks by a curious sound overhead.

"Pssst," called the noise.

Arthur peered into the branches above him but saw no sign of its source.

"Pssst," it called again. If it was some other confused woodland creature, he did not recognize its call.

Arthur took a small step forward to adjust his vantage point and looked up once more. This time, he could just make out the shadowy face of a girl between the branches.

It was Ruby. And she was beckoning him to join her.

By the time he had clambered up the rubbery trunk and onto Ruby's branch some twenty feet off the ground, Arthur's hands and clothes had become as clean as they had been all day—apart from the strong smell of synthetic pine that now clung to them.

53

He took a seat beside Ruby, who turned to him with a smile. "Looks like you've found me," she whispered.

"I'm pretty sure it's the other way around," he said, panting from the climb. "You're quite the hider, aren't you? You've managed to stay hidden for nearly two hours."

Ruby shrugged. "Didn't really do it on purpose." She held up her copy of *Poise and Poisonousness*. "Just catching up on some reading." She lowered the book and clapped it shut. "You know," she added, "this is a bit like our very first meeting, isn't it? Though it was you up a tree stalking *me* then. Not far from where we are now, I reckon."

"Yeah," said Arthur, rubbing the back of his shoulder. "Glad to see the branches on these new trees are a bit sturdier."

Ruby gave a smirk. "I seem to recall it wasn't the fall that sent you running away screaming that night. Come on now, was I really that terrifying?"

"Sort of," said Arthur. "I mean you did look a bit like . . ." He shifted his gaze toward the ground and mumbled the rest of the sentence under his breath.

"What was that?" said Ruby. "I don't think I quite heard you."

Arthur cleared his throat. "I may have kind of thought you were . . . a ghost."

"Really?!" Ruby snickered. "Do you see ghosts often?"

"Well, no," Arthur said defensively. "But you must admit—you didn't look completely un-ghostlike back then, what with all the black nail polish and eye makeup.

And have you ever considered it might have been easy in that particular setting to mistake *anyone* for the vengeful spirit of a child murdered by a toffee mogul? I mean, surely you've heard about the Crosley ghosts."

"Can't say I have. But if that's the sort of conclusion you come to every time you see a defenseless girl sitting alone in the woods, you probably shouldn't be leaving the house. Quite the sensitive type, aren't we?"

"Hey—*I* wasn't the one crying my eyes out, if you recall."

As the words left Arthur's mouth, the haunting image of the ghost girl's swollen green eyes and tear-stained cheeks suddenly filled his mind. "By the way," he added, "why *were* you crying?"

"I don't know if that's a very polite thing to ask someone."

"No. You're right," said Arthur. "I'm sorry."

Ruby nodded—then closed her book and set it beside her on the ledge. "Well," she said, "if you really want to know—that was the day I found out about the trees."

Arthur's brow furrowed. "Found out *what* about the trees?"

"That they were all going to be cut down, and replaced with—" Ruby knocked on the hollow-sounding Sim-o-Tree branch beneath them "—these man-made monstrosities. Just when I thought I was going to have actual trees of my own. . . . It was such a beautiful grove, wasn't it?"

Arthur thought back to the gnarled, gloomy entanglement of vegetation that had nearly served as his final resting place. "'Beautiful' may be a *bit* strong. . . ."

"Ah, what do you know, anyway?" snapped Ruby. "Your house has more trees than you know what to do with. This was going to be my first real house, you know. I thought it was going to be different from the compound, but it's turned out to be more or less the same. They didn't have real trees there either."

"Wait—what do you mean *compound*?"

"The place we lived before we moved here. Elite fitness facilities, world-class tutors, electrified fences—that sort of thing. What, you never had to grow up in a remote high-tech training station?"

"Um—no?"

"Of course you didn't. You got to have a *normal* childhood."

Arthur bristled at the accusation. "Look, you don't have to get personal. I was only asking a question."

Ruby's fiery expression dimmed. "I know," she sighed. "Sorry for getting worked up. It's just that . . . Arthur, have you ever felt like you were a stranger in your own family? Like maybe you were adopted or switched at birth or something?"

"Gee, I hope I wasn't. I mean, I don't *think* I was. They appear to be telling the truth when they recount the story of my recordless birth—they do seem to remember every detail. . . . But then again, I *am* awfully different—so I guess it's possible. But why should you think *you're* adopted? You're a world-record holder just like everyone else in your family."

"I don't know. I guess I just feel out of place—like this can't be my *real* family . . . like I'm an impostor. And I guess sometimes I just *wish* I was adopted—that my real family was out there somewhere, and that someday they'd come and rescue me."

"Why would you wish that?" Arthur puzzled. "I mean, if you actually did have an alternate family, they surely wouldn't hold half the world records your current family does. And then where would you be?"

"I don't know—truly and utterly content?"

"With no world records in your family? I doubt it."

"Arthur, have you learned anything since I've met you?"

"What do you mean? I know being a record holder doesn't automatically make you a saint or something. But I just can't believe it's better *not* to have records than to have them."

"Even if it means living a lie? Tell me, Arthur, how did you like dinner tonight? Satisfying, was it?"

Arthur swallowed. "Perhaps it wasn't the Most *Filling* Meal of All Time, but it was a satisfying world record nonetheless." The thought of food sent up an audible growl from his belly.

"Hmm," Ruby grunted. "You know what the Goldwins really had for dinner, just before your family arrived? Nutrient-rich, powdered protein shakes."

"Wow," said Arthur. "You've got your own shake machine? Your family's got *everything*, haven't they?"

Ruby let out an exasperated sigh. "Anyhow, I guess I just

imagine my real family as being a bit more like me." Ruby glanced down toward her dangling shoes. "You know—not so perfect."

"You seem pretty perfect to me," said Arthur. "I mean, you're a world-record holder . . . you live in the house of the future . . . you're a first-rate junior detective . . . oh, and your hair—it really is a pleasant shade. And have you ever noticed how perfectly it goes with your name? Your parents really outdid themselves coming up with that one."

"Actually," said Ruby, "they named me Rubilda."

"Oh," said Arthur. "Well, then you have the perfect *nick*name."

Ruby sniffed and gave a subtle smile, then glanced again toward the ground.

After several seconds of silence, she picked up her book again and flipped it open.

"Can you even see the words?" Arthur asked. "It's completely dark out."

"It isn't *completely* dark," said Ruby. "One can hardly consider herself a serious reader until she's read by moonlight."

"If you say so," said Arthur.

"Back on the compound," Ruby explained, "moonlight was usually the only light I had. Reading for pleasure was prohibited till we'd finished all the books on the Academy's required reading list. But who wants to slog through a tower of boring, tedious books when there are so many wonderful others out there? Sometimes, the only way to read what I wanted was to wait until everyone else had gone to sleep—and then sneak past the guards and security alarms out into the moonlight."

"Isn't that a bit drastic?" said Arthur. "I mean, it's only *reading*."

"*Only* reading? *Reading* was the one thing that kept me from completely losing my mind in that place. Books were all I had. In fact, they'd *still* be all I had, if it weren't for—well, if it weren't for certain recent events and certain people involved in those certain recent events."

Arthur scrunched up his brow. "What events now? Which people?"

Ruby let out a frustrated sigh. "Never mind," she said.

Convinced he had missed something, but not sure what, Arthur fiddled with a plastic twig for a few moments, then let out a sigh of his own. "All right, then. Well . . . let's go."

"What do you mean, 'let's go'?"

"Honestly," replied Arthur, "are you even remotely familiar with the basic rules of hide-and-seek? After tagging someone on the hiding team, a member of the seeking team escorts the captured hider back to base."

Ruby looked puzzled. "And why would you want to do that?"

"Because I've got to help my family stop yours from breaking the record for Longest Time to Remain Hidden in a Hide-and-Seek Match," Arthur explained. "I know that sort of thing might not matter much to you, but it does to me. It's bad enough I've never broken a world record of my own . . ."

59

"Why is that so important to you, Arthur?" Ruby shot back. "World records aren't so great, you know."

"That's easy for you to say; you've already broken one."

Ruby sighed. "I wish I could give my record back."

"You're not serious."

"You'd wish the same thing if you'd broken the record I have."

"But I don't know what record you've broken. Remember how you've never told me, no matter how many times I've asked?"

"Believe me," said Ruby, shaking her head, "you don't want to know."

"But I really do want to know," insisted Arthur. "And to be honest, I think it's a bit weird you won't just tell me."

"Rex and Rita would be seriously angry," Ruby scowled. "God knows, I've already shamed them enough—just ask them."

"I can't see how you could have shamed them so much, being a successful world-record breaker. And anyway, isn't it sort of your mission in life to make your parents angry?"

Ruby contemplated this a moment, then narrowed her eyes. "Do you promise not to tell another soul as long as you live?"

"I promise," said Arthur.

"Do you swear to gouge out your eyes and swallow them whole if you ever do?"

"I swear."

The truth was Arthur had often considered gouging out

his eyes and swallowing them whole, as a last-ditch attempt at getting his name in the *Grazelby Guide*—but he didn't mention this to Ruby.

After an extended pause, Ruby drew a deep breath and looked Arthur straight in the eye. "Well . . ."

At that moment, there was a bloodcurdling scream.

In his sudden confusion, Arthur could not tell whether the scream had come from the girl in front of him or from some other source. When he heard the next scream a split second later, it was clear it had not been Ruby.

"What on earth was that?!" she cried.

Arthur's face was now pale and panic-stricken. "I think it's one of my sisters," he spluttered. "She sounds close by—we've got to help her—come on!"

Arthur tore through synthetic leaves and branches as he scrambled down the tree. He dropped to the ground and dashed off toward the screams with Ruby trailing just behind him.

They burst through a wall of artificial bracken into a narrow clearing—and froze in their tracks.

Ten yards ahead, dangling by one arm from an elevated Sim-o-Tree branch, Arthur's little sister Abigail screamed in terror. While this in itself would have been distressing enough, it was the sight of what waited *beneath* his sister that turned Arthur's blood to ice.

Rearing up from the ground below her, its snapping jaws inches from Abigail's dangling feet, stood a gigantic blood-thirsty lizard, wearing a velvet smoking jacket and a monocle.

61

MIDNIGHT SNACK

Anyone who has previously crossed paths with an uncaged Komodo dragon is a lucky individual indeed—either lucky to be alive or lucky to be done with the dreadful business of being eaten by a Komodo dragon.

According to Dr. Scarwood, Arthur's Wilderness Survival instructor, the Komodo dragon is the World's Largest Species of Lizard—as well as one of its most brutal killers. Blessed with uncommon intelligence, the Komodo dragon is content using its sophisticated brain to think up the most insidious methods of making meals of its neighbors—devising such dishes as defenseless deer, wide-eyed water buffalo, unsuspecting village child, and, of course, baby Komodo dragon.

Arthur had needed little convincing that such a crafty,

cold-blooded creature should be avoided at all costs, and would have promptly run in the other direction—had the creature's menu that night not included his own sister.

"Help, Arthur!" Abigail screamed as her shoe slipped from her foot and fell through the air.

A split second later, the Komodo dragon caught it in its teeth, snapped its head back, and slung the shoe down its gullet, swallowing it whole in one revolting gulp.

Arthur and Ruby traded horrified glances, then grabbed whatever they could find to throw.

"Get out of here, you scaly sack of guts!" Ruby shouted as she released a stone into the air.

"Yeah," cried Arthur, hurling a fallen Sim-o-tree branch. "Go back to your own time, you reject from the early Cenozoic era!"

Ruby shot him a quizzical look, then turned and landed a direct hit on the beast's shoulder. "Take that, you slimy son-of-a-skink!" she yelled.

Unfortunately, Komodo dragons are endowed with incredibly thick skin—both physiologically and emotionally—and are not easily wounded either by small stones or disparaging remarks. And so, despite the children's best efforts, the beast did not budge.

Abigail, on the other hand, began to budge in a most worrisome manner.

"Arthur!" she cried. "My hand is slipping!"

The Komodo dragon, sensing the girl's swelling panic, rose to its tippy-toes and strained its neck, so that its forked yellow tongue flicked the bottoms of Abigail's feet.

Arthur knew he only had a moment to intervene before his sister became lizard food. He had one stone left.

He drew back his arm and flung the stone with as much force as he could muster. An instant later, it smashed into the side of the creature's head.

The Komodo dragon fell to all fours with a wobble. Armor-plated skin or no, nobody likes to be smacked in the face.

"Nice shot, Arthur!" Ruby cheered. "That'll teach him!"

But her cheering did not last long.

As the lizard recovered from its momentary daze, it turned its head and promptly noticed two new tasty morsels—plumper, juicier, and altogether more accessible than the one in the tree.

"Um, Arthur," said Ruby, "I don't like the way it's looking at us."

The monster locked its eyes onto the two children now only four yards away and shifted its ten-foot frame to face them.

"Me neither," Arthur agreed. He felt as though the hairs on the back of his neck were trying to make a break for it. They seemed to have the right idea.

Without warning, the lizard lurched forward.

"Run!" cried Arthur, scrambling over his heels in retreat.

The children darted in opposite directions, hoping to split the creature's attention, but the lizard quickly opted for the slightly larger slab of meat that was Arthur.

Arthur glanced backward and caught a glimpse of the beast charging after him with grotesque, ungainly strides.

"Arthur!" screamed Ruby.

"Go . . ?" Arthur cried between panicked breaths, "help . . . Abigail!"

"I've got her," Ruby shouted back. "You keep running, Arthur! Whatever you do, don't stop running!"

Now, as lizards go, Komodo dragons are exceptionally fast, with a top land speed of 12.4 miles per hour. Luckily for Arthur, the top land speed of a twelve-year-old boy running for his life from a hungry Komodo dragon is just about the same.

When Arthur realized he was maintaining a short but steady distance between the lizard's jaws and his own heels, he began to think he might be able to run the beast in circles just long enough for help to arrive. Sadly, his plans failed to consider the slender but rigid length of rubber root arching out of the ground just ahead of him.

The next moment, Arthur found himself sailing through the air. It was then the true terror struck him.

As Arthur landed face-first in the artificial underbrush, his skin prickled at the feeling of utter defenselessness. He seized the first object his fingers touched and flipped himself onto his back.

Luckily, he'd grabbed a sturdy, sizable Sim-o-Tree branch—because barely an instant after he'd shifted into position, the beast was upon him.

He braced the four-foot limb against his shoulder and

thrust the opposite end into the rushing reptile's face, crumpling the creature to a halt at his feet.

Now angrier than ever, and seriously tired of being bashed in the face, the Komodo dragon bit off the end of the faux tree branch and began clawing its way forward.

"Ahh!" Arthur cried in terror.

The monocle over the beast's right eye was now cracked and crooked, its velvet jacket hanging in tatters—along with any semblance of sophistication the show lizard may once have possessed. As the creature chomped through the rubbery tree limb, thick strands of saliva dropped from its mouth and seeped into Arthur's clothes.

"Ughh!" Arthur cried in disgust.

He struggled to back away from the oncoming creature—but his feet lay trapped beneath its scaly underside. He thrashed at the lizard's snout with the ever-dwindling Sim-o-Tree branch, but hard as he tried, he could not stave off the terrible truth: this was not a battle he would win.

As hope drained from Arthur's heart, a faint tinkling sound began to swell in the back of his mind.

The monster wrenched the synthetic stick back and forth, straining to rid its prey of the meddlesome object once and for all.

Arthur clutched the branch for dear life as the tinkling sound grew louder. He wondered if, being so near to death, he might be hearing the chimes of heaven filtering through from the other side.

With one final tug, the Komodo dragon ripped the

branch from Arthur's grasp and flung it into the trees.

A blast of putrid breath stung Arthur's nostrils, and he felt the monster's tongue flick against his cheek. The tinkling chimes of heaven rang out louder than ever.

It was then that Arthur noticed the giant dog leaping toward him through the Sim-o-Trees.

Like a hound out of Hades, the Whipples' Great Dane, Hamlet, bounded into the moonlight, dragging a jingling chain behind him—along with the uprooted stake to which it was attached.

"Sic him, boy!" shouted a voice to Arthur's rear.

It was Abigail. With Ruby rushing in alongside her, Arthur's sister cried again, "Sic him!"

There was a flurry of furious barking, followed by a brutal collision.

As Hamlet's jaws clamped down on the lizard's throat, the force of the attack flung the creature through the air and onto its back, freeing Arthur from the monster's clutches.

Arthur scrambled to his feet and ran to Ruby and his sister. There, the children watched powerlessly as the two titans of the animal kingdom battled for dominance, one determined to devour them—the other to defend them.

It was a terrible, savage sight. The monstrous lizard, unable to free its throat from Hamlet's grasp, thrashed and writhed, pulling the towering dog to the ground beside it. The Great Dane struggled to stand, but the lizard's constant flailing kept him from rising. Still, the dog held his grip.

"Get him, Hammie!" Abigail shouted through glistening tears. "Good boy, Hammie!"

As the beasts rolled across the fake forest floor, the dragon clamped its jaws onto Hamlet's front leg. The dog yelped but kept his hold and quickly resumed his snarling.

"Hammie!" cried Abigail. "Don't let him get you!"

Each creature clung to a mouthful of its opponent's flesh as reptile and mammal struggled to outlast the other's grip.

The battle raged on for several moments, and then, little by little, the flailing subsided. From where the children stood, it was impossible to tell which creature was weakening: the lizard, the dog—or both.

Abigail buried her face in Arthur's tattered shirt. "Oh, Arthur," she wept, "he'll be okay, won't he? He's got to be okay!"

Arthur wrapped his arm around his sister, but said nothing.

The once thrashing creatures were all but still now, their savage sounds reduced to muffled gurgling. Arthur held his sister close and exchanged a woeful glance with Ruby.

Then the dog began to stir.

"Abigail, look!" Arthur cried.

As the girl turned her head to see, Hamlet drew his hind legs beneath his body and, with a quick twist of his midsection, raised his hindquarters into the air. With far greater difficulty, the dog straightened his front legs and hoisted his neck off the ground. In his jaws, Hamlet still gripped the wrinkled throat of the Komodo dragon, its head now dangling to one side.

"Hammie!" cried Abigail.

The dog gave the lizard's neck a feeble yet triumphant shake, then tossed its lifeless body to the ground. With his tongue hanging happily from his mouth, Hamlet stepped over the carcass and limped toward his human companions.

As the dog drew near, Arthur sensed something amiss in his appearance. In the light of the moon, he could just make out a large dark patch of matted fur on the dog's chest and left front leg.

When he reached the children, Hamlet licked Abigail's face, then collapsed exhaustedly at her feet. As the dog lay panting proudly, the little girl knelt down beside him, wrapped her arms around his neck, and pressed her nose into his fur.

"Good boy, Hammie. Good boy," she whispered.

"Thanks, boy," said Arthur, scratching the dog between the ears. "If it weren't for you, I'd be lizard food."

There was a rustling noise from the nearby Sim-o-Trees, accompanied by the bobbing beam of a flashlight. The next moment, Uncle Mervyn burst into the clearing.

"I heard screaming. . . ." he spluttered.

His flashlight beam quickly shifted from the children's filthy faces and torn clothes to the massive, twisted corpse of the Komodo dragon.

"Oh my!" he exclaimed, rushing toward them. "Children, are you all right?!"

"We're fine, Uncle Mervyn," said Arthur. "Thanks to Hamlet."

69

"And Arthur," added Abigail. "The lizard would've grabbed me long before Hammie could get here, if it weren't for him . . . not to mention Ruby. She helped me out of the tree—and she's not even a member of my team."

Ruby smiled bashfully.

"Well done, all of you," said Uncle Mervyn. "Your parents will be horrified when they hear what's happened."

Uncle Mervyn raised his megaphone to his mouth and depressed the button. "Game over!" he called, his voice echoing through the empty night air. He removed a pistol from his pocket and shot a burning red flare into the sky overhead. "I repeat—the game is over! There has been a serious incident! All competitors reconvene at once!"

Before he had even finished the announcement, Mr. and Mrs. Whipple and several of their children rushed into the clearing.

"What's happened?" inquired a distraught Mrs. Whipple.

"We heard screaming and barking from the other side of the estate," her husband added. "We came as fast as we . . ."

Uncle Mervyn shined the flashlight on the monstrous heap of scales and teeth. Arthur's parents gasped.

"Abigail! Arthur!" cried Mrs. Whipple. "Are you—"

At that moment, Rex and Rita Goldwin rushed in with a group of their children. Each of their faces was smeared with camouflage paint, and leafy Sim-o-Tree branches had been fastened to their clothes, so that—though they were only standing a few yards away—Arthur could hardly see them.

70

"What's the meaning of this?" demanded Rex Goldwin, his voice devoid of its usual charm. "Here we are, well on our way toward the Longest Time to Remain Hidden in a Regulation Game of Hide-and-Seek, and your man calls the game! Someone better have been killed, or I'm reporting this to the Intercontinental Hide-and-Seek Commission!"

"Indeed," said Malcolm Boyle, the Ardmore lawyer, as he stepped out from behind his client, "this is in clear violation of Section 83 of the IWRF Officiator's Manual."

"Honestly," Rita Goldwin added, "I don't know if I've ever heard of such—" Her face filled with horror as she noticed the body of her prized show lizard. "Ridgely!" she shrieked.

She tore the branches from her clothes and rushed to the lizard's side, cradling its drooping head in her arms. "What have you done to him?!" she howled.

"He just appeared out of nowhere," said Abigail. "He had me trapped in a tree, and he was going to eat me—but Arthur and Ruby saved my life. Then he trapped Arthur, and he was going to eat him too—but then Hamlet came to the rescue."

"I see," Rupert Goldwin said, scowling as he turned to his father. "Ridgely was the World's Largest Living Lizard, and now their dog has *murdered* him!"

"Precisely," Rex agreed, turning to face Mr. Whipple. "Have you any idea how difficult he was to acquire—or how important that record was to us? You should never have brought that slobbering dog with you in the first place!"

71

"I must say I'm rather glad we did bring him, Mr. Goldwin," snapped Arthur's father. "If we hadn't, what would have become of Abigail and Arthur—or your daughter Ruby? Are you honestly suggesting you'd rather have had your lizard eat our children?"

"Well, no," Rex said curtly. "But your dog didn't have to *kill* him!"

His daughters Rosalind and Roxy pulled each other close, scrunching up their faces in dramatic sorrow.

"What choice did he have?" demanded Mr. Whipple. "It was the children or the lizard. You're the one who chose to house a deadly Komodo dragon on your estate. Which reminds me—how *did* it get out, Mr. Goldwin?"

"Isn't it obvious?" said Rex. "Being the last to leave Ridgely's living quarters, your animal-obsessed daughter failed to lock the door behind her, and the poor critter simply followed her scent, unaware of the terrible fate that awaited him. Komodo dragons have a phenomenal sense of smell, you know—just another of the many traits that make them so endearing."

At this, Rita Goldwin's sniffling swelled to a sob, but Mr. Whipple remained unmoved. "Hmm," he said. "And would you include your lizard's hunger for human children among those traits as well?"

Rita's sobbing reached another crescendo.

"How dare you mock Ridgely's memory in our time of grief!" snarled Rex.

"Forgive me, Mr. and Mrs. Goldwin," Arthur's father

growled. "It's just that I'm beginning to believe you are somehow mixed up in my family's recent misfortunes—including this latest mishap!"

"Really, Charlie!" cried Rex. "First your mangy dog murders our beloved family pet, then your record-certifying crony robs us of a well-deserved world record—and now you're suggesting I'm guilty of sabotage? I resent the implication! Face it, Charlie—you've never forgiven me for Norbury, and now you're blaming your present failures on me as well. Surely it's not *my* fault your family is cursed!"

Arthur's father took a threatening step forward, but Mrs. Whipple held him back—then stepped in front of him.

"Mr. Goldwin," Arthur's mother declared, "while I am grateful to you for saving my husband's life at our Birthday Extravaganza, I'm afraid your actions since that time have negated any good turns you have done us and voided whatever good will we may have owed you. I have tried my best to be neighborly, however insulting you and your wife have been, but I refuse to endure it any longer. Though I do not entirely know what transpired between you and my husband in the time before I knew him, as far as I can tell, he has been right to mistrust you."

"Well!" huffed Rita Goldwin.

Mr. Whipple placed his arm around his wife and nodded. "Thank you, dear."

A guileful grin slowly stretched across Rex's face. "I'm sorry you feel that way, Mrs. Whipple," he said, the unctuous charm returning to his voice. "And I thought we were getting on so well."

By this time, all the hiders and seekers had arrived on the scene and grouped themselves into two divided lines. Mr. Whipple turned to the line that had formed behind him and announced, "Come now, Whipples. Some of us require medical attention—and it seems we'll get no help from our new neighbors. Mr. and Mrs. Goldwin, allow us to show ourselves *permanently* off your estate. Henry and Simon, would you assist our wounded hero?"

Arthur's brothers nodded and turned to Hamlet, who still lay panting proudly at Abigail's feet. The dog's tail began to wag as the boys drew near, but when Henry wrapped his arm around Hamlet's front legs, the dog let out a sharp whine.

"It's all right, boy," Henry said softly. Then, with Simon's help, he hoisted the Great Dane into his arms.

"Roland! Rupert!" called Rex Goldwin, gesturing to the deceased Komodo dragon.

His sons walked to the giant lump of lizard flesh and heaved it off the ground. This proved a far more awkward task than they'd expected, but they managed it with as much dignity as possible for two boys with dead lizard limbs poking out of their arms in every direction.

"Well, Charlie," Rex concluded, "it appears our friendly rivalry has just been escalated to a blood feud. I've always thought blood feuds were the very best sort of feud—haven't you?"

74

Mr. Whipple did not answer.

Mr. Boyle removed a sheaf of papers from his leaf-covered briefcase and handed it to Arthur's father. "I'll need this Blood Feud Escalation form completed within the next twenty-three hours, as per Article 48 of your Intention of Rivalry form."

Mr. Whipple took the papers and stamped off to gather his children.

"Don't worry, Mr. Boyle," said Uncle Mervyn. "You'll have it before the ink has even dried."

"Or shouldn't Blood Feud Escalation forms be signed in blood?" snapped Mrs. Waite. "Afraid it might take a while to draw blood from all the Whipples; I'm sure they'd be more than happy to use yours instead, Mr. Boyle."

The corners of Mr. Boyle's mouth twitched upward.

As the two families marched off in separate directions, Arthur looked to Ruby just in time to share a fleeting, troubled glance.

. . .

Cordelia had barely bandaged the last of her brother's wounds when Arthur bolted from the Whipple house.

"Thanks, Cordelia," he called behind him as he threw open the garden doors and burst outside.

"Easy, Arthur!" his sister called back. "You've had quite a shock and—"

But Arthur was too eager to get back to Hamlet and the others to heed her warning.

75

He hurried off across the estate and eventually arrived at the facility where Mr. Mahankali, manager of the Whipples' private zoo, cared for sick and injured animals. As Arthur rounded the corner, however, he heard a noise that spun his head toward the thick copse of trees that abutted the menagerie wall.

His heart stopped as he watched a giant shadowy figure disappear behind a tree trunk.

Arthur's mind raced. The impossible height of the figure left little doubt. It could belong to no other person but Mr. Overkill, the mysterious giant clown who—along with his dwarfish partner, Mr. Undercut—always seemed to turn up whenever the Whipples were plunged into terror.

"Hey!" Arthur shouted. "What are you doing here?! Why won't you leave us alone?! Come back here!"

He suddenly felt so outraged he completely forgot to be afraid. He charged after the retreating figure, ready to capture the giant and dwarf once and for all—or to die trying. But when he rounded the tree, he saw no sign of anyone. He darted to the next tree—and then the next—searching frantically for another glimpse of the figure, but again found nothing. Arthur panted in disbelief. Either his mind had been playing tricks on him, or the giant had simply vanished into thin air.

Arthur scurried back toward his original course, more exasperated than ever. As he passed the first tree a second time, he now noticed a small, light-colored object ensnared in its roots. He plucked the article from the

76

ground and discovered it to be a crumpled piece of paper.

He smoothed out its creases to reveal a typewritten note on a sheet of stationery. Below the familiar-looking seal of a flaming five-pointed crown, Arthur could just make out the following text in the moonlight:

Dear Messrs. Overkill & Undercut,

My patience is wearing thin. Though you have succeeded in creating a moderate amount of chaos, you have yet to eliminate a single one of your targets. This time, I'll make it very simple for you:

[**X**] 14:30—Get out of bed.
[**X**] 21:00—Retrieve the key.
[ ] 23:00—Feed the lizard.

I would hate to have to inform the CHAIRMAN OF THE BOARD if your failure continues.

Signed,
The Treasurer

Arthur's hands trembled as he folded the note and slipped it into his pocket. He repeated his search of the area, but found himself all alone once again.

FEUD FOR THOUGHT

Apart from the sinking sense of dread he now carried in his bones, Arthur had escaped the Goldwins' dinner party with only a few small bandages over some minor scrapes and scratches. Hamlet, however, would not be so lucky.

The scariest thing about Komodo dragons, it turns out, is not their quick speed or enormous size, nor their powerful jaws or serrated teeth, but rather a fifth weapon in their arsenal—a weapon virtually invisible, yet far deadlier than any of the others, and located in the unlikeliest of places: Komodo dragon drool.

Inside the mouth of every Komodo dragon lives a microscopic legion of lethal bacteria just waiting to be deployed. Consequently, the creature needs only to land a superficial bite anywhere on an animal's body and simply wait for the bacteria to do its work. Soon the wound festers, and the unwary animal is dead within a week. The Komodo dragon consults its appointment book to see which animal it nibbled on the week before, and thus what will be on the evening's menu, then uses its super keen sense of smell to track down the corpse. And voila! Buffalo buffet.

Of course, since the Goldwins' Komodo dragon was no longer around to claim its final bite-victim, Hamlet was in little danger of becoming Komodo dragon fodder anytime soon. If only there were some way to tell this to the bacteria.

Try as he might, Mr. Mahankali could not stop the infection in the dog's front leg. In order to limit the spread of gangrene, he was left with one terrible option.

"Is there no other way, Mahankali?" entreated Arthur's father.

"I am afraid not," Mr. Mahankali replied, his grave expression showing through the thick hair that covered his face. "The leg must be removed. Even then, there are no guarantees he will recover, but it is our best chance at saving him."

Arthur felt sick to his stomach as he considered the unfitting reward Hamlet would receive for such heroic actions.

"Please, Mr. Mahankali," Abigail cried, "he saved our lives. Don't hurt him anymore!"

"Do not worry, little one; I will make sure he does not feel a thing."

"How can we help?" said Mrs. Whipple, doing her best to keep her composure.

"Please, all of you, you must go and get some sleep. There is nothing more you can do for Hamlet tonight but pray."

• • •

The next morning, Arthur awoke before the sun. He checked under his mattress to make sure the Treasurer's note was still there, then returned it to its hiding spot. Before he could devote himself to detective work, however, he would have to clear his mind of another matter first. He threw on his robe and crept out into the corridor. There, he found Abigail already standing at the top of the stairs, holding a tiny hamster in an astronaut suit.

"What are you doing up so early, Abigail?" he whispered.

"Corporal Whiskerton and I are too worried about Hamlet to sleep," she replied.

"Yeah," said Arthur, scratching the top of the hamster's head with his finger, "me too. Let's go see what we can find out."

Just then, the intermittent sounds of clicking latches and squeaking hinges filled the hallway. One by one, each of the other Whipple children emerged from the row of bedrooms and quietly crept toward the stairs.

"Come on then," whispered Henry when everyone was accounted for. "Let's go."

The children found their father outside on the terrace, heading back toward the house.

"Dad," Abigail blurted, "have you spoken to Mr. Mahankali yet? How did the surgery go? Did Hamlet make it? When can we see him? Is he going to recover?"

Mr. Whipple smiled a warm but heavy-hearted smile. "The surgery went well. Mr. Mahankali has made up a recovery room within his quarters, so he can watch over Hamlet—though I'm afraid it's too soon to say whether or not he'll actually recover. You can see him now, if you like, but he is heavily sedated—and likely will be for some time. Come, children, I'll walk with you."

The sun's first rays shone through the trees as the Whipples made their way past the private zoo at the corner of the estate and crowded onto the doorstep of the small house beside it.

The door soon opened to reveal the hair-covered face of the Whipples' menagerie manager. In the light of day, Arthur couldn't help but notice the scarred section of dark skin below Mr. Mahankali's right ear where hair no longer grew. Until his fiery brush with death during the Birthday Cake Catastrophe he had indeed been the Hairiest Man Alive.

"Ah, children," the Panther-Man smiled, "come in, come in. We must honor our courageous friend, yes?"

Mr. Mahankali led the group through his elegantly decorated home, past exquisite textiles and artwork, ancient artifacts and yellowing Sanskrit parchments, each display carefully illuminated with museum-style lighting.

They passed through a door at the far side of the front room to find their giant Great Dane lying on a bed surrounded by glowing candles. Apart from the gentle rising and falling of his belly, the dog was motionless. Where once his front right leg had been, there was now only a short stub, wrapped in white gauze.

81

Abigail burst into tears and rushed to Hamlet's side. "Oh, Hammie," she cried, "what have they done to you?" She placed her tiny hand on the dog's massive chest and buried her face in the bed, where she continued to quietly sob.

Arthur and the other children looked on in silence, many of them fighting back tears, some of them unsuccessfully. Heartwarming as it was to see Hamlet alive on the other side of surgery, it was equally *heartbreaking* to find him in this new truncated state, lacking any of his usual exuberance.

Corporal Whiskerton stood on the bed beside Abigail and Hamlet, holding his little space helmet in his tiny clawed hands. Ever since Hamlet had rescued him from a neighbor dog after a test launch gone horribly wrong, the rocket-piloting hamster had become especially fond of his Great Dane comrade. The sight of the forlorn little corporal was almost as sad as the sight of the dog himself.

"So what's the prognosis, Mr. Mahankali?" said Henry, doing his best to sound practical. "What are Hamlet's chances at recovery?"

"Who can say?" the Panther-Man replied. "He was very, very weak, and yet, he made it through the surgery. This shows to me that his will is strong. Still, we must not forget that life is a fragile, mysterious thing, which does not worry itself with our silly predictions. We must wait and see."

• • •

When everyone had said their temporary goodbyes, Mr. Whipple led his children—all except for Abigail, who insisted on staying with Hamlet—away from Mr. Mahan-kali's cottage and back to the main house.

There, they were met by the scent of slightly burnt sausage and toast.

"What is that delightful smell?" said Beatrice.

"That," Mr. Whipple replied, "is your mother in the kitchen."

"But what about Chef Mulchmann?"

"Gave him the sack first thing this morning. Until we find someone better suited to taking Sammy's old position—impossible a task as that may be—your mother will be cooking the meals around here. I trust you will all find this agreeable."

There were no complaints. Amid the darkness of the previous night and subsequent morning, here was a tiny bright spot. The Whipple children took their breakfast in the parlor, where they enjoyed their first smiles of the day. Though the toast was a bit blackened and the eggs slightly runny, it certainly beat another one of Chef Mulchmann's casseroles.

Arthur realized, of course, what a major concession this had been for his father. His mother possessed many extraordinary talents, but cooking was not exactly one of them. Any cuisine-related records for that morning's meal had been effectively forfeited.

With this in mind, Arthur took another bite of burnt toast. It was a strange feeling to eat his food simply because he was hungry, without trying to break any world records in the process. Indeed, it felt rather refreshing.

83

In the chair beside him, his father sipped from a teacup while studying the newspaper. Arthur was glad to see him relax a bit after the week their family had had. His father then flipped to the headline on the second page.

WHIPPLE DOG KILLS WORLD'S LARGEST LIZARD!
DEVASTATED OWNERS REX AND RITA GOLDWIN MOURN LOSS, SUSPECT RETALIATION FOR RECENT UNSAFE SPORTS VICTORIES

Before Arthur could read any more, the paper was abruptly spattered with tea as his father burst into a fit of coughing.

"That does it!" Mr. Whipple spluttered, flinging the newspaper into the fireplace. "We must put an end to this mockery! Finish your breakfast, children. From now until the World Record World Championships, we shall do nothing else but prepare ourselves for the competition, that we may silence these Goldwins once and for all!"

• • •

And so, after a brief reprieve, it was back to business at the Whipple house. And then some.

When they had finished their breakfast, the Whipple children scattered across the grounds and set to work on their daily record attempts, which were now instilled with even greater purpose. Arthur, equally caught up in the fervor, rushed off to the terrace to meet Uncle Mervyn for his scheduled attempt at Most Wine Glasses Balanced on Chin.

After nineteen tries and a dozen bins of broken glass, however, Arthur was forced to sit himself on the steps for a breather.

Uncle Mervyn swept up the glittering remains of the latest attempt and smiled down at the melancholy boy. "That was a good one, lad. You had it—right up until the point when you didn't quite have it anymore. Very close, indeed." He laid down the broom and took a seat next to Arthur. "If you keep trying, you're bound to get it one of these days. . . . But perhaps, in the meantime, we should try to find a more suitable event for this year's championships."

"You think so?"

"My boy—not that it will make you any finer a lad—but if you want it, I believe you have the potential to be one of the great record breakers of our time. You've got the will, you've got the means—and you've certainly got the heart. The way I see it, the only thing standing between you and the *Grazelby Guide* is the right event—and we just need to find it."

"Wow, thanks Uncle Mervyn. Believe me, I do want to be a record breaker—more than anything. But if I've been searching my whole life with no luck so far, do you really think we'll be able to find such an event in just a few weeks?"

"Well, of course I can't say for sure—but it's certainly no less probable just because you've been looking for a long time. That's the nature of searching: one minute you haven't found something and the next minute you have. When Ikey Newton discovered gravity, he had gone his whole life up to that moment *without* discovering gravity—and it had been right beneath his boots the entire time."

"I'm pretty sure the only thing beneath my boots right now is broken glass, but I think I know what you mean. Just because I've gone all my life without breaking a record, doesn't mean it couldn't happen tomorrow, right?"

"That's the spirit, lad. Now, have you still got your magical domino?"

Arthur reached into his pocket and removed the small black tile he'd received from his uncle on his last birthday. "Always keep it with me," he said.

"And it's brought you luck so far, has it?"

"Er," said Arthur, thinking back to the uncommon run of catastrophes he'd endured since it had come into his possession, "I guess so."

"Well," Uncle Mervyn coughed, "never mind about that. The important thing to remember is that, like that domino in the Most Dominoes Toppled record, we all have our part to play—right?"

"Right," said Arthur, trying to believe what he was saying.

"Good. Now take the rest of the day and make a list of all the events that sound even remotely appealing to you. Tomorrow, we'll start at the top of the list and quickly work our way downward. If an event gives you too much trouble, we'll simply skip it and move on to the next—until we find the record you were meant to break."

86

"Thanks, Uncle Mervyn," Arthur said, smiling, as he jumped to his feet. "I'll get started right away."

"Very good, lad. Today begins a new chapter in the life of Arthur Whipple—a chapter entitled 'Success.'"

Arthur marched back into the house with his head held high, his hopes lifted by Uncle Mervyn's encouraging words and their new plan to get his name in the record books. With that settled, he could get back to thinking about even more important matters. He ran up to his room and grabbed his leather-bound copy of the most recent *Grazelby Guide* along with a notepad and pen. Then, after a quick glance at the clock, he retrieved the Treasurer's note from under his mattress, hurried back down the stairs, and headed for the front door. He did not want to be late for his midday appointment with Ruby.

On his way out, Arthur peeked into a room on the right, where his mother sat squeezed into a corner by the enormous pair of woolen mittens she was in the process of knitting.

"Mother?" he called. "I'm heading out to do some, um . . . research."

"All right, dear," came Mrs. Whipple's muffled reply. "Don't be too long, though. Penelope might need your help a bit later with her team of dancing centipedes. You know how they give her trouble sometimes, and we really can't risk any of your brothers' or sisters' fingertips at present, as we'll need all of them intact if we're to beat the Goldwins at the World Record World Championships."

"Of course, Mother," Arthur replied. "I'll be back soon to help out however I can."

With that, he strode purposefully out the front door. He had an investigation to resume.

• • •

Arthur arrived at the Undertakers' Graveyard at noon, just as he and Ruby had agreed the night before. Not immediately seeing his partner, he slipped through the creaky iron gate, then cautiously made his way to the winged statue of Obediah Digby Lowe, Father of Modern Undertaking, at the center of the cobblestone square.

Arthur was pleased to find the statue far less terrifying in the light of day than it had been in the light of a lantern at midnight. Indeed, as he sat himself down in the statue's shadow, he could hardly help but think of the gaunt figure holding the human skull above him as a wise old friend. After what had happened the last time he was there, the whole graveyard now seemed strangely peaceful—almost pretty somehow. Perhaps there was something to Mr. Lowe's fondness for the place after all.

And so, with a lightness of heart and a clear view of the graveyard gates, he resigned to sit and wait for Ruby.

A creeping thought began to nag at the back of Arthur's mind. He reached into his pocket and produced the sinister scrap of paper he'd discovered the night before. With a bracing breath, he opened the note.

Arthur's eyes fell on the flaming crown insignia that

opened the message. Illuminated in the midday sun, there could be no doubt.

It was the same seal he'd seen on the skeleton's ring in *The World Record.*

Either a new treasurer had written this diabolical note, or else the old treasurer's skeleton was not as dead as it had appeared. Arthur wasn't entirely sure which would have been worse.

Drawing a deep breath, he proceeded to the body of the note and began carefully rereading every terrifying word.

Dear Messrs. Overkill & Undercut . . .

There was, of course, no question to whom these names referred. This only confirmed what Arthur had seen the night before—that the dwarf and the giant had survived the wreck of the *Current Champion* and were still after his family. But plenty of other questions remained.

For instance, who was this "Chairman of the Board" mentioned in the last sentence? Arthur had heard a fair bit about the Ardmore Board of Directors recently, but he'd never learned anything about any of its members other than the one whose predecessor had turned up dead. Could it be that the board's leader had a hand in the Whipples' recent spate of calamity as well?

And what about the author of the note: the mysterious Treasurer? Until now, Arthur had imagined this rumored new treasurer as a faceless figure sitting at a desk counting coins and writing checks for stationery supplies. But in Arthur's current estimation, the Treasurer was the most menacing of the four characters mentioned. Indeed, it seemed this last figure was the one actually devising the plots that Overkill and Undercut carried out.

As Arthur reread the first paragraph a second time, his eyes stuck on the word "eliminate." *Though you have succeeded in creating a moderate amount of chaos, you have yet to eliminate a single one of your targets.*

There could be little doubt now that the giant and dwarf had intended at the very least to maim Arthur's family, most likely to murder them, and it had only been through grace and good fortune that they had all survived thus far. If only Arthur knew the Treasurer's identity, he might be able to protect his family against the villain's deadly tactics.

And then it struck him.

Who had the most to gain from a Whipple family downfall? Who had been present at the last four apparent attempts on the Whipples' lives? Who would benefit from their new rivalry contract were the Whipples unable to compete? And whom had Arthur's father openly accused of involvement with the Komodo dragon incident, just the previous night? The more he thought about it, the clearer it became to him. Rex Goldwin and the Treasurer were one and the same.

But if Rex Goldwin was in fact the Treasurer, then Ruby was living in the same house as a murderous madman. Arthur checked his watch. She was now fifteen minutes late. What if her absence was the result of some terrible happening at the Goldwin estate? It was too awful to consider.

Arthur returned the note to his pocket and flipped open the *Grazelby Guide* in an effort to distract himself. He thumbed through the pages and began jotting down possible record attempts on his notepad as he continued to wait. Soon, Arthur had filled nearly ten pages with prospective records. Looking up from his list, he saw that the sun now sat rather lower in the sky than it had when he'd arrived, enveloping him in the shadow of the winged undertaker. Ruby was still nowhere to be found.

He packed up and started for home.

When Arthur had reached the main road, however, he paused, then turned in the direction of the Goldwin estate. He could hardly return home before determining whether or not Ruby was all right.

In a matter of minutes, the Goldwin house loomed overhead. Arthur walked directly up to the front door and rang the bell.

Now that he believed Rex Goldwin to be the Treasurer, this was truly a terrifying prospect—but Arthur took comfort in the fact that Rex remained unknowledgeable of Arthur's newfound knowledge. As far as Arthur could tell, Ruby's father had no reason to deviate from his charming, if arrogant, public persona.

The door swung open, sending Arthur's heart pounding against the walls of its cage. A dark figure stood in the doorway.

Rita Goldwin was dressed in mourning. She wore a black, slim-skirted suit and matching black veil. Pinned to her lapel, an emerald brooch in the shape of a Komodo dragon hinted at the source of her grief.

Arthur's anxiety somewhat subsided. But when he noticed the expression on Mrs. Goldwin's face, he began to wonder if he wouldn't rather have taken his chances with her husband after all—however murderous he might be.

"*You*," hissed the woman in the doorway.

"Um, hello, Mrs. Goldwin," Arthur said with a forced smile.

Rita Goldwin did not smile back. "You've got a lot of nerve coming here after the devastation your family caused last night. I should sic the lizards on you—and let *you* explain to them what happened to their brother!"

"I'm terribly sorry, Mrs. Goldwin. Please don't sic any more lizards on me. I was just hoping to catch, I mean, I thought maybe, er, is Ruby in?"

"I'm afraid Rubilda does not want visitors at the moment," Rita Goldwin replied curtly. "She's extremely busy preparing for the World Record World Championships. Frankly, I'd have thought you'd be doing the same, knowing the competition you'll be up against this year."

"So then, she's all right, is she?"

"Well, of course she's all right. What sort of question is that? She's simply sacrificing her time for the sake of the family. Is that such a foreign concept to you? Now, if you have no other business here, I really must get back to my own affairs. And please know, the next time I catch you so much as setting foot on our property, I *will* sic the lizards on you."

"Oh, right—well, fair enough. Sorry to disturb you, Mrs. Goldwin," Arthur said shakily. Then, remembering his original mission, he blurted, "Maybe you could just tell Ruby I dropped by?"

But before he could get out this last, feeble request, the door clapped shut in front of him. It seemed a bad idea to test the house's mourning mistress any further, so he turned on his heels and headed for home.

On the way back, Arthur thought about the excuse Mrs. Goldwin had given for Ruby's unavailability. From what he could surmise, the girl had not been harmed but was presently living under a certain degree of duress within her own home. He only hoped she managed to find a way out of it soon, or he'd be forced to face the investigation alone— a prospect to which he was not looking forward. Of course, there was also the fact that Ruby had quickly become the best friend he'd ever had and he was already starting to miss her—but he did his best not to think about that.

Upon his return home, Arthur spent the rest of the day compiling his list of world record possibilities, his mind wandering periodically to the predicament of his missing partner, or to unravelling conspiracy of giants, dwarves, and neighborhood supervillains upon which he had stumbled. With his cheek plastered to the pages of the *Grazelby Guide*, he finally drifted off to sleep, his dreams inhabited by cheering crowds and glistening golden trophies.

• • •

The next several days went very much the same. Arthur woke up, visited Abigail and Hamlet at Mr. Mahankali's cottage, shared a quick breakfast with the rest of his family, started down his list of potential records with Uncle Mervyn, headed over to the Undertakers' Graveyard to wait for Ruby, then—when she failed to arrive—headed back to the house to continue down the list until he was too tired to proceed.

The exhaustive search for a world record to finally call his own kept Arthur occupied and somewhat contented, but as each day passed, Ruby's absence weighed heavier and heavier on his soul.

Out of desperation, Arthur formulated a plan to both contact his partner and expedite their investigation.

On the seventh day, he set his plan into action.

That morning, his family had planned a trip into the city to stock up on supplies for their pre-championships surge in record breaking. It was just the thing his plot required.

Arthur rose earlier than usual and drafted a copy of the letter he'd received in the birthday cake from Sammy the Spatula. He then sketched two copies of the Treasurer's note, taking extra care to replicate the details of the fiery crown on the Treasurer's seal.

After tucking Sammy's original letter and a copy of the Treasurer's note beneath his mattress for safekeeping, he sealed the copy of Sammy's letter and the original Treasurer's note, along with a brief explanatory message, inside a large envelope. He addressed the envelope to Detective

94

Sergeant Greenley and placed it inside his knapsack. Then he hurried downstairs to join his family as they marched outside and piled into the car.

The drive from the Whipples' country house to the city took a little under an hour, and Wilhelm parked the car just off Haggle Street, the main thoroughfare in the District of Distinctive Objects.

While the rest of his family searched the shops for the World's Strongest Rope and the World's Lightest Running Shoes, Arthur ducked into The Fearsome Feather: Record-Breaking Books and Uncommon Collectibles.

There, he traded a mint-condition Cannibal King rookie card for a unique printing of Joss Langston's *Manslaughter Park*—certified to be the First English-Language Novel Illustrated in Color—which he had inquired about by telephone the day before.

Arthur secured a table outside a nearby café while he waited for his family. He retrieved a black pen, a handwritten note, and a small shipping box from his knapsack. Arranging the items on the tabletop beside his newly acquired copy of *Manslaughter Park*, Arthur opened the unsealed shipping box and slid out a typewritten letter that he had produced the night before:

Joss Langston Appreciation Society
International Head Office

Dear Miss Rubilda Goldwin:

95

Thank you for your entry in the Joss Langston Appreciation Society's recent essay contest. We are pleased to inform you your essay entitled "Secret Codes & Hidden Messages in the Works of Joss Langston" has won our Grand Prize! Enclosed, please find a highly-collectible, RECORD-HOLDING copy of Miss Langston's gripping novel *Manslaughter Park*.

Congratulations on your win! We look forward to hearing more from you in the near future.

Yours Sincerely,
Art H. Urwin
President,
Joss Langston Appreciation Society

Arthur set the letter aside and opened the leather-bound novel to its first page. He uncapped the pen and set about encoding the contents of his handwritten note into the pages of *Manslaughter Park*, using the simplest cipher he could think of.

On the first page, he selected a *d* and an *e* within the novel's existing text and drew a short line beneath each of the two letters. On the second page, he underlined the letters *a* and *r*. On the third page, he underlined a space and then another letter *r*.

Slowly flipping through the book, Arthur continued the procedure, methodically underlining two characters per page, and then crossing out the corresponding characters on his handwritten note. He felt a bit guilty defacing a world-record-holding artifact in this manner, but "desperate times" and all that.

A half hour later, Arthur finally crossed out the last handwritten character on his note and closed the book with a sigh of satisfaction. All his partner had to do now was string the underlined characters together into words and sentences to uncover the following message:

dear ruby, i really hope you are not dead. i went to the graveyard on saturday at noon as we discussed, but you did not turn up. i dropped by your house, but your mother informed me you were not seeing visitors. i have gone to the graveyard every day for the past week, but have yet to see any sign of you. i will continue to visit the graveyard every day at noon until you arrive or send word. i have made some breakthroughs in the case that i am eager to share with you. on the northern wall of your estate, at the one-hundred-thirty-seventh spike, you will find a hollow stone. inside, i have enclosed a

facsimile of a mysterious note i found
the night of the komodo dragon attack,
after catching a glimpse of the giant
mr. overkill. i suspect it to be a clue of
vital importance. i have sent the original
to d.s. greenley for analysis and now
await his reply. if you are in fact alive,
i have reason to believe you may be in
some danger, so please be wary. yours
sincerely, arthur

His only hope was that Ruby's parents would not open the book for much more than a superficial glance. Indeed, he was counting on Rex and Rita Goldwin's disdain for their daughter's taste in literature to keep the message hidden from unwanted viewing, and their love for record-breaking objects to keep the message safe from the rubbish heap. Only time would tell if his strategy worked.

Arthur slipped both the freshly encoded novel and the fake cover letter from the Joss Langston Appreciation Society into the shipping box, then closed the package and sealed it shut with a strip of packing tape.

He left the café, dropping the parcel addressed to Ruby and the envelope addressed to D.S. Greenley into a nearby post-box, then made his way back to the car to rejoin his family.

After returning home later that evening, Arthur concealed his other sketch of the Treasurer's note inside one of the ceramic rocks he had received for his birthday and stole away to the outskirts of the Goldwin estate. He scaled the wall and planted the rock beside the 137th iron spike as he had described in his message.

There was nothing left to do but wait.

• • •

On Tuesday, after three days with no word from Ruby, Arthur finally received a letter.

He ran up to his room and shut the door behind him, then tore open the envelope and unfolded the enclosed piece of paper. Unfortunately, it was not a message from Ruby. It was, however, the next best thing.

The note read as follows:

> A.W.—
> Communication received. Meet in the
> city—Friday, 21:00 at the Broken Record.
> Ask for a "Mr. Green." Will discuss further.
> —D.S.G.

Arthur smiled. The investigation was back on. Now he only had to retrieve his partner.

• • •

When Friday morning arrived, Arthur had yet to hear from Ruby.

He waited at the graveyard for nearly an hour before

finally accepting the fact he'd be meeting Sergeant Greenley alone that night. Arthur rose from his lookout spot with a frown, brushed himself off, then turned around—and practically collided with a dark-haired, green-eyed girl.

"So, how's the investigation going, Detective Whipple?" Ruby asked nonchalantly, as if two full weeks had not passed since their last meeting.

"What?" Arthur said with a start. "Where did you come from? Where have you—?"

"Sorry it took me so long to get away. Ever since the hide-and-seek disaster, Rex and Rita have had the house on lockdown. Nonstop training every day. They've only just eased up enough to let me out for an 'oxygen renewal session.' Honestly, I'd almost rather be back on the compound. It's been absolutely killing me not being able to get out here to the graveyard, which, I might add, is even better than the one in *Manslaughter Park*—though, of course, you can't really beat the one in *Southanger Cemetery*. It's good to see you, by the way."

"Wh—yeah," Arthur stammered, still recovering from the shock of Ruby's abrupt appearance, "it's good to see you too. I was starting to wonder if I'd ever see you again . . . but, I take it you deciphered my message?"

"Yep—though I think my baby brother could have figured that one out. You might want to work on your ciphers a bit."

"Well," said Arthur in an injured tone, "I had to make it simple, didn't I? How else could I be sure you'd get the

100

message, since we hadn't established a set code language? I know lots of codes. Have you heard of the one where you list the letters of the alphabet in one column, then reverse their order in a second column and then use the corresponding letters to write a hidden message? Yep? Just an example. What about the one where you assign a letter to each key of the piano and then record a tune with a secret message encoded in it? Didn't think so. That's a good one. Maybe next time you won't be so hasty to judge someone on his knowledge of ciphers without taking a look at his codebook first."

By this time, an impish grin had formed on Ruby's lips.

"What?" Arthur demanded.

"I'm only teasing, Arthur," Ruby giggled. "You did great. I mean, I'm here, aren't I? I got *this*, didn't I?"

With that, she held up Arthur's hand-sketched copy of the Treasurer's note, which he had planted atop the Goldwins' wall for her to find.

"Ah, you did, didn't you," said Arthur, his tone softening. "Sorry for getting defensive. I guess I take a bit too much pride in my ciphering skills."

"As well you should."

Arthur smiled bashfully, then moved on to more pressing matters. "So. You've read the Treasurer's note."

"I have indeed," Ruby replied.

This was what Arthur had been dreading. How did he tell his friend and partner that he suspected her own father of being a maniacal villain and the key player in a plot to

101

murder his family? If only there were a greeting card for this sort of thing.

"So," Arthur stalled nervously, searching for the right words, "what did, er, how did you—"

"Yeah," Ruby said matter-of-factly, "I'm pretty sure Rex is the Treasurer."

"What?" exclaimed Arthur. "You too?"

"It seems fairly obvious, doesn't it? I mean, who else has as much to gain from your family's demise? Who always happens to be around when something goes wrong with them? Not to mention the fact he's just painted a ten-foot canvas of that flaming crown symbol and hung it over his bed."

"Wow. Really? Well, are you all right then?"

"What do you mean?"

"I mean, knowing your father might be a lawless criminal—are you all right?"

"He's not my father, Arthur."

Arthur frowned. "I know you *think* he's not your father, but this is a serious situation. You probably shouldn't be relying on hunches here."

"I'm completely serious," protested Ruby. "It isn't just a hunch anymore. They've as good as said it."

"Really?" Arthur replied, suddenly intrigued. "What did they say?"

"Well, the other day I was hiding in a cupboard to avoid afternoon calisthenics, and I overheard Rex and Rita discussing the World Record Championships of the World—"

"World Record World Championships," Arthur corrected.

"Whatever. And Rex was going on about how easy it would be to defeat your family, but that he was a bit worried I would somehow destroy everything he'd worked for—which is a typical topic of discussion for him. 'Rubilda is definitely a weak link,' he said. 'If only there were a way to make up for her embarrassing lack of ambition. We really should have adopted another daughter when we had the chance.'"

She paused here as if expecting a response, but Arthur just stared at her blankly.

Ruby bristled. "Well? That proves it, doesn't it?"

"Does it really?" Arthur replied. "I mean, granted, it probably won't be earning him any records for World's Best Father, but I don't quite understand how it proves you're not his daughter."

"Didn't you hear me? He said 'we should've adopted *another*.' Why would he say '*another*,' unless they had already adopted a daughter?"

Arthur's brow furrowed. "Are you sure he didn't mean 'adopted another *daughter*?' Like, in addition to the biological daughters they already have?"

"That's not how he said it. I could tell he meant 'adopted *another*.'" Ruby exhaled, then snapped, "Look—you weren't there, were you?"

"Hold on now," Arthur objected. "I didn't mean to offend. You could be right; I just thought it might upset you to find out Rex is the one behind the attacks—regardless of whether or not he's your actual father."

"Look, Arthur, even if I wasn't adopted, God knows I don't belong *here*. So I'm either waiting around for my real family to turn up and save me, or until I'm old enough to escape this one on my own. Maybe this is my chance. And besides, even if Rex *were* my real father, is there anything I can do about it if the man decides he wants to be a murderer?"

Arthur shrugged. "I guess not."

"Then why should I be upset?"

"I don't know, I just thought. . . . Well, anyway, I'm glad you're all right."

Ruby's expression softened. "Thank you for your concern," she said sincerely. After a short pause, she added, "So what do we do now?"

"Oh—right," said Arthur, remembering why he'd been so anxious to regain his partner that day. "As I mentioned in my message, I have recently been in correspondence with Detective Sergeant Greenley, and he's arranged a meeting with us tonight at twenty-one hundred hours in the city. We can bike to Farfield Station and take the train from there. Do you think you can get away?"

"Are you joking? They'll have to shackle me to a dungeon wall to keep me from this one."

"Be careful," Arthur warned. "If Rex really is the Treasurer, there's no telling what he's capable of."

"Hey. I've survived this far."

"Well, keep up the good work then."

After arranging to meet back at the graveyard in six hours, Arthur parted ways with Ruby and headed for home.

He ambled up the drive and spotted Uncle Mervyn walking toward the house alongside Mrs. Waite, the house-keeper. This was not the first time Arthur had seen the gray-haired couple strolling alone across the grounds together.

"Uncle Mervyn! Mrs. Waite!" he called, quickening his pace to catch up to the pair, who turned and stopped to wait for him. "Uncle Mervyn," Arthur called again when he was within a few yards, "I was just coming to see you. Are you ready to pick up where we left off on our potential-record list? I've got a good feeling about this next series of events. Seems the magical domino's working. Today just might be the day, right Uncle Mervyn?"

"Aye, lad. It may indeed," Uncle Mervyn said with a smile. His expression was warm as ever, but there was something unfamiliar in his tone. Something somber. "But if not today," he continued, "you must promise me you won't give up—not before trying every item on this list. Do you swear it, lad?"

Arthur was dumbstruck. "I—I swear," he stammered. It was then he got his first clear view of Mrs. Waite's face. Her eyes were red and swollen. She gave a faint sniffle and brushed away a tear with her handkerchief.

Arthur, confused and increasingly anxious, stood petri-fied as Uncle Mervyn continued.

"If this is important to you, lad, you must keep after it—until you have exhausted every possibility. You may find someday that these things no longer matter, and on that day you may hang up your hat with pride—but you mustn't give up now, simply because the task is difficult. Battle on, lad—never give up and never give in!" Uncle Mervyn's voice reached a crescendo here and quickly fell off into a deep, reflective sigh. In a frustrated whisper, he asked himself: "How do you cram a lifetime of advice into a few short sentences?" Then, with sudden resolve, he offered his right hand to the boy and said, "Arthur, you are a fine lad, and I am honored to call you my nephew."

Arthur took the man's hand and the two shared a heartfelt handshake. "Thanks Uncle Mervyn," he said sincerely. "I am honored to call you my uncle. But please, what on earth is the matter?"

"Come, lad. We must go and see the others."

• • •

Arthur's family was in the study, seated around a large table with a small stack of egg crates at its center. It appeared to be a typical family meeting, except that, instead of eggs, the egg crates were filled with hand grenades. Arthur feared his family had taken their rivalry with the Goldwins a bit too far.

"Now," said Mrs. Whipple, "who'd like the first throw?"

All the children's hands shot up at once.

"Ah, come on," pleaded Edward, pointing to the one blank spot on a sleeve otherwise covered with embroidered patches. "I'm only three tosses away from my Young Grenadier's badge!"

"Very well, Edward," his mother said with a nod and then handed him a grenade, much to the displeasure of her other children. As she turned to see Arthur enter the room with Mrs. Waite and Uncle Mervyn, a sudden smile formed across her face. "Mervyn, you're just in time!" she beamed. "We've just finished planning the World's Largest Simultaneous Live Grenade Toss. Wait till those Goldwins see *this*!"

Arthur breathed a small sigh of relief. Disturbing as his mother's plan sounded, he was glad to hear his family had not yet entered into all-out military conflict.

"So, Mervyn," inquired Mr. Whipple, "how was your meeting with old man Grazelby this morning? He's no doubt regaled you with endless stories of his latest trip to the Congo; I only hope he's made it worth your while. Tell me, has the miser finally come to his senses and offered you a raise?"

Mervyn cleared his throat. "He has indeed. A whole twenty-five percent."

While the words themselves were undoubtedly positive, Uncle Mervyn's tone was hardly indicative of a man whose income has just been increased by one quarter.

"Well, well," Arthur's father said with a smile. "Congratulations, old boy! I've always said they were paying you a mere fraction of what you're worth. Of course, it's still true—but at least the fraction's a bit larger now, eh?"

"Aye, well, unfortunately this is not the sort of promotion I had hoped for. The increase, you see, is contingent on my taking a new position—a position I am required to

107

accept if I am to remain in the employ of Grazelby Publications. It seems—" Uncle Mervyn struggled with the words "—it seems I have been transferred to Moscow. I'm afraid I've only come to say goodbye."

The Whipples' smiles turned to looks of shock and dismay. Arthur's heart sank.

"What?!" exclaimed Mr. Whipple. "How is this possible?"

"Apparently," Mervyn explained, "my impartiality has been called into question. Several days ago, Grazelby's head office received a letter from an anonymous tipster, in which my split role as godfather, friend, and record certifier to this family was challenged. The letter charges that I have shown favoritism toward you in past decisions and accuses me of stopping an official record-contending competition without proper cause—namely, the hide-and-seek match with the Goldwins last month."

"So *they're* involved, are they?" Arthur's father growled. "Well, that nearly explains it—but what on earth has that blasted game of hide-and-seek got to do with anything? Our children were being attacked by a Komodo dragon, for pity's sake!"

"This morning," Uncle Mervyn continued calmly, "Mr. Grazelby asked me if I had indeed stopped the match. I told him I had. He reminded me that while such a call is generally left up to the officiator, the technical rule is that no event, once started, should be stopped for any reason, save for the loss of human life or by mutual consent of all competing parties. Since no human being had been killed, nor

108

had a halt been agreed upon by both teams, the game technically should have been allowed to continue. Had there been no official complaint, Grazelby might have been able to look the other way on the matter—but with this anonymous letter, they had no choice but to declare a 'conflict of interest' and reassign me to another branch."

"Anonymous letter, my foot!" shouted Arthur's father. "Rex Goldwin will not get away with this!"

"Now, now, Charles," Uncle Mervyn insisted, "don't do anything you'll regret. I'm afraid Mr. Goldwin is well within his rights this time. Save your fury for the championships. And as for me—I can't really complain; Moscow is a very prestigious post. In fact, in my younger years, before I was appointed here, I repeatedly requested that very assignment. I just wish they hadn't chosen now to honor me with it."

Arthur looked up at his uncle. "When does your new position start, Uncle Mervyn?"

"I'm to leave first thing tomorrow morning. But no tears now. Grazelby will be assigning a new certifier to your family before the week is out. I'm sure that whomever they choose, he or she will soon become just another member of the family. You'll no doubt forget all about me in a week or two."

At this, Mrs. Waite could no longer control her tear ducts and burst into weeping, subsequently triggering a slow-swelling outpour of tears from all of the Whipple girls, as well as a few of the younger Whipple boys.

After much crying and hugging and handshaking, Uncle

Mervyn announced, "Well, I'd best be off. Packing up my life to do and all that. I'll see you in a couple of months at the championships—standing on the winners platform above a defeated family of Goldwins, with any luck."

The Whipples walked their uncle to the front door, where Arthur's father said a final farewell.

"You will be sorely missed in this house. But our loss is Moscow's gain. Godspeed, Mervyn. Until we meet again."

"It has been my honor and pleasure," concluded a watery-eyed Uncle Mervyn, "to serve as your humble certifier. Goodbye for now, dear Whipples. May all your wishes come true."

With that, he winked at Arthur. He flashed one last melancholy smile to Mrs. Waite, then turned and headed back down the drive. And then he was gone.

• • •

Arthur tried continuing down his list of record possibilities alone, as he had promised his uncle—but his heart just wasn't in it. With Uncle Mervyn no longer around to offer encouragement, Arthur felt he had lost the one person in the world who actually believed in him.

As the day wore on, he began to focus more and more on his quickly approaching meeting with Sergeant Greenley. He decided his only hope of ever getting his uncle back—or his favorite chef, for that matter—was to take down Rex Goldwin for good.

THE BROKEN RECORD

Arthur and Ruby set off from the graveyard on bicycles, pedaling down scenic country roads under a slowly darkening sky.

During the hour-long journey to the train station, Arthur told Ruby of his uncle's reassignment to Moscow and her father's probable participation in the matter—to which Ruby hardly seemed surprised, yet offered her sympathies nonetheless.

The duo chained up their bikes upon reaching their first destination and purchased a pair of transfer passes into the city, then boarded the train.

One hour and three transfers later, Arthur and Ruby reached their final stop, venturing out of the underground station and into the electric night air of the bustling city street.

They made their way through the mobs of club-goers, pub-crawlers, theatre patrons, and fight fans, eventually arriving at a dingy stone wall marked by a large sign that read, THE BROKEN RECORD. Beside it, a blocky, dark-suited man with a broad, shaven head stood guarding a pair of double doors, his knobbly, hairy-knuckled hands clasped at his waist.

"So this is the place, is it?" asked Ruby.

"Yep. The World's Oldest Continually Operated Night-club. I've always wanted to see the inside of it. Hopefully, we'll get the chance tonight."

They approached the door, and Arthur addressed the doorman as politely as possible.

"Excuse me, sir, we're here to meet a friend of ours. I don't suppose we could peek in for just a moment and see if he's gone in already? We wouldn't want to keep him waiting."

The doorman did not look down. "What's his name, this friend of yours?" he asked in a deep, gravelly voice.

"Uh, Green, sir," said Arthur. "A Mr. Green."

"Hmm," grunted the doorman. "You'll have to wait outside. Stand yourselves to your left there while I get somebody to fetch him for you."

"Yes, sir. Thank you, sir."

The doorman disappeared past the doors, which the children promptly heard him bolt shut from the other side. Arthur and Ruby shuffled down the pavement, stopping

112

several paces to the left of the door, and leaned themselves against the dimly lit wall to wait for the detective.

The area was free of any other bystanders, but Arthur began to get the strange feeling he was being watched. He turned to look down the wall to his right, where a heap of rubbish spilled out of a shadowy corner a few yards away. In the darkness between the rubbish and the wall, he detected a hint of movement—and then, the distinct figure of a person skulking in the shadows.

Arthur's heart rate quickened. As his eyes adjusted to the lack of light, he realized he was staring at the grimiest-looking man he had ever seen.

At that moment, the man stepped out of the shadows. He gave a strange smile that revealed a rather incomplete collection of teeth and began stumbling toward the children.

"Hello," wheezed the filthy-faced, scraggly-bearded man. "What're a couple of nice kids like you doing out on the street at this hour?"

Arthur took a deep breath and stepped out from the wall, squaring his shoulders in an attempt to shield Ruby from any abrupt attacks. "Pardon us, sir," he replied nervously. "We're waiting for someone."

"Funny, I don't remember giving you permission to stand in front of *my* wall," said the man.

Frightened as he was, Arthur couldn't help but take exception to such a claim. "Now, sir, if you were to talk to the proprietor of the Broken Record, I'm sure you'd find the wall actually belongs to *him*—but, of course, we'd be

113

more than happy to wait somewhere else, if that suits you."

"I'm afraid that won't suit me at all. See, I'm looking to add some members to my street gang here. . . ." He gestured to the empty corner behind him. "And I must say the two of you fit the bill quite nicely."

"We do, sir?" Arthur gulped.

"Oh, most definitely. You're just the right size for snatching purses off the streets and slipping down the sewers with the loot. Anything you bring back gets split between the three of us—and, in turn, I provide protection from rival gangs and roving murderers and such. Could be a very promising business opportunity for the pair of you."

"Ahh—I'm very flattered, sir," said Arthur, "but I, um, well, I don't think my parents would approve of me leading a life of crime."

"Yeah," Ruby said with a nervous smile. "Not really a sewer person myself."

"Well, that is a shame," said the man. "Because now that you've heard my gang's plans, we can't just let you walk away from this, now can we?"

"Well, yes, sir," said Arthur, searching in vain for anybody who might help them. "I think you could, actually."

"Oh, I don't think so," said the man. He stepped forward, wringing his hands menacingly. "Honestly, what kind of gang would I be leading if I went round allowing potential squealers to just go on living? Not a very good gang at all, if you ask me. I'm sure you see my point, though—don't you, Arthur?"

114

"I—I can't say I do, sir," Arthur replied, his voice beginning to quiver. "You see, we're just. . . . Hold on a minute—what was that you called me?"

"It *is* Arthur, isn't it? Arthur Whipple?"

"Yes," Arthur replied cautiously. "How do you know my name?"

"Ah, but lad, Gutterpipe Garrett knows all," the man said, squinting slyly. "Or perhaps you know me by my other name."

The man's hands shot out, causing Arthur and Ruby to flinch with fright. But to their surprise, he simply reached up to his own head—and tore off his hair and beard.

"Ahh!" cried the children, recoiling in horror.

As Arthur took a second glance, however, he began to notice something strangely familiar about the beardless, short-haired man now standing before him.

"Detective Sergeant Greenley?!" he blurted in disbelief.

"At your service!" the man replied with a bow.

As Greenley stood upright again, the children remained frozen, their eyes and mouths locked open. The detective looked puzzled. After an extended silence, he spread his arms and added an enthusiastic "Ta-da!"

When there was still no response from his young audience, Greenley gently prodded, "Well . . . so what do you think—had you going for a tick, didn't I?"

Arthur and Ruby nodded mechanically.

"Sorry if I frightened you there a bit—afraid I tend to get rather carried away on these undercover jobs. Ever since I

115

played Mercutio at my village Stage and Stewmeat Festival, it's like my inner actor just keeps crying to get out."

Greenley retrieved a handkerchief from his coat, then set about wiping the dirt from his face and scrubbing the shoe polish from his blacked-out teeth. "All part of a grand tradition, of course, set down by the great dramaturgical detectives: Sir Justin Trouper, D.I. Guise, Basil Scrimm. We never start any case without a cast of undercover identities at the ready. Ahh—I've waited months for the chance to try out this new tramp character. And Inspector Smudge said the costume was a waste of resources. He'll be eating *his* words right about now, I think."

The children stood speechless as Greenley returned the now grubby handkerchief to his pocket. "But enough with the theatrics for the moment—we've got business to attend to." He removed his tattered scarf and ragged overcoat to reveal a freshly starched shirt and tie, then motioned to the building's entrance. "What do you say we get this meeting underway?"

"Yes, please," said Arthur.

The detective stopped at the entrance and addressed the neckless doorman, who had since returned to his post. "Cheers, Philip," Greenley said under his breath, tapping the side of his nose twice with his index finger.

Without shifting his gaze, Philip gave a nod and said, "Mr. Green." Then he pushed open the door and waved the three through the threshold.

Arthur and Ruby followed the detective down a steep series of steps and through a winding, poorly lit corridor. They pushed past a velvet curtain at its far end to find themselves in a large, smoky room pulsating with activity.

Like a brotherhood of master snake charmers, the four-piece jazz band in the back corner coaxed the dance floor to shimmy and sway to its every whim, while the bony barman in the foreground flipped bottles in time with the music. Dim lamps dangled above red vinyl booths at the room's edges, where slick-haired scoundrels belched cigarette smoke into the faces of their dates—sultry, smoldering women who promptly belched it right back.

It wasn't exactly a place for children—but apparently the distinction had not occurred to Greenley. Arthur, however, was surprised to find that in an establishment designated for adults, most people behaved more or less like unruly schoolkids. The patrons all chattered in obnoxiously loud voices, some twirling around the floor as if they'd had too much sugar, while others stumbled about like it was past their bedtimes.

Mixing into the crowd like a splash of water in the World's Largest Pot of Grease, the children and the detective made their way to an empty booth at the back of the club.

"My apologies again for the false names and disguises," Greenley whispered. "You never know who might be watching round here." He peered cautiously around the room. "When Inspector Smudge and I are stationed nearby, this is where I meet with all the mob informants, reluctant

117

witnesses, underworld ruffians, and other necessary evil-doers upon whom we coppers must sometimes rely."

"Wow," the children murmured, impressed by the detective's thrilling exploits.

"That is to say," Greenley added, "I haven't actually *met* with any of them yet—not as such."

"Oh," said Arthur.

"I mean, there *was* that slightly dodgy boxing promoter, but I was only meeting with him to purchase a second-hand fish fryer he'd listed in the *Weekly*. You would not believe how much they want for a new one these days—practically criminal, if you ask me. . . . But, anyway, when I do get a proper meeting with one of these underworld types, this seems a good location for that sort of thing, doesn't it? I mean, cutting deals with gangland snitches, ransom drops with kidnappers, off-duty dance-offs with Russian mobsters, and all that. Not really *my* cup of tea, mind, but it provides the appropriate atmosphere—don't you think?"

Arthur and Ruby nodded in bemused agreement.

"Anyhow," said the detective, his voice suddenly serious as he leaned in, "on to more important matters." He reached into his trouser pocket and retrieved a worn-out, folded-up piece of paper, which Arthur recognized to be the Treasurer's note.

"You were right to send me this, Arthur," said Greenley. "As much as it pains me to neglect an order from Inspector Smudge, I believe you've come up with a lead worth following here, and as an officer of the law, I would be remiss to ignore it. Indeed, I've been able to glean a fair bit from this little scrap—more, I dare say, than all the clues we've gathered so far." He peered suspiciously over his shoulder, then leaned in further toward the children, lowering his voice so they could only just hear it over the noise of the club. "It would seem your little note here is the first concrete evidence substantiating rumors of a new treasurer on the Ardmore Board of Directors."

Arthur and Ruby traded sideways glances.

"As you may be aware," Greenley continued, "the public face of the Ardmore Association is relatively well-known—what with their *Ardmore Almanac* and so on—but the inner workings of its board have been shrouded in mystery ever since it went underground some twenty years ago. Hard as we've tried, the Association's senior ranks have proved impossible to infiltrate. At least with this note, we've now been clued in to some of their associates, with whom we are a bit more familiar."

"Messrs. Overkill and Undercut?" said Arthur.

"Precisely," said Greenley. "Though I think it's safe to say these exceptional-sized chums of yours are operating under assumed names—which is bound to make recapturing them difficult. At the end of the day of course, they are almost certainly low-level henchman or hired thugs, simply following the orders of their employers. It is the *employers* who are important to us. If we find the puppeteers, we shall find the puppets as well."

119

"How many puppeteers do you think there might be, Detective?"

"Well," Greenley replied, "the note's reference to this 'Chairman of the Board' suggests we're dealing with the wishes of the board's director at least, if not the entire board itself. But, of course, until we start learning the identities of its members, we've got no one to charge. Can't rightly arrest a man's job title without the man himself, can we?"

"Guess not," said Arthur. "But what about the Treasurer then? Any clues as to his identity?"

"Ahh—that's the question, isn't it?" grinned the detective. "Well, my boy, thanks to your tip, I believe we have. You see, when I looked into Rex Goldwin's background, as your letter suggested, I made some startling discoveries. A quick inspection of his accounts reveals that our Mr. Goldwin has been receiving massive monthly payments from the Ardmore Association for well over a decade—and yet Ardmore has only begun to sponsor him publicly just this year. There's apparently been some sort of long-standing covert collaboration here."

"Well," said Ruby, "that would explain the compound."

"What's this now?"

"Until just a few months ago," Ruby replied, "Rex and his family lived at a secluded training facility. That facility must have been secretly funded by the Ardmore Association."

Greenley looked puzzled. "I've been investigating Goldwin all week, and I never came across anything like this."

"Mr. Goldwin is Ruby's father, sir," Arthur explained.

Greenley's face was instantly painted with shock and

embarrassment. "Oh dear. I—I'm so sorry, miss. I didn't realize. If I'd have known, I—"

"He's not my father," Ruby insisted. "Not my real one anyway. And if he's guilty of these crimes, he needs to be stopped—who*ever* he is."

"I don't know, miss. Are you certain you should be here?"

"Don't worry about me, Detective. I can look after myself. I've been doing it practically my whole life."

Greenley sighed. After an extended pause, he reluctantly conceded, "Well, if you're certain you can handle it. I've just never worked with a suspect's daughter before—"

"He's not—"

"—biological, or otherwise," Greenley clarified. "It's not something to be taken lightly."

"I understand, sir. I can handle it."

The detective gave another disgruntled, but relenting sigh. "Well, anyhow," he resumed at length, "where were we?"

"Rex's secret partnership with the Ardmore Association," Ruby quickly replied.

"Right. So, this prolonged collaboration certainly supports the notion that Mr. Goldwin is our Treasurer—and the one behind your family's recent misfortunes, Arthur—but unfortunately, with the heavy secrecy of Ardmore's board, there's really no way to prove it."

"What can we do then, Detective?" Arthur asked.

"We'll have to try a different approach. If we're lucky, we just might be able to get him for something else."

"Like what?"

121

Greenley peered out from under his brow. "It has come to our attention that, over the years, Goldwin has periodically procured the services of a Mr. Neil McCoy, a forgery expert who specializes in counterfeiting official documents. At this point, we can't be certain exactly what it is McCoy has been forging for him—could be passports, could be banknotes, could be world record certificates—but McCoy is currently the target of a major sting operation organized by Scotland Yard, which should be drawing to a close within the next couple of months. Once the Yard has made its move, we'll be able to determine precisely what sort of forgeries Goldwin has commissioned—and then charge him accordingly. Of course, these relatively minor offenses won't put him away for long, but at least they'll give us reason for an arrest, and buy us some time to find evidence for his real crimes."

"But what about Sammy the Spatula?" Arthur protested. "Every day that goes by is another one he's forced to live as a fugitive from justice. Isn't there anything we can do *now*?"

"The only way to fully clear your chef's name is to prove that someone *else* committed the crime he's accused of—and that's going to take a bit more time. I've read Sammy's letter as well, and it's truly heartbreaking stuff. Believe me, there's nothing I'd like more than to prove him innocent and bring him back home. But we mustn't get impatient, Arthur. A man's life hangs in the balance here; Sammy will surely appreciate our diligence."

Arthur nodded slowly as the difficult truth sank in.

"Meantime," Greenley added, "keep your eyes and ears

122

open—but be careful. It's only a matter of time before our friends Overkill and Undercut turn up again. And one of these days, they might actually complete their objective."

After an ominous moment, Greenley perked up. "Well, I'd best be off. The missus is making my favorite tonight— just as she always does after I get back from these under-cover jobs—and I reckon I ought to have a shower and a shave. Dragged that old coat through a rubbish bin on my way here—for authenticity purposes, you understand— and I'm afraid a bit of it's rubbed off on me. But first," the detective concluded as he rose to his feet, "allow me to walk you to your train."

• • •

Once aboard, the children found their seats and glanced out the window in time to see Greenley enthusiastically waving them farewell from his position on the platform, which now slid steadily away to their right.

As the beaming detective disappeared from view, Arthur lowered his arm and turned to his partner. "That went pretty well, don't you think?"

"What, being nearly murdered by a thieving hobo who turned out to be an overtheatrical undercover cop?"

"Well, no—after that part, I mean."

"Yeah, I'd say so," Ruby concurred. "It was a good meeting; the investigation definitely seems to be moving forward. And actually," she confessed, "the thieving hobo bit wasn't so bad either. I feel sort of honored that someone

123

went to so much trouble just to make an entrance with us. Greenley may be a few bullets short of a full clip, but it's hard not to like him."

"Yeah," Arthur agreed, "and if he's got half as much passion for detective work as he has for amateur theatre, we'll be wrapping up this case in no time."

"Let's just hope he finds some decent evidence on Rex before we have to see Overkill and Undercut again. I'd take ten murderous hobos over those two any day. I don't know about you, but I'm really not looking forward to finding out how they plan on topping a Komodo dragon attack."

"Agreed."

"Speaking of which," Ruby added, "how's Hamlet doing?"

Arthur had not yet mentioned anything regarding his family's faithful dog. It was hard enough to think about. "Not so good, actually," he frowned. "He's barely been conscious since he had his leg amputated."

"What?! Oh, that's awful."

"Yeah. Abigail's taking it pretty rough. She and Corporal Whiskerton—that's our model-rocket-piloting hamster—have hardly left his side. I sit with them sometimes in the mornings and give Hammie a good scratch behind the ears—but it's hard to tell if he even knows we're there. Poor Hammie; he deserves to be out breaking canine world records, and he's stuck in bed with one less leg—all for saving our lives."

"Poor Hammie," Ruby lamented.

Amid the repetitive rumble and clank of the train, the children stared out the window in contemplation.

After a few minutes had passed, Arthur attempted to change the subject.

"You know, speaking of the Komodo dragon incident, that reminds me—just before the attack, you were right in the middle of explaining all about the world record you've broken. Hmm," he said, scratching his head not so slyly. "Now what was it again?"

"I never said."

"Oh, that's right," Arthur recalled, playing a bit too hard at ignorance, "you were just *about* to say, when the Komodo dragon so rudely interrupted—remember?"

"I remember."

"Well . . ."

"Well," Ruby retorted, "I've since decided against it. Honestly—I'd been sitting up a tree for two hours. I wasn't exactly in my right mind."

Arthur scowled. "You know, I can always just go look it up in the World Record Archives. Don't know why I haven't done it before, really."

"Arthur," Ruby implored, "if you consider yourself my friend at all, you'll stop trying to find out what record I've broken. It's not important, all right?"

Arthur let out a sigh. "All right. I'm sorry. I'll try to stop asking you about it. It's just that I find it terribly fascinating."

The two sat in silence for another extended moment—until Arthur suddenly blurted, "Hang on a second—that's it!"

125

"What's it?" asked Ruby.

"The World Record Archives."

"What about them?"

"The dwarf assassin, Mr. Undercut—wouldn't you say he's the shortest person you've ever seen?"

"Yep," Ruby agreed, clearly confounded by Arthur's disjointed line of reasoning. "He's pretty short."

"Mightn't he be the shortest person *anyone's* ever seen? And the giant, Mr. Overkill—mightn't he be the tallest?"

"I guess so—but what's that got to do with anything?"

"Well, if they really are the Shortest and Tallest Humans on Earth, their names—the *real* ones—should be cataloged somewhere in the World Record Archives. All we have to do is look them up."

"Couldn't we just check the *Grazelby Guide*?"

"No use," said Arthur. "I practically know the past ten years of Grazelby publications by heart. Most recently, the *Guide* listed the World's Tallest Human as Longwe Dounga—until four years ago, when it stopped listing the category altogether. The World's *Shortest* Human was still listed as Kurt Scantley—but then that category was removed two years later."

"So how do you know these aren't our guys?"

"Mr. Dounga is a member of the Masai tribe and also holds the record for the World's Largest Stretched Earlobes. Believe me, it's not something you can miss. And Kurt Scantley only has one arm. Poor little guy got a tough break."

"All right, then why do you suppose they're no longer listed in the *Grazelby Guide*?"

"Well, the annual publication is nowhere near exhaustive—it would be impossible for anyone to regularly publish every world record in history, of course—"

"Of course," Ruby interjected sarcastically.

"—yet it does seem strange," Arthur continued, "that *Grazelby's* would choose to omit such prestigious records as these. More likely, these records have been broken by a *new* pair of record holders—record holders whom, for some reason, *Grazelby's can*not or *will* not list. . . . But then, that's what the archives are for. An entire building dedicated to world-record keeping—housing artifacts and information on every world record that has ever been set or broken. Because it's run by the International World Record Federation, it not only covers Grazelby-sponsored records, but all the records sponsored by other record books as well. There's no guarantee we'll find what we're looking for, but it's worth a shot, isn't it?"

"Sounds better than anything else we've come up with."

"All right then," said Arthur. "Do you think you can sneak away again tomorrow so we can make another trip to the city?"

Ruby's eyes twinkled with determination. "I'll see what I can do."

As the train sped through the darkness, the two young sleuths pondered the day to come with the growing suspicion that it might just change everything. They would not be wrong.

THE WORLD RECORD ARCHIVES

The next morning, Arthur woke to the sound of screaming.

He threw back his covers, leapt from his bed, and made for the doorway.

By the time he entered the corridor, however, he began to notice something odd about the cries coming from the first floor: for once in his recent life, these were not screams of terror or agony, but screams of joy.

Arthur hurried down the stairs more intrigued than ever, his brothers and sisters following closely behind.

The Whipple children arrived in the great hall to witness an astonishing sight.

Their sister Abigail lay in the middle of the floor, squealing with laughter at the feet of Mr. Mahankali and their parents. Pinning her to the rug, an energetic Great Dane dragged its massive slobbery tongue across Abigail's face as a hamster in a space suit scampered around them.

"Hamlet!" the children shouted as they dashed forward and dug their hands into the dog's fur.

Hamlet gave a kiss to Corporal Whiskerton, sending the hamster rolling happily backward, then returned his focus to Abigail. The barrage of licks continued for almost a minute before the girl finally scrambled to her feet and threw her arms around the dog's neck.

"Oh, Hammie," Abigail cried, "I knew you wouldn't let that lousy lizard keep you down!"

Hamlet shuffled around to rest on his haunches, and Arthur and his siblings noticed the dog's front left leg for the first time. Where once had been merely a stub, there was now a narrow wooden shaft, ending in a curved metal spring.

"Where'd that come from?" said George.

Mr. Mahankali stepped forward, grinning through the hair that covered his entire face. "You will all be proud to hear that our canine friend has just become the First Quadruped to Successfully Receive a Prosthetic Limb—engineered, I might add, by your brother Simon." The Panther-Man gestured to Arthur's older brother.

"Happy I could be of service," Simon said with a nod. "But my design would have been useless without Hamlet's incredible courage and, well, doggedness."

"Yes," said Mr. Mahankali, "I fitted him with it last

night while he was still unconscious, just to make sure the measurements were correct—but then, this morning, I woke up to a cold nose and big wet kisses—and there he was, standing at my bedside, begging for a walk."

"Well then," said Mr. Whipple, "shall we ask Hamlet if he'd like to take his new leg for a test run out on the east lawn? What do you say, children?"

"Yeah!" came the reply.

Hamlet sprang to his feet and panted excitedly.

"Come on, Hammie," Abigail grinned. "Let's go for a walk."

She placed her hand on his good front leg and began leading him toward the door—but the dog did not seem to understand. With a sudden, longing whine, he lowered his neck and nudged Abigail's knee.

"No, boy," Abigail scolded. "I'll have to walk beside you now. I don't want to hurt you."

Hamlet's whining grew louder and more insistent.

"No, Hammie," she insisted, then turned once again toward the door.

But as soon as she had done this, the dog lunged forward, scooped the little girl up with the crown of his head, and tossed her onto his back.

"Hammie!" Abigail protested, grabbing onto the dog's neck to keep herself from toppling off. "You've got to put me down!"

Hamlet stood proudly on his new leg, his giant tongue dipping rhythmically from the side of his mouth.

The Whipples couldn't help but laugh.

"What should I do, Mr. Mahankali?" Abigail asked in frustration.

"After what he has been through," the Panther-Man replied, "I would not deny him his wish to bear his favorite human on his back. It would be a terrible thing to sever his spirit as well as his leg, would it not?"

"I suppose you're right," Abigail conceded, thoughtfully stroking Hamlet's fur. "Well then," she declared after a quiet moment. "You heard him, Hammie . . . let's go!"

With that, the dog lurched forward and bounded across the room.

Though the ride was a bit bumpier than usual, neither Abigail nor Hamlet seemed to mind at all.

• • •

Arthur and his family spent the next two hours watching their freshly mended dog frolic from one end of the estate to the other. They finally made their way back to the house with the hope of giving Hamlet a rest, but the dog had no intention of stopping so soon. He dashed out to his training area and returned with a mouthful of rubber rings.

"Barely back from death's door," said Henry, "and he's already asking for a ring toss!" Henry rubbed the scar on the back of his shoulder where he'd been skewered by a stray arrow at the Unsafe Sports Showdown. "There's a dog after my own heart."

"I'd say he's eager to start breaking some new records," Simon added, "and get even with the Goldwins for what their lizard did to him."

"Sounds like a good idea to me," said Cordelia. "Who's throwing first?"

Just then, Wilhelm entered the room and addressed their father.

"Excuse me, Mr. Vhipple—there is a gentleman to see you—from the *Grazelby Guide*, he says. Shall I show him in?"

Mr. Whipple glanced to his wife with mild trepidation. "No no, Wilhelm. I will meet him in the entrance hall."

As their father stepped out of the room, the Whipple children all exchanged looks of curiosity—and then promptly filed out after him, eager to catch a peek of their new visitor.

Mr. Whipple led the large cluster of children that had materialized at his back into the foyer. There, he offered his hand to the figure at its center—a hollow-cheeked, middle-aged man in a slightly outdated suit, with slicked-over hair that appeared to have been parted by a laser.

"Mr. Whipple," announced the man, peering through round, thick-lensed spectacles, "my name is Archibald Prim. I have been sent by Grazelby's head office for the purpose of becoming your permanent record certifier. I trust you've been expecting me."

"We have indeed, Mr. Prim," said Arthur's father through a half-forced smile. "It's a pleasure to meet you."

"Likewise, Mr. Whipple. I look forward to establishing

132

a mutually advantageous partnership between our persons. Certainly, with your prolificacy in record breaking and my expertise in record certification, this should make for a highly effective match."

Listening to Archibald Prim's nasal drone, Arthur couldn't help but yearn for the warm, charming baritone of his family's previous certifier. However effective this new match proved to be, it was hard to imagine it ever coming close to the affinity he had forged with Uncle Mervyn. At the same time, Arthur realized that Mr. Prim deserved the benefit of the doubt—and thus resolved to refrain from any further comparisons.

"Yes—well, I must say, Mr. Prim," Arthur's father replied, "you could hardly have arrived at a more fitting moment. Our dog was just about to attempt his first world record since pulling through a two-week coma."

"Well then," the certifier declared. "Let us not delay any longer. Kindly direct me toward the aforementioned animal, and I shall officiate whatever feats it endeavors to perform."

"Very good, Mr. Prim. Right this way."

As the Whipples led their new certifier into the great hall, Hamlet hurried into position, sitting himself on the far side of the ring-catcher's line, which Henry and Cordelia had marked on the floor. Stepping up to the ring-thrower's line with a ring grasped in her hand, Abigail readied her stance and waited for Mr. Prim's signal.

Mr. Prim removed a tape measure from his pocket and carefully stretched it between their respective toe lines.

"Hmm," he muttered. "Nine feet, eleven inches, and fifteen-sixteenths. Good thing I checked."

With that, Mr. Prim pulled up the strip of cloth tape that served as Hamlet's marker and meticulously repositioned it one sixteenth of an inch from its original position.

Examining his handiwork through squinting eyes, the certifier declared, "That's better," and reeled in the tape measure. As he rose to his feet, Mr. Prim swapped the measuring tape for a stopwatch.

"Now—Competitor Number One," he addressed Abigail. "Are you ready for commencement?"

"Ready, sir," she answered excitedly.

"Competitor Number Two," the certifier said, turning to Hamlet, "are you ready for commencement?"

"Woof!" replied the dog.

Mr. Prim looked to his stopwatch. "And . . . commence!"

The moment the word left Mr. Prim's mouth, Abigail flung the ring forward.

Hamlet's eyes locked onto the flying object. With unyielding focus, the dog lifted his new front foot into the air.

A moment later, the ring twirled around Hamlet's fabricated foreleg.

The Whipples cheered. Hamlet's tongue unfurled with pride.

"Good boy, Hammie!" cried Abigail, reaching for another ring.

Just as she prepared to release it, however, Mr. Prim called out, "Hold!"

134

The Whipples turned to the certifier in confusion.

"I'm afraid you'll have to start again," he said. "Competitor Number One preceded my mark by nearly three hundredths of a second."

Mr. Whipple's brow furrowed. It appeared he might protest—but then, he simply turned to his daughter and smiled. "It's all right, Abigail. Do as Mr. Prim says. One throw will be easy enough to make up."

Abigail nodded in agreement, only slightly less excited than she'd been a few moments before.

"Competitor One—ready for commencement?"

"Ready."

"Competitor Two—ready for commencement?"

"Woof!"

"And . . . commence!"

Abigail waited until Mr. Prim had clearly uttered the last syllable this time—and then tossed the ring. A perfect catch.

When the dog had caught five rings in a row, Abigail stepped aside so that Cordelia could have her turn. Four more perfect catches, and then—

"Fault! Competitor Number Three has touched the toe line. Competitor Number One must start again."

Mr. Whipple's eyes widened, but he gritted his teeth and said nothing.

On the third attempt, the children were much more cautious, making doubly sure not to start too early or get too near the toe line. Soon, they had racked up thirty-five successful catches—only four rings shy of the world record for

Consecutive Rings Caught on the Leg of a Canine. Charged with executing the actual record-breaking toss, Edward prepared his first throw very carefully, slowly inching his toes up to the mark and triple-checking his stance. When he was satisfied he was not guilty of any rule infractions, he cocked back his arm—and then pitched the ring into the air. But as soon as the object had left his fingers—

"Fault! Competitor Number Nine has failed to release the ring within the allotted sixty-second time limit. The attempt is forfeit."

Sensing yet another stoppage, Hamlet dropped his leg and let the accumulated rings tumble to the floor. He turned to Abigail and let out a distressed whimper.

"All right Hamlet," she groaned, "let's try it again. We'll all be extra careful this time—but not *too* careful."

"Oh, I'm afraid that will be all for now," Mr. Prim interjected.

"What ever do you mean, Mr. Prim?" inquired Mr. Whipple. "Hamlet's ready for another go."

"Unfortunately, he'll have to wait until tomorrow before he's allowed one. According to Grazelby Certification Section 852, Subsection 17B-6: 'an individual may not exceed three attempts at a given record within a period of twenty-four hours.'"

Arthur's father chuckled in disbelief. "Mr. Prim, please—everyone knows that rule was only created to prevent Striver's Mania in certain predisposed individuals; it has never been enforced for private record attempts made by

136

well-minded participants. Surely, you're not serious about applying it to us?"

The certifier's face grew suddenly stern. "Mr. Whipple, are you asking me to violate Grazelby regulations on your behalf?"

"Well, of course not. But honestly, Mr. Prim, it's only—"

"Because if you were, I would have no choice but to charge you with attempted corruption of a world record official and report you to the International World Record Federation disciplinary council. I'm sure we would all find it highly regrettable if you were to be disqualified from IWRF competition just before the start of the World Record World Championships—wouldn't we, Mr. Whipple?"

Arthur's father lowered his head and exhaled. "Yes, Mr. Prim. It seems our canine ring toss attempts will have to wait until tomorrow."

Hamlet slumped to the floor in defeat, resting his chin on his forepaws and whining softly.

"Very good," declared the certifier. "I'm glad we see eye to eye on the matter. Really, Mr. Whipple, there's no need to fret over any one record; I shall be here indefinitely to judge whatever attempts you choose to undertake. So now then—which event would you like me to officiate next?"

"Actually, Mr. Prim," Arthur's father sighed, "I think we might take a break for a while today."

"Suit yourself. My services will be available when you require them."

Mr. Whipple nodded, then led his family silently from

the room. Though they had not seen their rivals for weeks now, the Whipples once again felt the sting of the Goldwins' inescapable presence.

• • •

After a morning spent with Mr. Prim, Arthur was surprisingly glad to resume his search for Overkill and Undercut. Somehow, death by killer clown no longer seemed quite so awful when compared to death by nitpicking.

Of course, *neither* of these deaths sounded particularly appealing, and Arthur hoped he'd be able to prevent them both with a visit to the World Record Archives.

He met Ruby at their established rendezvous point at noon, and the two promptly set off for the city as they had done the night before.

The young detectives emerged from the train station two hours later and stepped onto the street. Jutting up from behind the modest rooftops in front of them, the hazy outlines of five stony spires stood out against the gray and gloomy sky.

"There they are," Arthur whispered in awe. "The Pinnacles of Achievement—the highest points of the archives building. We're nearly there."

In ten minutes' time, the children stood at the black iron gate that opened onto the archives' steps.

The building stretched from one edge of their view to the other, its face riddled with gothic arches and ornate carvings. A massive entrance hall at its middle shot upward into a series of soot-stained pinnacles that nearly reached the clouds.

Stuck atop the center spire, like a chunk of beef kebab, was a metal sculpture of the earth—on top of which stood the shadowy statue of a man, triumphantly clutching the skewer's point as it pierced the globe and exited the North Pole.

A tepid wind swept through the children's hair.

"Not the most welcoming place, is it?" Ruby observed. "I mean, is this a registry of world records—or a house of human sacrifice? Not that those are really all that different from each other when you think about it. But seriously, should I be worried about vampire bats?"

"You might want to be a bit more respectful. This is practically hallowed ground we're standing on here."

Ruby rolled her eyes. "*Shallow* ground, more like."

"Honestly," Arthur scowled, "all of the world's greatest feats catalogued and collected in one location, and you call it shallow? I don't think you know what you're saying. At the very least, it's bound to hold some clues for us. Can you try to keep that in mind—or would you just be happier waiting outside?"

"Just because I think it's all a bit pointless and completely creepy doesn't mean I don't want to go in. Come on. Let's go see where they keep the chalices of blood."

• • •

The children stepped though a towering archway and into a vast entrance hall, which boasted bronze and marble statues of legendary record breakers, stained-glass windows depicting historic record-setting events, and record-breaking artifacts displayed like religious relics.

"Wow—it's even scarier on the inside," Ruby muttered. Turning to her partner, she added, "So where to?"

Arthur shrugged. "I've only actually been inside once before, and it was a long time ago. I don't really remember where anything is."

"That's funny. I'd have thought your dad would drag your family here every chance he got."

"Not actually. He'd rather we spent our time getting our names in a museum than simply visiting one. He says we shouldn't dwell on the past, because it keeps us from focusing all our attention on the present."

"If you say so," Ruby replied. "I guess we'd better ask for directions then."

The children made their way to the large stone kiosk built into the entrance wall and labeled "Information." Behind the desk sat a pale, ancient-looking woman with sagging eyes and a tightly wound bun that grew from the top of her head like a horn.

"Be careful, Arthur," Ruby whispered. "Don't let her get within neck-biting range."

Arthur ignored the comment and proceeded. "Excuse me, ma'am," he inquired. "Can you tell us the location for records of Human Height?"

Without hesitation, the woman croaked, "Building Three, Hall A, Room Two, Wall C."

140

Arthur stared blankly for a moment—then flinched with fright as the woman's wrinkled arm shot toward him across the counter.

She pointed a bony finger to the pamphlet holder attached to the front of the kiosk. "Would you like a map?" she asked.

Arthur exhaled in relief and embarrassment. All this talk of vampires and human sacrifice had made him jumpier than he'd realized. "Oh," he replied. "Yes, please."

Ruby couldn't resist an impish giggle.

The children followed the map for a quarter of an hour, through various corridors, chambers, and courtyards before finally arriving at the Physical Anomalies and Human Oddities section.

"This is it," announced Arthur. "Just through that door over there."

Ruby followed Arthur's fingertip to the doorway in question, where she noticed the two-headed, four-legged human skeleton that guarded the room's entrance. She shuddered. "Do we *have* to?" she said with a groan.

Arthur looked at her in surprise. "Since when are *you* frightened by something as harmless as a few lifeless bones?"

"I don't mind the regular ones. It's the *extras* that get me."

"Without those extras," said Arthur, "this skeletal gentleman would never have been given the honor of a permanent place at the archives, now would he?"

"Some honor."

"Look, we've come a bit far to be scared off by a little skeleton, don't you think?"

141

"I guess so," Ruby conceded. "Let's just try to get this over with as quickly as possible." She raised her hand to shield her eyes from the bony view, then stepped forward and hurried through the doorway with Arthur following just behind her.

The room in which they now found themselves was crammed from floor to ceiling on every side with all manner of ledgers, binders, and books. The children promptly located Wall C, then started at opposite ends and began working their way inward.

After twenty minutes of searching and nearly falling from the ladder twice, Arthur managed at long last to locate the current volume of *Detailed Dimensions of the Human Body*.

"Got it!" he yelled, pulling the book from its shelf and scrambling down the ladder.

"Phew. I thought I was going to die of dust inhalation," Ruby coughed. "Let's have a look."

The two met at the center of the wall, where Arthur dropped the heavy tome on a nearby reading table. "If Overkill and Undercut are indeed the Tallest and Shortest Humans Alive," he announced, "their names will be listed in these pages."

Arthur shared a hopeful look with his partner, then opened the book. The crisp leather binding creaked as he flipped through to the index. "Let's see here . . . 'head' . . . 'heart' . . . 'heel' . . . 'height. Pages 631-694.'" He thumbed to the first page of the Height section. At the end of a lengthy introduction, the children read the last words on the page:

142

The current record holder for World's Tallest Human is . . .

Arthur flipped excitedly to the next page.

There, printed in small type at the center of an otherwise blank space, was the single word CONFIDENTIAL.

"What?!" Arthur cried in shock.

"Go to the next page," urged Ruby.

Arthur quickly complied, but this only revealed a multipage profile on the previous record holder, Longwe Dounga.

"What about the World's Shortest?" Ruby suggested.

Arthur flipped through the entries for the past ten holders of the World's Tallest record, but when he arrived at the World's Shortest section, the children's eyes were met by the same ominous inscription: CONFIDENTIAL.

Arthur shook his head in disbelief. "I don't understand."

"How can they not be listed?" asked Ruby.

Just then, a hunchbacked man pushed a cartful of books into the room and set about reshelving them.

Without a word to each other, the children scooped up the hefty volume from the table and strode purposefully across the room.

"Pardon us, sir," Arthur inquired as they approached the archivist. "We've found something, um, strange."

"Have you now?" snapped the pallid-featured man. "Well, I'm afraid I don't have time to help you with your little research project here. There are serious scholars and record holders who require my assistance."

The children looked at each other in shock.

"That's strange," retorted Ruby. "You don't look like

you're assisting scholars and record holders; you look like you're shelving books."

"Yes, well I have to keep myself available for any important people who might turn up, now don't I?"

"Well then," said Ruby, "you'll be happy to hear one of them has just turned up. Do you really not know who it is you're talking to? My friend here just so happens to be an esteemed member of the Whipple family—as in, the Whipple family who holds more records in your precious archives than any other family in the world."

"Really?" said the archivist. While his tone was still skeptical, a hint of uncertainty had crept into his voice. "Well, what's his name then?"

"Arthur, sir," the boy answered feebly.

"Never heard of you."

"Well, of course you haven't," said Ruby. "He's up-and-coming."

"Hmm. What is he, some distant cousin?"

"Distant cousin," scoffed the girl. "He's only the son of Charles Whipple himself."

"Charles Whipple?" the archivist exclaimed. "Charles Whipple is your father?"

"Yes, sir."

A panicked expression fell across the man's face. "Oh, I am so sorry. I didn't realize. . . . You *will* forgive me, won't you?"

Ruby gave Arthur an urging look.

"Well," said Arthur, "I might just be able to look past it—if you were to help us with our research."

144

"Anything, anything," spluttered the man. "What have you got there?"

"We were looking for the World's Tallest and Shortest Humans," Arthur explained as he offered him the book, "but all we could find is a pair of blank pages like this one."

Straightening his spectacles, the archivist flipped between the page in question and the one before it. "Ah, yes," he declared. "It seems you have discovered a sealed record."

Arthur scrunched his brow. "What exactly does that mean—'sealed'?"

"It means that the holder of this record has asked to keep his or her identity private. The name will still be listed in the alphabetical catalog of record holders, but this record—and any others the holder has had sealed—will likewise be denoted by the word *confidential* in his or her personal listing."

Ruby seemed especially intrigued by this. "Do you mean to say that people are allowed to opt out of the record books?"

"In order to ensure a complete inventory of world records," explained the archivist, "the IWRF is compelled to offer anonymity to those who request it. Otherwise, certain records would never be reported at all, rendering the creation of an authoritative catalog quite impossible."

"But sir," Arthur countered, with a pointed look to his partner, "why would anyone ever want to keep their records private?"

"While some wish to avoid the public scrutiny and media attention that world-record breaking affords, others wish to conceal certain unsavory pursuits in which they might have participated. Still, you'd be surprised how many criminals waive their right to confidentiality—and end up being caught solely through their world record documentation. Not the brightest bunch, I'm afraid; most of them are just too competitive to keep their achievements to themselves. The police would probably still be trying to charge Freddie 'False Face' Ferguson if he hadn't publicized his record for Highest Number of Unique Masks Worn by a Single Bank Robber."

"If only we were so lucky," Ruby grumbled.

Before the archivist could ask what she meant by this, Arthur interjected, "So sealed records are relatively rare then?"

"Very rare," the man confirmed, "probably one in a thousand. . . . Of course, with such an astronomical number of archived records in general, this isn't actually that small a number."

"And there's no way to find out the identities of these record holders?"

"I'm afraid the only people with access to sealed record information are the Senior World Record Archivists—and they may only use it for the purpose of authenticating new records. The law prohibits them from releasing any such data to the public."

"Well," declared Ruby, "I think that officially makes this a dead end. Thanks for your time, sir."

"Oh, of course. Anything for a member of the Whipple family. Are you certain there is nothing else I can assist you with?"

146

Arthur sighed. "That's it, unfortunately."

The man inhaled through his teeth. "I don't suppose you could still mention it to your father that Terence Slumpshaw, Associate Archives Assistant, did his very best to help you?"

"Of course, Mr. Slumpshaw," Arthur assured him.

The archivist's fingers wriggled with excitement. "Oh, fantastic! Mother will never believe me when I tell her my name has been uttered in the Whipple household! What a day!"

Arthur, unsure how to respond to this, simply said, "Thanks again for your help," then turned with Ruby and headed toward the door.

As they reached the threshold, however, Arthur stopped in his tracks and turned back to the archivist. "Actually, sir," he added, recalling the name Rex had brandished at his father during their doomed dinner party, "you haven't got anything on *Norbury*, have you?"

Terence Slumpshaw turned his head with a smile. "If it is here, Arthur Whipple, I will find it."

• • •

The archivist returned a quarter of an hour later, out of breath and clutching a dented, dusty film canister.

"Please . . . forgive me for . . . the delay," he puffed, handing the canister to Arthur. "This newsreel collection was the first thing I could find under the heading 'Norbury.' The dates range from twenty to thirty years ago, so it may be a bit old—but it does seem to feature members of your family, so perhaps you'll find something pertinent, hmm? Now, if you'll just follow me, I'll get you fixed up with a private screening room and anything else you may require."

Mr. Slumpshaw led Arthur and Ruby out of the Human Oddities wing and into a medium-sized room furnished with red velvet seats and a film projector, which faced a broad, shimmering screen.

"Here we are," the archivist announced. "Shall I get us some refreshments?"

"I think we've got it from here, Terence," assured Ruby.

"Very well then. But do bring the canister back to me when you're finished, so I may properly shelve it and offer you a personal farewell."

The archivist gave a final fawning grin, then left the room and shut the door behind him.

Arthur popped open the film can and made for the projector. As soon as he had threaded the film leader through the sprocket wheels and flicked on the projector's lamp, Ruby hit the lights. The two found their way to the front row of seats, where they sat themselves in the darkened chamber and stared into the glowing white window before them.

Arthur drew a deep breath. "Let's hope this tells us something."

Amid the whirr of the projector, a scratched and dusty IWRF logo flickered onto the screen. A tinny, distorted voiceover crackled through the speakers as the title faded up.

"Notable Moments in World-Record Breaking! This time: the storied and somber history of the live burial record.

"*For centuries, man has endeavored to test his mental and physical limits by digging a hole in the ground, burying himself inside it, and seeing how long he can remain there before destroying his health or losing his mind.*"

The picture cut between archival shots of men digging graves, men being sealed into coffins, coffins being lowered into the ground, and earth being shoveled on top of them.

"*Receiving air, food, and water through a narrow vent in the compartment's ceiling, contenders for the live burial record must reside in a four-by-four-by-eight-foot box, buried six feet beneath the surface for the duration of the attempt.*

"*Given the event's treacherous and time-consuming nature, few have succeeded in besting the record set before them—none advancing the record by more than a few days at a time. That is—until Agatha Whipple.*"

Flashbulbs illuminated a smiling young woman as she climbed into a large wooden box and reclined onto her back.

"Who's Agatha Whipple?" whispered Ruby.

"My grandmother, I think," Arthur replied. "I never knew her. Both my grandparents died before I was born."

The box was sealed and lowered into an open trench, which was promptly filled in with earth, so that only the top of the air vent remained above ground.

"*Seven years ago, the live burial record was shattered when Mrs. Whipple, wife and mother, remained underground for a remarkable one hundred and two days—twice the duration of the previous record.*"

Shots of the woman's face framed in blackness by the

149

vent's rectangular opening were intercut with shots of the changing seasons, followed by shots of men removing the earth around the vent, revealing the long-buried box beneath. A proud, mustachioed man pried open the lid and lifted the smiling woman into his arms. As he carried her frail body toward the camera amid the resumed popping of flashbulbs, a small boy ran to meet them. The woman wrapped her arms around the boy and kissed him.

"Is that your dad?"

"I think so. And the one with the mustache is my grandfather."

"*Reunited with her husband—fellow record-breaking legend Charles Whipple Sr.—and their son Charlie, Agatha would hold the live burial record for an incredible six years—until one year ago, when it was finally broken by Gregory Lyon, a newcomer to the world records game hoping to make a name for himself.*"

"Wait—*Lyon?*" puzzled Ruby. "That's the name of your family's curse. Peculiar, isn't it?"

Arthur slowly nodded, his eyes fixed to the screen as the film continued.

"*Mercifully, Mrs. Whipple would not live to see her cherished record pass to a new champion. One month before the start of Mr. Lyon's attempt, Agatha Whipple died suddenly of a pulmonary embolism, when an undetected blood clot from her cramped time underground dislodged itself and traveled into her lung, leaving her family shocked and heartbroken.*"

150

A quivering-lipped Charles Sr. stood beside a fir-wreathed gravestone with his teary-eyed son.

"Charles Whipple, taking Lyon's ill-timed triumph as an insult to his wife's memory, sought immediate revenge. He buried himself in an underground tomb less than a week after Mr. Lyon had emerged from his own—and remained there an astounding one hundred and thirty-two days, nearly a month longer than his competitor. With Agatha's honor effectively avenged, the live burial record returned to the Whipple family."

Arthur's grandfather climbed out of the unearthed box, his face marked with a somber sense of vindication.

"Wherever there is victory, however, there is also defeat. Gregory Lyon, stripped of his life's greatest achievement and dishonored, quickly spiraled into desperation. He rushed a new attempt at his former record—only to perish nine days later when his hastily-constructed compartment flooded during a freak rainstorm before rescuers could dig him out."

"Ughh," Ruby cringed. "What an awful way to die."

"Yeah," Arthur agreed.

"At a funeral attended only by his newly widowed wife and a handful of cemetery employees, Gregory Lyon was entombed once again—this time forever."

A sobbing, black-veiled woman draped herself over her husband's third and final coffin as it slowly sank into the earth. When two pallbearers attempted to usher her away, the woman began flailing hysterically, her fingernails scraping the coffin's lid on its way down.

"Yet some spirits simply refuse to rest. Ever since Mr.

Lyon's tragic death, misfortune has seemed to follow Charles Whipple Sr. wherever he goes, leading some to coin the term 'the Lyon's Curse.' In recent weeks, Mr. Whipple has been run over by a rickshaw, grazed by a falling chandelier, and nipped by a king cobra—causing him to grow increasingly reclusive and cynical."

"So there's your curse then," said Ruby. "Doesn't sound all that bad if you ask me."

Arthur shrugged.

In a high-up window of the Whipple mansion, Arthur's grandfather cautiously peered out from behind a curtain and then disappeared.

"There is, however, one Whipple who remains optimistic. Following in his father's footsteps, ten-year-old Charlie Jr. has vowed to keep the live burial title in the Whipple clan."

A soft-cheeked, fairer-haired version of Arthur's father addressed a crowd of reporters. *"If anyone tries to take my mother's record away again, I will bury myself for as long as it takes to get it back—just like my dad did."*

Ruby turned to Arthur. "Hard to believe your father was ever so young—or so adorable. Sort of reminds me of someone I know, actually."

Arthur glanced at his partner in confusion, then turned back to the screen.

"And so it seems for the foreseeable future, this revered yet deadly record will remain in the care of the Whipple family. Only time will tell how each will shape the other."

152

With that, a clacking sound sprang from the projector as a rough splice traveled through the film gate. There was a momentary stutter in the picture, and then a second newsreel began where the first had ended. A slightly more modern-looking title card jumped onto the screen, declaring: THE FALL OF THE HOUSE OF WHIPPLE!

"That doesn't sound good," Ruby muttered as the narrator's muffled voice-over commenced.

"*After years of unrivaled record breaking, it seems the Whipple family's reign has finally come to an end—its last days marred by failure and tragedy. The collapse began just one month ago when, nearly a decade after Charles Whipple Sr. brought his late wife's live burial title back to the family, the record was taken away a second time.*"

The lid of a coffin hinged open, revealing a young man with chiseled features and a familiar smile.

"*On the morning of January the twenty-seventh, upstart record-breaking contender Rex Goldwin emerged from a makeshift grave at the back of the Norbury Arms pub after one hundred and fifty-three days underground—successfully besting the Whipple record by a full three weeks.*"

"Aha," Ruby declared. "The handsome face of villainy rears its ugly head."

"*This time, the task of record reclaiming for the Whipple family would fall to nineteen-year-old Charlie Jr.—who had been schoolboy chums with Goldwin until the latter decided to set his sights on the Whipples' most cherished record. Having vowed to personally protect the family leg-*"

acy against all encroachers, young Whipple was quick to back up his word, burying himself within the week."

Arthur's teenaged father gave a smile and a salute, then retreated into a wooden box, which was promptly nailed shut.

"But after just one night underground, an anguished Charlie Jr. was forced to forfeit the attempt, due to an undiagnosed case of claustrophobia—much to his father's disappointment."

Emergency workers hoisted the box from its pit and pried open the lid, revealing the now pale, shivering figure within.

Ruby nudged Arthur with her elbow. "So that's why your dad was so hesitant to enter the Lizard Lounge. He can't stand tight spaces. Had you never seen him act that way before?"

"Guess he just got really good at hiding it. Before Rex came along, nobody's ever really made him do anything he didn't want to do. He's never liked graveyards, though, that's for sure. And no wonder."

"Yeah," Ruby said with a smirk. "Good thing he didn't pass that trait on to you, eh, Arthur?"

Arthur shot her a scowl, then returned his focus to the image on the screen.

Charlie Jr. climbed from the coffin-like compartment and stepped toward his onlooking father, smiling meekly through shame and remorse. But the elder Whipple merely turned and walked away.

"Charles Sr. refused to settle for his son's failure and

swore to undertake the record himself. Sadly, however, he would not get the chance to do so.

"Last week, en route to a secluded island location where he hoped to perform the record attempt free from all distractions, his plane mysteriously went down over the South Pacific. The remains of Charles Whipple Sr. were soon discovered washed up on the northern coast of New Guinea."

"Wow," whispered Ruby. "It's probably a bit late for this now, but—sorry about your grandfather."

"Thanks," Arthur said solemnly. "Guess it makes sense now why my father feels so guilty about the way he died."

"Speculators have been quick to blame Whipple's death on the so-called Lyon's Curse, named for the late Gregory Lyon, who died years earlier in a failed attempt to reclaim the live burial title after it had returned to the Whipple clan. Sources close to the family report that Charles Sr. had spent the last years of his life in fear of the curse, seldom leaving his home, lest he should come to a gruesome end. Unfortunately, it appears his apprehension may have been well-founded."

"I take back what I said about the curse," said Ruby. "Sounds completely horrible, actually."

"I'll say," gulped Arthur.

"But as one star fades," continued the narrator, *"another is born. Hot off his recent victory over the typically unbeatable Whipple family, Rex Goldwin now stands poised on the brink of fame and fortune. . . ."*

Rex's toothy grin faded from the screen as another

crude splice rattled the projector, signaling the start of a third newsreel.

This time the title card read: WHIPPLE NAME RESTORED AS CHARLES JR. ROCKETS TO STARDOM!

A fast-moving montage showed Arthur's father receiving various trophies, plaques, and awards.

"*Galvanized by his father's death early last year, Charles Whipple Jr. promptly embarked on a veritable record breaking rampage, smashing every record he attempted. Having successfully proved himself in the record breaking arena, Whipple soon turned his attention to avenging his family honor—by confronting the man who had robbed them of their most prized record.*

"*Over the following months, Charles Whipple sought out Rex Goldwin and systematically broke every record the newcomer attempted, catapulting the former into international fame in the process—while driving the latter into depression and drunkenness, and seemingly out of the world records game for good.*"

A muttering, unshaven Rex Goldwin stumbled out of a pub, then suddenly charged forward, grabbing the lens and knocking the camera to the ground.

The pavement filled the frame, and the picture cut to an exterior shot of the Grazelby Building.

"*With Goldwin effectively vanquished, the twenty-year-old Whipple quickly found himself being courted by the two largest world record publications on earth, each of them angling for exclusive sponsorship privileges. In April,*

156

Charles turned down the Amazing Ardmore Almanac of the Ridiculously Remarkable *to sign a record-breaking contract with* Grazelby's Guide to World Records and Fantastic Feats, *instantly cementing his stardom and simultaneously making him the World's Most Eligible Bachelor. That's right ladies, he's single! But try not to get your hopes up too quickly; he does hold the record for Longest String of Dates without Seeing the Same Girl Twice. Indeed, it's going to take a special woman to capture this lady-killer. In the meantime, however—the future is wide open for you, Charles Whipple!"*

With one final shot of Arthur's young, smiling father, the screen went black, then blinding white, as the tail end of the film slapped the projector on its way out.

· · ·

"Well," Ruby announced to Arthur as they exited the screening room, "it appears we've got a motive."

"Yeah. It looks like my father pushed your father out of the world records game when they were younger, and now Rex is trying to return the favor—using the dwarf and the giant to reenact the Lyon's Curse, which appears to have been responsible for my grandfather's death."

"And, meanwhile, your father is still angry that Rex took away the one record that really mattered to him."

"Right," Arthur puzzled. "Can this get any more complicated?"

"That's usually how it goes in the detective novels. It's

157

probably going to get a lot worse before it gets better—if it gets better at all, of course. Really depends on which subgenre we're talking about here." Ruby ignored Arthur's blank stare and added, "One thing seems clear, though: our suspicions were right about Rex, and to clear Sammy's name we just need to find a way to prove them beyond any reasonable doubt."

"Agreed," said Arthur. "But in the meantime, I'd better get these newsreels back to Mr. Slumpshaw. I imagine 'proving things beyond any reasonable doubt' could earn us some serious late fees."

"All right then," Ruby said, smiling. "I'll wait for you in the main hall. I've had my fill of the Human Oddities section for today—and I'm sure old Slumpy will be happy to have a few moments alone with his favorite celebrity."

Ruby was right. As soon as Arthur found him, Mr. Slumpshaw began asking all sorts of excited questions about his famous family. When Arthur finally managed to say goodbye, the archivist handed him a handmade business card—which read, TERENCE SLUMPSHAW, ASSOCIATE ARCHIVES ASSISTANT / SENIOR WHIPPLE FANATIC—and instructed him to give it to his father.

Arthur thanked the man one last time, then hurried back toward the main hall. In his haste, however, he inadvertently turned right at the Aeroplanes and Aeronautics wing when he should have turned instead at the Horrors of Horticulture branch—and soon found himself thoroughly disoriented.

He scanned the wall of books to his left, looking for a clue to his current location. His eyes stopped on a large volume entitled *A Complete Listing of World-Record Holders and Their Records, Sorted by Surname: GOLD— GOLE.*

Arthur's pulse quickened as he realized the significance of the book before him. Of all the items in the archives, he had just stumbled onto the book that contained the details of Ruby Goldwin's world record.

But what was he to do? Ruby had made it fairly clear how she felt about his attempts to uncover her secret. He had no desire to betray her trust—but then again, how could he pass up such a fateful discovery?

Arthur decided he should at least make sure the book was a recent edition, before worrying himself too much with any potential moral dilemmas. He placed his finger at the top of the book's spine and peered cautiously down the hall. Ruby was nowhere in sight.

Arthur slid the book off the shelf and flipped to the title page. The edition was only one year old.

This was the point at which he had planned to return the book to its shelf and walk briskly away—but now that it was open, he could not bring himself to close it.

Arthur slowly thumbed to the middle of the volume. Surely there was no harm in checking to see whether or not the Goldwin name was even listed.

It was.

Next, he began flipping through the entries for Ruby's

159

brothers and sisters and their various records. He no longer bothered with excuses.

Rodney . . . Roland . . . Rosalind . . . Rowan . . . Rowena . . . Roxy . . .

Arthur snapped the book shut. What was he doing? Here he'd finally found someone who'd stuck with him despite his obvious shortcomings, and now he was stabbing her in the back the first chance he got. What sort of a friend was he?

A shudder ran down his spine as he considered how close he had come to ruining everything.

At that moment, a familiar voice called out from behind him. "What's that you're reading there?"

Arthur whirled around with a start, losing his grip on the book as he came to stand face-to-face with Ruby.

The book hit the floor with a thud. Arthur fumbled to retrieve it, but Ruby got there first.

She picked up the book and proceeded to hand it over. "Couldn't get enough of all these exciting statistics, eh?" she said with a smirk.

It was then that Ruby noticed the name of the volume she was holding. Her face flooded with confusion as she looked up at Arthur.

"It's not—" Arthur spluttered. "I—"

Ruby's confusion quickly turned to heartbreak. "But I told you I didn't want you to know. I mean, how could you—?" And with that, she turned and dashed down the hallway, burying her face in her hands.

"Ruby!" Arthur shouted. "Wait! I didn't—"

He cast the book to the floor and charged after her—only to collide at full speed with an oncoming book cart.

"Oh my! I didn't see you there," Terence Slumpshaw shrieked from the handle-side of the cart. "Are you all right, Arthur Whipple? You won't tell your father about this, will you?"

Taking no time to reply, Arthur shoved aside the scattered heap of books, picked himself up off the floor, and limped onward as fast as his battered legs would allow.

"Ruby!" he called in vain, losing sight of her as she rounded a corner.

Arthur tumbled into the main entrance hall a few moments later, but there was no sign of his partner. He searched the adjacent rooms and courtyards, then ventured past the front gates and hobbled desperately back to the train station.

But it was too late. Ruby was gone.

Arthur's heart felt as empty as the platform in front of him. Of all the horrible things that had happened to him in recent months—from agonizing personal failures to traumatic near-death experiences—somehow, this was by far the worst.

QUALIFICATIONS

Mr. **Whipple pointed** to a large glass case atop a dark wood pedestal, at the center of which sat a vacant velvet pillow. "It may not look it on first glance," he said sternly, "but this happens to be one of the vilest, most contemptible objects you will ever encounter."

Arthur and his siblings looked to one another, then leaned in with morbid curiosity. Their father had yet to reveal his reason for calling the emergency meeting in the Whipple Hall of Records that morning.

"This, children," Mr. Whipple sighed, "is an empty trophy case. And this particular empty trophy case . . . belongs to me."

Arthur's brothers and sisters gasped.

"Now," he said, "I want you all to take a long hard look at it. This . . . is what failure looks like."

Penelope's eyes began to water. "But how did you get it, Daddy?"

"That's not important, dear. The important thing is that we never allow it to happen again."

Arthur, of course, knew exactly how the cursed artifact had come to be in his father's possession. Thinking back to the face of the boy who had vowed to defend his mother's legacy, only to fail miserably in the attempt, Arthur felt a newfound kinship with the man he called father.

The children studied the trophy case like cavemen around an electric toaster.

"Let this be a tangible reminder to you all—as it has been to me," said Mr. Whipple, "why we must never settle for anything less than total victory. With the World Record World Championships hardly three weeks away, and a certain *other* family conniving to supersede us, this has never been more important. Now—let us go forth and make these final days of training the most effective of our lives!"

The children applauded in agreement, then marched toward the door while their father called out the day's tasks.

"Franklin—your shipment of antique anchors should be here by noon. Cordelia—Mr. Prim will be taking measurements on your soup-can Acropolis; try to be agreeable. Arthur—why don't you stay behind for a minute?"

163

When the others had all left the room, Mr. Whipple sat down beside his recordless son.

"Now, Arthur, your mother and I have been talking, and we've noticed your efforts at finding a suitable record to break have dwindled in recent weeks. We know that before his reassignment, Uncle Mervyn was helping you work through a sizable list of record possibilities—and we'd like to see you get to the end of it before championships qualifications are over. If there is indeed some event you were destined for, that list is your best chance of discovering it. And what better way to spur you on to a record in such an event than competing at the championships? But in order to compete, of course, you'll first have to qualify."

"Of course, Father," replied Arthur. "The only thing is that, well, after three weeks, I'm hardly halfway down the list. But if I could have just another three days, I think I could manage it."

"Very well, Arthur. I'll inform Mr. Prim you'll be having an especially full schedule for the remainder of the week. Now, remember, we're not expecting anything from you; honestly, under any other circumstances, we wouldn't be troubling you at all. But with such bitter competition this year, we could really use all the help we can get—however unlikely it may be."

"Yes sir. I'll do my best—er, I'll *be* the best."

"That's the spirit, boy. Now go show that list of yours what you're made of."

"Yes, sir. I will do that very thing."

164

Arthur headed for the door, but stopped short.

"Sir?"

"Yes, Arthur?"

"Norbury wasn't your fault, you know. And neither is the Lyon's Curse."

At the sound of the first word, Mr. Whipple's face went white. "Wh—? How did you—"

"Whatever happens at the championships," Arthur continued, "you'll always be my favorite record breaker."

With that, he turned and walked through the door, leaving his father with eyes wide and mouth agape.

• • •

Arthur scampered up to his room on his way out of the house and grabbed a bulging bag of letters, all of which shared a single addressee: Ruby Goldwin.

In the five days since Ruby's departure, Arthur had managed to write 1,482 individual letters to his estranged partner—just 7,541 short of the record for Most Apology Letters Sent in One Month by a Single Person—in the hopes that she might find it in her heart to forgive him and rejoin the investigation.

The first hundred or so went something like this:

> Dear Ruby,
>
> Words cannot describe how horribly, terribly, truly sorry I am—but I shall give

165

it a try anyway: I am so horribly, terribly, truly sorry. What I did was utterly, completely, unimaginably reprehensible. If you are unable to forgive me, I shall have no cause for complaint whatsoever.

Having said that, I think you should know, as a matter of interest—not that it excuses my actions in any way—that I didn't actually see anything about you in that horrible book. I stopped myself just in time, when I realized what a terrible thing it would be to break your trust. Of course, my change of heart ultimately arrived far too late, as I have no doubt broken your trust nonetheless.

If there is anything I can do to make up for my foolish actions, please let me know as soon as possible, so I might make immediate amends. I will even read a Joss Langston novel if you want me to.

Sincerely Yours with Never-ending
Regret and Remorse,
Arthur

After the initial batch, however, the next fourteen hundred letters looked a bit more like *this*:

Dear Ruby,

Indescribably sorry. Please forgive...
I'll do anything.

Remorsefully Yours,
Arthur

Unfortunately, none of it seemed to be working. No matter how many letters he sent, no matter how long he stood outside her house looking for her, Arthur had yet to hear a single word or catch more than a few fleeting glimpses of the girl since she'd turned and run from him in the halls of the archives.

He was starting to grow desperate. Not only did he miss having Ruby for a friend, he missed having her for a detective partner. Without her, how was he to find proof of Rex's guilt and Sammy's innocence? She had always been the *real* detective. He had never gotten anywhere before she'd joined the case.

Inspired by his recent chat with his father, Arthur began to devise a new tactic to get his partner back. If he could only break a world record at the World Record World Championships, perhaps Ruby would be so impressed by it that she'd suddenly forget all about the pain he'd caused her and simply forgive him on the spot.

Of course, this strategy required ignoring the fact that Ruby had never once seemed even remotely impressed by world-record breaking in all the time he'd known her—but

167

somehow, this didn't stop Arthur from embracing it anyway.

He knew the investigation might suffer a bit while he focused on selecting and training for his event, but he assured himself it would all be worth it in the end.

If he could only break a world record, he would earn the respect of his family and regain the trust of his partner in one fell swoop. If he could only break a world record, he and Ruby would thwart Rex and exonerate Sammy in no time. If he could only break a world record, all of his problems would be solved.

• • •

Arthur left the bag of letters downstairs for the postman and made his way to the garage to grab some supplies. Then he dashed out to the south lawn, where Mr. Prim stood watching as Beatrice took the last bite of her thirty-seventh schnitzel.

"Time!" shouted the certifier, looking up from his stopwatch. "Now, I'll have to dock two schnitzels from your total for *illegal use of utensils*, but a score of thirty-five schnitzels in two minutes should still qualify you for the championships—probably third or fourth seed, if you're lucky."

Beatrice dabbed the corner of her mouth with a napkin and rose to her feet, her expression stoic and steely. She was not accustomed to being seeded any lower than first or second, and this came as a bit of a disappointment. Given Mr. Prim's pedantic tendencies, however, she was happy to have qualified at all.

The certifier turned from the table to find Arthur waiting for him there, a box of matches in one hand and a bundle of thin-shafted torches in the other.

"Um, hello, Mr. Prim," he said. "I'm ready for my fire-eating attempt."

• • •

Five minutes and one half-singed eyebrow later, Arthur forcefully crossed out the words *Most Torches Extinguished with Mouth in One Minute* from his list of record possibilities.

Next, it was on to ostrich-egg juggling—which ended rather messily—and then perpendicular pole climbing, which proved much harder to execute when covered from head to heel in ostrich-egg yolk.

And so it went for several hours: Arthur failing at various record attempts, while his siblings succeeded in others—all of them under the strict supervision of Archibald Prim.

By the end of the day, Arthur had eliminated nearly three pages of possibilities from his notebook. Discouraged that none of the day's attempts had been good enough to qualify him for a spot in the WRWC, yet comforted by the thought that the next day could only get better, he rounded out his evening by writing another 297 apology letters to Ruby, then fell fast asleep.

Unfortunately, the next day would prove no better than the first, with a total of seventy-three failures—eighteen of them being the direct result of Mr. Prim's meticulous deductions.

By the afternoon of the third day, with only a handful

of events left on his list, Arthur began to lose hope that he would qualify in anything.

After cleaning up the feathers from his pillow-diving attempt, he retrieved his magical domino from his pocket and rubbed it desperately for luck as he readied himself for his next event: knife-block speed stocking.

Originally created three years earlier by a group of enterprising chefs as a solution to the "too many cooks in the kitchen" problem, competitive speed stocking had only just begun to reach a wider audience and was set to make its WRWC debut.

Play is conducted as follows: a lone contender stands within the hollow center of a ring-shaped table with twelve kitchen-variety knife blocks facing inward around its inner ring. Each block—except for one—is preloaded with a standard twenty-piece knife set. At the start of play, the contender begins transferring knives into the empty block from the one beside it, taking care not to sever any fingers or important arteries in the process. When the empty block has been filled and the adjacent one emptied, the competitor pivots to the next full block and begins transferring its knives into the newly emptied one until it has also been filled—and so on. When the knives from all twelve blocks have been transferred, one revolution is complete; a regulation contest consists of seven revolutions.

Arthur had been involved in speed stocking ever since being introduced to the sport twelve months earlier by his family's former chef. Sammy the Spatula was one of the sport's originators and had—before his incarceration and subsequent disappearance—sacrificed much of his free time to coach Arthur on his technique. Arthur had recently worked his way to the top of his local speed stocking club thanks to Sammy's instruction—though he had yet to achieve anything like the scores required for international competition.

But now, as Arthur stood at the center of the table reaching for the handle of the first knife, something inside him snapped. Years of bottled-up frustration surged through his veins and into his fingertips. His hands became a blur. The rat-tat-tat of blade against block reverberated through the air like machine gun fire.

"Two minutes, 21.674 seconds," announced Mr. Prim as Arthur popped the last knife into place. "Well, well, well. It appears you may finally have a qualifying time here, Arthur Whipple. Nowhere near the top seed of course, but if no one records a better time before the championships begin, you may just scrape by in nineteenth or twentieth."

Arthur panted heavily with exhaustion and relief. "Thank you, Mr. Prim," he smiled.

"Don't thank *me*, young man," Mr. Prim said sharply. "I am merely a servant of the numbers. Despite what you may be accustomed to, you'll get no special treatment from *this* certifier."

"I'm sorry, sir—I didn't mean . . ."

"Your next attempt begins in four minutes thirty seconds. I'd have thought you'd want to put in a little prepara-

171

tion beforehand, considering your less-than-stellar success rate."

"Of course, sir. I'll go fetch the bucket of fiddler crabs and the first aid kit."

• • •

Despite his efforts, Arthur did not qualify in any of his remaining events. He took solace, however, in having not been completely barred from the championships. At least he would have a chance to contribute this year, even if it was only in one event. He would just have to make it count.

And so, for the next two weeks, Arthur endeavored to do exactly that. When he wasn't in his room writing apology letters to Ruby, he was out about the estate honing his knife-block stocking skills.

On the last day before the start of the WRWC, Arthur made a significant and unexpected development. He realized that if he simply worked counterclockwise instead of clockwise—as was the traditional direction of play—he could shave nearly fifteen seconds off his best time. It was enough to put him well in range of the current world record.

What Arthur failed to notice, unfortunately, were the two sets of eyes watching him from a nearby tree as he stood panting with surprise and joy at his newfound breakthrough.

172

THE WORLD RECORD WORLD CHAMPIONSHIPS

On the evening of the following day, the Sixty-Seventh World Record World Championships began.

The opening ceremonies kicked off with a legion of acrobats grouping themselves into death-defying formations to reenact five millennia of world-record breaking history.

Arthur gazed awestruck beside his family from the contender staging deck as one record-breaking triumph after another materialized at the center of the stadium—from the Great Pyramid of Giza to the Empire State Building—each of them composed solely of human figures. As the mass of bodies reconstituted itself into the Sputnik 1 rocket launch, rising in unison toward the top of the stadium, the floodlights abruptly went dark and the human fireworks began.

Five hundred cannons fired at once with a deafening blast, rattling the stands and launching a battery of living rounds into the air. One of the projectiles zipped past Arthur's face, and he could just make out the dark, crash-suited form of a man, his blurred body fused with metal frameworks and assorted colorful protrusions. A moment later, when the speeding figures had reached the optimum altitude, showers of sparks burst from each of them, causing the black oval of sky at the center of the stadium to explode with light and color.

Parachutes sprouted from the flaming figures as gravity began to pull them back to earth—but by this time, another round of pyrotechnic performers was already lighting up the sky above them.

The cannonade continued for a quarter of an hour, culminating in the Largest Simultaneous Human Cannonball / Human Firework Launch in History, when one thousand cannons in and around the stadium fired at the same moment.

The force of the blast and the resulting roar of the crowd shook the entire structure.

Then, as the finale fireworks began to fizzle, two parallel streams of light—one silver and one gold—shot straight up through the smoke at the center of the stadium, climbing higher than any other before them.

"There goes your father, children," Mrs. Whipple pointed out. "Shame he has to share the honor of Host-City High-Flyer with that scoundrel Rex Goldwin. Let's just hope your father flies highest."

174

Arthur and his family watched as the two soaring figures continued to climb. The next moment, a flurry of silver and gold sparks filled the surrounding sky, drifting down onto a sea of *oohs* and *ahhs*.

As the glittering faded, however, the crowd's response shifted from wonderment to dread. While one of the figures was now floating on the breeze under a billowed parachute, the other was plummeting toward the earth.

"Daddy!" cried Lenora.

The Whipples watched in horror as Arthur's father grabbed desperately at his pack.

"Come on—pull the cord, Dad!" shouted Henry.

But still, no parachute emerged.

Arthur tried to turn away, to shield his eyes from the gruesome sight to come, but he could not bring himself to abandon his father at such a critical moment.

With the ground only fifty feet away, the flailing figure continued its blistering descent, the Whipples' hopes for their father fading with every foot.

And then, a parachute.

Barely an instant before impact, the canopy fully inflated. Mr. Whipple's body collided with the ground, concealed from the crowd by the now-tangled mass of white cloth.

The stadium went silent. It was difficult to tell what sort of medical equipment the situation would require: a stretcher—or a body bag.

A distant baby's cry echoed in Arthur's ears as the boy and his family scoured the scene for signs of life. The

175

deflated parachute flapped lazily in the breeze, anchored to the earth by the motionless heap beneath it.

A team of paramedics rushed onto the floor.

They approached the site of the crash, then reached out to remove the parachute and inspect the damage.

But just before they could grasp hold of it, the cloth was cast aside—and the man beneath it leapt to his feet. The medics stumbled backward as Mr. Whipple raised an arm to the stadium in salute.

The World's Largest Collective Sigh of Relief rose up from the crowd. No one, it seemed, would be dying a horrific death before their eyes. At least not tonight.

• • •

When Mr. Whipple had rejoined his relieved family, the Whipples proceeded down to the stadium gate to join the Parade of Contenders as it snaked its way through the streets of the city.

By the time they'd exited the stadium and reached the grand entranceway, the parade had already begun pouring through the gate and onto the stadium floor. The Whipples, being from the host city, would be walking in the final group, so they promptly began the trek to the rear of the parade, while the stream of participants gushed past in the opposite direction.

For Arthur, it was like walking through a dream. All of his favorite record breakers from every corner of the globe were there, floating by and swirling around him.

176

Arthur struggled to retain as many details as possible—from the well-pummeled nose of Stavros "Hydra-Hands" Alamanos, the World's Longest Reigning Boxing Champion and Highest-Paid Athlete, to the World's Tallest Turban, bobbing along on the head of the legendary Sheik Alhid Aziz Wabul, to the bulging, overworked tires on the wheeled platform that carried Roberto and Bibiana Babosa, the World's Heaviest Husband and Wife.

It struck Arthur to keep an eye out for Messrs. Overkill and Undercut amongst the record-breaking faces, just in case the World's Tallest and Shortest Humans couldn't resist taking part in the championships. But unsurprisingly, he never glimpsed so much as a frizzy clown wig. It was hard not to be a bit relieved by this, but he hoped for Sammy's sake that he might catch up to the dwarf and the giant soon.

Further down the line, Arthur spotted the scarlet uniforms and beaming smiles of the Nakamoto family, bouncing vibrantly down the center of the street. The Whipples had always considered the Nakamotos their fiercest rivals, but after the recent run-ins they'd had with a certain other record-breaking family, it was difficult to think of the Nakamotos as anything less than old and dear friends. The two families bowed to one another as they crossed paths.

Arthur then noticed the red and gold colors of the Soviet flag, as well as the gray-bearded man walking alongside it with the Russian champions.

"Uncle Mervyn!" he shouted.

The man spun his head toward the sound. "Arthur!" he

177

cried. He turned and began working his way through the crowd. "How are you, lad?" said Uncle Mervyn, smiling as he reached the side of the parade.

"I qualified in knife-block speed stocking."

"Ah yes. I heard about that. Excellent news. I see you and Mr. Prim are getting on just fine."

"Well—" Arthur began, but he was promptly cut off by his father as the other Whipples joined the reunion.

"Mervyn!" cried Mr. Whipple, clapping the certifier on the back. "Are *you* a sight for sore eyes. How's Moscow treating you?"

At this there came a gruff Russian voice from behind Arthur's uncle.

"Comrade McCleary," said a stocky man in a fur hat. "Your presence is to be required in parade with Champions of Motherland."

Uncle Mervyn nodded to the man, then turned back to Mr. Whipple. "Can't complain," he said with a wry smile. "Not if I don't want to be sent to Siberia, that is," he added, chuckling under his breath. He began walking backward to catch up with the parade. "Actually, Moscow's a wonderful place for record breaking. Just wish you and your family were there with me. Can't wait to see you mop the floor with the Goldwins before I go back." He glanced behind him, then looked again to Arthur and called, "Remember the domino, Arthur. We all have our part to play." Then, with a parting wink, he was swept up in the crowd and disappeared into the parade.

Arthur had barely begun to reflect on the encounter with his uncle when he noticed the self-satisfied smirk of Inspector Smudge amongst the sea of faces to his right. Having no desire to receive another lecture, he ducked behind another passerby before Smudge had the chance to detect him.

When he looked up a few moments later to make sure the man had gone, a flicker of something familiar caught his eye on the other side of the crowd.

Arthur promptly reached the end of the parade and scanned the surrounding swarm for a further glimpse but he found nothing. He sighed and turned to his rear. There, hardly ten feet in front of him, stood Ruby Goldwin.

Arthur's heart beat faster. This was the most he had seen of her in weeks. He didn't know what to say to her, but he knew he had to say something.

He took a step forward—only to have his path blocked by another familiar figure.

"Charlie!" called Rex Goldwin over Arthur's head. "Glad to see you weren't severely maimed back there."

Mr. Whipple nodded warily. "Thank you, Mr. Goldwin."

Ruby broke her brief gaze with Arthur and retreated amongst her siblings.

Arthur couldn't help but be reminded of the first time he'd seen the girl standing with her family, a complete and utter stranger. Now, after all they had been through together since the night of the Birthday Extravaganza, Ruby seemed more a stranger than ever. It was almost as if they had never met—only worse.

179

Ruby's father pushed past Arthur and approached Mr. Whipple as the rest of the Goldwins filed in around them. "That *was* a bit close, though—wasn't it, Charlie?" Rex said with a grin. "Hate to see our competition prematurely expire before we've had a crack at them. Next time, you might try pulling the rip cord *before* you hit the ground. I can't always be there to catch you when you fall, you know."

Arthur's father fixed his jaw. "Mr. Goldwin, as much as I appreciate your invaluable advice on the subtleties of parachuting, I'll have you know I am not an imbecile. Upon pulling the rip cord, you see, it simply came off in my hand. The only way I survived the fall was by tearing open my pack and releasing the chute manually. Of course, I'm sure I needn't tell this to you. I don't know how you did it—I personally checked my pack half a dozen times before launch—but this clearly has your slippery stench all over it."

"Well, Grand Coulee Dam, Charlie! You're not seriously accusing me of being responsible for your own incompetence again? Really, Charlie, this is getting to be a very bad habit for you."

Mr. Whipple glared from under his brow. "Satisfaction," he grumbled.

"What was that, Charlie?"

"Satisfaction, sir!" Mr. Whipple repeated, his voice swelling to a snarl. "I demand satisfaction! You, Mr. Goldwin, have insulted my honor once too often, and thus—in accordance with our lawful rivalry contract—I hereby challenge thee to a duel!"

180

With that, Mr. Whipple tore the ceremonial victor's sash from his shoulder and threw it to the ground.

"Ah, Charlie," Rex Goldwin cooed in a sly, mocking tone, "I thought you'd never ask."

Reaching down and retrieving the strip of cloth, Rex promptly employed it in slapping Mr. Whipple across the face, then politely offered it back to him. "I believe you dropped this."

"Very well," said Mr. Whipple, regaining his composure as he accepted the sash. "I shall see you for Dueling Day on the final morning of competition."

"Wouldn't miss it," said Rex. "After murdering you in competition all week, I reckon it won't be much of a stretch to simply, ahem, *murder you*. I must say it'll break my heart to have to do away with such an old and dear friend—but then again, I'd hate to deny you your honor. And after all, it *was* your idea."

"Please, Mr. Goldwin, I doubt this is the first time you've considered doing me in—or indeed the first time you've attempted to do so. And furthermore, I would not be so certain it will be you who does the murdering; I am no stranger to deadly contest, as you will soon discover."

"Oooh," Rex goaded with glee. "Charlie, please—I can't take it anymore! It'll be hard enough waiting till the end of the week as it is, without you teasing me like that! Please, no more!"

"Fair enough, Mr. Goldwin. I shall henceforth restrict my means of communication to the blade or the bullet."

181

"Oh, do stop, Charlie!" Rex snickered. "It's just too much! Next you'll be threatening to bludgeon us to death with the Championship Cup! Still, I can hardly fault you for your wishful thinking. Surely you realize the nearest your family will ever get to the cup is admiring it in our trophy room—after your own untimely demise, of course. Ooh—I really cannot wait to get started! Tomorrow just can't come soon enough, can it?"

"Indeed it cannot, Mr. Goldwin."

"Come along then, children. Let's leave Charlie here to enjoy the parade with his family. I'm afraid it will be his last."

With that, Rex Goldwin turned his back and led his family through the crowd into the heart of the procession.

After a moment of angry silence, the Whipples followed suit, rejoining the parade as it wound its way back toward the stadium.

When the two rival families emerged through the gate and stepped onto the stadium floor, the arena thundered with applause as the crowd leapt to its feet. This was sure to be the Greatest World Record World Championships the World Had Ever Seen.

• • •

The next morning's car ride into the city was silent and tense. As they neared the tournament grounds at Champions Court Place Park, the Whipples prepared their minds for the first day of what promised to be the most challenging competition of their lives.

Upon their arrival, Arthur and his siblings silently followed their father through the complex. In the vacant courtyard between the winged statue of Lady Victory and the Totem Pole of Triumph, on the steps of the Fountain of Favorable Results, Mr. Whipple halted—and turned to face his family.

"Children," he declared, "you may be experiencing an unusual and rather unpleasant feeling at the moment— a feeling, I must admit, to which I presently find myself no less vulnerable."

"I don't like it, Daddy," Lenora groaned. "What is it?"

"I believe," Mr. Whipple replied, "this is generally referred to as 'stage fright' or 'the jitters'—a perfectly common condition, I am told, in normal individuals when facing a particularly testing challenge. We mustn't forget, however, that *we* are *not* normal individuals. *We* are Whipples. In recent months, we have been sabotaged, insulted, maligned, and assaulted, and the only way to restore our honor is to win it back in open competition. For there are those, dear family, who would have us stripped of our records and dishonored—those who would relish in robbing us of our accomplishments and rendering us ordinary. But we shall not so easily oblige them. Oh, no. *We*, my dear Whipples, will not go quietly into normality!"

A cheer sprang out from his family like the Bursting of the World's Largest Dam.

"Now come, my young champions," said Mr. Whipple. "We must be steadfast; we must be strong. Charlotte, darling—are you ready to eviscerate the competition in finger-painting portraiture?"

"Yes, sir!" Arthur's five-year-old sister declared. "The earth will run Winsor red with the spilt pigments of our enemies!"

"Indeed, little one—that's more like it! All right, Whipples—you heard your sister. Let's go gut some Goldwins, shall we?"

• • •

With paint dripping from her fingers and face, Charlotte slapped her palette down onto the table.

In just over four minutes, she had successfully reproduced recognizable representations of the art world's twenty-five most famous faces—from Vandini's *Mia Lona* to Flambeau's *Self-Portrait with Potatoes*—effectively nudging out Radley Goldwin for the first world record of the competition.

The Whipples jumped with joy. The crowd roared. The Goldwins sneered.

"That was a freebie," Rex remarked as the two families passed each other on their way out of the arts complex. "A little gift from our family to yours. It's only finger-painting, after all, and we're more than happy to part with it. I'm afraid, however, in the next event we won't be so generous."

He was not lying. Twenty minutes later, Roland Goldwin had broken the record for Farthest Rubber Boot Throw, surpassing Henry's phenomenal throw of 66.4 meters by just three and a half centimeters.

"Ha," snapped Rex Goldwin. "Boot throwing, now there's a *real* event!"

Mr. Whipple looked slightly nervous, but said nothing.

Fortunately, his nervousness would soon fade, after Penelope bested Rowena Goldwin in Junior Beer-Stein Carrying to keep the Whipples ahead by one.

As the little girl staggered across the finish line with six sloshing mugs in each hand, Arthur noticed the shimmer of pride in their father's eye—and longed for the moment when he might receive a similar shimmer of his own.

Of course, he would have to wait some time for the chance to make any personal contributions to his family's cause. Because knife-block speed stocking was new this year to the WRWC, it had been tacked on to the very end of the schedule. Arthur hoped that by the time his big attempt finally arrived, it might still be of some use to his family—or at least that someone might be around to actually witness it.

But for now, he was content to cheer on his family from the sidelines as they battled the Goldwins through one nail-biting round to another.

After nail biting had ended—with Cordelia nibbling out a win over Rodney by barely half a fingernail—it was on to heart stopping. This time, the record was broken by the Goldwin family, when Randolf managed to slow his heart rate to just nineteen beats per minute through Zen meditation.

As Arthur watched his family struggle back and forth with their rivals over the coming days, he couldn't help but feel he was headed for a stalemate of his own. Hard as he tried to cast it from his mind, the thought of Ruby hating him was making it more and more difficult to focus on his upcoming attempt. Sure, she was bound to offer him unconditional forgiveness when she discovered he was a world-record breaker, but in the meantime, he was dying for even a simple "hello." Every time he worked up the courage to try and talk to her, Ruby would suddenly disappear behind her siblings, effectively cutting off his approach before he'd begun it.

On the evening before the final day of competition, as the Whipples and Goldwins geared up for the yak-milking competition, Arthur's frustration finally reached its curdling point.

After catching a rare glimpse of Ruby, only to watch her immediately vanish into a cluster of her brothers and sisters once again, he decided he had been ignored long enough. Arthur straightened his collar and marched toward the gathering of Goldwins. He gently tapped Ruby's outermost sister on the shoulder.

"Um, pardon me," Arthur stammered, "um, Roxy?"

"It's Rosalind."

"Oh, right. Sorry about—"

"Look—what do you want?"

"Yes, of course—straight to business—we *are* mortal enemies, after all, so I'll only take a moment of your time. It's just that, well, I was wondering if I might speak to Ruby for a minute."

186

Rosalind sniffed. "What are you asking *me* for? The two of you are practically married, aren't you?" Rosalind glanced to Ruby, who looked furtively away. "Ahh. Had a lover's quarrel, did we?"

"We *are* talking about Ruby here, right?" Arthur asked, furrowing his brow in confusion, then pointing for clarification. "She's right there—green eyes, dark, reddish hair?"

"Dumb-looking dimples, lazy expression?" Rupert chimed in. "Yeah, that's Ruby all right. Why would you want to talk to *her*?"

"Well, that's sort of a private matter. Look, if it's too much trouble—"

"Hey, Ruby—you wanna talk to Mr. Winner here?"

Without looking up from the ground, Ruby quietly shook her head.

"There you go," concluded Rupert. "The freak doesn't want to talk to you anyway."

Arthur's jaw clenched. "You know, Rupert—if that is your real name—I don't think you should talk that way about your sister. I mean, if you spent five minutes trying to get to know her, you might see what a remarkable person she is—clever and honest and kind and—and well, completely extraordinary, however hard she tries not to be. And, as it happens, she's also the best friend I ever had."

Arthur took a breath, ignoring the Goldwins' looks of bored indifference. "Anyway, thanks for your time. I won't be bothering you again."

"I don't doubt it," said Rupert. "Oh, and by the way, good luck in speed stocking tomorrow. I'm sure you'll do great—at losing."

Not wanting to dignify the comment with a response—even if he'd actually had one—Arthur turned defiantly away . . . and stepped face-first into a sudden stream of yak's milk.

Ruby's siblings burst into laughter.

"Sorry about that," tittered Roland Goldwin from the bulging underside of one of the shaggy-bellied beasts nearby. "I guess that one sort of got away from me there."

Thoroughly soaked and sufficiently humiliated, Arthur wiped his face with his sleeve and proceeded on his path as the Goldwins continued their jeering behind him.

Much as he hated to part with Ruby in such a manner, he could not bring himself to look back, for fear he'd only find her laughing along with them.

• • •

Forty minutes later, the Goldwins had added Most Yak's Milk Extracted By Hand in Half an Hour to their list of world records, bringing their record tally dead even with their rivals as the day drew to a close.

"Well, Charlie," Rex Goldwin smirked at Mr. Whipple from the other side of the fence, "who knew this competition would be so close, eh? Really, I thought we'd have completely buried you by now. Ooh, poor choice of words—we all know how you feel about being buried, don't we? But no matter; after our appointment tomorrow, your family will fold like an origami frog with no head. By which I mean, I will leave your family crumpled and headless—by which I mean, I will kill you."

"Thank you, Mr. Goldwin," Arthur's father replied. "It's not every day one receives such explicit clarification of his adversary's killing metaphors. Would've been a pity to think you were merely referring to your paper-folding hobby."

"Nope. Just talking about murdering you."

"Yes, I see. Will that be all, then?"

"Oh yes, Charlie," Rex leered. "That *will* be all. Sweet dreams now."

Mr. Whipple turned to his family as the grinning man sauntered away. "We must get our rest tonight, children," he declared. "For if life as we know it is to carry on, we shall have to earn it on the field tomorrow. Wilhelm, fetch the car."

The drive was silent once again as the Whipples headed home for the last time before the championships' end. With their father's duel in the morning and the awards ceremony at night, not to mention the dozens of decisive events in between—including Arthur's own—the fate of the Whipple family now hinged on one final day of competition.

It would be the most horrifying day of Arthur's life.

THE FINAL DAY

Arthur sat on his bed, surrounded by blankets and pillows and wooden knife blocks.

The thought of his upcoming event had left him unable to sleep, so he'd decided to get in a few practice runs before the rest of his family had risen. Because he didn't want to wake anyone, however, he was forced to practice the thunderous, lightning-paced sport of knife-block speed stocking rather gingerly.

"Ahem," came a hushed voice from the far side of the chamber.

Arthur turned his head toward it. The plump silhouette of Mrs. Waite filled the doorway. In her arms, she held Arthur's baby sister, Ivy, who, in turn, held her stuffed bear, Mr. Growls. Dressed in the same frilly pink nightgown as his owner, Mr. Growls did not look pleased.

"So sorry to disturb you, Master Arthur," whispered the housekeeper, "but—er—well, your presence has been requested in the garden."

"Oh," Arthur replied. He climbed over his knife blocks and staggered out of bed. As he stretched an arm through the sleeve of his shirt, he asked, "By whom?"

"Shhh," Ivy whispered, holding her finger to Mr. Growls' mouth. "It's a secret. . . ."

Mrs. Waite gave an uneasy smile, then simply motioned Arthur to hurry.

• • •

Arthur followed Ivy and Mrs. Waite through the dim, silent house and out onto the terrace. Swirls of early morning mist revealed the first glimpses of the approaching dawn.

When they had reached the edge of the garden where the grass gave way to forest, the housekeeper halted.

"There," she said, pointing to one of the larger trees. "Your visitor awaits."

Arthur gave a quizzical look to the housekeeper, then stepped past her toward the tree in question. When he was within ten feet of the trunk, a shadowy figure emerged from the darkness beside it.

"Hiya, Arthur," said the visitor.

"Oh," said Arthur, stumbling backward. "It's you. Ruby."

"That is my name, yes," said the girl.

191

"Right," said Arthur. "What I meant to say is: it's good to see you—I mean, to see you and to hear you saying words to me at the same time. Do you know what I mean?"

Ruby paused. "It's good to see you too."

"All right," Mrs. Waite interjected. "I'm glad you two are talking again—but I'd better get back. Mr. Whipple would have me skinned and mounted to the trophy room wall if he found out I'd let a Goldwin onto the estate on the final day of championships."

"Champ-in-*ships*!" chirped Ivy.

Mrs. Waite patted Ivy's head and turned back to Ruby. "He'd only take you for a spy, I'm afraid. Perhaps I should be more wary myself, but something tells me you're no spy, are you, dear?"

"You needn't worry about me, ma'am," Ruby replied. "I'm no fan of the Goldwins either. In fact, I'm very nearly convinced I was adopted, actually—so my surname is really nothing more than a seven-letter lie. I'm only stuck with it until I can find my real family."

"Oh, my my. You poor thing," said the housekeeper. "I'm sure they're not far off, dear. You're bound to find them soon enough if you just keep looking. With a little bit of patience, one can accomplish anything."

"I hope so, ma'am."

"You can be certain of it, dear. All right, Arthur—don't be too long now. Your father will no doubt be wanting to get an early start for the championships today."

"Champ-in-*ships*!" repeated Ivy.

192

"Yes, Mrs. Waite. Thank you," said Arthur before turning to his sister. "All right, Ivy. You and Mr. Growls go get ready. It's sure to be a big day for humans and bears alike."

"Big day for bears!" the little girl laughed.

As the housekeeper departed back toward the house with his sister, Arthur and Ruby stood casting furtive glances back and forth at one another, until Ruby finally broke the silence.

"So, I just wanted to wish you luck on your record attempt today—and to let you know I'll be cheering for you. I know you can do it."

"Wow. Thanks," Arthur replied. "That really means a lot."

"Yeah, well, it's true. If anyone can break that record, Arthur, it's you."

Arthur smiled briefly, then shuffled his feet. "In case you didn't read any of my letters, please, let me say again—I am so sorry about the archives."

"Yeah," Ruby frowned, "that was pretty bad. But, you know, it's possible I may have overreacted just a bit. And anyway, I think you've suffered enough, so . . . I forgive you."

The words warmed Arthur's insides like a sip of Explo-Cocoa in the middle of a rainstorm.

"And I *have* enjoyed the letters, by the way," she added. "Of course, most of them are down to three or four words now, but there's something strangely poetic about a message that merely reads, 'Ruby, Sorry. Arthur.' It's like you've managed to reduce the medium to its most basic form. Are you sure you haven't accidentally broken the record for World's Shortest Letter or something?"

"Already been done. The Shortest Letter Conceivable was written in Morse code by Soviet secret agent Egor Stroganov to his wife, Elga, instructing her to meet him at Terminal E of Düsseldorf International. The entire message consisted solely of three dots."

"Ah. Unfortunate."

"Yeah," Arthur agreed. "I knew I wasn't going to get that one. I was, however, only 762 letters away from the Most Apology Letters Ever Sent in One Month."

"Oh, well hey, don't let a silly thing like forgiveness stop you. Feel free to keep sending them for as long as you like. They might come in handy someday—you know, in case I ever need to divert the flow of a major river or something."

"Thanks—but I think they all have to be authentic. Mr. Prim is pretty particular about that sort of thing."

"Hmm. Then I guess you'll just have to make up for it with your event today, now won't you?"

"I guess I will. I do have a good feeling about this one."

Ruby bit her lip and wrung her hands together. "You know," she added, "speaking of world records . . ."

"Yeah?"

"I—I think I should tell you about mine."

Arthur coughed. "Wh—? Oh, okay—I mean, you don't have to, you know—I mean, I really shouldn't have been so nosy and—"

"No. I want to. I've held it in for too long—I think it's

driving me a bit loony, actually. I've given it a lot of thought since the archives—and I've decided it might be better just to get it off my chest. But I'm warning you, you're not going to like it."

"Come on, now. I'm sure it can't be that bad—I mean, can it?"

"Oh, it's bad."

At that moment, Arthur thought back to his initial suspicions, and how the girl had failed to respond when asked if her record was worse than murder. It suddenly struck him that—after months of unquenchable curiosity—perhaps he didn't actually want to know her secret after all.

"Don't be silly," he said, chuckling nervously. "It's not like finding out your record will cause any sort of mental anguish or physical pain—right?"

"Depends on your definition of pain, I guess."

"What? Okay, hold on," Arthur protested. "Maybe—"

He flinched as Ruby put one hand over his mouth, then pointed to the ground with the other.

"Shocking, isn't it?" she said with a cringe.

Arthur scrunched up his eyes and looked down to discover that Ruby had kicked off her shoes and was now standing on bare feet. In the dreamy haze of dawn, Arthur sensed something slightly odd about the view before him, but he couldn't pinpoint exactly what. And then, he realized. On each of Ruby's feet, there were seven petite toes.

"I told you you didn't want to know," she said, removing her hand from his mouth.

195

Arthur blinked. "Wait. That's it? That's your terrifying secret world record?"

"Yep," Ruby sighed, giving her toes a nervous twitch. "Disgusting, aren't they?"

"Are you joking?" Arthur blurted. "I'd give anything to have toes like yours."

Ruby's brow furrowed. "Come on—seriously. You don't think they're vile?"

"Not at all."

"Rex and Rita have always said I should keep them covered, because no one wants to see such ugliness."

"What? Is that why you got so spooked by that extra-limbed skeleton at the archives? Gosh. Your parents just get stranger and stranger the more I find out about them. First the lizards, then the secret societies and murderous plots— and now this. Honestly, I don't know what they're talking about. Those are the best looking toes I've ever seen."

"But all the other Goldwins are completely perfect. Really, you can hardly blame them for being disgusted."

"I don't think they're perfect at all," Arthur retorted. "I mean, first of all, there's the whole homicidal mania thing— but even overlooking that—how many of *them* can say they have *world-record-breaking toes*? That's no small thing where I come from—in fact, it's pretty much everything. I mean, really, I'm starting to get jealous just thinking about it."

At this, Ruby's right dimple began to reveal itself—and was promptly followed by her left. "You really are weird, you know," she said.

196

"Hey," Arthur smiled back, "I'm not the one who's ashamed of my record-breaking toes."

The two stood smiling in silence for a moment, before Ruby slipped her shoes back on and announced, "All right, well, I'd better be going. Wouldn't want Rex and Rita to get suspicious. Which reminds me, actually—when can we get back to the investigation? Surely the forces of evil have gone unchecked too long by the sleuthing skills of Detectives Whipple and Goldwin?"

"Indeed they have. After the archives, I figured I wouldn't get anywhere on the case without my hard-boiled partner there to drive it forward. So I sort of buried myself in training for the championships and, well, writing you apology letters. Guess I hoped I could win you back onto my side or something. Sounds a bit silly now when I say it out loud."

"Ah, the fog of war," Ruby said with a nod. "It's affected us all as of late, has it not? Can't say I've managed any better myself. Apart from Rex having the house on constant lockdown, I've been so preoccupied making voodoo dolls in your likeness, I've hardly had a chance to do anything else. Rigorous production schedule, you understand."

"Hmm," Arthur scowled. "Well, I imagine we should get back to detective work as soon as possible—especially with the championships coming to a close today. There's no telling what Rex and the Ardmore Association might do if they don't get the results they're hoping for."

"Agreed. I have a feeling something major might be going down in the next several hours. Even with your big

197

event today, we'll have to keep our eyes doubly peeled for the slightest sign of foul play."

"Sounds like a plan."

"Okay then," said Ruby. "See you at the championships."

She turned and took two steps into the trees—but then promptly whirled back around.

"Oh, and, Arthur—again, good luck today. That record doesn't stand a chance."

"Thanks," Arthur said with a wave as he tried to ignore the growing knot in his stomach that seemed to coil tighter at every mention of his upcoming record attempt.

Ruby waved back, then continued on in her original direction. As Arthur watched her make her way through the grove, he thought to himself how good it was to have her back on his side.

And then, suddenly, Ruby vanished.

BENEATH THE SURFACE

At first, **Arthur** suspected the girl's disappearance to be a simple trick of the early morning fog—but when he heard the screams a moment later, he knew it had been no illusion.

"Arthur, help!" Ruby's voice called from some unseen location.

Arthur's heart jolted to full speed as he dashed forward into the foggy wood. He pushed through the mist to reach the spot where Ruby's body had vaporized. It was then he noticed the massive opening in the ground before him.

"Wait!" warned Ruby's voice. "Don't—"

The next moment, Arthur found himself admiring the hole's impressive dimensions from within as he plummeted through it.

He caught a glimpse of Ruby scrambling to get out of the way beneath him before his fall was brought to an abrupt and rather unpleasant end by a large mound of earth.

"Ughh," Arthur groaned when the dust had settled.

"Tell me about it," replied Ruby from her position on the floor a few yards away. "Are you all right?"

"I think so. You?"

"Never better," Ruby grumbled as she stood and dusted herself off.

"What happened?" asked Arthur.

"I don't know. I was just walking along and suddenly the ground gave out under my feet and I found myself down here."

Arthur stood up and examined their surroundings. They appeared to be in the middle of some sort of cavern, which stretched off into the darkness in either direction. The narrow opening in the ten-foot ceiling they'd just tumbled through was cluttered with protruding tree roots and fallen leaves. On either side of the hole, rough wooden arches reinforced the roof at irregular intervals, all of them connected by a sagging string of glass bulbs.

"But where exactly is *here*?" said Ruby. "Your father hasn't recently installed a coal mine on your estate, has he?"

"Not that I know of."

"Any tunnel-digging contests or human-worm events?"

"I don't think so."

Arthur turned to the earthen wall beside him and started to climb. When he was three feet up the gradually sloping face, his footholds disintegrated and he tumbled to the floor. He bounced back to his feet and promptly tried again but was met with similar results.

"Hmm," said Ruby. "I guess we're just going to have to see where it leads then."

The children started up the northerly leg of the tunnel, but before the light from the opening had completely fallen off, their path was blocked by a large, steel-barred door.

"Looks like we'll have to try the other direction— unless, of course, you happen to have a cutting torch in your pocket."

"Not today, I'm afraid."

"Hey, what's this?" Ruby blurted, pulling on a loose length of cord connected to a small metal switch box. She flipped the switch with her thumb, and the string of glass globes lining the cave flickered to life, casting a warm glow on its jagged walls. "Well," she added, "if we're going to be lost forever beneath the surface of the earth, at least we won't have to do it in total darkness, right?"

"Yes. That is very comforting."

The pair turned about and proceeded back down the tunnel in the opposite direction.

"We'd better hope this thing actually goes somewhere," Ruby said as they passed the opening in the roof where they had involuntarily entered the cave, "or we might have to get used to a diet of groundwater and cave crickets."

"Believe me, I'm hoping."

When the children had walked just over a hundred yards, Arthur spotted a peculiar object at the edge of the cavern floor. "What is that?" he asked, pointing to the bright-red, plum-sized orb beside them.

Ruby took a step closer. She squinted down at it for a moment, then stooped forward and picked it up. "Looks like . . ."

"Like a rubber ball?" Arthur suggested. "Maybe Simon's been doing a bit of subterranean juggling in his free time and left one behind?"

"It's not a ball, I'm afraid," said Ruby. She held the object between her thumbs and forefingers and spread them apart to reveal a large slit in the foamy red rubber. "No, this looks more like . . . Arthur, I'm beginning to think I might know what this place is."

"Really? Well, what is it then? Where are we?"

"Unless I'm mistaken," Ruby said gravely, "what we have here is an all-purpose clown nose."

"What?" Arthur gasped. "Are you sure?"

Ruby sighed. "One knows best what one fears most."

"Hmm," said Arthur. "So, wait—where does that put us? What's it doing down *here*?"

"Don't you see?" said Ruby. "This must be how the dwarf and the giant managed to get on and off your estate without being noticed—how they disappeared when the birthday cake started exploding—and how they vanished after you saw the giant sneaking around your family's estate the night of the Komodo dragon attack. There must be a hidden entrance above ground somewhere—among the trees, probably—on the other side of that steel door we came across. Yep, I'd bet anything: the tunnel we're in now is none other than Overkill and Undercut's secret passageway."

Arthur gulped. The dank cavern walls suddenly seemed even less agreeable, now that their sinister purpose had been revealed.

"Where do you think the other entrance is?" Arthur asked, his voice dropping to a whisper.

"I guess we're going to find out."

"But should we really keep going forward—knowing what we know now? I mean, they could be down here at this very moment."

"What choice do we have? It's our only way out. We'll just have to be careful."

"I don't think being careful is going to do us much good against a nine-foot-tall killer for hire—but I guess you're right. We don't really have a choice."

"That's the spirit, Arthur. Now let's get moving."

Cautiously creeping forward against the left side of the tunnel, the children proceeded into the dimly lit space ahead, expecting at any minute to be abruptly murdered by two exceptionally sized assassins.

Thirty minutes later, however—after walking nearly a mile underground—Arthur and Ruby were pleased to find themselves still very much alive and completely unmurdered.

In this happy and unexpected state, the children began to notice a subtle shift in the landscape overhead.

"There's something strange about the roots poking through the ceiling here, isn't there?" Arthur observed. "They don't look like the ones we've passed so far."

"Don't seem quite real, do they? And if you look at them from just the right angle—they're completely symmetrical."

"Sim-o-Trees," declared Arthur.

"Yep," said Ruby. "It appears we've ventured onto the Goldwin estate—or beneath it, anyway. Can't say I'm too surprised, really. Where else should the caverns of the underworld lead but into hell itself?"

Arthur shuddered. "That's a bit dramatic, don't you think?"

"You haven't had to live there."

As the two turned a slight corner, they began to discern an ending to the string of bulbs that had served to light their path.

Fifty yards hence, when they'd reached the lights' termination point, it became clear that the path itself had come to an end as well. There before them stood a door. And not the steel type, like the one at the other end of the tunnel but a typical wooden one, like the sort that might be found marking the entrance to any ordinary house—except for the fact that it was nine feet tall. On the ground in front of the door was a slightly soiled decorative mat, embellished with little blue flowers and the words HOME SWEET HOME.

"Rather quaint for the gates of hell, isn't it?" Arthur remarked.

"I'm guessing this is the back door."

"Hmm. Well, what do we do now?"

"We hope the denizens of hell don't keep their doors locked."

With that, Ruby turned the doorknob.

Before the boy could protest, the door creaked open. Darkness spilled into the corridor.

Ruby peered through the crack, then motioned to Arthur. "Come on," she whispered.

Doing his best to disregard the sinking feeling in his soul, Arthur took a deep breath—and followed Ruby through the door.

• • •

The children stood inside the doorway until their eyes had adjusted to the near-darkness, then proceeded down the short corridor in which they found themselves.

They stopped at the end of the hallway and peered around the corner. Before them lay a large, sparsely decorated room, not unlike a soldier's barracks—but decidedly less fragrant. The far wall contained the oddest bunk bed Arthur had ever seen. While the bottom bunk was barely bigger than a bassinet, the top bunk was the length of one-and-a-half king-sized mattresses. Arthur thought the beds to be occupied for a terrifying moment, but on second glance, he saw only tucked linens and vacant pillows.

He continued to survey the darkened room as Ruby reached for something on the wall beside them—something, Arthur realized, resembling a light switch.

"Wait—" he protested, a split second too late.

A single light bulb twitched to life at the center of the ceiling.

"Come on, Arthur," Ruby said as she stepped into the room. "There's nobody here."

Arthur peered one last time from left to right, then joined her in the chamber ahead.

205

When he had confirmed beyond any doubt that the bunks were indeed empty, he relaxed and turned to Ruby. "So, it looks like Rex hasn't just been *employing* Overkill and Undercut, but providing their lodgings as well—right below your house."

"Yeah," said Ruby. She reached down and picked up a mismatched pair of shoes—one nearly two feet long and the other hardly four inches. "What better way to keep your own personal henchmen nearby than to house them in the basement?"

"Lucky for us, they appear to be out at the moment. Let's hope it gives us enough time to find a way out of here."

"Hold on," said Ruby. "We can't leave right away. Not until we find some clues to their identity or a way to link them to Rex. This might be the break we've been waiting for." She held up her index finger. "I took the same oath that every junior detective takes—to honor my badge and to seek the truth wherever it is concealed—and I'm not about to break it now. Honestly, when are we going to get a chance like this again?"

"Wait," said Arthur in an injured tone, "when did you take an oath? Is there some reason I wasn't asked to participate? I mean, I really would have liked—"

"All right, so I might have just made up the Junior Detective's Oath—but isn't it the sort of thing we should be striving for?"

"Oh," said Arthur. "Well, yes—of course it is. But while we're looking for clues, we really should be looking for an exit as well. There's no telling when Overkill and Undercut might return—plus, my family will be leaving for the championships at any time now, and I don't want them to miss the start of competition just because they're off searching for me . . . not to mention the fact that my own event begins in just a few hours."

"Okay," conceded Ruby. "If we find a way out, we'll go. But in the meantime, I'm doing some investigating."

She walked to the nearest of the room's three visible doors and pushed it open, then poked her head through the threshold. "En suite bathroom," she noted. "Impressive. This is turning out to be quite the luxury basement dungeon, isn't it?" She stepped inside and began calling out her findings. "Small sink. Medicine chest. Toilet. No windows or doors. I'm going in for a closer look. Maybe they've got matching toothbrushes with their actual initials on them or something."

"All right. Good luck with that," Arthur called as he made his way to the large door in the corner. "I'll check the next one."

He tried the knob. It did not turn.

"Locked," he called in a loud whisper.

"Can we force it?" Ruby called back.

"Feels pretty solid. Maybe there's a key somewhere. Let me check the other door."

Arthur headed back toward the corridor through which they'd entered, then turned to his left and stopped in front of the room's final door. As he grasped the handle, he was surprised to feel it turn freely in his hand.

207

He pulled the door open.

A giant clown lunged at him through the darkness.

Arthur jumped backward. "Ahh!" he screamed.

A cold hand wrapped around his mouth.

"Shhh!" Ruby whispered coarsely in his ear. "Do you want the whole underworld to know we're down here?"

Arthur looked up in confusion. The towering clown stood frozen in place before him.

"Pretty sure he won't be doing us any harm any time soon," said Ruby.

Removing her hand from Arthur's mouth, she reached out and pulled the velvet glove from the clown's giant fingers—to reveal an oversized wooden hand.

Arthur exhaled. The terrifying figure in the doorway was merely a mannequin in a storage closet.

Ruby stepped further into the cupboard and crouched down beside the giant dummy, then turned back around to face Arthur. In her hands she now held a second clown mannequin—this one less than three feet tall.

"Looks like you've discovered where Overkill and Undercut store their clown costumes when they're not infiltrating birthday parties and blowing up birthday cakes."

"Mm-hmm," Arthur said with a wince. "But do you think you might put that thing down now? Just because it's not actually alive doesn't make it any less creepy."

"Ahh," Ruby grinned. "So you're admitting clowns are creepy then."

"Let's just say I'm warming to the idea."

208

"Booga-booga!" Ruby grunted, shaking the tiny clown in Arthur's direction.

"No, really," he said. "It's horrifying."

"Oh, all right," said Ruby, lowering the mannequin back to the floor. "Come help me sort through this stuff. It looks like clue heaven in here. I mean, honestly, if we can't find a clue in a gold mine like *this*, we don't deserve to call ourselves detectives."

Arthur avoided eye contact with either of the lifeless clown figures to his left as he joined Ruby in the storage space and set about rummaging through its contents.

The closet was crammed full with all sorts of hardware supplies, curious implements, small tools, and further pieces of clown costume.

"Look at this," said Arthur, fishing out a pink rubber belly and holding it up to himself. "Seems Mr. Undercut isn't content being the World's Shortest Clown; he wants to be the World's *Widest* as well."

"Wow," said Ruby. "They've got all kinds of these in here, in different shapes and sizes. Must be going for Largest Collection of Rubber Fat Suits or something"

"Those two do love their disguises, don't they?"

"Yeah, well, it's a good thing you discovered these before Overkill and Undercut had the chance to use them against us. Who knows, Arthur, you may have just saved both our lives. . . . Shame it wasn't something just a wee bit more incriminating, though."

"Yeah," said Arthur. "Or a key."

The two continued their search with little success, their only recovered evidence being two dozen fake rubber bellies, eight mustaches, fifteen red rubber noses, one back-scratcher, three sardine tins, five mismatched toy soldiers, and a spool of copper wire.

Arthur had begun to wonder if they would ever find anything even slightly useful, when he suddenly spotted a mysterious dust-coated volume in the far corner of the shelf.

His mind reeled with possibilities. Could this be the secret ledger that detailed every transaction ever made between Rex Goldwin and his hired henchmen? Or was it, perhaps, the personal diary in which Overkill and Undercut had confessed to all of their dastardly wrongdoings?

Arthur seized the book and blew the dust from its cover.

When the air had cleared, a smartly dressed young man smiled up at him from the printed surface between his thumbs. Arthur's heart sank. The book he held in his hands was nothing more than a mail-order catalog for Garber and Sons Fine Clothing.

Just as he prepared to fling the catalog to his feet, however, Arthur was struck by the strange familiarity of the young man's face. He scrunched up his eyes and realized he had indeed seen this likeness before—in a pair of framed photos from the Goldwins' trophy room.

"Look at this," Arthur remarked as he showed his find to Ruby. "Your brother is on the cover of this clothing catalog—one of the twins, I think—the ones with the scholarship or whatever it is. Is this Rayford, or Royston?"

"Beats me—I've never actually been able to tell them apart. They've been off traveling the world since I was a baby, so I've really only seen pictures."

Arthur opened the catalog and began thumbing through its pages.

"You'd think Rita would've mentioned the twins were clothing models," Ruby added, "after all she says about them."

Each two-page spread featured one of the handsome twins in a different sporting motif, showing off various knitted jerseys and athletic apparel. There was polo, and then football, and then golf—but when they reached the horse racing and tennis spreads, the pages containing Ruby's brothers had been completely torn out.

"This must be where your mother got the pictures for the trophy room—though it's a bit strange to find it down here, don't you think? I'd hardly peg Overkill and Undercut as the types to be interested in high-end sportswear."

Arthur tossed the catalog down onto the shelf, frustrated it hadn't yielded any relevant clues. The book landed with the back page open, and Ruby reached down to pick it up as Arthur continued rummaging through the closet.

"All right," Arthur grumbled to himself, "there's got to be a key in here some—"

"Hang on," Ruby interrupted, pointing quizzically to the catalog. "In the credits, only one name is given for the model, and it doesn't belong to either of my brothers. *Sven Jorgensen*, it says. Who in the world is *he*?"

"Let me see," said Arthur, taking a closer look.

Sure enough, at the bottom of the page was a small line of text that read: PHOTOGRAPHER: BRUNO LENSMAN, MODEL: SVEN JORGENSEN.

"That's strange," he agreed.

"So these *aren't* my brothers," puzzled Ruby, "but just some fashion model called Sven Jorgensen?"

"It certainly looks that way," said Arthur. "But if *those* aren't your brothers, then who—?"

Ruby's face suddenly went pale.

"What is it?" Arthur blurted.

"I'm not sure," Ruby said shakily. "But I don't want to stick around to find out. We need to leave, Arthur. Now."

Arthur could hardly remember ever seeing Ruby frightened before, but at that moment, she looked completely terrified. A wave of unknown dread rushed through his insides like a sudden gulp of ice water.

"Where do we go?" he cried as they turned to run. "We haven't got the key!"

"Back in the tunnel," shouted Ruby. "I don't know—anywhere but here!"

The children dashed for the entryway, Arthur's legs moving entirely of their own accord. He was confident he could keep running forever if so required. As it turned out, he would only have to run another five feet.

Ruby rounded the corner one step ahead of him—and jolted to a stop. Arthur skidded alongside her and looked up.

Filling the corridor in front of them stood a nine-foot giant and a two-foot dwarf.

212

RAYFORD & ROYSTON

The children gasped in terror while the dwarf simply smiled.

"Well, well," the tiny man remarked coolly from his perch on the giant's shoulder. "Look who's decided to drop in: it's our daring detectives." He looked much younger with his makeup off; it was clear he could hardly be older than twenty. The cockney accent he had spoken with aboard the *Current Champion* was now gone. His voice was high-pitched, yet gravelly—as if he had taken up chain-smoking in an effort to kick a lifelong helium addiction. "But why are they in such a hurry, I wonder? You're not leaving, are you, Sis? We've waited nearly twelve years for this little family reunion. Oh, do stay; we've so much to catch up on."

Ruby's mouth hung open in disbelief. "Rayford?" she stammered. "Royston?"

Staring blankly down at the girl through oversized spectacles, the giant said nothing.

The realization hit Arthur like a speeding circus train.

"Come now, Sis," smirked the dwarf. "Don't tell me you don't recognize your own dear brothers?" He paused briefly, then let out a long, dramatic sigh. "Well, I guess you're not completely to blame for that—what with Mother insisting on using those ridiculous photos to represent us. It's not as if she wanted it that way, you understand—it simply couldn't be helped. Some of us are just too *distinctive* for the rest of the world."

Ruby remained stunned. "What about the Clapford Fellowship—and the Ardmore Academy—and your world travels?"

"Yes," the dwarf replied, "I'm afraid that's another one of Mother's little embellishments. Though we were indeed recruited by the Ardmore Academy and awarded the Clapford Fellowship, only a fraction of those funds has ever gone to travel expenses. Since the very beginning, Father has used his influence with the Academy to grant us the pursuit of more *valuable* studies—such as Modern Combustibles, the Science of Sabotage, Advanced Weaponry Techniques, and the Art of Self-Concealment. It's a fascinating story, really—but hardly suited for the foyer. Please, won't you join us in the main chamber? I'll have Royston put the kettle on—though I'm afraid we can only offer you the instant variety. It's really not so bad after the first dozen sips or so—hardly a trade-off for the easy convenience of a military ration pack. And if you enjoy the powdered coffee and tea, Royston might even be persuaded to whip us up some powdered eggs and sausage while he's at it."

"Mmm," said Ruby, smiling uneasily. "As tempting as that sounds, Rayford, my colleague and I should probably be heading out now—you know, back up to the overworld and all that awful sunshine and icky fresh air."

"Yes," Arthur chimed in, wondering if their exit might really be this easy, "we'd love to stay and hear all your fascinating stories, but, unfortunately, I've got a world-record attempt to get to, and it's sort of crucial I make it there on time. I wish I could postpone it, I really do—but we'll just have to come back tomorrow, and you can tell us stories and prepare us hot beverages and we can all enjoy a delicious banquet of powdered foods—"

"Yes, that certainly sounds nice," replied Rayford the dwarf, "but of course, you won't have to come *back* tomorrow, because you'll already be here."

Arthur's terror swelled once more. "We will?" he gulped.

"You didn't really think we'd let you just leave, did you?"

Arthur gulped again.

The dwarf nodded sympathetically. "Believe me, this is not how we wanted it. We'd have been more than happy to simply get on with our lives and let you get on with yours. After today, your silly little investigation would not have mattered to us in the least. Our plans were all nicely back on track

215

after the unfortunate incident at the Mountain and Mole-hill with that insufferable big-mouthed dwarf, Mr. Lowe. We should never have been there in the first place, of course. Royston knows how loose my tongue gets when plied with a bit of gin—but he just had to take us out for a celebratory drink anyway." Rayford glared at the giant, who lowered his head and averted his eyes to the wall. "It was hard to deny the Birthday Extravaganza had gone rather well, so against my better judgment, I agreed. Who knew the friendly chat I'd have with Mr. Lowe that night would wind up getting your chef out of jail and on his way to acquittal? That's when Royston and I were forced to endure the shame of letting that imbecile, Smudge, think he'd arrested us, so we could shift the blame back onto Sammy, where we wanted it."

"Some plan," Ruby said, rolling her eyes.

"Not the simplest one I've ever devised, perhaps," said the dwarf, "but it worked out in the end. Our previously scheduled plot for Whipple destruction was running smoothly again. That is, until this morning, when we returned home from a routine trip to Sedgeley's All-Night Sabotage and Surveillance Supply for some razor wire and plastic explosive to find our tunnel collapsed and the two of you here, within the walls of our inner sanctum. It's forced us to shift our plans once again. I'm afraid we've no choice but to keep you here until Father decides otherwise. I'm guessing it might be a while. He can hardly have you blabbing our little secret to the authorities, now can he? Yes, I think it's safe to say there will be no record attempts for you today—unless, of course, you're attempting the record for Longest Time to Be Held Captive in an Underground Chamber. But try not to be too disheartened; living in a subterranean dungeon isn't nearly as bad as you might think. There's quite a lot of freedom in it, actually: freedom from sunburn, freedom from gardening—freedom from door-to-door salesmen. . . . Honestly, it's practically utopian when you think about it."

Ruby's eyes narrowed. "Let us go," she said.

"Perhaps I haven't made myself clear. We have a painfully short list of options here—and letting you go simply isn't on it."

Ruby glanced at Arthur with a strange, steely look. Though he wasn't entirely sure what it meant, Arthur did his best to match it.

Ruby turned to face her brothers. "I guess we'll just have to extend the list then."

With that, she snatched the shoe from her foot and flung it at the dwarf.

"Arthur," she cried, "run!"

Rayford jerked to one side to dodge the shoe—and promptly lost his balance.

The children charged for the narrow space between the giant's right leg and the wall. Arthur dove headfirst through the gap and rolled past the twins, then dashed for the exit.

The giant, meanwhile, had caught his brother by the back of the collar and lowered him safely to the floor.

"Roy!" shouted the dwarf. "Stop them! Now!"

Arthur threw open the door at the end of the passage

217

and turned to usher Ruby through. The girl, however, was no longer following him.

Ten feet to his rear, Ruby dangled by her ankles from the giant's monstrous right hand.

"Go, Arthur!" she cried. "Get out!"

Arthur glanced at the open cavern before him. In this frantic state, he might just be able to scale the tunnel wall and escape through the hole in the ceiling.

He looked again to his rear. The giant had turned about and was now advancing steadily toward him. Still hanging upside down, Ruby grabbed at the giant's trunk-like legs in an effort to stall them.

Arthur drew a quick breath, then squared his shoulders. "Let her go!" he shouted, and then charged the approaching colossus.

He leapt into the air and clasped his hands around the outstretched arm that held Ruby's ankles. The giant's arm dipped for just a moment, then lifted sharply toward the ceiling.

"Let . . . her . . . go," Arthur repeated stubbornly, his toes rising three feet from the ground.

He released his right hand and began grabbing for the giant's face. His fingers clutched at Royston's cheeks and nose, then settled on the giant's lower lip. Arthur pulled at the corner of the giant's mouth, causing Royston's face to look sad on one side and slightly bewildered on the other, like a badly painted pair of drama masks.

Otherwise, the giant appeared unfazed.

"Royston!" the dwarf snapped from the ground below. "Stop toying with the boy and bring them inside. We haven't got all day."

As soon as the words had left Rayford's mouth, the giant clutched Arthur by the collar with his free arm and plucked him from his body like a bothersome if somewhat oversized insect. He held the two children apart from one another at arm's length, regarding them with a silent stare. Then he pivoted his position and proceeded to follow his tiny twin into the main room.

The children no longer struggled.

"Sorry, Ruby," Arthur murmured. "He was just too big."

"Don't be sorry, Arthur," Ruby replied. "You nearly had him."

Rayford stopped and turned to his captives. "You're making it very difficult for us to remain hospitable here," he scowled. "If we're going to be sharing quarters for what's likely to be the remainder of your lives, we'll have to lay down some ground rules. Rule number one: no throwing shoes at us, then bolting for the door; it's just rude. Rule number two: no climbing on Royston; he's not a jungle gym. Now, until we can trust you to obey these rules, I'm afraid we've no choice but to take certain precautions. Royston—please show our guests to their new lodgings."

The giant carried the children to the darkest corner of the room and halted in front of a large rectangular object veiled by a canvas drop cloth. The dwarf shuffled past his brother and tugged at the corner of the canvas to uncover a rusty steel cage.

Arthur shuddered. He had known from Rayford's tone not to expect the Grand Royal Suite, but he had at least hoped for a musty vacant storeroom, or even a nice hollow pit in the floor. Rusty steel cage had really been toward the very bottom of his wish list—just before hungry lion's den and room with slowly intruding spikes.

Rayford stood on his tiptoes to unlock the cage door, then hinged it outward. "It's fitting, don't you think, that the two of you should have Ridgely's old room, seeing as it was the two of you who brought about his untimely passing? I can just picture his lovable lizard face smiling down at us now. Of course, it nearly broke Mother's heart at the time; she didn't speak to us for a whole week after it happened. But we're learning to cope. We just have to keep reminding ourselves that our darling dragon has finally been given his wings."

"I hate to say it, Rayford," Ruby snapped, still upside down, "but if Rita's lizard has received any extra appendages in the afterlife, it's definitely a pair of horns. I don't think they generally allow child-mauling monsters into the place that gives out the wings."

Rayford sneered. "I think it's about time you officially relocated to your new residence, don't you? Roy—would you like to give them the full tour?"

The giant stared quizzically at his little brother.

"By which I mean," growled the dwarf, "you may feel free to throw them in the cage at any time!"

220

Royston nodded in apology, then hunched forward and thrust Arthur through the cage door.

Arthur's spine hit the back of the cage with a clank. It was no more pleasant an experience than he'd imagined.

The giant then turned his attention to Ruby. He flipped her right-side up again, gripped her under her arms, and held her firmly in front of his face.

As Royston's eyes met his sister's, he paused and cocked his head one degree to the left. He scrunched up his brow and inched his nose forward.

Ruby stared unflinchingly back. Slowly, moisture began pooling at the bottoms of her eyes.

The giant drew nearer.

Without warning, Ruby lunged forward and wrapped her arms around his neck.

Royston flinched and drew back his arm to strike—but quickly relaxed when he realized he was not under attack. For a moment, he stood bewildered and motionless as the girl pressed her cheek against his own—and hugged him.

The moment did not last long. Rayford's patience, it turned out, was even shorter than his stature.

"Roy!" barked the dwarf. "Aren't you forgetting something?"

The giant's face flooded with shame and panic. Stumbling backward, Royston ripped the girl from his neck and tossed her clumsily into the cage. He slammed the door shut, then snapped the lock into place and promptly removed the key.

"That's more like it," Rayford grumbled.

221

Inside the cage, Arthur could hear faint sniffling coming from his new cellmate. He crawled up beside her and placed a hand on her shoulder. "Are you all right?" he asked.

Ruby looked at Arthur through glistening eyes. "I—I thought I was the only one."

"Ah, yes," the dwarf interrupted, his beady eyes glaring through the bars of the cage, "I take it you're referring to that minor surplus you've been granted in the toe department. That *is* rather amusing, isn't it? I'm not sure Mother would consider it to be in quite the same category as our own exceptional attributes, but I imagine you might be regarded as marginally special in some less discerning circles. That said, we exceptionals should really stick together, regardless of our varying levels of uniqueness. Indeed, I had hoped we might work as a team someday—Mother's three most special children, reunited at last. But I must say I'm sensing a bit of resistance from you on that now."

Ruby wiped her eye with the heel of her palm and raised her chin. "I hate to break it to you, Rayford, but Rita hardly thinks of us as *special*. She's simply trying to cover you up—like she's done with my toes since the day I was born."

"It pains me to hear you say that, Sis—but whatever makes you feel better." Rayford glanced at his watch, which could only have been a rubber accessory for a toy doll, then said, "Ah, well, look at the time. Royston and I really must be going if we're to accomplish all we have to do today."

Something in the dwarf's tone unsettled Arthur. "W-what exactly would that be?" he asked.

"Well, once we do a bit to beef up security around here, it's off to the World Record World Championships to finally put an end to this ridiculous rivalry." The dwarf giggled as he glanced to the bulging shopping bag the giant had retrieved from the entranceway. "But don't worry, boy, your family will go out with a bang—hee hee—believe me, it's going to be *a blast*."

Arthur's face went pale.

"Hmmm," Ruby scowled. "Don't know if you were quite clear enough there, Rayford. It's fine to take the subtle approach, but what's the point if no one can tell what you're talking about?"

"Well, excuse me, Little Miss Know-It-All. And Royston wonders why Father finds you so disagreeable. Very well then, how's this: if things don't go our way, somebody is going to get blown up."

"Better," said Ruby with a smirk. "But I still don't know if we completely understand. Could you maybe be a *bit* clearer?"

Rayford's face was quickly taking on the traits of the World's Largest Cherry Tomato, but before he could respond, Arthur interjected, "My family will notice the hole we made. They'll follow the tunnel back to us. They'll get us out of here and we'll warn them of your plans."

"Oh, really?" leered the dwarf, the coolness returning to his voice. "And what car is it your family drives? Triple-decker Hulls-Hoyst, is it? A bit like the one we've just seen speeding past us toward the city on our way home? Ah, yes—with everyone so focused on Daddy's duel this morn-

223

ing and the competition's final events, it seems your family has forgotten all about its poor, recordless son. I'm afraid you'll be getting no help from them today. And as for you, dear sister, well, I'm sure it's no surprise Mother and Father have left you behind as well. You really should try to be more of a team player if you want any chance at earning their love, you know."

"Is that so?" snapped Ruby. "And what exactly has 'earning their love' got *you*—a bomb shelter with a custom bunk bed?"

Rayford gritted his teeth momentarily, then resumed his speech. "Anyway, do try to enjoy yourselves. I hope your accommodations don't prove too intolerably dull or confining. You might try a game of 'I spy' or 'sit-down charades' to better help you pass the time. Royston and I have often found them to be just the thing. Oh—and if any jumbo-sized rats happen to wander into your cage, you'll want to refrain from petting them—I'm afraid Rocco hasn't had his vaccinations yet. Very well then—toodle-oo!"

At the snap of his brother's fingers, Royston grabbed the sinister shopping bag in one hand and hoisted Rayford onto his shoulder with the other. He lumbered over to the locked door and inserted a key into the latch, then pulled it open and ducked into the doorway.

The diabolical twins disappeared through the threshold as the door slammed shut behind them, leaving Arthur and Ruby altogether alone.

224

THE DUEL

Well, it's been *quite a blustery morning here at Champions Court Place Park—both meteorologically and competitively—as the final leg of the tournament is now well under way. The major story to come out of this morning's events, of course, has been the Whipple family's sudden surge forward in their race against the Goldwins for world-record breaking's most coveted prize."*

"That's right, Ted. After starting the day in a veritable dead heat with their rivals, the Whipples have managed to pull ahead of the Goldwin clan by nearly a dozen world records. At this point, they've earned such a lead that, to have any chance at the Championship Cup, the Goldwins would need to win virtually every one of their remaining

events—an unprecedented feat for any family behind by so much at this stage in the competition."

"There's no question, Chuck—this is definitely the Whipples' race to lose."

"Certainly, Ted. Of course, with Dueling Hour set to kick off in just a few minutes at the traditional high noon, there's really no telling what the final outcome will be. As Charles Whipple and Rex Goldwin prepare to square off on the main dueling field as per the terms of their rivalry contract, a massive crowd has gathered to watch them settle their dispute—an event that is sure to shape the future of record breaking for years to come."

"That's right, Chuck, this single contest can often mean more to a participant's career than the very championship itself. No loser of a premiere-division duel has ever gone on to win a major cup title. This is largely due to the fact that few defeated duelists—even those surviving the ordeal—have managed to overcome the acute humiliation of being beaten in a matter of honor on such a grand stage. Many have dropped out of the world records game altogether; some have struggled to remain relevant, only to become the objects of ridicule and derision amongst the world-record-breaking elite. And then, of course, there are those unfortunate few who have gone so far as to take their own lives."

"Never really a thing we like to see, is it, Ted?"

"Indeed, Chuck. Though, more often than not, it does end up being the best career move these poor devils could have made."

"Too *true*, Ted. There's nothing like dying a horrible death to help one recapture lost market share."

"Absolutely, Chuck. Let's just hope it doesn't come to that for one of our combatants here today; the loss of revenue on sponsorships alone would be truly tragic. But now, let's head out to the field, where Charles Whipple and Rex Goldwin are gearing up for their preselected event: motorbike jousting!"

• • •

Mr. Whipple strode toward the tent's exit, but his wife clutched his arm and pulled him back.

"Are you sure we haven't forgotten something, Charles? Hard as I try, I can't shake the awful feeling that something is missing. We haven't left George's bagpipes at home, have we?"

"No dear. I packed them myself."

"What about Ivy and Mr. Growls's matching diving suits? I don't remember seeing them this morning."

"I watched Wilhelm load them onto the roof rack just before we left. Please, darling—we're all a bit nervous here. It's only natural when one is faced with such a high probability of death and humiliation. But we mustn't lose our heads now—not when we're so close to our goal. I assure you, everything is perfectly in order."

"Oh, Charles—I'm so worried for you! Do be careful not to be killed!"

"You may rest assured, dear—I shall make every effort to that end."

227

With that, he kissed his wife and walked from the tent to the welcoming roar of the crowd.

Mr. Whipple cut a straight line across the tiltyard, zipping up his black leather jousting jacket as he approached his motorbike, where his two eldest sons stood waiting. He gave a nod to each of them, then straddled the vehicle and ground his boot into the kick-start lever, goading the engine to life.

When he had set his helmet in place and fitted his scarf, he motioned to Simon, who handed him his shield—a steel hubcap painted with the sable elephant of the Whipple family crest.

"Good luck, Dad," said Simon.

"Thank you, Son."

Mr. Whipple turned to Henry. "Electro-lance."

"Yes, sir," said the eldest. He hoisted the long, tapered spear into his father's right arm and connected it to the two electrical leads that ran to the bike's battery. "Bring us back a Goldwin kebab, Dad."

Mr. Whipple glanced to the opposite end of the list field where his opponent sat revving the engine of his gold-trimmed cycle.

"I shall indeed, Son," he said, then lowered his goggles and grasped the throttle.

As the flag boy approached the center of the field, Henry and Simon retreated to the sideline, leaving their father alone with his mechanical steed. A hush fell over the crowd.

The flag, held aloft in the boy's hand, flapped for a moment in the breeze—and then dropped.

228

The two motorbikes charged forward.

Mr. Whipple sped alongside the low fence that divided the two sides of the field. He lowered his lance and trained its point on his oncoming target.

He waited until he was close enough to see the fury in Rex Goldwin's eyes, then leaned into his handlebars and braced for impact.

The spring-loaded spearhead struck the golden lizard at the center of Rex's shield with a crash, sending sparks of electricity arcing across its face and into the arm of its bearer.

At the same moment, Rex snapped his own lance upward, skirting the top of Mr. Whipple's shield and striking his head.

Sparks flew from Mr. Whipple's helmet as the spear scraped a deep gouge in its left side. Though the insulated shell protected him from the electric shock, the force of the blow snapped his head back in a cruel, unnatural motion.

The crowd gasped. Mr. Whipple slumped to the rear of his cycle, his fingers clutching tenuously at one handlebar as his vehicle swerved to the right.

A cluster of field-level spectators dove from the path of the runaway motorbike, narrowly escaping death as it crossed the sideline and careened toward the concrete wall beyond. Looking on from the front row, the Whipples leapt to their feet and covered their mouths in panic.

Sparks showered from Mr. Whipple's handlebar as it struck the cement barrier.

Penelope and Charlotte buried their faces in their hands.

229

But just before the wheel made impact, Mr. Whipple regained his grip on the handlebars. He jerked the bike away from the wall and plowed through a row of hedges, nearly striking two referees before finally skidding to a halt on an empty patch of turf.

The crowd cheered. The Whipples sighed with relief.

Mr. Whipple caught his breath and peered down the field to see Rex Goldwin saluting the audience from his motorbike, entirely unharmed in the duel's first clash.

As the two men passed each other on the way back to their respective starting positions, Rex shouted across the fence, "Careful, Charlie! Don't go dying on me just yet—be a pity to spoil the fun so soon, wouldn't it?"

"Never you worry, Mr. Goldwin," replied the other. "The fun is only just beginning."

• • •

"Well, Ted, that marks the fourth straight round in which Charles Whipple has scored a clean shot to his opponent's shield—in spite of being struck on the helmet by his opponent's lance. Quite a strange tactic from Rex Goldwin, don't you think?"

"Very strange indeed, Chuck. Though head strikes are not illegal in motorbike jousting, only strikes to the shield count for points. It seems Goldwin is willing to sacrifice a showing on the scorecards for a chance at unseating Whipple and engaging him in close combat. If he manages to deal a death blow, of course, he'll have no need

for points—but I've never seen a combatant focus so heavily on unseating an opponent so early in a duel. It's a tactic usually reserved as a last resort—when one can no longer win the duel on points. Rex Goldwin, however, has shown no interest from the very start in a victory by scorecard. I'd say what we've got here, Chuck, is a man out for blood."

"No question, Ted. I guess we'll see how badly Charles Whipple wants to keep his own from spilling."

"That we shall, Chuck. This should be a good one!"

• • •

For the next five rounds, Mr. Whipple continued to rack up points on his opponent's shield—while Rex Goldwin persisted in pummeling Mr. Whipple's head, like a sweet-toothed child battling the World's Most Stubborn Piñata.

It was in the tenth round that Rex's persistence finally paid off.

Having grown accustomed to his opponent's repeated shots to the head, Mr. Whipple had learned to lessen the impact by dodging to one side or the other. This, routine, however, left him entirely unprepared for a direct blow to the chest.

The tip of the spear compressed against Mr. Whipple's steel-studded jacket and catapulted his body backward, while his motorbike rode on without him. Mr. Whipple floated in midair for a split second, then thudded to earth on his back.

He lay stunned for several moments. But then he noticed the man on the motorbike charging at his head.

Rex hunkered into his seat and cranked the throttle as the fallen man struggled to move.

Mr. Whipple reached for his lance. He anchored its handle in the earth and popped its point upward.

The maniacal grin on Rex's face froze as the spear struck his ribs.

Mr. Whipple rolled to his right. Wind blasted his face as Rex's tires whirled past him.

An instant later, Rex hit the ground. His unmanned motorbike collided with the center fence and plowed into the earth, its front wheel still spinning as the vehicle clattered to a standstill.

In the space between the two immobilized machines, their riders lay motionless in the dirt.

Then, slowly, the figures began to rise.

"Touché," Rex croaked as he staggered to his feet and removed his jacket. "I've got to admit, Charlie—you're harder to exterminate than I'd thought."

Mr. Whipple tossed his own jacket to the ground. "Why, Mr. Goldwin," he panted, "that may be the nicest thing you've ever said to me." The two men circled one another and removed their helmets, gripping the hidden handles inside to convert their headgear into small, rounded shields.

"Ah, Charlie," Rex chuckled. "What a shame you couldn't have died a bit easier." From a sheath on his belt, he drew a two-foot-long wood-and-metal shaft, not unlike a large cattle prod. "Death by zap dagger is quite excruciating I'm told." He pressed the trigger button and a blue surge of energy arced between the two electrodes at the tip of the rod.

Mr. Whipple drew his own, identical weapon. "You may be overstating your chances, Mr. Goldwin. I think you'll find I'm quite handy with zap dagger and blast buckler—though it's no great matter to me. I should gladly die a thousand deaths today to have my family honor restored."

Rex grinned. "Well, Charlie, I certainly wouldn't want to stand between you and your honor." And with that, he threw a handful of dirt in his opponent's face.

Mr. Whipple stumbled backward, shutting his eyes in pain and confusion. *Zap!* Rex's weapon struck his shoulder.

"Ahh!" cried Mr. Whipple. He flailed his buckler wildly and managed by chance to parry his foe's second thrust.

Rex countered with two quick strikes—*Zap-zap!*—one to the side and one to the stomach. Mr. Whipple doubled over in anguish. The crowd roared.

Rex drew back his weapon and brought it down with enough force to split the man's skull.

Crack! The sound of the blow echoed into the stands.

But instead of slumping to the earth, Mr. Whipple stood taller. Having caught the weapon an inch from his brow with his own zap dagger, he slowly pressed back Rex's hand. Mr. Whipple's eyes burned red with blood and fury as he lifted his head to face his enemy.

The two combatants struggled, weapons locked, until Rex deflected Mr. Whipple's blade and lunged for his rib-

233

cage. Mr. Whipple, however—having largely recovered his eyesight—simply repelled the blow with his buckler and took a stab of his own.

Zap! The weapon struck Rex under his arm.

"Arh!" he yelped. Stung for the first time, Rex's face flooded with rage. He leapt forward and lashed out with his weapon.

Crack-crack-crack! Mr. Whipple parried the blows as he stumbled backward.

Then, with a quick sideways swipe, Rex hooked the back of Mr. Whipple's buckler and wrenched it from his grasp.

The helmet/shield hit the ground, leaving Mr. Whipple painfully vulnerable.

Zap! Zap-zap! Electricity pierced his left arm as he struggled to defend himself. He blocked the next strike with his zap dagger, only to have Rex land a series of jabs like none other so far. *Zap! Zap-zap! Zap-zap-zap-zap-zap!*

Mr. Whipple's attempts at warding off electrocution grew more and more feeble with each jolt, a detail that did not go unnoticed by his opponent.

Rex put all his weight behind the weapon and lunged for the weakened man's heart.

Charles Whipple, however, was in no mood for dying. The instant the electrodes met his shirt, he grabbed the end of the zap dagger and spun to his left, guiding the weapon away from his body and wresting it from Rex's grasp. Using Rex's weight against him, Mr. Whipple flung his attacker to the ground.

234

Rex landed facedown in the dirt. As he wriggled onto his back, Mr. Whipple clamped a boot onto Rex's forearm just below the shield and swiveled his twin daggers into a downward grip.

"No, Charlie!" Rex squealed, covering his face with his free arm and blinking rapidly. "Please don't! I'll—I'll do anything!"

Mr. Whipple depressed the trigger buttons and two streams of blue energy reflected in his furious eyes. He raised his weapons into the air.

At that moment, a voice called out behind him.

"Mr. Whipple! Mr. Whipple!" it cried. "I can't find him anywhere! It's all my fault. . . ."

Mr. Whipple halted halfway through his strike and turned toward the source of the commotion. There, he saw a roundish, gray-haired housemaid holding up her skirts and charging toward him across the field.

The next thing he knew, there was a scuffling at his feet. He looked down to see Rex Goldwin clambering out from underneath his boot. He leapt after him—but Rex slipped from his grasp and scurried off down the lists.

Boos sprang up from the crowd.

Mr. Whipple stood panting for a moment, watching his opponent escape—then turned to face his housekeeper.

"Mrs. Waite, this is highly irregular!" he roared. "What in blazes are you yammering on about?"

"I'm terribly sorry, sir, but it's Arthur—he's gone missing! I'm afraid something dreadful has happened to him!"

235

Mr. Whipple glanced distractedly across the tiltyard in time to catch a glimpse of his rival's back as it disappeared through the door of the Goldwin tent.

"What do you mean he's gone missing?" he snapped. "Hasn't he been with us all morning?"

"I don't think so, sir. And I'm afraid I may be to blame for it."

Mr. Whipple's eyes narrowed. "Really? And how do you figure that?"

"Well, you see, sir, earlier this morning, before anyone else had risen, I, well—I may have shown one of the Goldwins onto the grounds."

"You may have done *what*?"

"It was only Arthur's friend, Ruby, sir. She said she needed to see him—and I know I should have sent her away, but I couldn't really see any harm in a quick visit—so I led her out to the edge of the garden and then brought Arthur to meet her. I left them alone to talk—with every intention of returning to check on them a bit later—but then I'm afraid I got caught up preparing for the day's events and forgot all about them. It only just struck me before the start of the duel I'd not seen Arthur since. I've spent the past half hour searching for him with no luck. No one can remember seeing him at all today." Mrs. Waite's face grew solemn. "You don't think that Goldwin girl's done something to him, do you, sir? I mean, I thought they were friends, but she is one of *them* after all, isn't she?"

"She is indeed, Mrs. Waite. This is truly a troubling report."

236

"Oh, sir—I feel awful! What are we to do?"

"I'm not sure there is anything *to* do, Mrs. Waite. In case you haven't noticed, I am presently engaged in a mortal duel—an activity, alas, which rather requires my undivided attention."

"But, sir—surely your son is far more important than some silly game of pride?"

"If you please, Mrs. Waite, I shall be the judge of what *is* and what is *not* important to this family. Now, I appreciate your account of the matter; it has been most informative—but I must insist you exit the field at once so I may be left alone to resume this *silly game* without further distraction."

"Yes, sir," the housekeeper sighed—then did as she was told.

• • •

"Well, that's certainly not something you see everyday, is it Chuck?"

"Indeed it isn't, Ted. Last time I saw a maid storm onto a dueling field, she was carted off in separate wheelbarrows. You've got to admit, Ted—this is one brave housekeeper!"

"Brave, Chuck—or just foolish? After denying the crowd their well-deserved death blow, she'd better be ready to defend herself."

"True enough, Ted. But though she may have inadvertently saved Goldwin from a swift and present demise, Charles Whipple has already secured a victory on the scorecards—and needs only to remain alive until the

237

end of the duel to doom his opponent instead to a long, slow death by dishonor. So, unless Goldwin can deliver a death blow of his own or force a surrender, it's all over for him anyhow. We'll just have to hope it's enough to appease the fifteen thousand dueling fans in attendance here today."

"I don't know, Chuck. This is the whole reason the IDA repealed the Mercy Mandate in the first place. It's common sense, really: duels to the death just make for better spectator sport."

"Can't argue with you there, Ted. Lucky for us, there's still time for that sort of end as well."

"We can only hope, Chuck."

"Absolutely, Ted. But death blow or no, this really has been a spectacular duel so far."

"Right you are, Chuck. Whipple has now scored the Widest Point Differential in the History of the Sport. He needs only to match Goldwin's scores for the remaining five tilts to officially clinch the record—an easy task, no doubt, seeing as he's outscored Goldwin in every round."

"No doubt, Ted. . . . Oh, hold on a minute—we're just getting a report here regarding the reason for the Whipple housekeeper's startling interruption. According to our sources on the field, Charles Whipple's twelve-year-old son, Arthur, has gone missing and may be in considerable danger—perhaps even the target of foul play."

"Who?"

"You know, Ted—Arthur Whipple—the only member of

the Whipple family to have never broken a world record?"

"Doesn't ring a bell, Chuck."

"You may remember him from the Junior Rocket-Stick Race at this year's Unsafe Sports Showdown. Foolishly sacrificed a shot at the title to assist an injured Jump Johnston?"

"Oh, that poor devil? Great Lakes! As if he didn't have enough problems—now he goes and gets himself kidnapped? Some people just can't catch a break, can they, Chuck?"

"Apparently not, Ted. And now it seems the lad's left his father with a bit of a dilemma: does he go for the world record and a chance to vanquish a dangerous opponent—or does he leave the duel immediately to search for his missing son?"

"Well, Chuck, given all we've come to know about Charles Whipple, I think we can rest assured he'll do the right thing."

"Absolutely, Ted. This is far too important a duel to simply walk away from. In a competition of this magnitude, every record counts—not to mention the honor at stake here—and Whipple is just too shrewd a competitor to be unnerved by something like this."

"I fully concur, Chuck. . . . Oh, and here he comes now, back onto the field—with a positively thunderous reception from the crowd. And yep, there he is, mounting his motorbike and revving the engine, ready to win glory once again. This is a true champion we've got here, Chuck."

"No question, Ted. Now he needs only to put the final

nail in his opponent's coffin to reclaim his throne at the forefront of world-record breaking."

"That's right, Chuck—and we get the pleasure of watching him do it. I hope you've brought your rubber ducks with you, folks; it's going to be a bloodbath."

• • •

Charles Whipple readied his electro-lance and fixed his gaze on the falling flag. The motorbike beneath him growled at his command, then charged forward.

As Rex Goldwin neared, Mr. Whipple could detect a shift in his enemy's posture. Rex's body slumped wearily over his handlebars. His lance wobbled loosely in his grip.

It was clear to everyone present that Mr. Whipple had won. If he simply finished the next five rounds, the duel was his. He would finally regain his honor from the man who had stolen it, ridding himself of Rex Goldwin once and for all. Surely, restoring the Whipple name was well worth any small sacrifices he had to make.

He sped faster.

By the time he reached his opponent, however, something had changed.

Mr. Whipple raised his spear and swerved sharply to his right. His enemy's lance grazed his helmet as he spun his motorbike 180 degrees—and sped back toward his own tent.

"Wait—where are you going?" called Rex Goldwin

from the opposite side of the fence. "Oh, that's it—go on, coward—run away when you know you're beaten!"

Ignoring Rex's jeers and the growing furor of the crowd, Mr. Whipple made a straight line for the edge of the tilt-yard, where his wife and children were already waiting.

Mrs. Whipple rushed forward to meet him. He jumped from his motorbike, cast off his helmet, then looked to his wife and said, "We've got to find Arthur."

"I know," replied Mrs. Whipple, her face creased with worry. "Charles, how could we have just forgotten him like that?"

"I'm not sure, dear—but I aim never to do so again."

With that, he walked toward his children, who stood looking on from the sideline with Mrs. Waite. The house-keeper stepped forward as he approached.

"I'm so sorry, sir," she said softly. "This is all my doing."

"Don't blame yourself, Mrs. Waite. It's not your fault. If I hadn't been so focused on this blasted duel, I might have realized I'd left my own son behind. Now—please help me muster the children."

"Yes, sir," she said, then set about gathering the young Whipples around him.

"Children," Mr. Whipple announced, "as you may know, your brother Arthur has gone missing. I fear, how-ever, that his disappearance is no mere accident. We all know our Arthur would never miss an event so important to this family unless something was dreadfully wrong."

241

"Poor Arthur," Beatrice whimpered. "How can we help?"

"We must set out to find him at once," her father replied. "We'll divide ourselves into search parties in order to cover as much ground as possible."

"But what about our events?" asked Cordelia.

"It seems we shall have to miss some of them. How can any of us continue on until we know your brother is safe?"

"But Dad," Cordelia argued, "it's not as if Arthur was going to help us win the cup anyway. I mean, I don't want him to get hurt or anything—but, honestly, this is the *championships*!"

Mr. Whipple shook his head. "My dear Cordelia, I wish I could say I had nothing to do with this callous single-mindedness of yours, but I'm afraid it's just as much my fault as it is your own. I fully intend to set a better example in future—but for now, you'll just have to do as I say. Though Arthur may not possess the abilities or accomplishments— or common sense—of the rest of us, he is a Whipple nonetheless, and as such, it is our duty to keep him from harm, whatever the cost. Would you not want us to do the same for you, were you in your brother's place?"

Cordelia sighed and looked away, then nodded reluctantly.

"I thought as much. So, either we win the cup together, or not at all. Now, enough talk—we've no time to lose. Let us get moving—and pray we are not too late."

THE DUNGEON

Arthur pressed his face between the rusty bars of the cage as he struggled in vain to pry them apart. The dank, musty air invaded his nostrils and assaulted his stomach.

From the cage's opposite corner, Ruby remarked, "I assume they haven't grown any less steel-like in the past few hours."

"Nope," Arthur groaned as he loosened his grip on the bars. Dropping his hands, he added, "You know, it's funny—of all my brothers and sisters, I never thought *I* would be the one to have to worry about this sort of thing. I mean, who's going to abduct the one Whipple nobody has ever heard of before, right? I know it might sound strange—but I almost feel honored actually."

"I guess I can see that," Ruby replied. "But then again, you *are* locked away in a rusty cage on the floor of a dungeon with no sign of rescue. So it's sort of a mixed blessing, isn't it?"

"Yeah," Arthur sighed. "And they're not exactly trying to ransom me either, are they? Argh!" he cried abruptly, punching the roof of the cage. "I can't even get kidnapped properly!"

Clumps of hardened black sludge dislodged from the ceiling and dropped onto Arthur's face. Snarling, he flicked the debris from his forehead with the back of his hand.

"And what's worse," he continued, "the one time my family could actually use my help, I'm stuck in here, unable to warn them they may be attacked at any moment by twin assassins with advanced explosives training!"

"Hey, don't forget that those two assassins are actually my own dear brothers," Ruby added sarcastically, "and quite possibly the long lost family I've been searching for my entire life."

The girl paused. Arthur noticed her eyes grow watery.

"Ruby?" he called softly.

"Ahh," she said through a quivering smile, sniffling briefly as she brushed away the tears. "It hurts to say that bit out loud."

Arthur's heart sank. He wanted desperately to comfort his friend, but struggled to find the words. "I—I'm so sorry," he said.

"No, it's all right. Just sort of sneaked up on me there for a moment. I'm okay."

Arthur felt a sudden surge of rage well up inside him.

"Ahhh!" he cried. "Why doesn't anything ever work out the way it ought to?!"

He grabbed the bars at the front of the cage and shook them with all his might, then promptly collapsed against the cage door.

There was a small *click*—and the lock on the outside of the cage fell open.

The once-despairing children glanced at each other in astonishment, then immediately scrambled up to the door for a closer look.

The heavy steel padlock swung gently back and forth before their eyes, dangling from one side of its U-shaped stem.

"What just happened?!" cried Ruby.

"I think the lock unlocked itself."

"Wow. How hard did you shake it? And how long have you been living with super-human strength?"

"I never knew I had been. But I guess it's either that—or this is one remarkably defective lock."

"Can you reach it?"

"I think so."

Arthur extended his arm through the bars at the bottom of the door and reached up past the steel mesh that protected the latch. He grunted in concentration as he strained to grasp the end of the hook and push it out of its slot.

"Got it!" he exclaimed.

The lock clattered to the floor. Arthur retracted his arm through the bars and gave the door a push. The rusty hinges squealed in protest as the door swung open.

245

The two exchanged smiles, then rushed through the opening.

"Nicely done, Arthur!" cried Ruby.

In the relative freedom of the open dungeon, Arthur crouched down and retrieved the fallen padlock. Closing the cage door behind them, he slid the lock back into place and popped it shut with a *click*—then pulled on it as hard as he could.

"Seems to work just fine," he puzzled.

"Hmm," said Ruby. "Looks like Royston forgot to actually *lock* the lock when he was locking us in the cage. I guess it's no wonder he's never learned to speak. Don't report me to the Global Guild of Dwarves and Giants for saying this—but giants aren't really known for being the World's Brightest Thinkers. I mean, look at Frankenstein, or the *Jack and the Beanstalk* giant—or the 50 Foot Woman. None of them are exactly geniuses, are they?"

"I can see your point," said Arthur, "though it's hard to be *too* critical—I mean, after all, we're the ones who never bothered to check the lock."

"If it's all the same to you, Arthur, I'd rather not think about the part where we spent all morning inside a cramped rusty cage for no reason at all. But anyway, come on—let's see what else our cunning captors may have overlooked."

The two children scurried over to the door that had served as the twins' exit. Arthur tried the handle. "Still locked," he said.

"Maybe you should try shaking it," smirked Ruby.

246

Arthur scowled. "I've got a feeling that's not going to work this time." He shook the handle to no avail. "Happy?"

"Yeah, well," said Ruby, "we could hardly hope to be so lucky twice in one abduction, now could we?"

"Hardly. Which means it's back into the tunnel for us. We'll just have to find a way to climb out through the hole in the cave ceiling. If only we had a ladder or a pole or something tall we could climb up."

Ruby smiled slyly. "I think I might know just the thing."

• • •

Arthur and Ruby scrambled across the earthen floor of the tunnel, each of them carrying one end of a nine-foot-tall giant clown mannequin.

"How did I get stuck with the head end, by the way?" Arthur grumbled. "I can already feel the nightmares forming."

"Exposure therapy," said Ruby. "It's good for you. And you won't think it's so creepy when our wooden friend here singlehandedly saves our lives."

"We'll see about that."

The children began to notice a bluish glow on the cavern walls ahead.

"We're nearly there," said Ruby. "Come on—let's hurry!"

In five minutes' time, the two found themselves peering up at the same gaping hole that had provided their unexpected entrance several hours earlier.

"Dear, sweet sunlight," said Ruby, placing her right hand on her chest, "after facing the possibility of losing you

247

forever, I now realize what an ungrateful recipient of your warmth and beauty I have been. It is my solemn promise never again to take you for granted as long as I live. This, I do swear."

"Me too. Let's get out of here," said Arthur.

The pair planted the clown's massive feet on the tunnel floor directly beneath the opening and hoisted the towering mannequin into position. When it was fully upright, the top of its head scraped against the ceiling, holding it shakily in place.

"You go first," insisted Arthur. "I'll hold its legs."

"Hmm. I can't quite tell whether you're being chivalrous—or if you're just trying to put off climbing up the clown for as long as possible."

"I really don't think a lady should question the motives of a gentleman," Arthur replied. "But yeah, it's probably a bit of both."

"Your honesty is noble indeed, good sir. Now, if you would be so kind as to give me a leg up onto this evil clown here."

Arthur smirked. "*There's* a phrase you don't hear every day."

He steadied the makeshift ladder with one hand and cupped the other against his thigh. Ruby clutched the back of the clown's stained, ruffled shirt, then planted her shoe in Arthur's improvised foothold and pulled herself up.

"There you go," said Arthur. "If I didn't know otherwise, I might mistake you for a professional clown climber."

Ruby scaled higher up the mannequin, while Arthur worked to counterbalance her weight and keep the whole thing from toppling sideways. Soon, Ruby had reached the clown's shoulders and wrapped her arms securely around its neck. She was now only a few short moves away from the surface.

Just then, a strange shuffling sound caught Arthur's attention.

"What was that?" he said.

"What was what?" said Ruby.

"I thought I heard something."

Arthur looked around him but saw nothing out of the ordinary. Ruby climbed another foot higher.

There was another noise. Arthur looked down a second time. Scrunching up his eyes, he peered into the shadows on the far side of the sunlight—and started in terror.

There in the darkness, hundreds of gleaming eyes peered back at him.

It was not, of course, the eyes themselves that made Arthur's hairs stand on end—but rather, the *owners* of those eyes. As his vision further adjusted to the darkness, he began to discern an army of scaly-skinned creatures creeping steadily toward him from the northern leg of the tunnel.

It took little time for Arthur to recognize the new invaders: a monitor lizard in a tattered cocktail dress, an iguana with a crooked bow tie, a Mexican beaded lizard in a mud-covered mariachi jacket. They were the remaining residents of the Lizard Lounge—and they had come for revenge.

"Ruby!" Arthur whispered frantically. "We're not alone!"

"What?"

249

From Ruby's elevated position, the chirping of birds overhead drowned out the growing chorus of hisses and grunts below.

"Just hold still!" insisted Arthur. "Whatever you do, don't move!"

Ruby, however, was not one to follow an order without knowing the reason behind it. She shinnied her way down a bit and lowered her head, craning her neck to see whatever it was that had so agitated her partner.

The moment she ducked her head beneath the roof of the cave, she had her answer. A large lizard shot toward her face, skittering upside down across the cave ceiling.

The frilled dragon snarled and extruded the broad collar of skin and scales that encircled its neck, giving itself—in combination with its Elizabethan costume—the appearance of a demonic William Shakespeare: a startling sight, no doubt, in any situation.

Ruby screamed and jerked backward. The top-heavy mannequin teetered.

Arthur pushed against the clown's legs with all his might, determined not to let his friend fall. But in his effort to force it upright, he overcompensated slightly.

The next thing he knew, Ruby was falling forward, past the one annoyed reptile on the ceiling toward the horde of furious lizards on the floor. Arthur grasped frantically at the clown's trousers, but it was no use; he could not stop the momentum of the giant figure.

Clown and girl crashed to the ground, where Ruby

found herself face-to-face with a massive crocodile monitor. For a moment, the creature's broad, rounded face seemed simply to smile at her. That is, until it opened its mouth.

With a harsh hissing sound, the air around Ruby's head rushed into the black hole created by the monster's gaping gullet.

"Ruby!" Arthur cried. He stood terrified and helpless four yards behind her. He searched desperately for something heavy enough to throw at the creature—but found at his feet only loose clumps of earth.

He fumbled through his pockets as a last resort, and his fingers landed on a small rectangular object. It was his magical domino.

Arthur closed his hand around the tile and drew it from his pocket. If ever he needed its help, this was the time. He gave the domino one final rub for luck, then took aim and flung it with all his might.

As the tiny missile sped fast and true toward the enormous lizard, Arthur's mind flashed with notions of a modern-day David and Goliath—he, the young and unlikely hero with deadly aim; it, the cruel and unconquerable giant with an uncommonly tender forehead.

Any biblical notions he may have had, however, were completely dashed a moment later, when the creature caught the domino in its mouth—and bit it in two.

"Ahh!" cried Arthur.

He hurled himself forward, as his best hope at helping

Ruby crumbled before his eyes. He had no choice now but to take on the pack of lizards with his bare hands.

Luckily for him, his first plan had not failed half as badly as he'd imagined.

As the crocodile monitor continued chomping the small ebony block to bits, the other lizards quickly turned on the creature, each demanding a share of whatever delicious treat it was he'd been given.

By the time Arthur had reached Ruby, the creatures were so preoccupied fighting over the imaginary morsel, he was able to help her to her feet and shepherd her a safe distance away before any of them had even noticed.

The confusion, however, did not last long. Before the children could make a full retreat, the lizards managed to forgive their ungenerous brother—and shifted their anger to the two-legged intruders who had not bothered to bring enough treats for everyone.

Arthur stepped in front of Ruby as the creatures crept closer. "I suppose this is what your brothers meant by *beefing up security*."

He reached down and grasped the arm of the fallen mannequin. The lizards hissed with indignation from its far side.

"Those two really take their jobs seriously, don't they?" said Ruby. "So what do we do now?"

Using the mannequin as an inhuman shield between himself and the lizards, Arthur began prying its arm away from its body. "You use the mannequin to climb out—then get to the garage and fetch a ladder. I'll—" Arthur snapped the clown's arm from the shoulder socket and began sliding it out through the end of its frilly sleeve. "I'll try to fend them off for as long as I can." He held up the newly severed arm like a blunt, five-fingered sword, then clenched his teeth and arched his brow.

Ruby looked concerned. "I don't mean to doubt your skills with a wooden mannequin limb or anything, but don't you think you're a bit outnumbered?"

"It's our only chance of getting out of here."

Arthur jabbed the makeshift weapon at one of the bolder, larger lizards. The lizard snapped at him menacingly.

"But what if you get bitten?" asked Ruby.

"I'm pretty sure only one of them is poisonous—that one in the sombrero there; I'll try to stay clear of him."

"Well . . . all right," Ruby sighed as she took hold of the mannequin. "But I'm not happy about it."

Arthur brandished the severed wooden arm before him, forcing the lizards backward. "Back you beasts!" he commanded. He turned to Ruby with a grin and added, "I think I've got this."

His grin faded a moment later.

As the front line of larger lizards retreated, a swarm of smaller lizards poured into the resultant gap.

Ruby gasped—and promptly dropped the mannequin.

The new reptiles were each roughly two feet in length with blunt snouts and lumpy black skin covered in sickening scarlet blotches. They looked like the unholy offspring of a black widow spider and a king cobra. On their heads, they wore tall, cylindrical caps, giving them the appearance of monstrous Mexican soldiers. They made the other lizards look almost cuddly by comparison.

"Arthur—we need a new strategy!" Ruby cried. "You can't afford to be bitten by one of *these*."

"What—what are they?"

"Rita's newest pets. When the Komodo died, she decided to fill its spot with the World's Largest Private Collection of Venomous Lizards. They're Gila monsters."

"Uahh. Exactly how venomous are they?"

"One bite is excruciating; a few bites are enough to cause respiratory failure—though no one's ever really been bitten more than twice. Seeing as we're surrounded by hundreds of them, though . . . well, you've always wanted to break a record, haven't you?"

Arthur retreated with Ruby toward the cavern wall behind them, waving the wooden arm as the army of Gila monsters advanced.

"If dying was all I had to do," he grumbled, "I might be up for it; it's the *excruciating* part that gets me."

"Would it comfort you to know that—according to *The Big Book of Lizard Breeding*—the Gila monster is a typically sluggish, idle creature, unlikely to attack without provocation?"

"I don't think these ones have read that book. They look pretty energetic to me."

Indeed, the creatures before him were lively and volatile—snapping at one another and clawing over each other's backs. There was no doubt they were entirely capable of inflicting lethal harm. Of course, this is true of any mob; while one bad-tempered individual may prove largely innocuous, a *mob* of bad-tempered individuals is sure to turn savage every time.

Unfortunately, any such insights into the shared psychology of lizards and men did nothing to ease the children's minds toward the gruesome end that awaited them.

Soon, the Gila monsters were climbing over the clown mannequin barricade that served as the children's last line of defense.

"Stay behind me," Arthur called to Ruby, holding out his arm-shaped saber.

He lunged at the first of the creatures to cross the barrier and flung it backward—only to watch two others take its place.

Arthur struck again and again, but the creatures continued to spill forward, pressing the children further and further against the wall.

"I'm sorry I got you into this," Ruby said gravely.

"No," said Arthur. "Really, it's the other way around. If I hadn't betrayed your trust, you'd never have had to sneak onto the grounds this morning—and we'd never have fallen into this tunnel."

"Oh, right," said Ruby. "I guess it *is* your fault."

"What?"

"Just joking."

Ruby kicked a clump of earth in the face of an oncoming Gila monster and backed as closely as she could against the cavern wall. They were completely surrounded.

"Look, Arthur," she said, "it doesn't matter whose fault it is we're here. The fact is, given the choice between never knowing you and dying a horrific death by Gila monsters, I'd choose the Gila monsters every time. Before you fell out of that tree on the Crosley estate, my life was hardly worth a pile of dragon droppings—and, well, now that we're about to literally become a pile of dragon droppings—I think you should know how I feel. . . . Arthur, I—"

"Ruby, look out!"

Arthur dove across his partner. Lashing out with the mannequin limb, he struck the Gila monster that had crept up behind Ruby and was preparing to bite into her ankle.

The creature flew several feet backward and landed in the heart of the horde, where it was welcomed back into the ranks by the snapping and snarling of its nearby comrades.

Arthur, however, now lay prone and helpless in the dirt, gazing directly into the dead black eyes of his demon attackers.

The monsters rushed forward.

Arthur had no time to stand. The stench of toxic lizard breath seared into his senses.

"Arthur!" cried Ruby.

His vision filled with black scales and snapping snouts. It was hardly the image he would have chosen to be the last thing he ever saw in this world.

Then suddenly, the image changed.

From out of nowhere, a small mechanized contraption

256

appeared before him. With its geared treads and pivoting turret, it somewhat resembled a miniature tank.

The Gila monsters shifted their attention away from Arthur and began hissing and snapping at the new metallic invader. One of the creatures climbed onto the machine's front face and clamped its jaws around the red nozzle that protruded from the turret. No sooner had it done this, however, than the creature was blasted to the back wall by a jet of white foam.

Arthur watched in astonishment as the machine tilted its foam cannon downward and proceeded to blast the line of lizards directly in front of his face. As soon as this cluster had been flooded with foam and expelled backward, the machine's turret pivoted left and continued its assault on the rest of the legion.

Seeing his chance, Arthur staggered to his feet. Just then, a tangle of rope struck him on the shoulder.

"Arthur—" a voice called overhead, "grab on!"

Arthur looked up in confusion—and saw three familiar figures peering down at him from the upper edge of the opening. While his mother stood panicked with her hands over her mouth, his brother Simon frantically manipulated the controls of a long-antennaed remote control device. Beside Simon, the Whipples' butler, Wilhelm, stood grasping the top end of a rope ladder.

Arthur shot Ruby a look, and the two leapt at the ladder, clutching onto it with every limb.

A moment later, they had left the lizards behind and

were ascending through the upper rim of the hole, out of the shadows into the warmth of the afternoon sun.

When they'd reached the surface, the pair collapsed to the ground with relief and exhaustion.

Wilhelm pulled Arthur up by the shoulders and said, "Are you hurt, Master Arthur?"

"No—I think I'm all right," Arthur panted, checking himself for any undetected mortal wounds. "Thanks to you two."

"I am sorry vee did not get here sooner; no boy should have to be nearly eaten by lizards so many times in so few days."

"Yeah," Simon agreed. "You've certainly had more than your fair share of life-threatening lizard attacks lately." He pressed a button on his remote control and a tiny grappling hook shot up from the pit. He caught the hook, reeled in the attached cable, and hoisted up the tank-like contraption that had saved Arthur's life. "It's a good thing my DSX Machine was operational. After we discovered the pit and Wilhelm went to get the ladder, I ran to my workshop and grabbed it—just in case. I built it as a 'Detached Salvager and Extinguisher' to put out rocket-kart fires and retrieve parts from unstable wreckage—but apparently it works as a reptile repeller as well."

"Whatever it is," said Arthur, "it has just earned itself free cleaning and polishing for life. If it weren't for you and your machine, we'd still be at the bottom of that pit."

At this, Arthur's mother ran forward and hugged him as he had never been hugged before.

"Oh, Arthur, thank God you're safe!" she cried. "We were so worried. What an awful mother I was, not to notice you weren't with us this morning. My dear, sweet boy, can you ever forgive me?"

Arthur closed his eyes and breathed a contented sigh.

"I forgive you."

He could have remained in the warmth of his mother's embrace many minutes longer—but he was soon struck by a puzzling thought.

"Hang on," he blurted, "what are you all doing here? What about the championships?"

"When your father discovered you were missing," explained Mrs. Whipple, "he walked off the tiltyard in the middle of his duel. We all split into search parties to look for you."

"He did . . . ?" Arthur's mind swirled with equal parts confusion, joy, and terror. "What about your events?"

"We've missed them."

"Oh no! We've got to get back before you miss any more! Where are the others?"

"Ivy and the octuplets stayed with Mrs. Waite to search the championship grounds in case you somehow turned up there. Your father has gone with Henry and Cordelia to check the Goldwin estate. We can fetch them with the car on our way back to the city."

The others nodded in agreement—but before they could take their first step toward the house, Arthur's father emerged through the trees with Henry and Cordelia. The moment he saw his recordless son, Mr. Whipple cried out and ran to meet him.

"Arthur!" he exclaimed. "Are you all right, Son?"

"I am now," said Arthur. "But . . . your duel with Mr. Goldwin?"

"Seems I'm not the dueling type in the end," his father said with a smile. "I nearly tried to keep going after I'd heard you were missing, I'm sorry to say. But it's funny what one's mind gets up to when one is hurtling forward on a motorbike with an electric spear in one's hand. . . ." His voice softened as his eyes narrowed. "Suddenly, I was back inside the coffin. I've a feeling you know the one I mean, Arthur. I could practically hear myself gasping for breath as I clawed at the walls. I saw the dozens of hands reaching in to pull me to safety, and then I noticed the one pair that was missing. I looked up to see where my father was—only to watch him turn his back and walk away. He was a great man, my father, and I've spent my whole life trying to match his greatness. But today I realized I'd rather simply be a *good* man myself. So I left Mr. Goldwin to finish the duel on his own. I am so sorry to have left you behind, Son—and so glad to see you unharmed. But where have you been?"

"He got attacked by lizards again, Dad," said Simon.

"Oh dear," said Mr. Whipple as he clutched Arthur's shoulder. "How ever—?"

At that moment, Arthur's father noticed Ruby, who was standing to the boy's rear and had thus far been ignored by the rescue party. "Wait a minute. What on earth is she doing here? She's a spy for the Goldwins!"

"What?" Arthur replied in shock.

"That girl has schemed to detain you in an effort to terrorize and cripple this family!"

Ruby raised her hands in humble protest.

Arthur stepped in front of her. "No she hasn't," he insisted. "They locked her up as well. She's on our side."

Mr. Whipple cocked his head slightly, his expression shifting from outrage to puzzlement. "Locked up? Who did?"

"Overkill and Undercut."

"They're still alive? The clownish giant and dwarf who said they were working for Sammy before they went down with the *Current Champion*?"

"That's them. But Sammy's completely innocent. Everything they said about him that night was a lie. After Undercut mistakenly spilled his story to Mr. Lowe at the Mountain and Molehill, he and Overkill had to get themselves arrested so they could shift the blame back onto Sammy. Ruby and I have been privately working with Sergeant Greenley to try and apprehend them on our own. They're the ones who let the Komodo dragon loose; they're the ones who shot Henry with the arrow at the Unsafe Sports Showdown; they're the ones who sabotaged the birthday cake—using a tunnel they'd dug from the Goldwin estate onto ours. Ruby and I fell into it this morning by accident."

Arthur pointed over his shoulder to the pit, which his father had not noticed until now. Mr. Whipple and his newly arrived children walked to the edge of it and looked down. The floor crawled with ill-tempered, foam-covered lizards.

"Whoa," said Henry.

"This . . . is *incredible*," Mr. Whipple marveled.

Arthur retrieved the copy of the Treasurer's note that he kept in his trouser pocket and offered it to his father. "The night of the Komodo dragon attack," he explained, "they used the tunnel again to get back to our house. I think I scared them away, but they dropped this in the trees. It's a list of instructions from their boss—signed and sealed by Ardmore's new treasurer."

"We deduced," said Ruby, speaking for the first time, "that Rex was the Treasurer and he'd hired Overkill and Undercut to sabotage your family."

"But it turns out he didn't have to hire them—they're his *sons*."

"What?!" exclaimed Mr. Whipple.

"My brothers," said Ruby. "Rayford and Royston."

"The twins Mrs. Goldwin is always talking about traveling the world on scholarship," continued Arthur. "They've actually been living this whole time under the Goldwin house and carrying out Rex's bidding. The pictures of them in the trophy room are fakes—just like the names Overkill and Undercut. Royston and Rayford are really the Tallest and Shortest Humans on Earth. After we stumbled onto the tunnel, we followed it to their secret lair in the Goldwins' basement."

"But just when we'd uncovered the truth," added Ruby,

"they turned up and threw us in a cage. After they'd left, however, we managed to escape back into the tunnel to discover they'd filled it with deadly lizards—which proceeded to attack us, of course. Luckily, Simon and Wilhelm found us in the nick of time."

"Thanks for that, by the way," said Ruby, turning to the boy and the butler. "If your lives ever need saving, I hope you'll let me return the favor—or, at least bake you a cake or something."

"Please, miss," the butler replied. "The pleasure vas ours."

Mr. Whipple pondered the children's report, shaking his head in disbelief and disgust. "I've always known Goldwin was up to something—there was no question about that—but never in my darkest dreams did I imagine it would prove so utterly sinister."

"Yeah, Arthur," Cordelia scowled, "you might have mentioned some of this before. I mean, it would have been nice to know our neighbors were actually trying to murder us."

"I am sorry about that," said Arthur, "but the last time I spoke up, Sammy the Spatula was nearly shot to death, and the rest of us almost drowned. I wanted to wait until the case had been fully solved before saying any more about it, so no one else would be hurt by my mistakes."

"The case, eh? So you're back to playing detective again, are you?"

"Cordelia—that's enough," scolded Mr. Whipple. "It seems your brother has indeed made more progress on this case with his friends than the 'World's Greatest Detective'

has managed to accomplish with the full resources of Scotland Yard at his disposal. Well done, you two. Miss Goldwin, I am sorry I took you for a spy. You seem to be as good a friend to this family as any."

Ruby smiled. "I'm a friend to the truth, sir."

"Indeed, there is no better friend to have," Mr. Whipple replied. "So tell me, where are these Rayford and Royston characters now?"

"They left for the championships with a sack of explosives," Arthur explained.

His father gave a sardonic snort. "Seems the joke's on them then. Because *we* are not at the championships."

"But Dad," cried Arthur, "we've got to get back!"

"I'm afraid it's too late for that, Son," Mr. Whipple said with a sad but comforting smile. "The competition is all but over. The important thing is you're safe."

"No," insisted Arthur. "We can still make the last event if we leave now. I can't let you lose to the Goldwins on my account. And as for me—well, I've dreamt of joining you in the championships all my life. Now that I've finally got that chance, you aren't going to take it away, are you?"

"But what about the Goldwin twins and their explosives?"

"They said they plan to use them against our family if things don't go their way. But now that we know their schemes, it might be our only chance at catching them in the act and proving Sammy's innocence. And anyway, are we really going to let them scare us off like that?"

Arthur's father wrung his hands in contemplation. "Very well then," he growled. "I guess we'll just have to keep an eye out for our two volatile friends—as I have not the slightest intention of giving the Goldwins *their way*." His eyes burned with fury and determination. "Come, we must get back to the championships at once!"

• • •

"You really have to wonder, Ted, if Charles Whipple took one too many blows to the head in the early rounds of that duel."

"Absolutely, Chuck. First, to walk off the dueling field a mere four rounds from an all-but-guaranteed victory, and then to have his entire family disregard their remaining events in order to search for one recordless son—this is a man clearly disconnected from reality."

"No question, Ted. And what's worse, this sudden lapse of logic has allowed Whipple's archrivals to claw their way firmly back into the competition."

"Indeed it has, Chuck. What a remarkable display of resiliency the Goldwins have exhibited by winning every single one of their events since the Whipples' departure—and drawing the score line level between the two families once again. I certainly never would have bet on them this morning—but it now appears the Goldwins will indeed be this year's champions."

"And let's not forget, Ted, the stakes are even higher for these two families, what with the official rivalry contract they've signed. Whichever family loses the cup will be dis-

265

qualified from any events the winner is participating in for the next two years, making the cup that much harder to win back at the next championships."

"That's right, Chuck. Seems we're about to witness a long-term regime change here."

"It certainly does, Ted. With only one contest remaining—the newly added knife-block speed stocking event—even if the Whipples were to actually turn up for it, they would face an almost insurmountable battle, as the individual representing them in this event is none other than Arthur Whipple: the missing member of the family who has not even one world record to his name."

"It's quite tragic, isn't it, Chuck? We knew the Whipples' reign had to end someday, but to end like this—with hardly a whimper, much less a roar—I just never thought I'd see it."

"Nor I, Ted. Nor . . . Oh—hang on, what's this? Oh—oh my! We've just received word that the Whipples have arrived—with their son Arthur—only a moment ago at Champions Court Place Park—and are indeed heading toward the speed stocking arena as we speak!"

"Unbelievable, Chuck! It seems they're actually trying to go for it. Can this competition get any more sensational?"

● ● ●

As Arthur and his family approached the competitor's entrance to the speed stocking arena, the great double doors swung open. A man stepped through the doorway.

"There you are, Charlie!" Rex Goldwin grinned as he

sauntered toward the group. "Where ever have you been? We've missed you terribly—but I'm afraid we've had to go ahead without you; as you well know, the championships wait for no one."

"Of course, Mr. Goldwin," Arthur's father replied. "You clearly had no choice in the matter. But why do I get the feeling you know *exactly* where we've been?"

"Honestly, Charlie—I have no idea what you're talking about. I must thank you, however, for finding my daughter. Sorry for any trouble she's given you; she can make quite a nuisance of herself when she wants to. Come on, dear," Rex said as he reached toward Ruby, "let's get you back with your brothers and sisters. Your mother has been worried sick about you."

Ruby pulled away as Rex's hand came close.

"Not so fast, Mr. Goldwin," said Mr. Whipple. "I'm afraid Ruby will be staying with us until you've had a chat with the authorities. You see, she and my son Arthur seem to think you've had them thrown into a cage by your twin sons, Rayford and Royston, who are not in fact traveling the world on the Clapford Fellowship as you have claimed, but are indeed living beneath your house and doing your dirty work—including the numerous acts of sabotage recently perpetrated against my family. Furthermore, they insist the twins are not the handsome pair you have pictured in your trophy room, but in fact the exceptionally sized duo we met aboard the *Current Champion*: the sinister Messrs. Overkill and Undercut. So tell me,

Mr. Goldwin—does any of this sound familiar to you?"

At his father's mention of "the twins," Arthur thought he'd caught a glimpse of some darker emotion in Rex Goldwin's eyes—but it was gone as quickly as it had appeared and replaced by a sly smile.

"You've got me, Charlie," Rex smirked. "So the twins aren't quite as handsome as we've made them out to be. I'm afraid that was Rita's doing, mostly. It just kills her to think that those two actually came from her womb, you know? But really, Charlie, that's hardly a crime. You no doubt feel the same way about that little loser of yours—and I'm sure you would have covered him up as well if you'd had the chance."

"I'll not have you talk that way about my son!" Mr. Whipple shot back. "I've made the mistake of grossly undervaluing Arthur for over twelve years now, and I refuse to let anyone else ever do so again. And as to your crimes, Mr. Goldwin, I'd say sabotage and kidnapping are easily enough to have you arrested."

"Please, Charlie. What the twins do in their spare time is hardly any concern of mine. They're big boys now, you know—well, at least the one—and I can hardly be held responsible for their actions. Of course, if you want to talk to them, I'm afraid you'll have to find them first. As you may have discovered, despite their freakish sizes, they have a way of disappearing when they want to." Rex snorted. "I'm surprised at you, Charlie! Just when my family and I are set to walk away with the championship, you try to

268

dredge up some silly scandal in a ridiculous attempt to slander us. Afraid your failure of a son won't win the last event for you, eh?"

A moment after the words had left his mouth, Rex Goldwin found himself flat on his back with a very sore jaw. Mr. Whipple stood over him, fist in the air, his knuckles red from their impact with Rex's chin.

"I asked you, Mr. Goldwin," said Arthur's father, "not to talk that way about my son. Whatever happens here, we are proud of him."

Rex wiped a spot of blood from his lip. Neither the blow nor the fall had dislodged the charmingly sinister smile from his face. "Ah," he smirked, "spoken like a man about to lose."

Mr. Whipple ignored Rex's comment and turned to Arthur. "Come now, Son. We've not much time. We must get you to your event."

Arthur looked at his father in amazement. "Yes, sir," he said.

Arthur could hardly believe his ears. Had he really gained his father's respect without breaking even a single world record?

This was an unexpected turn of events. As far as Arthur could tell, his greatest dream had just come true—though not in any sort of way he had ever imagined. It wasn't easy to process.

Arthur hurried with his father through the doors of the speed stocking arena, suddenly struck by a strange sense

269

of loss—as though his purpose in life had been abruptly drained away. With his chief aspiration fulfilled, did his big event really even matter anymore?

It took only a moment for him to find the answer—and with it, all sense of purpose he thought he had lost.

Breaking a world record, he realized, was now more important than ever before—but for quite different reasons. Though he had gained the respect he'd needed from his father, now his father needed *him*.

And this time, Arthur would not let him down. He would fight to repay the seemingly unconditional pride his father had expressed in him; he would teach his father's enemies they could not mock his dad and get away with it; he would show the world he was his father's son.

Arthur started up the rear steps of the speed stocking stage, but Mr. Whipple stopped him and clutched his shoulders.

"I have every faith in you, Arthur. You are as fine a Whipple as ever there was. Now get out there and do what you were born to do."

"Yes, Father. I'll—"

"Positions!" screeched Mr. Prim from the certifier's podium. "Any competitor not in place at precisely 16:02 will forfeit his spot! There shall be no further warning!"

Mr. Whipple snapped his attention to Wilhelm and Mr. Mahankali, who followed just behind him. "Wilhelm; Mahankali," he ordered, "the three of us will stand guard and watch for this dwarf and giant. They're bound to be here somewhere. And this time we're ready for them."

He turned back to his son with a thumbs-up and a smile.

Arthur waved quickly to his father, then scrambled onto the platform and ducked into position at the center of his knife-block ring.

He reached instinctively into his pocket, only to be reminded that his magical domino was gone, lost forever in the belly of a giant lizard. A wave of panic crashed over him—but quickly subsided. *Perhaps*, he thought, *the magic of the domino was never in the domino itself.* "*We all have our part to play,*" he heard his uncle saying. His domino's part, in the end, had been to help him and Ruby when there was nothing else for them. Perhaps his part was a similar one. Perhaps he was his family's magical domino.

He took a quick breath to settle himself and looked out at the crowd for the first time.

What should have been a smattering of spectators for an inconsequential last-minute event had become a legion of fanatics gathered to witness the deciding moment of the championships. Fortunately for Arthur, there was no time for stage fright.

"Ready. Set . . ." *Bang!* Mr. Prim's starting pistol echoed into the stands.

Time stopped. The world became clear. Arthur knew what he had to do.

He seized the hilt of the first knife, then drew back his arm and slid the gleaming blade from its sheath.

271

THE LAST ATTEMPT

Arthur became a flurry of fingers and steel, ripping the knives from the first block and popping them into the empty one beside it. *Rat-tat-tat-tat-tat-tat-tat!* The clattering of wood and metal echoed into the stands.

The instant the empty block was full Arthur swiveled thirty degrees left and set to work on the newly emptied block before him. When the second block was full he proceeded immediately to the third.

He had discovered in practice that working counterclockwise gave him a considerable advantage over the traditional direction of play. The preparation had paid off. He felt more comfortable in the ring now than he ever had before. The knives were merely an extension of his own body. He could hardly tell where his fingertips ended and the blades began.

As he completed the first revolution, Arthur allowed himself a quick glance around the stage. Nineteen other competitors stood at the centers of nineteen other knife-block rings, all of them frantically flinging blades from one block to the next.

He glanced up at the giant scoreboard—and could barely believe his eyes. There, beside the letters A. WHIPPLE, was a bright blue light. He was in first place. His technique was working.

He quickly checked the spinning digits of his Knives Transferred Count, then compared it with the numbers beside the glowing red light further up the board. The second place competitor was only four knives behind him. It was no surprise who it was.

At the start of his third revolution, Arthur risked another glance, this time to the knife-block ring directly to his right. There at its center; stood Rupert Goldwin.

As the Goldwin boy finished one block and pivoted to the next, Arthur realized something: unlike the other competitors, Rupert was moving counterclockwise—just like him. The Goldwin boy had stolen his technique and was now using it against him.

At that moment, Rupert turned his head, and the two locked eyes. Rupert smiled, scornfully.

Arthur smiled back. Though he would normally have been intimidated by such a menacing grin, he was strangely encouraged by this brief exchange with his rival. For the first time in Arthur's life, someone was imitating *him*.

273

And besides—had Rupert even bothered to check the scoreboard? Unless he especially liked being in second place, it didn't seem he had much to smile about. Arthur, on the other hand, had very good reason to smile. He had finally gained the one thing he'd always wanted: his family's acceptance. And now, he was having the race of his life. Rupert Goldwin could smirk all he liked. This event belonged to Arthur Whipple.

Just before the boys turned back to their own rings, Rupert's grin faltered ever so slightly—but Arthur's grin only grew wider. He had no need to fake it. He could not remember ever enjoying a record attempt so much.

As he completed his third revolution, Arthur checked the scoreboard again. His ranking was still the same; his lead, however, had increased substantially. Rupert was now a dozen knives behind him; the third-place competitor was a full knife-block behind Rupert.

Arthur tried not to get too excited. He had failed enough record attempts to know his luck could take a turn for the worse at any moment. Still, it was hard not to be optimistic. He had never had a lead like this before. It would take quite a catastrophe to rob him of it now.

It was at that moment, of course, that the cleaver sliced into his hand.

He scarcely realized what was happening until it was already too late. As he watched the edge of the blade slip across his left palm, he felt only a bit of pressure and a hint of cold. Something told him, however, he would not

274

escape so easily; his payments in the pain department had merely been deferred—and he'd be made to settle them shortly.

Yet, as he waited for the inevitable pain to arrive, he managed not to miss a beat. His hands continued to fly in front of him as though nothing had happened. . . . But *oh*—there it was. A searing fissure shot through his hand like a stream of lava. He gritted his teeth—but continued on at the same breakneck pace as before. It was going to take more than a bit of shooting pain to shake him from this competition.

He reached for the next knife—but his fingers merely slipped from its handle. It was then he noticed the blood.

Scarlet drops dripped from his fingertips and spattered the surface of the wooden block before him. He reached out a second time, but again, the handle only slipped from his grasp.

Arthur's mind flooded with panic. Was this how it would all end? Would he be unable to even complete the event?

In desperation, he reached for the handle once again. Tightening his grip this time, he drew the knife from its sheath and drove it into the empty slot in the block beside it.

Arthur glanced at the scoreboard. His lead had slipped by a few knives—but he was still in first place. He continued plucking knives as fast as he could, careful to clutch each one firmly.

His rhythm returned and he proceeded around the ring with ease and precision. Though the added effort slowed his pace ever so slightly, his lead was large enough that even the Goldwin boy had no hope of catching him.

That is, of course, had Arthur not cut himself a second time.

"Ah!" he cried as his grip on a carving knife slipped a fraction of an inch. There was no delay in pain this time. But the stinging in his hand was the least of his concerns. With both hands crippled now, his fantastic lead no longer seemed so unbreakable.

Blood dripped down the blocks and onto the floorboards. Arthur pushed the pain from his mind and launched into his sixth revolution.

Come on, he urged himself. *Just two more revs. Don't think about the blood. This is what you were born for. Just stay ahead—and don't think about the blood. You can do this. . . .*

A chef's knife chipped a chunk out of the knife block as Arthur forced it into its slot.

Keep going. Stay in front. Focus.

He could feel Rupert Goldwin slowly gaining on him out of the corner of his eye. He glanced over to see that Rupert's smile had returned and was now wider than ever.

"Looks like you've got a bit of a scratch there, Whipple," the Goldwin boy called without looking up from his knives. "Feel free to step out and get a bandage if you like. Don't worry—I'll let you look at my trophy when you get back."

Ignore him, thought Arthur. *Don't let him get to you. Don't say anything. . . . Okay, well, maybe just one quick*

276

thing, to make sure he knows he's not getting to you.

"What—*this?*" Arthur called back. "This is nothing. I've had worse *paper* cuts. I just like to bleed is all."

"So you're bleeding on purpose, then?"

Arthur paused, realizing he'd talked himself into a bit of a corner here. He tried to imagine what one of his brothers might say in such a situation, but nothing came to him. He was on his own.

"Yep," he said with perfect confidence.

"Brilliant," Rupert snickered. "Good luck with that."

Arthur wished more than ever that he'd been blessed with his family's trash-talking skills. But then, it struck him. There was only one thing left to say.

"Scoreboard, Rupert," he said plainly. "Scoreboar—"

And with that, Arthur slipped on the wet floor and crashed to his knees.

The crowd gasped. The front runner had fallen—and in his final lap.

"Ha!" snapped Rupert, then surged forward.

Arthur watched in horror as the blue light that had marked his name from the start suddenly abandoned A. WHIPPLE—and cozied up alongside R. GOLDWIN.

For a split second, Arthur wanted just to stay down and collapse beneath the pressure of shame and embarrassment piling onto his shoulders. But something forced him to his feet. He hadn't come this far to give up now.

Arthur seized the next knife handle and launched himself back into the race. His family was counting on him. He wasn't going to let them down. Not this time.

His hands whipped through the air.

Four knives behind. Only three more blocks to fill. . . .

He willed himself forward.

Two more blocks. . . .

He was catching him. Rupert was only one knife ahead.

One more block. . . .

It all came down to this.

Thwack!

Arthur slotted the final blade home—and dropped to his knees.

He looked to the scoreboard. The blue and red ranking lamps had been extinguished.

Arthur checked Rupert's time. 1:57.32.

His eyes darted to the digits beside his own name. His heart stopped.

1:57.32.

The scoreboard showed an even draw—but of course, the board only displayed hundredths of a second. The official times, Arthur knew, were kept by the certifier. His heart started up again.

He turned to see Rupert raising his arms in presumed triumph.

As the last of the other competitors finished the race, the crowd clamored for just a moment—then hushed, in anticipation of the judge's decision.

Archibald Prim made some final marks on his score-cards, then straightened the stack against the podium.

Unseen at the back of the crowd, an impossibly tiny man stood beside his enormous, hunching companion and readied his thumb over a small red-buttoned device.

Mr. Prim cleared his throat and addressed the arena.

"By a margin of eight thousandths of a second," the certifier's voice echoed into the stands, "the winner of the first ever knife-block speed stocking event at the World Record World Championships—and new record holder in the sport—is . . ."

Arthur closed his eyes and held his breath.

". . . Rupert Goldwin!"

Arthur opened his eyes. A drop of blood mixed with a bead of sweat and dripped from his eyelid.

A wave of applause rose up from the crowd.

Rupert's family stormed the stage. The Goldwins hoisted their son onto their shoulders and raised their arms to the arena.

The tiny man at the back of the crowd lowered the small red-buttoned device, having never pressed the button. He gave a satisfied smirk to his companion and slunk off beside him into the crowd.

Flashbulbs and fireworks went off in every direction.

Arthur's heart dropped. He fell to the floor and wrapped his arms around his face. Confetti rained down on him like volcanic ash on a ruined city.

From his position at the podium, Mr. Prim looked entirely unsurprised. "Mm-hmm," he remarked—and ticked his clipboard.

279

Arthur tried to block out the sounds of the Goldwins' celebrations, but he couldn't cover his ears tight enough. Why on earth had God not seen fit to provide lids for ears as well as for eyes? Surely, in His infinite wisdom, He'd known how useful a pair of earlids would have been at a time like this. Arthur wanted nothing so badly as to shut his senses down. He never wanted to see anyone again. He never wanted to hear anyone again. He wanted to stay on the floor forever. They could disassemble the stage and transport the pieces to some secluded storage facility somewhere, and they wouldn't even have to bother moving him. Just give him a quiet corner of the warehouse without too many rats or spiders and let him stay there in the dark. He wouldn't take up much space. He'd hardly breathe. He just never wanted to see anyone ever again. Especially not his family. Oh no, his family! How could he ever face them? They had given him a chance to finally belong—and he had failed. He had let himself down; he had let them all down. How would he ever be able to stand again?

Amid the cheering and pyrotechnics, Arthur began to detect a muffled voice above him. Slowly, cautiously, he uncovered his face and tilted it upward.

Silhouetted against the flash of fireworks, Arthur's father stood leaning over the edge of the knife-block ring. He smiled warmly and stretched out an arm toward his son.

"Well done, Arthur," he said.

Arthur stared at his father's hand. "I—I've failed you," he said.

"You've done what now?"

"I've lost you the Championship Cup. I've failed you."

"Nonsense! You've done nothing of the sort. You, son, have fought harder than any mere record breaker has done all week!"

Arthur sighed doubtfully and lowered his eyes.

"Arthur," his father insisted, "it's true. Just look at your hands, Son. Look at this stage! You've practically painted it red. Clearly, you've left it all in the ring here—and then some. Do you think any of the other competitors would have done so well with an injury like that? You are stronger than all of them. It's just that your strengths are, well—not so easily quantifiable. I know I've failed to see it in the past—and for that I'll be forever sorry—but today my eyes have been opened. There is something in this world even more valuable than the ability to break world records—and you, Arthur, have got it. We should all be so lucky."

Arthur peered up from the floorboards.

"Now," said his father, "take my hand. The floor is no place for a Whipple. You should be standing. Your place is with us."

Arthur wiped his brow and drew a deep breath, then reached his bloodied arm toward his father's hand.

Mr. Whipple clutched Arthur's forearm and hoisted him over the outer edge of the ring-shaped table. He helped him to his feet and clasped a hand on his shoulder.

"I know you were wishing for a slightly different out-come here today, Son—and I'm sure that stings a bit.

There's no way around it, I'm afraid; we Whipples like to win. But know this: I could not be any prouder of you right now had you just broken every world record in the *Grazelby Guide*."

Arthur looked into his father's face and knew it was true. "I—" he said. "I . . . Thanks, Dad."

Mr. Whipple smiled and squeezed Arthur's shoulder, then glanced over his own.

At this, Arthur's mother rushed past her husband and embraced her son.

"Arthur—my darling boy," she said, kissing his forehead. "How are your hands? Let's have a look at them. Oh, you poor dear! You must be in horrible pain."

Arthur shook his head.

"What a brave boy you are," his mother said, smiling. "Come on then—we'll get you fixed up good as new."

She draped her arm around his shoulders and led him to the first aid station.

● ● ●

Arthur emerged from the booth with both hands bandaged to find his brothers and sisters gathered outside to meet him. They stood in a row, doing their best to ignore the continued celebrations of the Goldwin family directly behind them. Cordelia seemed to be having a particularly difficult time of it and would glance back in annoyance any time the Goldwins shrieked or hooted with even the slightest bit of overenthusiasm.

As Arthur walked down the line, his siblings patted his back and shook his hand and tousled his hair.

"Good try, Arthur," said Beatrice.

"You were the best one out there by far," said Simon. "You were just unlucky, that's all."

"If you hadn't slipped," said George, "Rupert wouldn't have stood a chance."

But Arthur could not quite bring himself to make eye contact with any of them.

At the end of the line stood Ruby.

"Hi, Arthur," she said.

"Hi," he replied. Then the words began pouring out. "I wish you hadn't seen that. I—"

"You—were amazing," she cut in. "I had no idea you could use knives like that. I mean, don't get me wrong, I believed in you and everything, but I guess I never expected you to be so, well—*good*."

"Look," Arthur sighed, "I appreciate what you're trying to do, but you don't have to try and make me feel better about it. I know how I must have looked."

"What are you talking about?" snapped Ruby. "When have I ever tried to make you feel better about anything? I'm only saying it because I mean it. That was really impressive, Arthur. And in case you've forgotten, I am not someone typically impressed by world-record breaking. At all. But watching you today—it made me think I might actually be missing something."

Arthur squinted. "You do realize I didn't win, right?"

"Ah, come on, Arthur—it was obvious that on any other day you would have destroyed them all. Today just wasn't your day. But the way you kept fighting, even when the stage was covered in your own blood—it was really, well . . . extraordinary."

Arthur scrunched up his face. "You think so?"

"I know so," Ruby said with a smile.

She took a step closer and leaned in toward Arthur.

At that moment, Rupert Goldwin appeared at Ruby's back—and promptly nudged her aside. "Good game, Whipple . . ." he said, offering his right hand to Arthur.

"Thanks, Rupert," Arthur sighed, politely taking the boy's hand. "Good—"

". . . Not quite good enough though, was it?" Rupert continued. "But don't beat yourself up about it; you were always going to lose against us—and you can hardly change fate, now can you?"

Ruby glared at her brother. "Do you take lessons in being despicable, Rupert—or does it just come naturally?"

"Ah, Ruby," said Rupert, turning to face his sister. "Now you, on the other hand, had a chance to choose your fortune, didn't you, Sis? You must feel pretty silly now, having betrayed your own family only to end up picking the losing side. Not to worry, though; we might still be persuaded to take you back—if you ask *real* nice."

"Don't hold your breath, Rupert—"

"Well, I do have the record for breath holding, so—"

"Yeah, I may have heard you mention it—about a thousand times. But still. Unless you've figured out how to hold your breath for, well, *ever*—I wouldn't try it. You'll never hear me asking to come back. You know, on second thought, maybe you *should* hold your breath. Just make sure you're chained up in a shark tank when you try it. Be a shame to let yourself go to waste when there are so many poor, starving sharks in this world. And then no one could ever say again that you've never done anything generous with your life."

"Oh, Sis," Rupert smirked. "I really will miss our little chats when you're gone—won't you?"

"I don't know how I'll get by."

"Ah, well—c'est la vie," said Rupert. "Now, try not to be too disappointed if the Whipples aren't completely keen to keep you around." He shifted his gaze to Arthur. "They've already got *one* loser in the family, you know."

With that, Cordelia—who'd been standing just within earshot—lunged past Ruby and caught Rupert across the nose with her knuckles.

"Shut your mouth, Goldwin scum!" she cried and promptly tackled the boy to the floor. "Nobody talks that way about my brother but me!"

As she proceeded to pummel Rupert about the chest and face, the members of both families flocked to the commotion and began grappling against one another.

"Come on, losers!" shouted Roland Goldwin. "Back for another beating already?"

"*I'll* show you a beating!" Henry roared.

285

"Get her off me!" cried Rupert.

The incident surely would have escalated to an all-out brawl, had Mr. Whipple not swooped in the next moment and pulled his daughter off the battered boy beneath her.

"Enough!" he shouted.

The families stopped their scuffling.

"This is not how we concede a competition!"

Mr. Whipple stepped back a few feet and lowered the struggling girl to the ground. "Cordelia—stay back."

"But—"

"Back."

Mr. Whipple gave his daughter a firm look, then turned and approached Rex Goldwin. "My apologies, Mr. Goldwin. I'm afraid Cordelia tends to be a bit excitable."

"Excitable?" scoffed Rex. "I thought I was going to have to fetch the fire hose."

"Yes, well I'd hate for you to think of us as unsportsmanlike after all we've been through. So please, hear me out. Though I must say I utterly and completely despise your methods, winning the World Record World Championships is a remarkable accomplishment—by any means. It's not easy for me to say this, but . . ." Mr. Whipple extended his right hand. ". . . congratulations, Rex."

Rex tilted his head in pleasant surprise. "Well now," he smiled, "that's more like it, Charlie. There's no need for hostility. Honestly, I don't see any reason we shouldn't all be the best of friends—now that our contract's been fulfilled and this whole rivalry nonsense is behind us."

"Neither do I," said Mr. Whipple. "Well, unless of course, you count the time you tried to crush all our party guests—or the time you had our chef sent to prison—or the time you maimed our dog—or the time you kidnapped our son and held him in your dungeon—or, come to think of it, *any* of the numerous times you tried to murder us in cold blood. Apart from these minor examples, though, I can't see a reason in the world we shouldn't be friendly."

"Goodness, Charlie—it almost sounds like you blame *me* for all that."

"I'm afraid I do, Mr. Goldwin. And I'm afraid we'll still be contacting the authorities just as soon as tonight's festivities have ended. It may be difficult to catch you in the act as we had hoped, now that your plan to have your two sons murder us has been precluded by your win here, but we will not stop until we've proved you guilty of the crimes you've tried to pin on our poor chef Sammy. You may have got away with the cup, but you won't get away with your criminal deeds as well. Not if I have anything to say about it."

"I'm sorry to hear that, Charlie," said Rex, feigning a concerned sigh. "I just can't see why you'd want to pursue such a pointless course of action. If there was any foul play, I've already told you: it was the twins' doing. You'll never pin anything on me."

"It won't stop me trying."

"Fair enough. It's your own time you'll be wasting. Thanks to our little rivalry contract, you're now barred from competing against us in any event we choose to enter for the next two years—and believe me: we'll choose to enter a lot of them. All the extra time you've got will have to be spent scraping up other events to take part in, if you hope to even come close to your current rate of record breaking. Meanwhile, we'll only get better and better. And pretty soon, you'll have no chance at beating us in anything."

"There are more important things than beating your family, Mr. Goldwin," said Arthur's father. "But yes," he added with a sigh, "you must be very proud of getting me to sign that contract now. It was my own pride, of course, that drove me to make such a foolish agreement. And for that, I must apologize to my family. I've made things unduly difficult for them, I'm afraid." He turned to his wife and gave a sad smile, but she returned it with a twinkling nod of forgiveness. He looked around him to find similar expressions on the faces of Arthur and the rest of the Whipple children. Arthur's father turned back to Rex with a gleam in his eye. "Still, I wouldn't count us out just yet. We've overcome bigger obstacles—many of them this very day, in fact. But for now, we'd best be off. Enjoy the awards ceremony, Mr. Goldwin."

"You too, Charlie," grinned Rex. "I hope your evening isn't marred too terribly, knowing the cup will be going home with somebody else this year—and likely every other year as well."

"Your concern is much appreciated, Mr. Goldwin. Good

288

evening, all of you. Competing with you these past months has been . . . eye-opening—to say the least."

And with that, Mr. Whipple turned and led his family out of the arena as the fireworks continued above them.

● ● ●

"Must we really go to the awards ceremony, Dad?" Cordelia pleaded as she trudged through the courtyard. "I don't think I can stomach seeing the Goldwins for one more minute today—much less seeing them presented with the Championship Cup."

"Cordelia," scolded her mother, "where have you learned such dreadful sportsmanship? It's bad enough you've already assaulted one of the Goldwins—though I'm sure he more than deserved it—but now to suggest we skip the awards altogether simply because we haven't won the top prize? Honestly, I know it's new to us, this losing business, and bound to cause some discomfort, but I wonder sometimes if so much winning has actually done us a fair bit of harm."

Cordelia sighed and hung her head, and the Whipples resumed their march across the courtyard. They had not gone far when Arthur stopped them again.

"I don't mean to be contradictory," said Arthur, "but I have to say I'd rather not go either. I know it's unsportsman-like—but I just feel so awful about losing the cup for all of you. You've all been really great, not calling me names or disowning me or anything—but I still can't help feeling I've let you all down. I don't think I'll be able to sit through the ceremony without being physically ill."

"Ah—don't feel bad, Arthur," replied Cordelia. "Look on the bright side. Now that the Goldwins have won, at least we don't have to worry about being blown up by those lunatic twins of theirs. And besides—it's not your fault we didn't win. We all lost events this week—a whole lot more of them than you did."

"Yeah, Arthur," Simon agreed. "You had all the pressure on your shoulders only because we failed to win so many of our own events."

"And you were really incredible out there," added Henry. "You lost in far better style than any of us managed to do this week. I mean, all that blood sloshing about the stage—that looked completely fantastic! You really made us proud today, Brother."

"Absolutely," said Cordelia. "You were great, Arthur. It's not the losing I mind so much—I mean, I do, I really do, it's killing me inside—but I'll get over it. The truly agonizing part, though . . . is losing to *them*."

"Yeah," the other children sighed.

"All right," snapped Mr. Whipple. "That's enough self-pity for one evening. We're all going to the awards ceremony tonight, and we're all going to enjoy ourselves. First: because we are not a family of unsporting milksops—and second: because we've earned it. Regardless of the final outcome, we've all made some incredible accomplishments this week. We were cursed with opponents who regularly resorted to sabotage and violence—and yet, we very nearly beat them, without ever sinking to their level. And when we were forced to choose between winning the cup or rescuing our family, we made the right choice. And for that, I am exceedingly proud. Indeed, I am prouder of *nearly* winning this cup than I am of all the cups we've ever actually won. Because it was *this* cup that made our family whole for the first time."

Mr. Whipple looked to Arthur and smiled. Arthur couldn't help but smile back.

"Don't misunderstand me," his father added, "this family has not lost its zeal for record breaking—certainly not after the way it's brought us all together today. First thing tomorrow, we begin the task of winning the cup back from the Goldwins at the next championships, in spite of their precious rivalry contract. But tonight, we celebrate everything we accomplished this year. Let's enjoy second place while we've got it; we're not likely to have the experience ever again, now are we?"

Arthur and the other Whipples shook their heads.

"Very well then, let's get ourselves cleaned up and ready for the ceremony. The Goldwins may have placed first in the competition this year, but they've got another thing coming if they think they can top us tonight—in dignity or in style!"

THE WHIPPLES ACCEPT DEFEAT

As the **Whipples**' triple-decker limousine slowed to a halt outside the entrance of the Opulerium Theatre, Arthur's heart swelled with excitement and dread.

Though he had attended several WRWC Awards ceremonies before, this was the first time he had actually participated in the tournament—and thus, the first time he had not felt completely out of place there. And yet, these were not at all the circumstances under which he had hoped to attend his first awards ceremony as an official competitor. His participation in the tournament, after all, had ended rather disappointingly—and now, the legions of reporters and photographers swarming around the red carpet before him only served to remind him of that fact.

He felt his father's hand on his shoulder.

"Arthur," Mr. Whipple said with a smile, "will you do us the honor of leading us out?"

"I—I don't know, sir," Arthur replied. "Do you really think that's appropriate? I mean, wouldn't you rather have someone representing us who actually won an event?"

"Indeed, I would not," answered his father. "Do you still not believe me, boy? When I said I could not be any prouder of you, I meant it. Perhaps you'll doubt me less when you see your entire family following you up the red carpet. So now then . . . after you."

Mr. Whipple gestured to the car door, and Arthur drew a deep breath. "Well, if you're absolutely certain you want me to . . ."

Mr. Whipple nodded.

"All right then," Arthur nodded back.

Wilhelm appeared outside the car window, and Arthur quickly straightened his bow tie and adjusted his lapel. A moment later, the valet opened the door.

Strobing blasts of white light struck the boy as he stepped from the car, freezing his limbs and face in various poses: his foot meeting the plush pile of the crimson carpet; his hand tugging on a cufflink; his top lip curled in startled astonishment.

The frequency of flashbulb-fire decreased considerably as the cameramen realized the boy's identity—but it was still more media attention than Arthur had ever received, so he thought nothing of the falloff and simply walked through the parted sea of celebrity seekers.

293

"Arthur," shouted one reporter, "that was quite an attempt you made this evening! You really had the crowd on the edge of their seats!"

Arthur turned to the reporter and smiled. Not only was this the first time he'd received a compliment from a reporter, it was the first time he'd ever been addressed by a reporter at all. He felt so honored and privileged, he could scarcely remember why it was he'd been feeling so disappointed.

"Thank you," he said. "I'm glad people got to see a good speed-stocking match. I hope it helps spread awareness of this fine, underappreciated sport. Of course," he added with a smile, "I'd have liked to have won it as well, but I'm afraid tonight just wasn't my night."

"Indeed it wasn't," the reporter said, frowning. "Does it trouble you to think you may have missed your last chance to live up to your family's now-fading reputation? And what do you say to speculation that your loss today could be the final nail in the Whipples' coffin?"

Arthur's mouth hung open. "Er . . . I . . ." he stuttered.

The reporter pressed the microphone into Arthur's chin. "I—well . . ."

At that moment, Arthur's father stepped in front of him. "My son, I am happy to say," Mr. Whipple interjected, "has no need at all to prove himself a part of this family. He is—and always will be—as valued a Whipple as any other."

Arthur looked back to see his entire family standing behind him, smiling in agreement with their father as flashbulbs went off around them.

294

"And as for our family's reputation and future," continued Mr. Whipple, "you can rest assured we shall not be leaving the world records game anytime soon—though we do hope to be known henceforth for more than just record breaking. In fact, tonight we would like to announce the beginning of a new era in our family's history. From now on, we . . ."

But before Arthur's father could finish his sentence, the reporter yanked the microphone away—and joined the rest of the crowd in a sudden scurry back toward the street.

Arthur and the other Whipples turned just in time to see a gold-plated car eleven doors long pull up to the curb and stop.

For several seconds nothing happened, save the continued pop of flashbulbs. But then, in perfect synchronization, all eleven doors opened at once—and out stepped the Goldwins, one through each door.

The crowd of reporters swarmed about them.

"Rex!" one man shouted. "How does it feel to have finally put an end to the Whipples' reign?"

"Rupert!" shouted another. "Is it true you've been chosen as *The Record*'s Boy of the Year?"

Though the Whipples were too far away to hear the Goldwins' responses, the questions were upsetting enough in themselves. Left alone at the top of the red carpet, Arthur and his siblings looked to their father in dismay.

Mr. Whipple only smiled. "It's all right," he said. "Let the dog have his day. Tonight our sole concern is having fun. You remember *fun*, don't you? It's that thing we used to have before we became completely obsessed with beating the Goldwins. Now, I realize I was largely to blame for that; I have not exactly been 'Mr. Fun' these past months. But tonight, that all changes. Tonight, I am indeed Mr. Fun—no, *Dr.* Fun. Dr. Fun, with a doctorate in Funology. And a master's in Leisure Sciences."

Mr. Whipple gripped his lapel and pulled a comically serious face. "Hey, look," he suddenly exclaimed, pointing through the lobby doors. "With everyone off chasing the Goldwins, there's no wait at the Chocolate Bar! Who wants first bite of a chocolate barstool?"

And with that, he dashed for the doorway.

The Whipple children raced after their father and into the theater lobby, leaving all thoughts of the Goldwins behind them.

● ● ●

When George had finished the last drop of chocolate sauce from the chocolate hip flask he had sneaked into the darkened theater under his jacket, he took a bite of the flask itself, then passed it to Arthur.

After biting off the top corner, Arthur offered a bite to Ruby in the seat to his left, then handed it back to his little brother, who proceeded to pass it to the rest of the Whipple children to his right. As it reached the other end of the row, Mr. Whipple glanced disapprovingly at the chocolaty lump of contraband—then grinned slyly and finished it off in one bite.

A spotlight popped on at center stage to reveal a short,

balding man behind a microphone. Arthur recognized him instantly as "Nonstop" Norman Prattle, the same man who had hosted the Whipple Family Birthday Extravaganza several months earlier.

"Welcome, ladies and gentlemen," said Nonstop Norman in his rich, nasally voice, "to the fifty-eighth World Record World Championships Awards!"

The audience applauded.

"And what a year it's been for world-record breaking, has it not? Let's see. . . ." The announcer scratched his head. "We've had tragic falls, epic rises, villainous treachery, and vulgar scandal . . . and that was just at the Whipples' birthday party!"

The audience hooted with laughter.

Arthur looked to his father, expecting to see a picture of outrage—but to the boy's surprise, his father simply stood from his seat and bowed playfully to the crowd.

The audience laughed even louder.

"That's right folks," shouted Nonstop Norman, "enjoy him while you can—this may be the last we'll ever see of him!"

The laughter swelled again.

Mr. Whipple saluted the announcer with a wry smile, then returned to his seat.

"And there he goes, ladies and gents—a member of a vanishing species: *Whipplus obsoletus*!"

This time, the laughter sounded a bit forced.

"All right—I'd better get on with it then. Wouldn't want

297

the Whipples to sic their sabotaging chef on me, would I? Oh wait—he's off in hiding now, isn't he? Word on the street is he's been taken in by a family of sewer rats—but they're afraid to eat his cooking!"

The crowd fidgeted in their seats. Even they, it seemed, had *some* standards.

"Ahem," coughed Nonstop Norman. "Presenting the first award of the evening, for Extraordinary Achievement in Records of Human Strength—five-time beef-lifting champion and founder of the Prime Cut Butcher Shop and Alternative Gym—Tony Stoutberger!"

• • •

Over the next two hours, a team of celebrity presenters distributed awards in each of the eighty-five IWRF-recognized categories of world-record breaking.

Despite the rather grating comments of the show's host, Arthur and his family managed to enjoy themselves in a way they had never managed to do before. Seeing for the first time that the Championship Cup could be taken from them, the Whipples were all the more grateful for the awards they did receive. Though it was difficult to watch the Goldwins' trainer, Rinaldo Fabroni, win the Human Strength award over their own dear butler, Wilhelm, the Whipples could hardly contain their pride when the award for Extraordinary Achievement in Records of Unsafe Sport went to their son Henry. And while they had to sit through Rupert Goldwin accepting the award for Extraordinary Achievement in Records of Hygiene, and then his sister, Rosalind, being honored for Extraordinary Achievement in Records of Bone Structure, the Whipples also got to watch Beatrice receive the award for Extraordinary Achievement in Records of Food Consumption—and Franklin, for Extraordinary Achievement in Records of Seafaring.

In fact, the Whipples enjoyed themselves so much, that Arthur nearly forgot about all the harrowing ordeals he'd suffered before the awards ceremony had begun. That is, of course, until the award for Extraordinary Achievement in Records of Reaching High-Up Objects went to a certain Royston Goldwin.

Unsurprisingly, Royston was not available to accept the award in person—but Rex happily accepted the award on his son's behalf, explaining that Royston was "traveling abroad at present" and that he expressed his regrets. Arthur and his family did their best not to lose their composure as they watched their rival lie through his teeth into the microphone.

Luckily, the next award was for Extraordinary Achievement in Records of Diverse Disciplines, presented to Arthur's little brother George for Holding Records in More Categories than Anyone Else on Earth. As the Whipples applauded their youngest son's accomplishment, their hearts grew lighter once more.

● ● ●

By the time the show's closing segment arrived, Arthur's family had amassed quite a substantial haul—larger, in fact, than they'd managed to collect at any previous competition. In trying to defeat the Goldwins, it seemed, they had become better competitors in general. It was only a minor consolation, but it did give them some comfort as they prepared themselves for what was to come next.

When all the other awards had been presented, Nonstop Norman approached the microphone one last time. "And now," the host announced, "to present our final— and most prestigious—award of the evening: the World Record World Championship Cup, please welcome—star of *Cleopatra's Cats!* and the upcoming *Song of Salome*— the World's Highest-Paid Actress—Bianca Bainbridge!"

The audience applauded loudly.

Arthur looked down the row at his family and thought about everything that had brought him to this point.

As much as he had enjoyed himself that evening, it was difficult not to focus on his regrets. He wished he could have given his family that last world record they'd needed to win the Championship Cup. He wished he could have known the feeling of holding a world record trophy in his hand. He wished he could go back and do it all differently. . . .

Arthur stopped himself.

True, it had been the most horrifying, heartbreaking day of his life—but, somehow, it had also been the very best. Today, he had been reunited with a true friend, with whom he had outwitted a pair of highly skilled assassins bent on their demise. Today, his family had forfeited their own events to come and rescue him. Today, his father had been truly proud of him, in spite of his recordlessness.

300

Indeed, he had had more wishes granted in one day than he had ever had granted in his entire lifetime. How could he complain about *that*?

Up at the front, a long-legged woman in a diamond-studded gown strode onto the stage. Slowly, a giant golden trophy emerged from an opening at the stage's center.

Perched on a broad wooden pedestal, the Championship Cup stood nearly four feet tall and measured thirty inches wide from one handle to the other. Its finish was so highly polished it appeared to be forged from a golden looking glass rather than any sort of metal.

Arthur's jaw dropped at the sight of it, while the audience oohed and aahed in reverence.

When Bianca Bainbridge approached the microphone, every eye in the theater shifted to her. That the woman was not completely upstaged by the trophy beside her was a powerful tribute to her own beauty and elegance.

The moment she spoke, the crowd fell silent.

"For more than a century," she began in her smooth, sultry voice, "the Championship Cup has been bestowed upon the single Family to Possess More World Records than Any Other Family on Earth. An elite group of persons sharing both a common goal and a common name, the recipients of world-record breaking's highest honor must endure constant toil to earn their title. No competition is fiercer than this. Indeed, many families do not survive the race intact. For the winners, the resulting fame and fortune more than make up for the struggle; for the losers, there is only shame and regret.

In the end, only one family can reign victorious."

The woman held up an envelope.

"It is my privilege to be the first to congratulate them," she smiled. "This year's World Record World Championships champions are . . ."

She slid her slender forefinger under the envelope's seal, revealing the embossed card beneath, amidst the obligatory drum roll.

Though Arthur had largely come to terms with his performance that day, the sound of the drum still managed to churn his stomach. It was hardly suspenseful. Everyone in the audience knew exactly whose name was on the card.

Bianca Bainbridge opened her mouth to speak—but then paused abruptly, squinting at the card in front of her.

Oh no, Arthur thought. *Nobody's told her.*

Miss Bainbridge, being a friend to the Whipples, was clearly shocked to see another family's name printed on the card.

While it was hard not to appreciate her sentiment, Arthur couldn't help but wonder why the WRWC Commission insisted on hiring celebrity presenters who hadn't the slightest interest in what they were presenting.

The actress stood staring at the card for an extended moment—then turned away from the microphone and walked inexplicably toward the wing at stage left.

The crowd murmured loudly.

Arthur slumped down into his seat. *Oh*, he groaned to

302

himself, *how embarrassing.*

It was bad enough he had to live with being the one to lose the cup for his family, but now, to have his failure dragged out like this in front of thousands of people—it was absolute torture.

As Bianca Bainbridge neared the side of the stage, a flustered-looking man with curly gray hair and a purple sash stepped out from the wing to meet her. The pair exchanged alternating looks of concern as they whispered back and forth to one another. After a few moments of this, the actress closed her eyes and nodded. The man, smiling nervously, gestured to the microphone, then followed Miss Bainbridge back to the stage's center.

By this time, the unseen drummer was well on his way to achieving the World's Longest Continuous Drum Roll—and Arthur was feeling every beat of it.

"Do pardon the interruption," Bianca Bainbridge insisted as she returned to the microphone. "Just a bit of a shock, I'm afraid. But I now have official confirmation from Commissioner Helms. And so, with your permission, I shall now resume the announcement."

She held up the card and raised her chin to the balcony.

"The Family to Hold the Most World Records on Earth, and thus, the WRWC Champions are . . ."

The Goldwins rose from their seats.

". . . the Whipples!"

Rex Goldwin and his family had already begun waving at the crowd when the words actually sank in. The gratified

303

expressions fell from their faces, leaving behind stunned outrage.

Arthur and his family exchanged bewildered glances. Mr. Whipple looked to his wife in shock.

Tepid, confused applause rose up from the audience.

Arthur's father slowly rose from his seat and made his way down the row, his face wrinkled with confusion.

At the sight of Mr. Whipple starting for the front, Rex Goldwin leapt into the aisle and darted up the stage steps before his rival could reach them. He stormed onto the stage and charged straight for the man with the purple sash.

"There must be some mistake!" shrieked Rex. "It's the Goldwins who have won the championships, not the Whipples—the Goldwins!"

"I'm sorry, Mr. Goldwin," the commissioner replied calmly. "I'm afraid there is no mistake."

"Look. You've got it wrong here—understand?"

"Mr. Goldwin, I'll have to ask you to leave the stage now—or I shall be forced to summon security."

Rex shaped his mouth into a snarl and took another step forward, then noticed the two hulking men in dark glasses stepping out of the wings on either side of him. He halted his advance and straightened his jacket.

"Very well," he seethed. "But if you insist on proceeding with this nonsense, you will soon find yourselves the target of the Largest Lawsuit Ever Filed! You won't be fit to host a tic-tac-toe tournament by the time I've finished with you!"

With that, Rex spun around and stormed off the stage,

knocking shoulders with Mr. Whipple as he passed him on the stairs. "This is far from over, Charlie," he hissed over his shoulder.

Mr. Whipple, dazed and bewildered, stumbled up the steps and onto the stage, then walked cautiously to the microphone.

His face glowed in the spotlight as he slowly began. "I—I'm afraid I don't know what to say. For once, it seems I am in agreement with Mr. Goldwin. Surely, the Goldwin family—not the Whipples—have won this year's champ-ionships."

Bianca Bainbridge touched Mr. Whipple's elbow and said, "I'm as surprised as you are, Charles—but Commissioner Helms assures me your family is indeed the winner."

"Please, Commissioner," said Mr. Whipple, turning to the man with the purple sash, "I don't understand. The Gold-wins have clearly broken more records than we have. Indeed, we have already come to terms with our loss today and are actually quite satisfied with our efforts here this week—so if this is some kind of prank or a careless error of some sort . . ."

"I assure you, Mr. Whipple," said the commissioner as he approached the microphone, "this is no prank. Perhaps Mr. Prim will be so kind as to explain."

There was some fussing with the curtain, and an awkward moment later Archibald Prim stepped onto the stage. The certifier's brow was so deeply furrowed, his expression could be read from the rear of the topmost balcony.

Mr. Prim strode up to the microphone, cleared his throat, and addressed the crowd. "Really, this is most irregular," he protested. "I have never once been made to explain a

305

decision publicly before. However, if the commission truly requires it, my explanation is thus . . ."

Mr. Prim dabbed his forehead with his handkerchief.

Arthur and his family leaned forward in their seats.

"Near the end of the competition," the certifier began, "I became aware of an additional Whipple world record. Unfortunately, this record took several hours to certify, so an official award for it could not be presented prior to tonight's ceremony. But since the record itself was indeed broken during an official event before the end of competition, it must be included in the standings for the overall championships. The record in question, of course, is for the Highest Number of Unsuccessful Official World Record Attempts, broken this afternoon by one Arthur Whipple."

Arthur's heart froze. What had Mr. Prim just said? The words turned to mush in Arthur's mind. It seemed for a moment he had caught their meaning—but now, he couldn't quite seem to put them together. Surely, Mr. Prim could not have said what he'd thought he had said.

Arthur felt Ruby's hand on his arm. He turned to see a look of surprise and joy on the girl's face.

Arthur's heart jolted back to life. He turned again toward the stage as Mr. Prim continued.

"I have been tracking the Whipple boy's failed attempts as a matter of procedure ever since I was assigned to his family one month ago. Astounded by the boy's extraordinary number of failures, I decided to conduct further research—and discovered him to be quite close to breaking the late Tad Biltmore's record in the same category. When the Whipple boy failed his attempt at knife-block speed stocking earlier today, he officially broke Biltmore's record of 6,391 Official Failures—adding another record to his family's total and tying the Goldwins' score in the competition. Being the boy's first world record, however, this also gave the Whipples the distinction of becoming the Family with the Most World-Record *Holders*, with all fifteen of their family members holding records, as opposed to the Goldwins' total of fourteen. It was this record that broke their overall draw with the Goldwins, further distinguishing the Whipples as The Family to Hold the Most World Records on Earth, and naming them this year's World Record World Championships Champions." Mr. Prim shook his head. "Honestly," he grumbled, "it's so simple, it hardly requires explanation."

Arthur's heart was pounding so hard now, it seemed his ribs would be unable to cage it any longer.

There was a brief moment of stunned silence—and then, the audience erupted into tumultuous applause, the likes of which Arthur had never heard before.

A rush of cool water washed over the boy's soul.

He turned to Ruby. She flung her arms around him and kissed his cheek.

The next moment, he found himself hoisted onto the shoulders of his siblings and paraded into the aisle.

"Arthur! Arthur! Arthur!" they chanted.

The theater leapt to its feet. Smiling faces and clapping hands swirled around him. Arthur's heart soared.

307

As he neared the stage, a warm, familiar face caught his eye.

"You've done it, lad!" his uncle Mervyn called from the edge of the aisle, eyes sparkling with tears. "You've done it!"

Arthur smiled and waved to his godfather—but was promptly whisked up the stage steps and onto the stage.

The Whipple children set Arthur down at the stage's center, where their father waited beside the giant golden trophy.

The crowd hushed.

Mr. Whipple beamed down at Arthur. "Well, my son," he said, "it seems your strengths are rather more *quantifiable* than I had imagined. And here is the proof." He hoisted the Championship Cup off its pedestal. "This . . . belongs to you."

He offered the trophy to his son.

Arthur's hands trembled as he wrapped them around the cup's curved handles. Mr. Whipple released his hold, and Arthur felt the full weight of the cup in his arms. This was no dream.

His father stepped back and gestured to the microphone.

Arthur stepped forward, doing his best to keep the towering trophy from toppling sideways. He rose to his tiptoes and pressed his mouth against the microphone as he looked out at the audience. After a suspenseful pause, Arthur's distorted voice echoed over the loudspeakers.

"Thank you," he said. Then he lowered his heels and stepped away from the microphone.

The crowd roared.

Arthur's father clutched him by the waist and lifted him

off the ground, then sat him on his shoulder. Amidst the clamor, Arthur's mother and siblings gathered around them.

"Well done, my darling!" Mrs. Whipple cried as she embraced her son.

"You did it, Arthur!" shouted Beatrice.

Ivy and her matching toy bear, Mr. Growls, traded high fives with Arthur from their perch on Simon's shoulder. "Wurld wecord! Wurld wecord!" chirped the littlest Whipple.

Cordelia clutched Arthur's ankle and smiled. "It's just like you to wait till the last second to save our skins, isn't it, Arthur?!"

"Better late than never, Brother!" cried Henry. "For the first time in my life I was actually content with losing—but how much better is this?!"

Arthur grinned and looked into the audience.

Amongst the thousands of cheering spectators he spotted many of his heroes and past competitors—all applauding *him*. The Cannibal King, Jump Johnston, the Nakamotos. Even Bonnie Prince Bobo was grinning a big chimpanzee smile and slapping his hairy hands together.

Arthur's gaze then fell on the empty row where his family had sat only moments before. On the far end, Ruby stood on her seat, clapping her hands wildly and whooping at the top of her voice.

Arthur's eyes glistened in the spotlight. All of his dreams had come true. Everything was perfect.

It was then that the stage exploded.

TROPHIES & CATASTROPHES

There was a blinding, deafening blast. The next thing Arthur knew he was flat on his face under a blanket of splinters and soot. He gasped for breath as a fifty-pound stage light crashed into the floorboards five feet from his head.

"Everybody up!" his father's voice bellowed behind him. "Off the stage—now!"

The audience, momentarily stunned by the explosion, now broke into a chorus of screams and shouts as they raced one another for the exits.

"Not again!" cried Nonstop Norman Prattle as he scurried down the stage steps and into the crowd, knocking over an elderly woman on his way.

Arthur glanced behind him to see a massive hole where

the rear quadrant of the stage had been. Smoke and flames poured from the chasm.

Arthur picked himself up off the floor and turned to his family. His parents and older siblings struggled to help the octuplets to their feet amidst fits of coughing and crying. Arthur noticed Charlotte lying on the floor to his right. He grabbed her under her arms and helped her up.

"Come on!" shouted their father. "Let's—"

Another blast shook the theater, knocking the Whipples back to the floor.

"Help!" called a small frightened voice.

Arthur opened his eyes. Clinging to the front edge of the stage before him were two tiny sets of fingers.

"Charlotte!" he yelled, scrambling toward the edge. "Dad—come quick!"

Mr. Whipple sprang to his feet. "Wilhelm—get the little ones down! Mahankali—assist Mrs. Whipple. Henry and Simon—help where you're needed. We'll be just behind you!"

Arthur's father rushed to the front of the stage while Wilhelm scooped the other seven octuplets into his arms and led the rest of the family to the stairs.

Arthur grabbed his little sister's left arm as her legs dangled over the orchestra pit, its floor strewn with abandoned instruments and jagged music stands fifteen feet below.

"Help!" Charlotte cried again, looking up at her brother with eyes full of terror.

"Hold on!" Arthur shouted.

311

He strained to lift her, but their father arrived a moment later, clutching both of Charlotte's arms and pulling her back onto the stage.

"All right, you two," said Mr. Whipple, holding Charlotte to his chest, "let's get out of here!"

They were ten feet from the stairs when the third blast struck. Charlotte spilled from Mr. Whipple's arms as he hit the floor.

Arthur looked up just in time to see a large chunk of the set crash down on his father. "Dad!" he cried.

From beneath the rubble, Mr. Whipple groaned weakly. "Get—get your sister off the stage. . . ."

"But Dad, what about—"

"Arthur, go—now!"

"Daddy!" cried Charlotte.

Arthur turned away from the wreckage and grabbed his sister, then ran for the stairs. "Come on, Charlotte!" he yelled.

As he and Charlotte reached the steps, Henry and two bearded gentlemen—one in a top hat and the other in a bowler—rushed past them.

"Get Dad!" Arthur called to Henry.

"We're on it," Henry replied. "Just get Charlotte down to Wilhelm with the others!"

Arthur nodded and bounded down the stairs, his little sister clasped in his arms.

He caught up with Wilhelm and the rest of the family ten yards up the aisle, then turned with the others to watch the rescue effort taking place atop the stage.

Lighting cans and hunks of scenery rained down around the three rescuers as they struggled to free Arthur's father. Henry and the man with the top hat hefted the fallen piece of set off the floor, while the man with the bowler reached down to grasp hold of Mr. Whipple's arms.

Just as the stranger pulled Arthur's father clear of the debris, another blast sent a lighting rig crashing to the stage in a shower of sparks, obliterating the space where Mr. Whipple had been trapped.

"Charles!" Arthur's mother cried in panic. "Get down here this instant!"

Henry and the benevolent strangers lifted the dazed man to his feet. They now stood on the only section of stage that had not been demolished. One more blast was all it would take.

As Arthur watched the men limp for the stairs, something caught his eye in the private balcony near the curtain at stage right.

There, standing on one of the seats, was a tiny man with a crooked mustache, cursing and pounding his fist on a small black box with a silver antenna.

Arthur's eyes narrowed. "Rayford," he spat. He turned to the others, pointed upward, and shouted, "There—in the opera box! He's got a remote! We've got to stop him!"

Wilhelm glanced overhead and cried, "Mahankali—stay vith the others! Keep them avay from the stage!" Then he dashed down the aisle, leapt onto the giant crimson curtain, and began to climb.

313

At the sight of this, the dwarf let out a shriek and hopped off his chair, then scurried through the doorway at the back of the compartment.

The butler swung himself up and over the balcony railing and chased after him.

Henry and the pair of hat-wearing good Samaritans walked Mr. Whipple down the stage steps as Wilhelm reappeared at the balcony's edge, holding the dwarf in one hand and the remote detonator in the other.

"And just vhere did you think you vere going, mein kleiner Freund?" smiled the butler.

"Put me down, you brute!" screeched the dwarf.

"Very vell," replied the butler. "Let's get down together, shall vee?"

And with that, Wilhelm vaulted over the rail.

"No—wait—what are you doing—you barbariaaaaaaaan!"

A moment later, the butler landed on his feet in the aisle below, the dwarf clutched safely in his arms. Rayford's face, however, had turned several shades paler.

"There vee are," said Wilhelm, setting the little man on the floor beside Henry.

Henry crouched down and grasped Rayford's shoulder. "You might want to think twice before making any more requests of the family you just tried to blow up. I'd say your best bet is to hold still and keep quiet till we can get you to the police. Understand?"

His lip quivering with rage, the dwarf nodded.

314

Just then, the stage's sprinkler system came on behind them and began to put out the scattered flames.

Arthur's parents rushed to meet each other.

"Charles!" cried Mrs. Whipple. "Don't frighten me like that! Are you all right?"

"I'm fine, dear. No more than a scratch."

"Argh," Mrs. Whipple grumbled. "If I never see another stage on fire again, it'll be too soon!"

"Agreed," replied her husband. "I must say, we're still too close to this one for my liking. The crowd certainly seem to have the right idea; shall we join them?" He offered her his arm.

"Please," she said, and took it.

"Come, children," called their father, "we've had enough catastrophe for one evening. Let's get out of here."

Mr. Whipple led the group toward the rear of the still-retreating crowd, then turned to the two men who had helped save his life. "Gentlemen," he said, "it is a rare thing indeed to be the recipient of such selfless heroism— and from complete strangers, no less. I am truly in your debt."

"Don't mention it, my good man," replied the top-hatted gentleman in a cheerful, aristocratic tone. "It's the very least we could do for a chap such as yourself. Though I must tell you—"

At that moment, Arthur noticed a curious sight up ahead. While the rest of the crowd hurried up the aisle and

315

through the lobby doors, one man stood stationary in the shadows.

It took another moment for Arthur to realize the man's identity—and yet another for Arthur to spot the gun in the man's hand.

As Rex Goldwin raised the pistol out of the shadows and aimed it at Mr. Whipple, Arthur cried out at the top of his voice.

"Dad!"

But it was too late. The shot echoed through the auditorium before the man could heed his son's warning.

And yet, Arthur's father did not fall.

The moment Rex squeezed the trigger, something struck his hand and threw the gun from his grasp.

"Leave them alone, Rex!" shouted Ruby, clutching a long-handled pair of opera glasses.

The already retreating crowd screamed and ducked for cover.

Amidst the chaos, Rex glanced to his pistol, lying on the carpet a few yards away—then fixed his eyes on the girl standing between them. "You . . ." he hissed.

Ruby had stared into the eyes of many savage reptiles that day, but none of them could have looked half so cruel as her father's did then.

She raised the metal opera glasses a second time, but Rex swiftly knocked them to the floor. Before she could recover them, Rex struck her across the face with the back of his hand.

"Ruby!" Arthur cried from twenty yards away. He raced toward her, though he knew he would never reach her in time.

The girl fell backward into a row of seats, then crumpled to the floor. Gasping for breath, she watched Rex pick up the opera glasses and step closer. The next moment, he was towering over her, thumping the heavy-framed glasses against his palm.

"After all I've done for you in spite of your obvious defects," Rex sneered, "this is how you repay me? It's time I taught you some gratitude, you little freak. . . ."

He raised the opera glasses into the air—then brought them down with as much force as he could muster. There was a loud *crunch* as the lenses shattered from their frames on impact. Ruby, however, remained unharmed.

When Rex tried to raise the weapon again, he discovered he could not. It was then he noticed the giant hand clasped around the end of it.

Rex turned to see a hulking figure crouching over him.

The figure plucked the metal handle from Rex's grasp as if removing a pinwheel from a petulant child, then opened its massive fist and emptied out the contents. Twisted bits of metal and glass spilled to the floor.

A look of terror came over Rex.

Then, the figure spoke.

"You should know better, Father," said Royston.

Ruby's face filled with surprise at the sound of her brother's voice.

317

And with that, the giant grabbed Rex by the throat and lifted him off the ground.

The dangling man gasped for air, clutching and clawing at Royston's hand. But his son's grip was too strong.

Rex's struggling slowed as his face turned purple.

"Royston," cried Ruby, "Royston, no!"

The giant looked down at his sister, then back up at the bulging, bloodshot eyes of their father.

"You've got to let him down," Ruby pleaded.

Royston closed his eyes and nodded—then began to lower his arm. But before he could return Rex's feet to the floor, a voice called out behind him.

"Stop, villain—in the name of the Law!"

Ruby and her brother spun around to see a team of twelve uniformed policemen burst through the lobby doors and into the aisle.

At the head of the pack strode Inspector Hadrian Smudge.

"Unhand that man at once, Mr. Overkill!" cried Inspector Smudge. "You have already attempted to shoot one innocent man; I shall not let you strangle another!"

At that moment, Arthur and his family rushed up from the opposite direction and halted beside Ruby and Royston.

The giant released his father's throat and Rex fell to the ground, coughing and gasping for breath.

"I," Rex wheezed, "I saw him aim the gun at Charlie, and I tried to stop him—but he's just too big for me. To think he'd turn on his own father. . . ."

318

"His *father?*" the inspector gasped.

"I'm afraid so," coughed Rex. "He—he's out of control, Inspector. Surely you can see why I was too ashamed to admit he was my son. . . ."

"He's lying!" shouted Ruby. "*He's* the one who tried to shoot Mr. Whipple—Royston was only protecting me from *him*!"

"Pardon me, miss," the inspector frowned, "are you not the same girl who, only a few months back, would have had me arrest the prestigious presidents of the Global Guild of Dwarves and Giants simply because you and your friend Angus thought they fit the description of a particular pair of party clowns? Oh, I don't think I'll be taking your advice any time soon. And besides—isn't this precisely what you wanted all along—for these villains Overkill and Undercut to be arrested? I should think a simple 'thank you' might be more in order here."

"But Inspector," cried Arthur, "they were only working for Mr. Goldwin! He's the real culprit!"

"The children speak the truth," said Mr. Whipple. "Mr. Goldwin has clearly been the mastermind from the beginning. Please, Inspector—as the one who hired you in the first place, I beg you—do not arrest the wrong man a second time."

"Mr. Whipple," said the inspector, "I'm afraid the Law cannot be hired or unhired at your every whim. Do you honestly believe you can call it off now, simply because it has chanced to find an offender whom you regard as inconvenient? I doubt

319

you are so naive. Your chef and his associates must pay the price for their misdeeds—and it is my duty to ensure it. Now," he said, turning to the task force behind him, "please take the tall man into custody. You may let Mr. Goldwin go free."

The officers stepped forward and handcuffed Royston—paying no regard to the giant's father.

"No!" cried Arthur. "You don't know what you're doing!"

Mr. Whipple looked helplessly at his son.

"Thank you, Inspector," Rex said coolly, ignoring the boy's outburst. "It's a good thing someone so reasonable was here to protect a man so cruelly slandered and falsely accused as myself. My daughter, unfortunately, is a very troubled girl. Seems she'll say anything for a bit of attention—no matter who it harms. Perhaps a bit of attention from her father will finally straighten her out."

Rex held his hand at his side, clenching it so tightly it began to shake.

Arthur looked to Ruby with a desperate glance. After all their hard work, Rex Goldwin had managed to escape justice once again. There would be no one to protect Ruby from his retribution. Arthur's heart sank. He had never felt so powerless.

"Please, Mr. Goldwin," the inspector insisted, "I am happy to do my part in the molding and instruction of today's youth. It pains me to see someone of your position saddled with such defiantly wayward offspring. You, sir, are free to go."

320

The inspector gestured toward the exit.

"Not so fast, Smudge!" came a voice from the crowd.

At that moment, the bearded man in the top hat leapt into the center of the aisle.

The inspector, as well as the surrounding crowd, reeled around in surprise. It was then that the bearded man in the top hat tore off his beard and top hat.

"Greenley!" cried the inspector. "What on earth are you doing here—and in that ridiculous costume?! Have I not made it clear you were to stop purchasing those dreadful things?"

"You have indeed, sir," said D.S. Greenley. "I'm afraid, however—you will have to come with me."

"What?!" squealed the inspector. "Go with you where?"

"To the station, sir."

"To the station?! Have you gone mad? How dare you speak to me this way, you insolent little cuss!"

"My apologies, Inspector—but I'm afraid you've been under investigation by the Yard's Inspector Inspection Squad for some time now."

"What the devil are you talking about?!"

"I hate to say it, sir, but it seems your record for Most Solved Cases in History has been achieved through unlawful means. The IIS have discovered that in each of your cases for the past decade, you have ignored vital evidence in order to make a quick arrest—instead of diligently pursuing the truth. Indeed, it appears you've broken a new record, sir—for Most Innocent People Wrongly Convicted."

321

"Preposterous!" cried Inspector Smudge. "I'll not have my conduct appraised by some insignificant sergeant—a sergeant who, I might remind you, is meant to be my assistant!"

"I understand it makes for an awkward situation, sir—but I'm afraid neither of us has any choice in the matter. Top brass, you see, have personally ordered me to inform you of the charges and bring you in."

"You ungrateful little rat!" the inspector snarled.

"Oh, on the contrary, sir," said Greenley. "I truly appreciate all you've done for me these past months. Indeed, I've learned more from you than you know."

He retrieved a pair of handcuffs from his coat.

Inspector Smudge's eyes grew wide. He froze for a moment like a hunted fox—then whirled around and fled back up the aisle.

He had not taken two steps, however, before he was stopped and seized by the wall of uniformed officers he had commanded only a moment earlier.

Greenley took hold of the inspector's arms and slapped the first cuff onto his wrist.

"No!" the inspector whimpered. "I've done nothing wrong! I'm innocent!"

Greenley sighed. "You can't hide from the Law, sir." He clapped the other cuff shut and announced, "Inspector Hadrian Ulysses Smudge—I am arresting you on suspicion of criminal negligence and perverting the course of justice."

"This is outrageous!" cried the inspector. "I can't be

322

arrested! I am the recipient of the Golden Magnifying Glass Award!"

Greenley shrugged. "I reckon the Academy of Qualified Award Givers will be wanting that back, sir." He transferred his hold on the captive's wrists to a nearby officer and said, "Take him away, lads."

A pair of policemen escorted Smudge through the small crowd of brave theatergoers and intrepid reporters that had gathered around the commotion.

Greenley then turned to Ruby's father, who had begun inching his way into one of the rows. "Now, as for you, Mr. Goldwin," he said, "I'm afraid you're not going anywhere."

The sergeant nodded, and a second pair of policemen closed in and handcuffed Rex, who immediately began struggling against his bonds.

"What do you think you're doing?!" Rex shouted. "You have no idea who you're dealing with here! I'll have your badge!"

"Rex Goldwin," Greenley said calmly, "you are under arrest for the attempted murder of Charles Whipple, as well as multiple counts of conspiracy, aggravated assault, sabotage, fraud . . ."

At that moment, Rita Goldwin pushed her way through the crowd to see her husband in handcuffs. "What—what's happening?! Rex!"

The Goldwin children arrived beside their frantic mother as Greenley turned to her and said, "Ah, Mrs. Goldwin—

323

glad you could join us. Lads—you can go ahead and put the bracelets on this one as well."

Two more policemen stepped forward and flanked Rita Goldwin, whose face filled with panic.

"Wait—why are you arresting *me*?!" she shrieked as the officers clapped a matching set of handcuffs around her wrists. "I had nothing to do with any of Rex's business dealings!"

"That remains to be seen, Mrs. Goldwin. But in the meantime, we have a charge that will more than suffice." Greenley touched his fingertips together and narrowed his eyes. "This morning, you see, I had a chat with a friend of your husband's—a Mr. Neil McCoy: the infamous forgery expert. As it happens, Mr. McCoy has been the focus of a longstanding Scotland Yard investigation—which has only just yesterday been brought to a successful close. Though we've known of your husband's connection to McCoy for some time now, we've as yet been unable to glean the precise nature of their dealings. That is—until today. In exchange for a reduced sentence on his other forgery convictions, Mr. McCoy has provided us with copies of a certain series of documents he's been commissioned to produce for your family over the years—the first dating back nearly two decades and the last, not quite twelve months."

From the inside of his jacket, Greenley retrieved a large Manila envelope—out of which he produced a small stack of official-looking documents. "Namely, these birth certificates here," he said. "Now—I asked myself—why should anyone want to forge their children's birth certificates? At first, I figured it was simply to cheat on various age-based world records or some other petty offense. You can imagine my surprise, then, to discover that the dates on these certificates correspond to the birth dates of nine missing children, each of whom was abducted from a different hospital shortly after birth."

Rita Goldwin's face went white.

"And that's when it struck me," declared Greenley. "The couple I'd been investigating for a simple bit of forgery were in fact the infamous Maternity Ward Marauders, whom law enforcement agencies across the world have been struggling to apprehend for the past seventeen years."

The crowd gasped.

The faces of the Goldwin children filled with confusion.

"No . . ." murmured their mother.

"According to these certificates, madam," the detective continued, "it would seem that nine of your twelve children are not your children at all. And so, it should come as no surprise to hear the following: Rita Anne Goldwin, in collaboration with your husband, Reginald Richard Goldwin, you are under arrest for the kidnapping of . . ." Holding up the certificates, the detective called off each birth name as he flipped through the stack. ". . . Johan Maarten Van der Meer . . . Astrid Oda Skoglund . . . Francois Louis Moreau . . . Sally Jane Peterson . . . Vladimir Pavlovich Ivanov . . . Jurgen Lukas Müller . . . Kasper Marek Jankowski . . . Dominique Marie Dubois . . . and Nigel Thomas Winterbottom."

"No, please," cried Rita Goldwin. "My babies!"

"I'm sorry, ma'am—but they were never yours to keep. They have been terribly missed, these children you've stolen. Think of all the misery their parents have been made to suffer these past years."

"Those people never deserved them!" Rita snarled. "These children would have been nothing without us! You're so worried about their parents' misery—but what about their own? Rupert would have been a turnip farmer if we hadn't saved him; Roland would have been forced to take over the family cabinetmaking business; and Rowena was destined to become a schoolteacher! Now *that* is misery! You can't subject them to such a cruel fate—I won't let you!"

Rita lunged at Sergeant Greenley with her fingernails—but was easily restrained by the officers. Her spirit broken, she collapsed in their grasp and began to sob.

Greenley offered Rita his handkerchief, then turned to the officers and said, "Take her to the car, lads."

The Goldwin children looked to one another in shock and disbelief as the men carried the woman they called "mother" from the theater.

Ruby stepped forward.

"Sergeant Greenley," she said with wide eyes, "does one of those birth certificates belong to me?"

The detective placed a hand on Ruby's shoulder. "I'm sorry, luv," he said. "I'm afraid yours is the real thing. Yours—and those of your two brothers: Rayford and

Royston. It would appear the three of you are in fact the only actual children of Rex and Rita Goldwin."

Ruby's eyes dimmed. "I see."

Arthur stepped up beside her and put his hand on her other shoulder.

Rex sneered. "Don't look so disappointed, *Daughter*."

Rayford pulled against Wilhelm's grip and blurted, "I told you we were the special ones, Sis! You should have believed me! We would have been unstoppable!"

"Oh, I almost forgot," said Greenley, turning to the dwarf. "Rayford Goldwin, I am arresting you for multiple counts of attempted murder, sabotage, conspiracy, and kidnapping. Looks as though prison is to be quite the family affair."

One of the officers took the dwarf from the butler, handcuffed him, and proceeded to escort him outside.

"I'd do it all again, Father," Rayford cried over his shoulder, "if only to hear I'd made you proud!"

Rex Goldwin said nothing.

The lobby doors swung shut.

D.S. Greenley turned to the giant. "Royston, though it pains me to do so after what you did for your sister, I'm afraid I've no choice but to arrest you on the same grounds as your brother."

"I understand, sir," said the giant. He lowered his head and held out his hands.

"Very well then," Greenley replied. "Royston Goldwin, I am placing you under arrest for multiple counts of

327

attempted murder, sabotage, conspiracy, and kidnapping."

Two policemen stepped forward to flank the giant. Royston nodded to Ruby, then turned and walked with them up the aisle.

Ruby watched her brother until he disappeared into the lobby.

The Goldwin children stirred restlessly.

"Is it really true, Dad?" asked Rosalind. "Are we adopted?"

Rex stared at the floor.

"Come on, Dad," said Roland, "tell me those two aren't really Rayford and Royston. This is all just some sort of joke, right?"

Rex, whose head had sunk lower and lower with every moment since his arrest, now looked up from under his brow and glared at the detective. "Bravo, Sergeant. You have succeeded in destroying everything I have ever created. How does it feel to break up the World's Most Perfect Family?"

He turned to his children and sighed. "Yes, children— I'm afraid it's true. But I promise you, everything I did was for the sake of our family. I only wanted to make ours the very best in all the world. That's hardly a crime, is it?" Rex's attempt at a sympathetic expression came off as merely pathetic. "When Rita first gave birth to those two mutants," he continued, gesturing to the lobby doors, "we could hardly take them out in public with us, now could we? Yes, we wanted to be a record-breaking family—but not like that. And of course, we couldn't risk having any more freakish children, so we simply selected a few perfect specimens and then took you off the hands of your unremarkable, undeserving parents. And look what we made of you! We should have just kept going, but after we'd successfully adopted Roland, Rosalind, Rupert, and Roxy, Rita got the bright idea we should try to have another 'natural' child. This time we were blessed with a fourteen-toed misfit." He nodded at Ruby. "Of course, she wasn't quite as bad as the first two—at least we could keep those hideous feet covered up—but that was the last time I was going to leave the fate of my children up to 'nature.' Rita went back to wearing her collection of false pregnant bellies as we waited to bring our next child home. . . ."

Arthur looked to Ruby. "Guess those weren't clown costumes after all," he whispered.

"Guess not," she said. "Who'd have thought the real explanation could be weirder than *that*?"

Rex sighed. "We kept collecting until we figured we had enough record breakers to dethrone the 'legendary' Whipples. My only regret is not collecting a few more of you. . . . Well, that—and not murdering every last Whipple when I had the chance."

Rupert Goldwin groaned with impatience. "So what's to happen to us then?" he demanded. "Hold on," he added excitedly, "does this mean we'll get the house to ourselves?"

Greenley gave a reassuring smile. "Not to worry, lad— we'll make certain you won't have to live alone. At this very

329

moment, agents from the ASRCAI are waiting outside the theater. They'll have each of you reunited with your respective birth families in no time—just as soon as you complete the mandatory ninety-day deprogramming camp. Just think, Rupert—before you know it, you'll be back on your family's turnip farm, gearing up for your first harvest!"

The full weight of Rupert's situation seemed to strike him for the first time. The hopeful expression drained from his face.

Just then, a large piece of the set crashed to the stage behind them. Though the stage's sprinkler system had doused most of the fire by now, several sections of the structure still appeared dangerously unstable.

"Come on then," said Greenley. "Let's get ourselves outside, shall we? Nobody's going to get to enjoy their new turnip farm if the roof comes down on our heads."

• • •

The Goldwin children made their way through the crowd of shell-shocked patrons and out to the street, where uniformed agents wrapped them with woolen blankets and ushered them into a van marked AGENCY FOR THE SAFE-KEEPING AND RESTORATION OF CHILDREN ABDUCTED AS INFANTS.

Arthur watched as Rupert (aka Francois Louis Moreau) took one last look around him, hung his head, and climbed through the van door. Even after all the torment the Goldwin boy had made him suffer, Arthur couldn't help but feel just a little bit sorry for him.

330

As the ASRCAI van pulled away, Greenley opened the rear door of an awaiting squad car and loaded Rex Goldwin inside.

The rage in Rex's eyes had now been replaced by a heavily glazed stare.

"There was only ever room for one of us at the top, wasn't there, Charlie?" he muttered. "And why shouldn't it have been me? All I've ever wanted is absolute perfection—is that too much to ask? Surely, it's no less than I deserve. Have you any idea how difficult it is to succeed when you're constantly surrounded by lesser individuals? And yet, look how close I came to winning it all. . . ." He snorted and turned to Arthur. "Who'd have thought your little failure of a son would be the one to ruin all my years of hard work?"

"Now now, Rex," Mr. Whipple replied. "Surely, even you can see there's only one failure here now—and it's certainly not any member of *my* family. Let's see here: you've failed as a world-record breaker, you've failed as a kidnapper, you've failed as a murderer—and you've failed as a father. I wonder what the Ardmore Association will think about so much failure in their one perfect champion? I should say you're due for a rather drastic demotion after this. But I guess you won't have to worry much about that where you're going, will you, Mr. Goldwin?"

Arthur's father paused.

"Or should I call you . . . the *Treasurer*?"

Rex's eyes snapped toward him.

Mr. Whipple smiled. "What ever did happen to the

331

Treasurer before you, Rex? Did you do the same to your predecessor as you tried to do to me?"

Rex Goldwin's ever-deepening scowl suddenly melted away. "Well, well, Charlie," he said with a sly grin. "You've really figured it all out, haven't you? The Association's board of directors was crazy to ever go up against *you*; they just never had a chance, did they?"

There was something unnerving in Rex's tone. Something that made his capture seem somehow like less of an accomplishment.

But before Mr. Whipple could inquire further, Rex simply said, "Oh well. Have a nice life, Charlie." He gave a smug final salute with his fettered right hand, then slid to the far side of the seat and stared out the opposite window.

The group stepped away from the car, and Arthur's father turned to the detective with a long sigh of relief.

"Well, Sergeant," he said, "I really can't thank you enough for all you've done here. If not for you, we should still be at the mercy of that madman."

"Just doing my duty, sir. If you'd like to thank somebody, thank your boy and his mate Ruby there. They're the ones who brought the clues to my attention and set the whole thing in motion. Surely, there'd have been no case without them."

"Indeed, Sergeant," agreed Mr. Whipple. "I owe them more than I can say." He looked to the two children and smiled. "I only hope I may yet prove it to them."

Just then, a shrill voice at their backs caused the group to whirl around.

332

The Goldwin twins, Rayford and Royston, approached the curb with a trio of policemen and stood waiting for transport.

The dwarf did not appear happy.

"This is all your fault, Roy!" he shrieked up at this brother. "If not for your repeated failures, we'd be holding the Championship Cup ourselves now, instead of being hauled off to jail! How is it possible that someone with such elite training can make so many idiotic blunders!"

The giant opened his mouth to speak—but the dwarf cut him off before he could say the first word.

"Oh, save it, Roy," Rayford snapped. "What makes you think anyone wants to hear what you've got to say? You've made a mess of every single task you've been given since the day we left our secret bunker on the Compound! First, it was the birthday party, where—despite having a doctorate in Explosives Rigging—you couldn't manage to get a few oversized birthday candles to actually fall at the *same time*. Then, it was the Unsafe Sports Showdown. There you are, a certified Deadshot in foot archery—and yet, the moment you're called on to take out one defenseless boy, you can't be bothered to hit a single lousy organ! And tell me—what *did* happen the night of the Komodo plot? The plan was to release Ridgely as soon as one of the Whipples passed by—but by the time you'd let go of his tail, the girl had already spotted him, run to a nearby Sim-o-Tree and begun to climb it! Did you suddenly forget everything we'd ever learned in Animal Assassins 201? Professor Wilde would

333

be mortified; you were his star pupil, for crying out loud!"

"Listen, Ray," said the giant. "I wasn't—"

"Listen Ray nothing!" screeched the dwarf. "You've lost the privilege to even address me! Because despite all your prior ineptitudes, none of them can even begin to compare with the utter incompetence you've demonstrated today! This morning, you were charged with the simple task of locking two kids in a cage—and yet, somehow, they were able to escape without so much as one self-severed limb! I wonder—did you even bother to lock the lock? It's a good thing I sent you for the car while I emptied the Lizard Lounge into the tunnel, or your blundering would surely have made it even easier for them!"

With that, he turned to Arthur and Ruby.

"Just look at those two," he sneered. "Does it not make you sick to see them here now—happy and free—cheating Mother and Father out of their rightful victory and splitting our family apart? But then, it's difficult to tell if you care about this family at all, when you're told to guard the rear exits to prevent our enemies from escaping—and you end up assaulting our own dear father instead! Honestly, Roy—what sort of son and henchman are you, anyway? All I can say is: you'd better watch your back, Brother. I've got friends on the inside; I'll be leader of the Dwarven Brotherhood in no time. And don't think the GGDG will protect you; I've got half the board in my pocket! Oh, you'll pay for your failures, Brother. You'll pay dear—"

But before Rayford could finish this last word, the giant

simply cocked back his leg and kicked the dwarf through the open door of the awaiting squad car.

Arthur and Ruby couldn't help but giggle.

Rayford collided with his handcuffed father on the car's far side, before landing flat on his back in the empty seat beside him.

"Watch yourself, you little mutant!" snarled Rex.

"So sorry, Father," the dwarf whimpered as he struggled to right himself. "I hope I haven't hurt you. Oh, do forgive me."

Back on the pavement, the giant tilted his head to face his little sister and the two locked eyes for a moment. Slowly, Royston's mouth revealed a faint smile, but his eyes remained sad as he looked back at the outraged dwarf now sitting upright in the back of the squad car.

"How dare you!" Rayford screeched at him. "You've just crossed the wrong dwarf, Brother! You're a dead man! Do you hear me, Royston? You're—"

Just then, the attending officer snapped the door shut in Rayford's face and climbed into the driving seat. A moment later, the car started up and lurched forward into the street.

As Arthur and the others watched the car pull away from the theater, they could see the enraged dwarf jumping up and down in the rear window, shouting back at them at the top of his lungs—his screeches heard by no one but his father and the poor policeman tasked with transporting the two villains to jail.

Shortly after the car disappeared from view, the van

arrived that would convey Rayford's giant brother to a similar destination.

"All right then, Royston," sighed Greenley. "That'll be your ride, I'm afraid."

The giant nodded. He stepped forward, then turned back to face Mr. Whipple.

"I am sorry, sir," the giant said in a deep but clear voice, "for the terrible harm I have inflicted on your family. I knew it was wrong what we were doing; I wanted to stop it. I should have found my voice sooner. They—they were all the family I had. But I should have stood up to them." He shifted his gaze to the ground. "For all my size, I'm afraid—I just wasn't big enough."

Mr. Whipple looked up into the giant's face.

"Your crimes are serious indeed," he sighed, "there is no question. Many of those I love have suffered dearly at your hand. And yet, today, that same hand has saved your sister from a brutal beating—and saved me from a second bullet. I cannot say for certain, but I imagine that counts for something. It's up to you to decide the sort of work your hands will do from now on. Will it be of the former sort—or of the latter?" Mr. Whipple took in a deep breath, then slowly exhaled. "Indeed Royston, it seems today may prove to be a turning point for more than one of us."

Royston pondered these words a moment, then, giving a nod to Mr. Whipple, turned and ducked through the rear door of the van. Once he'd managed to fold himself inside it, the giant's frame nearly filled the entire rear compartment.

336

Royston shared one last look with his sister, raising his cuffed hands in an attempted wave before the driver shut the door behind him.

Ruby watched in silence as the van drove away and vanished into the night.

Arthur put a hand on her shoulder. "Seems he wasn't just another mute ogre after all," he said.

"No," said Ruby. "No, he wasn't."

After some moments had passed, D.S. Greenley stepped up alongside her. "Well, Miss Goldwin," he said, "seeing as you're the only one in your family who's not been a victim of baby snatching or been placed under arrest, it seems you've no place to go. I'm afraid we'll have to take you to the orphan shelter for now, until we can figure out a more permanent arrangement. But not to worry; it's not half as bad as you may think. I try and volunteer once a month myself—putting on original one-acts for the orphan kids and offering free acting lessons for some of the more imaginative ones. In all my time there, I've only witnessed three stabbings and two medium-sized riots—all of them occurring right in the middle of my performances, oddly enough. Just their way of crying for help, of course—poor little buggers. But no, it's a fine place. I reckon you'll really—"

"I don't think that will be necessary, Detective Sergeant," interrupted Mr. Whipple. "We've got plenty of room for Miss Goldwin at our house—that is, if she would do us the honor of staying with us."

"I don't know, Mr. Whipple," she smirked, "after all

337

Greenley's said about the orphan shelter, it's a tough choice, really. Of course, I'd hate to take any honor away from the Whipples by declining such a generous invitation. . . ."

"Very well then," smiled Mr. Whipple. "It's settled. You'll stay with us for as long as you like. It's the least I can do for the girl who saved my life."

Greenley laughed. "Well, how do you like that? Couldn't have come up with a better scenario myself. All's well that ends well, eh?"

"Indeed, Sergeant," said Arthur's father, his face growing suddenly stern. "There is, however, one final matter which has yet to be resolved—and requires our urgent attention. Now we've proved Rex and his sons are to blame for the sabotage, we really must—"

"Say no more, Mr. Whipple," Greenley interjected. "I believe I've just the man to help settle such a matter."

The detective donned a strange smirk, then turned to face the nearby crowd of onlookers.

"Mr. Smythe," he called out, "perhaps you'd like to formally introduce yourself."

Out of the crowd stepped the bowler-wearing gentleman who had aided the detective in protecting the Whipples during the stage explosion.

"Fank you, Sergeant," said the stranger. "I'd be much obliged."

And with that, the bearded man with the bowler removed his beard and bowler.

"'Aven't forgot about your old chef, 'ave you?" smiled the man.

"Sammy!" shouted the Whipple children.

Arthur's heart nearly burst with joy.

"My goodness!" cried Mr. Whipple, rushing forward and embracing the man. "Is it really you, old boy?"

"I can 'ardly believe it meself," grinned the chef. "'Acquitted of all wrongdoing,' says Greenley 'ere. Free as a bloomin' bird, I am!"

"He was a hard man to track down, your chef," chuckled the sergeant, "but I am not without my connections in the underworld. Turns out the chap who played Lord Capulet when I was Mercutio now runs a sort of underground answering service and was able to get a series of messages to Mr. Smith for me. After I relayed to him the evidence condemning Mr. Goldwin, along with details of the case against Inspector Smudge, Mr. Smith kindly agreed to join me for my little production of 'The Big Reveal' this evening. Little did I know, he'd wind up risking his own life to help save you lot from an exploding stage!"

"Please, Sergeant," said the chef, grinning bashfully. "It were all my pleasure, I assure you."

Mr. Whipple's smile grew strained, then faded. He let out a low sigh. "I'm so sorry I ever doubted you, Sammy. It's absolutely inexcusable the way I've acted— and I can't say I don't deserve it if you never forgive me."

Sammy the Spatula smiled. "It's all right, guv. I've missed you lot as well. And I know it weren't you who done me in.

339

No—that were Smudge and that Goldwin dog, weren't it? And them two are all taken care of now, ain't they?"

At this, Mrs. Whipple ran in and wrapped her arms around the man. "Oh, we've been utterly lost without you, Sammy," she cried. "I've been doing the cooking!"

"Well, that is ravver drastic, ain't it, Mrs. Whipple?" the chef said with a wink. "But you'll not 'ave to ever worry about that again, now I'm back. I've used me time in 'iding to write a cookbook filled wiv all sorts of new recipes for colossal cuisine. I can 'ardly wait to get back in me kitchen and start giving 'em a go!"

The Whipple children's faces all lit up.

"But before I run away wiv meself 'ere," Sammy continued, "there's somefing I got to say."

He turned and walked directly to Arthur and Ruby, who stood admiring the reunion from a few steps away. "Don't believe we've officially met, miss," he said, offering his hand to Ruby. "Sammy the Spatula."

"Ruby Goldwin," she said, smiling.

"Pleasure," said Sammy with a nod before turning to the boy beside her. "I knew I could count on you, Arfur. Greenley says you and your mate 'ere were the only ones 'oo still believed in ol' Sammy, even after everyfing what happened, eh?"

Arthur blushed, and Sammy's eyes grew watery.

"You are an extraordinary lad indeed," sniffed the chef. "If you ever need anyfing—anyfing at all—just say the word, mate. I owe you me bleedin' life, I do."

340

He wiped his eyes and grinned. Then he held out his hand, and Arthur promptly shook it.

"It's good to have you back, Sammy," said Arthur. "We'd have fought for you forever." A smile crept onto the boy's face. "Though I can't say my mother's cooking had nothing to do with that."

Everybody laughed.

"Fair enough, lad," grinned the chef. "I've surely done far less admirable fings for the sake of me own stomach!"

When the laughter had died down, D.S. Greenley turned to Sammy and said, "Well, Mr. Smith, on behalf of Scotland Yard, allow me to formally apologize once again for your treatment over the past few months. You can rest assured Inspector Smudge will be held accountable for his actions. I sincerely hope you'll develop a better opinion of the Yard in future."

"Most definitely, Sergeant," Sammy replied. "You 'ave truly given me new faiff in the law."

Greenley's eyes lit up. "Have I? Well, thank you for saying so. I do my best, of course, but it's hard to know sometimes if I'm really making a difference out there."

"Absolutely," Sammy insisted. "Keep up the good work, mate."

"Indeed I will," the detective said, grinning proudly. He took a deep contented breath, then turned to Arthur's father. "Now, Mr. Whipple, if you and your wife would just come with me for a moment so I can get a proper statement, we'll be done with all this mess and you can enjoy the rest of your evening."

341

"Of course, Sergeant."

Arthur's parents followed the detective toward one of the parked squad cars, while the octuplets bombarded Sammy with questions about the perils of life in the underground.

Arthur turned to talk to Ruby for the first time since the award ceremony had begun. "Phew," he exhaled. "Quite a day, hmm?"

"Yeah," said Ruby, "I think that might be the World's Biggest Understatement."

Arthur smiled. Over Ruby's shoulder, he then noticed a man with laser-parted hair striding toward them. In one hand, the man carried a neat stack of papers, which he pored over as he walked. In the other, he carried a moderately sized golden trophy.

"Ah, there you are, Arthur Whipple," said Archibald Prim as the pair turned to face him. "Here is the trophy for your recent record, young man—directly from the engravers." Then he handed him the trophy.

Arthur marveled at the weight of it. So this was what a world record felt like.

"Thank you, Mr. Prim," he said.

"Yes," replied the certifier. "I left as soon as the final award had been presented in order to fetch it for you. My apologies for the delay. So many items to check and recheck and check again, you understand." He looked to his watch. "Yes, well—I must be off. Next year's paperwork will not complete itself, now will it? I shall see you and your family

342

tomorrow." Mr. Prim peered over the children's heads for the first time. "Oh," he said. "Is the theater on fire?"

"I'm afraid it is, Mr. Prim," said Arthur.

"Well, who ever let that happen? I shall have to have a serious talk with the safety director—he is clearly in violation of his contract here!"

And with that, Archibald Prim stormed off in search of the man soon to be known as the *former* safety director.

Arthur's eyes followed the certifier as he departed.

"Kind of hard to believe, really," said Arthur. "I'd have never imagined I'd receive my first world record because of *him*."

"Life's funny that way, I think," said Ruby. "Never works out quite how you'd expect."

Arthur nodded.

Their gaze then fell on the trophy. Its mirrored finish and curved handles gave it a look not unlike a smaller sibling of the Championship Cup itself. Inscribed on the base below Arthur's name were the words: HIGHEST NUMBER OF UNSUCCESSFUL OFFICIAL WORLD RECORD ATTEMPTS (6,392).

"Shiny, isn't it?" said Ruby.

"Yeah," Arthur agreed. "Somehow it's even better than any of the trophies I ever imagined . . . probably because it's *real*."

Ruby smiled. "You've earned it, Arthur. Let me be first to congratulate you on what is sure to be the first in a vast collection of trophies with your name on them."

343

Arthur flashed a smile, then turned to Ruby with an earnest expression. "Hey," he said. "Thanks for saving my dad's life. And sorry about . . . you know, your family."

"Oh . . . yeah," said Ruby. "It's all right. At least I know the truth now. I mean, I've always suspected something wasn't quite right—in a way, it's nice to find out I wasn't just losing my mind, you know? I think that's all I ever really wanted. . . . Well, maybe not *all* I ever wanted. It's going to be hard to accept the fact that my real family isn't out there waiting for me somewhere. But, you know—*mostly* all."

"Well," replied Arthur, "for what it's worth—I mean, I know it's not the same thing—but there's a family waiting for you here now . . . if you want it."

Ruby smiled. "Yes. I think I'd like that."

Arthur smiled back. "Couldn't hurt to have a second junior detective on hand, what with all these mysteries that keep sprouting up around my family." He scratched the side of his head. "You know, we never found out exactly how Rex became the new treasurer, did we?"

The sly sparkle returned to Ruby's eyes. "Consider it priority one for Detectives Whipple and Goldwin," she said, tucking her hair behind her ear. "Now that we're no longer under constant attack by clown assassins, we should have a lot more time for detective work. If you're not too busy fending off all your new record breaker fans, of course."

"Of course," Arthur said with a smirk.

His parents returned a moment later to gather up their family and friends.

Wilhelm and Mr. Mahankali shared laughs with Sammy the Spatula, while Mrs. Waite stood looking on with tears in her eyes.

"Come on, Mrs. Waite," Sammy said as he noticed her crying. "Dry your eyes, luv. No 'arm done. I'm back now—and you and me 'ave the privilege of working for the Greatest Family in the World!"

"I know," sniffled the housekeeper. "I'm just so . . . happy!" And with that, she burst into tears all over again.

"Ah, Mrs. Waite," Sammy chuckled as he hugged her and patted her back. "There, there, luv."

Everyone smiled at the housekeeper's unguarded outpouring, and some wiped away tears of their own.

Mr. Whipple took a deep breath and cleared his throat. "Surely, it's been an emotional day for all of us; I'd say we deserve a bit of a treat, wouldn't you? So," he announced, "in honor of Arthur's first world record and our subsequent championships victory, as well as to celebrate Sammy's freedom—and to apologize for hiring an immoral inspector who falsely accused him of sabotage, threw him in jail, and nearly had him shot and drowned—I've booked us the Myriad Room at P.T. Evermor's Infinite Spoon. They'll be expecting us shortly."

"Yay!" cried the octuplets. (Home to the Largest and Most Diverse All-One-Can-Eat Smorgasbord on Earth, P.T. Evermor's had long been the Whipple children's favorite restaurant.)

Arthur's stomach grumbled with joy. After a day of foiling

345

kidnappers, escaping lethal lizards, surviving explosions, and breaking world records, he had worked up quite an appetite.

• • •

The Whipples returned home well after midnight, having had more than their fill of food, drink, and all-around merriment.

Cordelia lent Ruby a set of her nightclothes and showed her to one of the guest rooms, where Arthur and his family bid each other a most joyous goodnight, then retired to their respective bedchambers.

Once in his room, Arthur placed his new trophy on the bedside table, changed into his pajamas, and got into bed. He took a long, disbelieving look at the golden statue beside him, then switched off the lamp.

For several minutes he simply lay in the dark, smiling.

And then, Arthur Whipple slept the best sleep of his life.

18

THE DAY AFTER YESTERDAY

WHIPPLES WIN!
AT WRWC AWARDS CEREMONY, WHIPPLES DEFEAT ARTIFICIALLY CONSTRUCTED SUPER FAMILY, SURVIVE EXPLOSIVE REVENGE PLOT, DELIVER MATERNITY WARD MARAUDERS TO AUTHORITIES—ALL THANKS TO PREVIOUSLY RECORDLESS SON

The Whipple family celebrated their fourth consecutive win at the World Record World Championships Sunday night—but it was almost not to be.

The Championship Cup had been universally expected

to go to the Goldwin family, until it was revealed the Whipples' then-recordless son, Arthur, had managed to break the record for Highest Number of Unsuccessful Official World Record Attempts in the competition's final event.

It was during the Whipples' acceptance of the top prize that a series of explosions destroyed much of the stage and hurled the theater into chaos.

Luckily, the alleged saboteur—publicly concealed son of the Goldwins Rayford Goldwin—was identified and detained before any more explosives could be detonated, and no one was killed in the blast.

Soon afterward, the suspect's father, Rex Goldwin, fired a pistol shot at the stage, just missing Charles Whipple—and was promptly apprehended himself.

Shockingly, Goldwin and his wife, Rita, were then charged with the kidnapping of nine newborn children over the past seventeen years—revealing the couple to be the fugitives commonly known as the Maternity Ward Marauders.

The stolen children, selected for their perfect scores on the Igor Test (which assigns a numerical value to the quality of each body part in a newborn), were then raised as the Goldwins' own. The abductees would ultimately account for three-quarters of the Goldwin brood, making the Whipples' victory even more remarkable, considering the hand-picked nature of their rivals.

It was Scotland Yard's Detective Sergeant Callum Greenley who uncovered the plot and made the arrests.

"It's a relief to see the curtain finally close on this case," said Greenley. "Of course, it was hardly a one-man show. There were many players involved in reaching this finale and I am proud to have played but a supporting role. I can only hope my supporting role as Raffers in the Little Orb's production of *East End Tale* goes half as well."

As to the involvement of the Ardmore Association in the Goldwins' plot, Greenley added, "That investigation is ongoing. I can only say we suspect the Association had some part to play in all this—and that we've reason to believe Mr. Goldwin has in fact been on the Ardmore Board of Directors for many years, succeeding the deceased Bartholomew Niven as their new treasurer. Indeed, Goldwin is currently the prime suspect in Niven's murder, given his clear motive for the crime. Due to the board's highly secretive nature, this will not be an easy inquiry to make—but we shall continue to pursue it for as long as it takes to uncover the truth."

Malcolm Boyle, chief legal representative for the Ardmore Association, was quick to deny any such collaboration on the part of his clients.

"The Ardmore Association is shocked and appalled to hear of the purported actions of Mr. Goldwin and his accomplices. Though it's true the Association has served as the Goldwins' sponsor, it has never had any knowledge of their alleged criminal pursuits—nor has Mr. Goldwin ever served on the Ardmore Board of Directors. These rumors are simply one more attempt by the Association's power-hungry rivals to tarnish the respectable Ardmore name."

Titus Grazelby, head of the Grazelby Publications

empire, is one man, however, who finds it difficult to believe anything coming from the Ardmore publicity machine.

I trust Mr. Boyle about as far as I can throw him—which is from here to that plate glass window there, if he actually had the nerve to stand in the same room with me. No, I'd not be surprised at all if this Rex Goldwin villain was on their board of directors. The Ardmore Association has been—and always will be—a corrupt organization. But enough talk about Ardmore. They're the losers here; tonight is all about the Whipples.

"Charles Whipple and his clan have won a fantastic victory today," Grazelby continued, "for themselves and for the entire Grazelby Publications family. Of course, I must send a special note of gratitude to Arthur Whipple, whose spirit and determination won the day for us. Naturally, a full profile of the Whipples' newest record breaker, as well as a detailed report on this year's championships will all be included in the new volume of *Grazelby's Guide to World Records and Fantastic Feats*—on shelves this November."

Grazelby is clearly not alone in his appraisal of the Whipples' achievement. Following news of the family's stunning victory Sunday night, shares of Grazelby Publications (GRAP) promptly hit an all-time high Monday morning. The Whipples, holding one-third of the company's shares, are set to see their personal fortune more than double by the close of market Monday.

But besides the thrill of victory and the massive payday,

the members of the Whipple family have another thing to celebrate: their very lives.

With the Goldwins' incarceration, the Whipples have seemingly survived another chapter in the saga of the Lyon's Curse—a fanciful term given to the string of tragedies that has followed the family ever since rival record breaker Gregory Lyon was killed competing against Charles's father, some thirty years ago.

But with this last spate of violence, could the curse that claimed Charles Sr.'s life finally be over? Only time will tell. For now, the Whipples seem perfectly content living in the present.

"Today marks the start of a new era for the Whipple family," stated Charles Whipple, "an era in which character comes before accomplishment, and people are prized above plaques. Of course, it should always have been this way; I am sorry I did not realize it sooner. But then, it is only because of my son Arthur that I have realized it at all."

Arthur Whipple, hero to the Record-Breakingest Family on Earth—and rising star to the world, had this to say about his sudden success:

"Um—wow. Yeah. I—I can't believe it. I mean, yeah. Wow."

Considering the circumstances of his triumph, truer words may never have been said.

For one boy at least, a new era has certainly begun.

• • •

351

Arthur woke to find the first rays of sunrise shimmering through his window, filling his room with a bright natural glow.

When he'd convinced himself the events of the prior evening had not simply been a dream, an involuntary grin formed across his face. This was the dawn of his new life as a world-record holder; more importantly, it was the first morning he had woken up feeling truly at home.

Arthur stretched his arms and yawned a deep, satisfying yawn. He cast off his covers and rose from the bed, then headed to the wardrobe. He paused a moment before the mirror to examine his reflection.

There was the same clump of light brown hair sticking stubbornly out from the side of his head; *there* were the same spindly arms—and yet, there was something decidedly different about the boy in the mirror this morning. Something lighter, less burdened—something clearer.

His very surroundings, it seemed, had changed as well. Overnight, the world had become a brighter, better place, in which absolutely anything was possible. He could hardly wait to get started on world record number two.

Arthur began sliding an arm through the sleeve of his robe when his nose was struck by the spicy scent of sausage. *Sammy!* he thought and ran to the window.

Sure enough, there on the outdoor breakfast table lay the World's Largest Sausage Link—and beside it, an industrial cement mixer filled with what appeared to be the Largest Batch of Eggs Ever Scrambled.

352

For one terrifying moment, Arthur feared he'd somehow slept through the breakfast bell—but he promptly realized that nobody else had arrived at the table either. *What's everybody waiting for?* he thought to himself. *Surely, we've been deprived of Sammy the Spatula's colossal cuisine long enough. Let's eat!*

He slipped the other arm into its sleeve, grabbed his new trophy off the nightstand, and darted for the door.

As soon as he had crossed the threshold, however, Arthur was forced to a halt by a wall of people.

There, in a semicircle around his doorway, stood his parents and the octuplets, as well as Simon, Cordelia, and Henry. Ruby stood with Wilhelm to their left, rubbing her half-closed eyes with the back of her hand.

All of them, Arthur realized, were wearing party hats.

"Good morning, Arthur," said Mr. Whipple with a smile.

"Oh," Arthur started. "Good morning."

"And how is our newest world-record breaker today? You've slept well, have you?"

"Very well, thank you. I'm sorry if I've kept you waiting." He looked again at the party hats. "Have I forgotten a holiday or something? It's not Haberdashery Day already, is it?"

"No indeed, my boy. Why, today belongs to you."

"Oh. It does?" Arthur scratched his cheek. "How exactly have I come to possess it?"

"Last night," his father explained, "it occurred to your mother and me that, in the matter of birthday parties, you have been rather shortchanged—nine of them in all you've

353

missed, by my count—and now, we mean to remedy that. Starting tonight, you'll be having a birthday party every day for the next nine days. You decide the theme for each, select the food, invite whomever you like. And henceforth you will have a birthday party every year—not just in leap years. Do you find the terms acceptable?"

Arthur could hardly speak. Before his throat closed up altogether, he managed to say, feebly, "Quite acceptable, sir."

"Good," said Arthur's father.

He removed a foil-and-paper crown from behind his back and proceeded to place it on his son's head. "Arthur," he said, "for the next week and two days, I hereby pronounce you Birthday King of All Christendom—and us, your loyal subjects."

At that, everyone bowed low, leaving Arthur to stand and marvel. In his wildest dreams, he had never imagined this.

After a few moments, everyone straightened up again, and Mr. Whipple said, "Now, we shall begin planning the first of your parties out at the garden table. To kick off the Arthur Whipple Birthday Party Extravaganza, Sammy's made a special breakfast in your honor. But before we commence with the celebrations, there's one last order of business that needs tending. So, if you would all follow me downstairs please. . . ."

Mr. Whipple turned, and the others followed.

At the stairway, Ruby filed in alongside Arthur. "Happy first birthday," she said. "I must say, you seem surprisingly capable for a one-year-old."

354

"I'm glad you think so. It's not easy feeling twelve times your actual age, you know."

Ruby smiled, then rubbed her eyes again. "So I take it people don't sleep in around here either," she yawned. "Perfect. I escape one loony bin only to end up in another. . . . Hey—perhaps you could use your authority as Birthday King to set the alarm clocks a few hours forward, eh?"

"Listen to you—I've been Birthday King for all of thirty seconds, and you're already trying to corrupt my power. Some royal advisor you'll make," Arthur grinned. "But honestly, why would you ever want to sleep in, when there are so many amazing things to be done in this world?"

The girl looked skeptical.

"You'll see," said Arthur. "You're with the Whipples now. We'll make a morning person of you yet."

Ruby bulged her eyes and shook her head. "Loony bin," she whispered.

The party wound its way through the house, its destination soon becoming clear. Upon reaching the entrance to the Whipple Hall of World Records, Arthur's father heaved open the massive wooden doors and ushered the group inside.

Arthur filed in with Ruby and his siblings, staring in awe at the enormous wall of trophies and plaques before him. For as long as he could remember, he had gazed up at that wall dreaming of the day when he'd finally find a place of his own there. And now, it seemed, that day had arrived.

Mr. Whipple closed the giant doors behind him and strode to the center of the wall.

355

"The Great Wall of Whipple," he said reverently. "The place where all our greatest accomplishments are displayed—for the pride of this family and the respect of the world. All the Whipples are represented here. . . ." He paused and turned to look Arthur in the eye. "All, of course, but one. Indeed, there is one name missing from this wall: the name of Arthur Whipple."

Arthur's siblings patted his back and mussed his hair, while Arthur grinned bashfully and glanced to the ground. This was the moment he'd waited for all his life.

Mr. Whipple continued. "I have long dreamt of the day when our wall would at last be complete—when all our names could finally be written upon it. . . . And yet, in spite of recent events, I'm afraid it will have to do without Arthur's name for a while longer."

The Whipple children's excitement turned to confusion. Arthur looked up from the floor.

"Though it's true Arthur has now broken a world record of his own," their father explained, "I simply don't feel it belongs here on our wall."

Arthur's stomach felt hollow. After all this time, he had just begun to believe that maybe he really did belong there. Had it all been an illusion?

Mr. Whipple raised an arm and gestured over the children's heads. Arthur and his siblings turned to see Wilhelm walking toward them, pushing a large wheeled object veiled by a purple velvet cloth.

The crowd of murmuring children parted to make way

for the mysterious artifact. When the butler had rolled it to the very center of the room he locked the wheels in place, then stepped back into the shadows.

Arthur's father walked toward the object and halted beside it. Then he slid away the cloth.

Underneath was a large glass case, set atop a dark wood pedestal. At the center of the pedestal sat a vacant velvet pillow.

"As you know," Mr. Whipple addressed his family, "I have kept this empty trophy case in order to remind myself of that which I have not won—of the attempts I've failed—of the opportunities I've missed. . . ."

Arthur's father stared into the glass for a moment, running his fingertip along the rim of the pedestal, then slowly pulled it away.

"I have recently come to realize, however, it was not the things I thought I were missing that I truly needed to find. And now—thanks to one formerly recordless boy—I no longer feel I am missing anything at all. As such, I have no further reason to keep this case empty."

Mr. Whipple looked to his son with twinkling eyes. "Arthur, my boy—would you be so kind as to lend us your new trophy, that we may finally put this case to its proper use?"

The pit in Arthur's stomach vanished as his heart swelled in his chest.

"It—" he started, holding back tears and holding up his trophy. "It would be my great honor, sir."

357

Mr. Whipple smiled. "I had hoped you'd feel that way."

He gripped the tall glass dome of the display case and lifted it from the pedestal.

Arthur stepped forward and, savoring every instant, placed his trophy at the center of the pillow, then slowly backed away.

Mr. Whipple lowered the dome back onto its base, then gestured again to Wilhelm, who turned and flipped a switch on the wall behind him.

A spotlight shone down from the ceiling, illuminating Arthur's trophy like a golden beacon at the room's otherwise shadowy center.

Arthur's eyes sparkled as his siblings oohed and aahed around him.

"Well now, that looks rather marvelous, doesn't it?" Mr. Whipple observed. "Thank you, Arthur, for contributing such a fine centerpiece to our distinguished collection."

Arthur, unable to speak, simply smiled and nodded. His father grinned back at him, then gave an affectionate wink.

When they'd all stared at the new fixture for several moments, Mr. Whipple turned to the others and said, "Well then—now that's settled, who's hungry for a bit of colossal cuisine?"

The children all raised their hands.

"Let's go get some then, shall we?" their father said, smiling. "Arthur's first birthday breakfast awaits!"

The octuplets bounced up and down with excitement as their mother turned to the butler.

"Wilhelm," she said, "go and fetch Mrs. Waite, would you please? Tell her she and Ivy may continue whatever it is they're working on as soon as Ivy has had her breakfast. Surprise birthday gift, I believe she said. Hard to tell *what* Mrs. Waite was saying last night, the poor woman was so emotional, bless her heart."

"Right avay, ma'am," the butler replied as he made for the door.

"Thank you, Wilhelm," said Mr. Whipple. "Now, everyone else—to the breakfast table!"

• • •

Taking his dinner fork in one hand and his dinner machete in the other, Arthur carved off a large lump of sausage and dropped it onto his plate. Sitting there with his family, he couldn't help but be reminded of a particular morning months back, when Sammy had served French toast, and all of their adventures had begun.

Arthur cut himself another bite, pausing for a moment to make sure the fifteen-foot sausage link wasn't wobbling just a bit more than it should be.

". . . And after the fire-breathing porcupines finish their routine," his father continued, "it'll be time for cake. Now, if Sammy gets to work straight away, he may just have enough time to break the size record we set at the Birthday Extravaganza. What do you think? Shall I have him get started?"

Arthur thought back to his experience with his family's last birthday cake. "Actually," he said, "I was thinking we might

359

do something a bit smaller this time—still record-breaking, of course—but with a little less potential for destruction. I don't know—World's Fluffiest Cake, perhaps?"

"Hmm. I'd never thought of that one before. Won't be nearly as dramatic, of course—but then, I suppose we could benefit from a fresh approach on the matter of cake. Wouldn't want our guests to think we're becoming predictable, would we? All right then—World's Fluffiest it is."

Arthur smiled and had another bite of breakfast. It was hard to believe how far he'd come in the span of just a few months. Before today, he'd barely been given a party at all—and here, he was about to be given the Best Birthday Party of All Time.

Breaking a world record was one thing—but now, wishes he'd never even made were coming true. Finally, things were going his way. The constant turmoil that had plagued him from birth seemed like a distant memory. For the first time in his life, his heart was truly at peace.

Arthur began dreaming of ways to make each of his other eight birthday parties even better than the one before, when he happened to notice Wilhelm approaching across the east lawn.

The butler had never been one to convey himself sluggishly, but his current pace struck Arthur as being rather more hurried than usual.

Wilhelm stopped when he reached the table and stood panting at the lawn's edge. Alone in a sea of green, the champion strongman appeared much smaller than Arthur had remembered him to be. His typically rosy cheeks were now all but white.

In his hand, he clutched a small sheaf of papers.

Upon seeing the butler, Arthur's father wiped his mouth with his napkin and exclaimed, "My goodness, man—you're white as a sheet! I hadn't noticed earlier—but it looks as though you could use a bit of sun and a good meal, eh, old boy? Come on then, pull up a chair—and try not to eat the whole thing in one bite!"

The butler did not move, but opened his mouth to speak.

"They—" he wheezed, "they are gone."

Mr. Whipple rose from his seat with a puzzled expression and approached his valet. "What's that you say, Wilhelm? Who's gone?"

"I—I vent to fetch Mrs. Vaite," the butler replied, "as Mrs. Vhipple asked, but nobody answered when I knocked. I began to vorry that something vas wrong, so I opened her door, just to make sure everything vas okay—but there vas nobody there at all."

The other Whipples, troubled by Wilhelm's tone, excused themselves from the table and came to stand behind their father.

"Please, Wilhelm," said Mr. Whipple, "this hardly seems reason for alarm. She's no doubt off somewhere with Ivy planning Arthur's birthday surprise as Mrs. Whipple suggested."

"I'm afraid," said Wilhelm, "it is not the sort of surprise you are thinking of. Before I decided to search Mrs.

Vaite's quarters, I had already searched all the other places I thought they might be. Vhen I finally vent inside, I found the room tidy and the bed made, but there vas still no sign of them. And then—then I found this."

The butler held out the papers.

"Well, what is it, man?" Mr. Whipple asked impatiently, panic seeping into his face.

"It's . . . a letter, sir. From Mrs. Vaite."

Mr. Whipple took the papers from Wilhelm and held up the first page so he and the others could see it. Neat lines of handwritten text cut back and forth across the thin parchment.

Arthur's heart lurched at the sight of the familiar seal. It was a crown made of flames.

"Dad!" he cried. "That's the seal that was on the Treasurer's note!"

Mr. Whipple turned to his son with a look of powerless dread, then shifted his eyes back to the letter—and began to read aloud.

My Dearest Whipples,

You needn't worry about your precious little Ivy. I have taken it upon myself to look after her for the foreseeable future. I assure you, she is quite safe. For now.

By the time you read this, we shall

*be a thousand miles away from this
godforsaken house of yours, so you may
spare yourselves the trouble of searching.*

Arthur's mother gasped. "I—I don't understand! What is she talking about? Oh, Charles—what has she done?"

Mr. Whipple looked at his wife, then dropped the letter to his side—and dashed back toward the house.

The others set out immediately after him.

Arthur's father threw open the terrace doors and burst inside.

"Ivy!" he shouted into the great hall before racing up the stairs. "Ivy, where have you gone?"

When Arthur and the others finally caught up to him, Mr. Whipple was in the nursery, standing over Ivy's bed. The bed was neatly made, with pink-and-white-striped sheets peeking out from the top of a white quilt embroidered with pink-flowered vines. On the pillow sat Ivy's stuffed bear, Mr. Growls, dressed to match its owner as usual. But something about the toy struck Arthur as strange. As he stepped closer, he realized the bear's eyes and mouth had been crudely stitched shut with thick black yarn.

Arthur shivered.

Mr. Whipple lifted the bear from the bed, staring helplessly at it for a moment, then turned and handed it to his wife, whose knees nearly buckled at the sight.

"Oh, Ivy!" she cried. "Our poor little girl! Why would

363

Mrs. Waite do this, Charles? It makes no sense! Have we ever wronged her in any way?"

"I—I don't know, dear," Mr. Whipple replied, putting a comforting arm around his wife.

His other hand trembling, Arthur's father raised Mrs. Waite's letter to eye level once again. He drew a deep breath and continued reading.

> *Oh, I can just see your faces now. "But what have we ever done to Mrs. Waite that should cause her to behave in such a dreadful manner?" You really are so predictable, you Whipples. With all your extraordinary powers of perception in matters of competition, you so often fail to see what's right in front of you in everyday life. Since you asked, however, I shall indulge your primitive curiosity:*
>
> *It all started the day you killed my husband.*
>
> *You remember Gregory, don't you? Fearless face, steely gray eyes? Ah, but of course you don't. You have surely forgotten all about him—apart, perhaps, from his bearing the name that would be given to your fiendish family's curse. But I do not forget so easily. When my dear Mr. Lyon*

364

*was drowned in a box, trying to win back
his rightful record from the villain you call
"grandfather" . . .*

Arthur's mind flashed back to the black-veiled woman
from the archives reel, clawing at her husband's coffin as it
was lowered into the earth.

Arthur glanced to Ruby and shared a look of horror.
"Hang on," he blurted, turning back to his father. "Gregory
Lyon? As in the Gregory Lyon who tried to steal our grand-
mother's live burial record? As in the *Lyon's* Curse? Mrs.
Waite is Gregory Lyon's *widow?!*"

"Oh, no," said Arthur's father. "How could I have been
so blind?"

Mr. Whipple stared forward for one solemn moment,
then returned to the letter. As he continued to read through
each of its half dozen pages, the others listened in stunned
silence.

> *. . . When my dear Mr. Lyon was
> drowned in a box, trying to win back his
> rightful record from the villain you call
> "grandfather," I secretly vowed revenge
> (as any good wife would do) upon the man
> responsible for murdering him. It took a
> few tries—concealing king cobras, rigging
> runaway rickshaws, et cetera, et cetera—and*

a lot of talk about some "Lyon's Curse"—
but in the end, I had my revenge. When I
heard the joyful news of your grandfather's
horrific plane crash, my Gregory and I
were finally able to rest. . . .

That is, until a few years later, when
a certain Charles Whipple Jr. began
appearing in the headlines.

You can imagine my horror to find
that—after leaving me a childless widow—
my husband's murderer was now living
on through his record-breaking son.
Clearly, I could not ignore such injustice.
Unfortunately, I had exhausted the last
of Gregory's estate on eliminating the first
Charles Whipple (disposing of a Whipple,
mind, is hardly an inexpensive enterprise).
Indeed, I should have been powerless to do
anything—if not for the generous support
of the Ardmore Association.

As luck would have it, there had been
a recent shift in power on the Ardmore
Board of Directors, clearing the way
for new members. I forwarded a letter
of interest through one of Ardmore's
aspiring young lawyers, a Mr. Malcolm
Boyle, and the Chairman of the Board
quickly recognized the benefits of my

singular expertise. And soon I had managed to secure a coveted seat on the board myself—a seat once held by a certain Bartholomew Niven, long before he ever turned up as a skeleton in a sea cave.

(Well then. Now that you've no doubt guessed my title, I imagine you're curious as to how exactly the position came to be open. How exactly did Mr. Niven go from a respected member of the Ardmore board to a forgotten pile of bones on a beach? Seeing as I wasn't there, I can't tell you exactly. But I can tell you this: it certainly wasn't Rex Goldwin's doing. No, Mr. Goldwin is far too obsessed with keeping his perfect hands clean to really get blood under his nails. But rest assured—the Chairman of the Board is not so squeamish. Haven't had the pleasure yet, have you? Well, never you worry; with any luck, you'll be meeting him soon. . . . But back to the story.)

With the full resources of the Association now behind me, I retrained my sights on Charles Whipple's son—only to find he had coaxed some witless woman into becoming his wife and giving him record-breaking sons of his own.

It still pains me to think of it. Here,

367

the family of the man who had robbed me
of my husband and any chance of my own
family was fast becoming one of the most
celebrated families in the world. Instead
of paying for their misdeeds, they were
rewarded with fame and fortune. My desire
for vengeance burned brighter than ever.

And yet, if I were to simply dispose
of the murderer's son now, I should only
be forced to contend someday with the
murderer's son's children. Of course, I
toyed with the idea of killing them all at
once—but then, I had no desire to make the
entire Whipple family into martyrs. The
public, you see, have an obnoxious habit of
worshipping their fallen heroes—and I
was not about to grant the Whipples eternal
idol status.

Fortunately, my colleagues and
I realized there was a much better
option. Instead of destroying individual
Whipples—we would destroy the name of
Whipple itself.

All our plan required was a champion.

By the time Rex Goldwin received
our recruitment letter, he was already
seeking revenge upon the man who had
ousted him from the world records game.

His "involuntary adoption" scheme was well under way, and he and his wife had successfully liberated two preselected infants from their unworthy birth parents. What the Goldwins lacked, however, was the means to properly mold their children into the record-breaking machines needed to ensure the Whipples' destruction.

We were more than happy to oblige.

Once Rex had accepted our offer, the board of directors stationed the Goldwins on an advanced training compound, while the unfortunate twins Rayford and Royston were taken underground to study military tactics and the deadly arts.

As the Goldwins' training progressed, we assisted them in their acquisition of infant family members until we had collected enough children to match yours—save one. By this time, news of the Maternity Ward Marauders had spread across the globe, and every high-charting newborn on the planet was being given its very own security detail. Regrettably, we were forced to stop the Goldwins one child short of our minimum goal—before our luck ran out and they were discovered by the authorities. Still, we were convinced the Whipple boy, Arthur, posed not the slightest threat to the record books or to our plans—and so we proceeded with confidence.

Mr. Whipple paused for a moment and flashed a melancholy smile to Arthur. Arthur tried to imagine how it might have felt under different circumstances to know he had proved their enemies wrong about him.

His father resumed his reading.

With our family of champions assembled at last, all we had left to do was infiltrate the Whipple household.

What a shock it was your former housekeeper, Mrs. Scrubb, came down with that dreadful case of malaria. I wonder if it had anything to do with that parcel full of African mosquitos she received. Whoever sent it must have gone to considerable trouble to get it through customs. Poor Mrs. Scrubb. In her advanced age, she had no choice but to opt for early retirement.

It must have struck you as rather odd to receive only a single applicant for such a distinguished position. But then, of course, all my references checked out, and my late

370

husband had himself been a world-record breaker (you did not bother to inquire further), and so, you hired me.

Having worked my way into your home at last, our years-old plan could finally be set into action. It all began, of course, with an oversized piece of French toast. . . .

My, what a glorious time my employment at your house has been. From sabotaging your breakfast table, to helping the Goldwin twins blow up your birthday cake and then framing your chef, to planting the poison on your boat and disconnecting the rip cord on your parachute, these have truly been some of the most fulfilling days of my life. It was especially satisfying, of course, writing the "anonymous" letter that saw your dear Uncle Mervyn—poor, trusting fool— shipped off to Moscow.

But perhaps the memory I'll cherish most was the look on your face, sir, when you first saw me running onto the dueling field. I must say I was a bit nervous trotting myself out there in front of such an angry crowd—but then, I couldn't have you finishing off my champion before he'd completed his primary objective,

now could I? It's a good thing the twins
had managed to inform me of your son's
little predicament—or I really don't
know what I'd have told you. Even so,
I had serious doubts the news would do
anything to stop you from continuing the
duel. Your reaction, however, proved most
enlightening.

Until yesterday, I was not entirely sure
what level of importance you placed on
the lives of your children. But when you
left the championships in search of your
son—the recordless one, no less—it became
clear to me you cared at least enough
about your offspring to sacrifice your own
reputation to keep them from harm. (This
new knowledge, as you will soon discover,
has factored rather significantly into our
present strategy.)

In the end, of course, Arthur's
unexpected success proved to be the
Goldwins' undoing, and our first plan
failed—but I am hardly one to cry over
spilt milk. Indeed, I am inclined to
congratulate the lad on his accomplishment.
Even I—who have sworn to destroy every
last Whipple on earth—can appreciate
a good, heartwarming underdog story

when I hear one. And besides, without this first bit of failure, we should never have landed upon our new and improved plot to annihilate the Whipple name.

Which brings me at last to the real aim of this letter. As much as explaining the details of such a long-running and meticulous plot has been necessary—not to mention surprisingly therapeutic—it pains me to think you've had to wait so long to get to the really exciting part.

And so, without further ado, allow me to present my inevitable list of demands.

As I have already assured you, your daughter Ivy is presently safe and sound in my care. If you wish, however, to ever see her alive again, you will adhere to the following condition: From this moment on, every member of the Whipple family shall refrain from the act of world-record breaking.

There shall be no individual records; there shall be no family records; there shall be no world records of any kind. Unless, of course, you wish for little Ivy to break a record of her own—say, for Greatest Height to Plummet without a Parachute—or, perhaps, for Longest

Time to Survive on the Open Ocean before Sinking to the Sea Floor. You can imagine what a logistical nightmare this last one will be to certify—so please, do us all a favor and just heed the demands, won't you?

I must also ask you, of course, not to mention our little arrangement to anyone outside your own household. You can see how defeating it would be to our purpose to have the whole world suddenly sympathizing with you, as you nobly abstain from record breaking in order to save your poor kidnapped daughter. No, I'm afraid it just won't do. Breathe a word of this to the papers, and you'll soon find your daughter's story concluded in the obituary column.

And in case you're thinking of attempting to break records without my knowledge, you can forget about that right now. The Association has eyes everywhere. If you so much as twirl a plate on a stick, we shall hear of it.

Very well then. Goodbye for now, dear Whipples. If you have not already thought to do so, you may consider this my official resignation. I apologize for *the limited warning, but surprise abductions hardly lend themselves to a two-weeks' notice.*

Sincerely Yours,
Mrs. Lyon-Waite
The Treasurer

Mr. Whipple looked up from the letter. His face was hollow and lifeless, save for the smoldering glow of fury gleaming through his eyes.

Arthur's brother Simon ground his fist into the palm of his hand. "So Rayford and Royston were henchmen all along to the Goldwins—but the Goldwins were henchmen all along to Mrs. Lyon-Waite!"

"And she was the Treasurer from the start," Arthur murmured, shaking his head in disbelief as he looked to Ruby. "Under our noses the whole time."

Tears poured down the cheeks of Arthur's mother and many of her children. Mr. Whipple pulled his wife close to him.

"Oh, Charles," Arthur's mother sobbed, "what ever shall we do?"

"I do not entirely know, dear," the man replied. "But I can tell you this: we shall not sit idly by and surrender our daughter to traitors and madmen! We shall track them to the ends of the earth if need be—and rescue our little girl from the clutches of the Association, wherever they may dare to hide!"

375

"But, Dad," said Henry, "how will we ever get to her without breaking any records along the way? It's all we know how to do!"

"Yes," their father sighed. "It does seem a cruelly impossible task, does it not? Honestly, we may as well have been commanded to refrain from breathing in and out! Either way, we shall have to unlearn all that is natural to us. Left to ourselves, I fear we'd be unable to manage such a feat. But there must be a way. If only we had someone to keep us on track—to guide us away from our instincts. Someone not so prone to constant overachievement. . . ." A small spark caught fire at the back of Mr. Whipple's eye. "An expert, if you will, in *not* breaking records. . . ."

Arthur stood waiting to hear the next step in his father's plan. Where would they find such a person? Could someone like this really help them bring back their sister?

Arthur searched his family for an answer.

Slowly, every eye in the room turned—and looked at him.